Last Christmas in London

Last Christmas in London

Eleanor Pilcher

Bedford Square Publishers

First published in the UK in 2026 by Bedford Square Publishers Ltd,
London, UK

bedfordsquarepublishers.co.uk

A CIP catalogue record for this book is available from the British Library.

ISBN
978-1-83501-563-6 (Paperback)
978-1-83501-564-3 (eBook)

2 4 6 8 10 9 7 5 3 1

Typeset in 11.35 on 14pt Bembo Std
by Avocet Typeset, Bideford, Devon, EX39 2BP
Printed and bound in Great Britain by
CPI Group (UK) Ltd, Croydon CR0 4YY

FSC www.fsc.org MIX Paper | Supporting responsible forestry FSC® C013604

The manufacturer's authorised representative in the EU for product safety is Easy Access System Europe, Mustamäe tee 50, 10621 Tallinn, Estonia
gpsr.requests@easproject.com

For Auntie Ann

Chapter 1

'HAPPY ASSISTMAS!' JOSH AND I YELLED into my phone camera, our voices competing with the strain of an old jukebox belting Christmas music from the pub corner, and the cacophonous cheer of Friday-night revellers. It was a blend of chaos and joy that only a traditional London boozer can conjure up, a pub where, every time you sat on the ancient banquette, a waft of dust would rise half an inch into the air, mingling with the lingering scent of cigarette smoke from the nineties.

'How dare you leave us!' Josh wailed theatrically, flinging himself across my arm with the exaggerated flair of someone three cocktails deep. It was a miracle I could hear him over the sound of the post-work drinkers, dodging their spouses, housemates, and perhaps sobriety, by having one more drink at the bar.

'I'm sorry!' I cried, pocketing my phone, already planning which TikTok sound to slap over the moment and which effects might brighten the dim, overhead lighting. I hugged Josh's head, which promptly disappeared under the table to rest on my lap. I was drunk. No, scratch that, I was *very* drunk. Five hours of drinking will do that, especially when you start at 2.00 p.m.

I had left my boss, Pim, at the St Pancras Hotel spa and

taxied her Chow Chow, Gerald, to her ex-husband's house in Clapham for his custodial visitation. Glamorous, right? But now it was just me, Josh, and my other best friend, Megan.

'I wouldn't leave you if I could help it. Either of you,' I told them firmly.

Megan, who'd joined us an hour ago, sat across the table nursing a large sauvignon blanc, her face etched with the kind of pained resignation usually reserved for completing jury service. She wasn't enjoying our choice of venue. This was *definitely* the wrong end of Greek Street for her tastes. Megan was more The Ivy than the Hand and Shears, but there were limits to how often I could leverage my connection to Pim Hardcastle, the once-BAFTA-nominated-actress-turned-TV-personality to get us into high places.

'You could just stay here?' Megan lifted her glass to her perfectly lined lips. 'And not go to Canada.'

I raised my eyebrows in reply. 'I'm hardly getting head-hunted in London. I've barely spent any time here since I started working for Pim. No one knows who I am.'

Josh threw up his arms. 'We do!'

'I know, babe.' I kissed the crown of his head. 'But not the industry. It's one of the downsides of the life of a nomad – but there have been perks!' I added, less insistently. There was something about my job and life choices that I always felt I had to defend, especially to Josh and Megan, who, if they had their way, would have my 'Find My Friend' always pointed to London. But that hadn't been the case since I was twenty and I got the job with Pim Hardcastle, as her hard-working – saint of an – assistant.

My time with Pim had been an adventure. She had once been hailed as a bright young thing in the eighties, some heralded her as the next Maggie Smith after her bold, gender-bending turn as a female Heathcliff in an audacious LGBT+ retelling of *Wuthering Heights*. But in the unforgiving nineties, a decade that was particularly cruel to ageing starlets, Pim became infamous rather than famous for her countless on-set tantrums, a series of ill-fated marriages to men who loved their vices more than her, and a tabloid legacy of drama that she wasn't getting any nominations for.

Since then, Pim had tried everything to cling to relevance. She'd written scandalous tell-all autobiographies that alienated her from the industry even further, appeared on C-list celebrity shows across the globe, and re-invented herself as often as she needed to, to keep her fortune, if not her fame. Now, thirty-five years after her last major success, she was travelling like a Real Housewife without the franchise, flitting from one country to the next, sponging off production companies, and ensuring she wrung every ounce of luxury from contracts and ex-husbands' alimony. And dragging me around to organise her battered Dior suitcases, manage her chaotic schedule and make sure she never left a hotel room with mismatched earrings or shoes that clashed with her outfit. But that was about to change.

This was my last month as Pim's assistant, and it happily coincided with Christmas. Making this my last ever 'Assistmas', as I and my 250,000 TikTok followers had christened my series of TikTok videos about working in the glamorous world of TV during the insanely busy festive season. Viewers loved seeing the behind-the-scenes of production companies, offices, and studios, from the perspective of an average assistant. No aesthetic content here, what you see is what you get – but that seemed to resonate with people online.

I tried to suppress the grin that came with the remembrance that this was my last month of being a personal assistant. Soon I would be a Broadcast Production Assistant – okay, *still* an assistant, but a company one with an actual career ladder to climb, not just climbing another escalator with a Chow Chow in a carrier making a bid for freedom.

'It's been a good few years,' I said, allowing my grin to develop as Megan and Josh stared sadly at me. 'I've seen more of the world than most people could dream of. Sure, it's been for work, but I'm not unhappy with how things have turned out.' I put my head on Josh's shoulder.

I knew both of them thought my life was a catastrophe and inconsistent, but I truly was happy with it. I never understood societal pressures to get a degree, go travelling for a year, get a nine-to-five job, date some losers, then find a winner to marry, and have children. That was never going to be the life I had. I decided that early on, ever since I saw *Eat, Pray, Love.*

I had always wanted the nomadic, no-strings and no-pressure lifestyle and that was precisely what I got with Pim. Yes, she wasn't the perfect boss and yes, there were days I was incredibly lonely but TikTok and sharing experiences online helped with that. Viewers commented and had conversations with me in my DMs, asking me questions and valuing my opinion. A novelty in television and film. It helped to know that there was a community of people who valued my advice and insights into the industry, who *actually* wanted to hear from me and not just for me to hold the door open for them.

Originally, I had started the channel in the hopes it would get me noticed by people in the industry. It wasn't long before I discovered my channel reached more people trying to break into the industry instead. But that wasn't a bad thing; it gave me and my TikTok channel a purpose. To be educational as well as entertaining.

It did open *some* doors for me, just not career-based ones.

And I got to document all the days that I got to experience the world of television, which is truly exciting. I had to remind myself regularly that, while my job wasn't the most glamorous day to day, it did allow me the chance to spend time talking to icons on television sets and in green rooms, attend premieres with A-list celebrities walking the carpet, to pee in toilet stalls next to Oscar winners, and to hand out shots to the entire England football team.

My life has been a whirlwind of activity that no one could ever plan for.

I was sad to be leaving Pim behind, and I imagined she was just as stressed as I felt because I was leaving her.

But it was time. More and more, the loneliness was creeping in with TikTok and online interactions only going so far, and the exhaustion of travel and setting my watch to new time zones every day, while making short-term friendships with staff members was draining me to the point of carelessness.

After all, I'd grown up with the reality that time could slip away without warning. My mother died in her early forties. It was a reminder that life wasn't a guarantee; and I shouldn't wait forever to start doing what mattered to me. That's why I wanted to start fresh and settle down, finally open my arms to the universe and say, 'Come on in!'

Megan took a breath and seemed to shake herself out, back into supportive friend mode. 'I'm really proud of you.'

She lifted her wine glass in cheers. But then her lip twitched. 'I mean, it's about time,' she added, her trademark sarcasm slipping through.

'Oh, Megan, it's okay!'

'It's *not* okay,' she shot back, scrunching her face in exaggerated disdain. 'You've been with Pim for nearly eight years, and in all that time, the only raise she gave you was to meet legal inflation. That and when you went viral the first time.' TikTok content as Pim's assistant was perennial. My life was quite glamorous to an outsider – jet-setting across continents, staying in hotels, fancy dinners, mingling with a revolving door of celebrities – but the reality was… different. Still, I couldn't complain; I'd loved it. 'You couldn't even afford rent in London on that salary,' Megan pressed on.

'Good thing Pim covers my hotel expenses,' I muttered breezily.

Megan's eyes raised further and even Josh groaned in a way that translated to *Did she though?*

Okay, fine, so Pim would put herself up in a five-star villa while I would sleep on the sofa, or occasionally have to taxi to and from the local B&B.

'I got to see the world!' Both knew they couldn't counter that. While Megan had been building her own consulting empire – consulting on *what*, I still had no idea – marrying her perfect university sweetheart, Alex, birthing my joyful godson, Alfie, and building up her Nectar club points as the all-round queen of middle-class living, I'd been travelling across Malta, Australia, South Korea, and Canada.

It was in Toronto, during Pim's stint as a guest judge on a Canadian cooking show, that I made the life-altering decision to apply for a new job in television production.

Somewhere between watching a contestant cry over a collapsed soufflé and fetching Pim her fifth flat white of the day, I slipped my CV filled with anecdotes more than experiences to HR and tried not to think about it too hard in case I didn't get it.

A fortnight ago, I learned I'd landed it.

The email had sat unopened in my inbox for a full seven minutes while I paced the length of the latest hotel room, my stomach fizzing with an entirely new feeling; a mix of high anxiety and extreme excitement. Maybe fear? Maybe relief?

It was like riding a rollercoaster when you realise you're not strapped in properly just as it sets off from the loading bay.

'I love London,' I said. 'It's truly my favourite place, but I can't wait to go back to Toronto and start afresh. And I would never have had the opportunity to interview at Salient if it wasn't for Pim's hosting gig there.' Salient Studios was my new place of work.

'And your TikTok channel.' Megan nodded towards my phone and the unfinished Assistmas video in need of editing. My TikToks had somehow reached the Head of Content while I was filming some B-roll and editing trailerised 'days-in-the-life of a PA' videos. I'd been experimenting with new edits, but he'd like the content enough to suggest I apply for the production role. 'You're an influencer, babe.'

'Hear, hear,' Josh chimed in, lifting his near-empty glass.

I grinned, clinking my tequila sunrise against his old-fashioned. 'Content creator, actually,' I corrected, and Megan laughed as she raised her glass with a smile.

'I *am* proud of you,' she repeated. 'I hate that it's in Canada, but this new job sounds perfect for you.'

'I know!'

In one month, I'd be starting the new year in a new role. I already had my visa sorted, thanks to years of constant travel, and my familiarity with the Salient team from working with them on Pim's TV show meant I'd be stepping into a role I knew I'd love. After eight years of being an assistant, TikToking my way to a viewership of thousands of followers and learning the ropes one terrible reality TV show at a time, I was finally going to apply my media-studies degree to an actual in-house job.

Best of all, I wouldn't be living out of a suitcase any more. I could finally put down roots, something I hadn't truly had since I was a child.

Denise and Bob, my foster parents, had never made me feel unwanted, but being fostered quietly teaches you to be grateful and behave, to never take up too much space. Always remembering that everything could be temporary and not to get too comfortable.

Now, getting this job in a new country and with a new house, I could exist without the unspoken labels. I wasn't an orphan, or the girl who was spoken of in hushed conversations and given sympathetic looks, as I was in childhood. Nor the dependable assistant who fetched coffee and fixed crises while everyone else got promoted around her as I was as an adult.

In Toronto, I would be my own person, an ex-pat and a Brit, but not an orphan or the assistant of Pim Hardcastle. If I did move back to London, I would always feel like one or the other – and I would struggle to get a job. Eight years as a personal assistant had given me plenty of skills – and content for my TikTok – but in London it mostly gave people permission to underestimate me. There, I'd always be Pim Hardcastle's PA first and anything else second. Someone who had got stuck in an entry-level position for eight years, who lacked ambition and drive to even get so much as a pay rise. Moving abroad meant a clean slate, more opportunity to climb the ladder, and the freedom to re-invent myself entirely. That's what I wanted, or rather, needed.

Josh threw his arms around me, burying his face in the now-familiar chasm under my boobs.

'My parents are bloody over the moon.' Megan swirled her drink before pausing at the look on my face. 'Okay, maybe not *over the moon* that you're leaving to live in a far-off country – again – but they're really proud of you.'

I flushed. My gut had dropped at the idea that Denise and Bob – Megan's parents and my guardians growing up – were thrilled I wouldn't be in the same time zone. They weren't my biological parents, but we were close enough that they wanted to FaceTime every week, usually to tell me about Denise's ophthalmology appointment and Bob beating his mates at snooker (a rare occurrence, so worth a FaceTime).

'Honestly, Mum won't stop bugging me for more details,' Megan carried on. 'She hasn't asked me this many questions since I told her I'd started dating Alex.'

I laughed. 'I love Denise and Bob.' They were easily the most wonderful people on the planet. No contest.

When I lost my mum to cancer just as I was starting secondary school, I thought my world had ended. No dad worth mentioning, no grandparents to speak of – it felt like there was no one left to care for me. But when I landed with Denise and Bob, everything changed.

They'd been foster parents on and off before I'd arrived.

Denise had me wrapped in her arms before I'd even unpacked my limited belongings, and Bob was assembling IKEA furniture for my new bedroom like he'd been preparing for me his whole life.

Megan had been my best friend since nursery when she threw Lego at my head, and I broke her dolly's arm in retaliation; the respect was mutual. Our mums had been the only two sane parents at the school gates, thick as thieves from the moment they met. I can see now that they must have planned everything behind-the-scenes long before Mum passed. And thank God they did.

Mum had made sure I was housed, clothed and loved, and Denise and Bob took to it like ducks to water. A stranger would never have been able to tell that they weren't my mum and dad, the way they always included me and made me feel a part of the family.

But I always knew.

There was love – so much of it – but it came with an unspoken pressure to deserve it. I felt like I owed them something, constantly. I couldn't afford to get it wrong. I had to stay polite grateful and quiet. Never make too much noise. Never remind them I wasn't really theirs.

It was a lot of pressure, to always be on my best behaviour, to not let Mum down. Even now, decades since she passed. I could still hear her voice in my head – *'Mind your Ps and Qs'*, her phrase for 'please and thank you'. *'Be a good girl.'* It was the last thing I remembered her saying to me. And I'd built my life around trying to be just that.

I got good grades, tried not to act up, just listened and watched, never getting in the way. Putting Megan first, it was her family after all, and I got by until I could get out of the way. The job with Pim was perfect for the latter.

Denise meant well. But she didn't always get me. She'd hand me Megan's old clothes with a proud smile, not noticing that the flowery skirts and pastel cardigans made me feel like I was dressing in someone else's skin. Bob once signed me up for a maths tutoring programme without asking, because he thought it might 'open doors'. They wanted the best for me, but it always felt like *their* version of 'best', and my job was just to go along with it.

The job with Pim, ironically, had been the first step in getting out from under all that – into something that was messy and mine.

'They're amazing,' Josh chimed in, reappearing from my lap, looking dazed. 'I wish I'd had parents like Denise and Bob. Or even an aunt or uncle. Growing up in a Kingdom Hall full of Witnesses, watching my every move for even the slightest hint of a hip wiggle, wasn't exactly warm and fuzzy.'

Josh said it lightly, but there was a constant edge to it. Being raised as a Jehovah's Witness came with conditions and Josh broke those conditions from the day he could reach the handle of his mother's wardrobe or change the channel on the TV in order to copy dances by female pop stars.

His personality was not one that could be bottled or suppressed, even if he tried. He was too authentically himself, and it was his authenticity that drew me to him on a night out at university. He was the friend who could fill rooms with laughter and colour, who turned pain into spectacle and holidays into events, who refused to let anyone dim him again. In my life, he was the person who made everything fun – even if it did occasionally get him into trouble for being *too* much or too honest.

I smiled, grateful for his lightness, but I couldn't help

thinking, Denise and Bob *were* amazing. That didn't mean it had been easy.

'Oh, honey.' I gripped his arm tightly.

'No!' Megan slammed her glass on the table with the authority of a judge's gavel. 'This is not a pity party. We are *not* going down the road of sadness and sentimentality. We are here to celebrate.'

'And to plan!' Josh shot upright like a puppet whose strings had been yanked.

'Plan?' I repeated.

'Yes!' Josh shouted over the growing roar of the bar. 'It's your last Christmas – sorry, Assistmas – in London.'

'And my first.' In all my years working for Pim, I'd never spent Christmas in a place colder than twenty degrees Celsius. Pim despised three things above all else: being cold, being crowded, and being cheerful. Christmas in London, naturally, was her worst nightmare.

'We need to go all out.' Josh pulled out his phone and his Filofax – yes, a *Filofax*. 'I have made a list.'

'Of course he has.' Megan smirked at me.

'Well, actually.' Josh flipped open the well-worn leather binder. As he did, threads of tinsel and swatches of various shades of red velvet spilled onto the table. 'It's *your* list.'

'My list?' I picked up a piece of tinsel, eyebrow raised.

'Yes, it's all the things you, me, and Megan have always talked about doing in London but have never actually got around to. I've been a great friend, jotting them all down.' He lifted his list, on which every corner was doodled with little snowflakes and ribbons. He was right, all the items on the list were things we had all planned to do but never got around to. Some from years ago.

'Wow!' I played with the tinsel between my fingers.

'But, Josh,' I said, lifting a swatch a red cloth from the table. 'What is all this?'

He plucked back the swatch. 'We're still trying to find the perfect shade of red for the Harrods Santa costume. Someone left a review last week calling the current one *blood-coloured*. It's a Christmas display, not a Quentin Tarantino set. I won't have my Santa described as *bloody*. Not today, not ever.'

'You're really invested in this, huh?'

'Being in charge of the Christmas visuals for Harrods is no joke,' he said dramatically. He tapped the list again, regaining my attention. 'This is a big deal, okay? You could say we've been planning this for *years* and this is finally *the* year. We're doing this.'

'Hand it over.' Megan snatched the Filofax and cleared her throat before adopting the deep, dramatic tone of a movie-trailer voice-over. 'Evelyn – better known as Evie – Frost,' she said, pausing for effect. 'You have thirty days to complete this list.'

'In between filling out my notice period,' I reminded the two of them. One of the reasons Pim and I were back in London over Christmas was for me to hire my replacement. Though every time I tried to raise the subject with Pim, she waved it off, changed the topic, or insisted we'd talk about it later, as if ignoring it might make me run out of time and force me to stay.

It wouldn't.

Thankfully, despite the stress of hiring my replacement, spending a Christmas with friends and family was a big plus.

'Fine, but don't ruin the moment!' Megan dropped her voice. She scanned the list, her face lighting up. 'I can't believe you made a list of this!' She was laughing as Josh took a mock bow.

Clearing her throat, Megan began reciting the list. 'You have to – or, rather, *we* have to – drink mulled wine at Covent Garden.'

'A classic.' I leaned forward, a memory of texting Josh my desire to enjoy a quick mulled wine in Covent Garden during a stopover in London from Zürich, a stopover that never happened, due to Pim deciding to extend her stay by two weeks.

'Visit the light installations in Carnaby Street.'

Josh made an *ooh* sound as Megan's eyes twinkled with delight – that was her request. 'Go to a Christmas carol concert. Watch the New Year's Eve Fireworks,' she rattled off, and I recognised more of my suggestions – all the things I had never done with friends or family and had avoided when living solo abroad. It was hard to find a Christmas market in December in Capri or Cape Town.

'Have a Christmas movie marathon,' Megan continued.

'Of course!' Josh was a big fan; he began reciting his top choices on his hands.

'Eat dinner in an igloo.'

'Is that a thing?' I asked.

'It's a must these days.' Another one of Josh's choices.

'Go ice skating,' Megan read on.

'Aww, definitely.' I had always wanted to recreate the ice-skating scene in *Serendipity*. 'I can't believe you wrote all this down.' I hugged Josh's arm tightly, feeling the warmth churning in my stomach.

'It's *so* romantic.' He squeezed my arm back. 'Ooh questions!' Megan paused, rolling her eyes at Josh's dramatic lightbulb moment. 'Could we add a Christmas romance?'

I laughed so hard I might have burst my lung. 'Who for? You – yes.'

'No! You—' He pushed me. '*Please*, let's make this Christmas a Hallmark experience.'

'I don't think that is how that happens?'

Megan had frozen and I could see her contemplating whether to write it down or not.

'Don't even.' I raised a finger in warning, and she resisted the temptation.

'Maybe we need to visit a Christmas Tree Farm or find a run-down country pub,' Josh continued, enjoying plotting my make-believe romance.

'Darling, no.' I gently grabbed his chin and began shaking his head for him.

'Where would we find a Christmas Tree Farm in Britain?' Megan added as if this solved the suggestion, and not my glaringly dry dating life. It had been a while since I had even opened a dating app. I was pretty sure the ones I used to use had gone out of business or were just full of incels by now. Leslie Jones was right, we just need one dating app called *What's Left* and be done with it.

Dating, for me, was more of a diversion than a pursuit for anything lasting. A way to pass time in strange cities or to find some semblance of company in the loneliness of hotel rooms. Half the time the guys I dated wanted to move swiftly on to sex or commitment, and those were two things I had little to no interest in.

I wasn't sure I'd ever be interested, at least not in the way most people were. I'd realised in my early twenties that I wasn't wired for relationships the same way others were. It wasn't something I *needed* to feel complete, not like Megan, who fell head over heels for Alex – her first boyfriend, now husband – and seemed to decide on day one that he was *the* one.

Maybe one day I'd feel something similar; I always thought it would happen after a friendship developed or possibly if lightning struck. It was something that I had started to think about more as I approached my thirtieth birthday, the stupid biological clock I had done a good job ignoring so far was ticking louder. More and more I started reacting like Captain Hook hearing the crocodile every time I got my period and realised I was edging closer to having less of them ahead of me than the ones behind. I wasn't suddenly desiring to become a mother but I did wonder, if I didn't start dating properly soon, would I miss the boat to settle down in time to become one, should I so choose?

I knew from watching Denise and Bob growing up what a real happy marriage and relationship looked like. But for years my life hadn't seemed to be missing anything I couldn't live without, and staying unattached had felt simpler than wanting more than I was ready to give. Now I was back in the UK, though, surrounded by loved ones who were all loved up, I did wonder if maybe there was a feeling of loneliness inside me that I was plugging with work. But I didn't need the added pressure from Josh and Megan to do what I was already doing, and I didn't want to have to explain myself when for so many years I had played the 'happy singleton', authentically I might add. My priorities were shifting, I recognised that, but I wasn't entirely comfortable with admitting it out loud.

Trying to sound less defensive and move the topic on to something I did feel comfortable discussing five drinks deep, I smiled. 'Okay, anything else *doable* on this list?'

Megan cleared her throat, reviewing the list and smiling with sudden glee that unnerved me. 'Drum roll, please.' Josh and I dutifully rattled our hands across the sticky table. 'You must take part in the Great Christmas Pudding Race.'

'Oh, no!' A grin spread across my face, betraying my eagerness.

'Oh, yes!' Josh and Megan shouted in pantomime-like unison.

The Pudding Race had been on my bucket list since university: a ridiculous relay race in Covent Garden, where people in often hilarious Christmas costumes raced while carrying Christmas puddings to raise money for charity. Disorganisation and a particularly virulent year of norovirus during our final year of university had thwarted our attempts to join before, but this year it would finally happen.

'I've already roped Alex in to be our fourth,' Megan said, passing the Filofax back to Josh. There was the smallest flicker of hesitation in her voice when she said her husband's name, though she quickly covered it by busying herself with her coat. I squinted at her, but she avoided my eye.

'And I've booked our slot. I had a feeling you'd be back for Christmas this year,' Josh added excitedly.

'You did not!' I nudged him with my shoulder. 'You just booked in blind hope.'

'And my Christmas wish came true,' he said, fluttering his eyelashes. I slung an arm around him.

'I love you guys.'

'And we love you.' Megan winked. 'Now hurry up and finish those drinks so I can take us somewhere modern.'

'Ooh, *Heaven*?' Josh suggested hopefully.

'No.' Megan shot back instantly.

'You're no fun,' he replied, tossing back his drink.

'Don't forget, I've got to get Pim to her tech rehearsal at the Southbank Centre by ten tomorrow.' The other reason Pim was back in town with me in tow was for her to do a one-night-only event to celebrate the fortieth anniversary of her iconic performance in *Wuthering Heights*. A show that both of us had been surprised to find had been in demand – especially as it was taking place on Christmas Eve. Turns out the LGBT+ community still loved her, years after her decline in the eyes of the mainstream, and if it was a choice between watching *Meet Me in St Louis* (for the hundredth time) or hearing Pim Hardcastle speak at the Southbank, they'd choose the latter.

'Oh, pish! Stop worrying about work,' Megan said, slipping off her stool and pulling her Burberry coat around her shoulders.

'Says the consultant who's *always* on the clock.'

Megan smiled, adjusting her wedding ring absent-mindedly before quipping, 'I own my business, which means I also own my clock.' And striding out of the pub as quickly as possible.

Josh stared after her, eyes squinting as if deep in thought. 'If she owns the clock but takes a work call while she's with us, does that mean she doesn't want to be with us in that moment?'

'Yes, Josh,' I laughed. 'I think it does.'

'How rude!' he gasped, clutching his imaginary pearls. 'I love it.'

Chapter 2

'Megan! Don't leave us!' Josh implored childishly, as we tried to peel his grip from around Megan's arm.

'Act your age.' Megan went straight into mum mode. 'You're not that drunk.'

'No,' Josh sighed, releasing her as he burped and rubbed his belly. 'That McDonald's hit the spot.'

'Classy.'

I laughed. 'I'll look after him.'

'Excuse me.' Josh turned to me. 'I'm the senior party here.'

'By three months,' I reminded him as Megan kissed me on the cheek. 'Get home safe, and text us when you're in.'

'Yes, *Mum*,' she replied playfully, though I knew she quite enjoyed being mothered for once rather than the other way round.

'Send my love to Alex.'

She nodded curtly. 'Don't give her alcohol poisoning, Josh.'

Josh rolled his eyes and began walking away backwards. 'It's mulled wine, hardly neat whisky.'

'Are you sure you can't come?' I asked quietly one last time.

Megan nodded. 'Sorry, hon. Alex has been home with Alfie all week. I need to give him a break.' What about *her* break? Josh had told me this was the first time he'd seen Megan since October; it was hardly like she was painting the town red every evening. 'I'll miss my train. Go, have fun.' She blew me a kiss again and walked away.

'Come on, come on!' Josh acted like a petulant child at Disneyland when he was drunk, even mildly so.

'I'm coming!'

The Covent Garden piazza was packed; though it was early December, it was heaving with frustrated-looking shoppers and wide-eyed tourists. The massive red Christmas tree sparkled in the open-air marketplace, looking much more festive than the barely decorated fir tree in Trafalgar Square, near my hotel. Inside the covered market, giant glitter balls and mistletoe hung from the ceiling, casting rainbows across the crowds. Stalls selling festive trinkets and tourist incentive gifts lined the market, while seasonal displays promoted a selection of West End musicals and children's pantomimes.

The air buzzed with the hum of conversation, broken only by occasional sleigh-bell sound effects and endless renditions of 'Let It Snow' over the ancient sound system.

'You're so lucky you get to experience this every year,' I said, watching Josh's face light up as his endless Christmas energy began to rise.

'Come on,' he said, grabbing my hand. 'Let's get the mulled wine before the snow starts at eight.'

'The snow?'

'Yes!' Josh grinned. 'They pump out a load of artificial snow around the tree every hour.'

'What time is it now?' I asked, glancing around. I spotted the clock above St Paul's Church. 'Quarter to. Plenty of time.'

Before I could offer to stay with him, he darted into the growing queue, leaving me to search for a table. I made a beeline for a pair of empty chairs, only to be beaten by a mother and her young son. He was wearing a Santa hat and a sweater vest with nutcrackers on it. I couldn't begrudge them the seats. Who could? Smiling awkwardly, I backed away, trying not to look as if I was sulking.

But then I walked into something. Actually, I walked into *someone.* A man, sending everything in his arms clattering to the ground.

'Oh my gosh!' I exclaimed, dropping to my knees to help. 'I am so sorry! I didn't see you!'

'It's fine,' the man mumbled, scooping up his things: a large black box, a tangle of wires, a hard-shell suitcase, and a microphone.

'Can I help you carry anything?' I asked.

Then he looked up.

Hello, gorgeous man.

'Hi,' I said, painfully aware of the breathlessness of my voice.

'Hi,' he replied, narrowing his eyes at me before straightening up.

'I'm so sorry, I—'

'Yeah, I heard you…' He didn't finish the sentence, and I could tell it wasn't exactly fine. His expression showed the internal struggle of someone trying not to be rude while undoubtedly thinking a few choice words.

'Seriously, can I help?'

He sighed, his gaze flicking over me and pausing briefly

when he noticed my red-and-white striped jeans. It was *a* look, I know. Finally, he gave in.

'Yes, I'd appreciate that,' he said, pulling over the black hard-shell suitcase.

Though I had offered, fairly insistently, I was still surprised when he accepted. Strangers rarely do, especially when another stranger has just barrelled into them.

'You can carry this,' he said, handing me the suitcase. It was much heavier than I expected. Without another word, he turned and began weaving through the crowd. I had to jog to keep up.

'Where are we going?' I asked, suddenly remembering Josh was waiting for me, and that I was supposed to be finding us seats before the snow started.

'Not far. Just by the church,' he called over his shoulder, slipping through the throng with practised ease. He stopped under the arches of St Paul's Church and began unloading his gear.

'You can put that there,' he said, gesturing to a neat pile of items at his feet.

I hesitated, glancing around. For a split second, I wondered if he was homeless, living under the arches with all his worldly possessions packed into tidy cases. But then I noticed the knife-thrower wrapping up his act nearby, thanking the crowd and collecting tips in an upturned hat.

The penny dropped. 'Are you a busker?'

'Might be,' he quipped with a small smile. He began to plug the wires into the black case, which I suddenly realised was an amp, before he began building a mic-stand.

'You're a singer?'

'Could be.'

'You don't talk much, do you?' I said, crossing my arms, now determined to coax more than two words out of him.

'Not with people that don't look where they're going.' He fiddled with the amp's dials, focusing on his set-up.

'I was!' I said indignantly, and then I remembered actually I *wasn't*. 'Okay, maybe not *this* time, but I usually do. I'm very responsible, I even check the streets before I cross on a green light.' This was such an overshare, but I wasn't going to have him think I was a clueless tourist with no manners or sense of direction. But he said nothing, he just kept preparing his amp.

I crossed my arms. 'I'm sorry.' He continued to say nothing, and I rolled my lips, trying not to laugh with frustration. He kept on with his set-up, but he wouldn't quit staring at me. It was unnerving, in a strangely enjoyable way. 'What? Are you saving your voice for the show?'

That made him smile – a proper smile – it lit up his face, making it impossible not to notice how handsome he was.

'No, I just don't usually talk to people before my shows. I'm not used to it.'

'No friends around to cheer you on?' I immediately regretted how that sounded. 'I mean… are they at work, or maybe they don't live nearby, or—'

'I don't have many,' he said, unfazed by my awkwardness. 'Not many who understand busking, at least.'

'That's a shame,' I said quickly. 'It's kind of cool, isn't it?'

His brow furrowed. 'Are you asking me?'

'No, I mean it *is* cool. I always thought busking was like begging. But then I learned how much work goes into it. In the city, I mean. You have to audition, right? Get a licence and everything for it.'

'Oh, really?' he replied sarcastically.

I was rambling. 'And Covent Garden is, like, extra-exclusive. Special licence, strict time slots...'

'That's true.' His tone was neutral but his expression became amused as I gave him a run-down of the procedure he had clearly already been through. It was full-on word vomit. I couldn't stop.

'... and you can only perform at specific times, like...'

'Like now,' he interrupted, nodding towards the knife-thrower, who was clearing the performance space.

'Oh, crap!' I stammered. 'I'm so sorry.'

'You say that a lot.' He was already picking up his amp and moving towards the centre of the space. 'Sorry. You say "sorry" a lot.'

'I'm British.' I shrugged. 'You know what it's like; it's a reflex. Especially abroad.'

'You're not from London?'

'Yes and no,' I replied, following him like a stray dog. The crowd from the knife-thrower had started to disperse, though it wouldn't take long for a new one to gather, I expected, there were so many people in the piazza. With the Christmas tree sparkling nearby and the first flurries of fake snow scheduled to start any minute, it was a prime slot, I imagined.

'I should leave you to your show.' I began awkwardly stepping back. 'Break a leg, I guess.'

'You say that to actors, not buskers.' He smiled faintly as he adjusted his mic.

'What do you say to buskers then?'

'Good luck.'

Funny, that.

'Good luck!' I added, before retreating into the crowd, hoping my face wasn't turning the same shade of red as one of Josh's Santa suits.

'Evie!' I heard Josh call. I turned to look for him, spotting him weaving through the crowd, holding two steaming cups of mulled wine. 'Hey, I thought you were getting seats?' He handed me a cup.

'Sorry. I lost them, and then…' I trailed off, glancing back towards the busker. 'Let's just say I'm feeling a little embarrassed right now.'

Josh raised an eyebrow. 'Why, what did you do?'

'I, uh… kind of told that guy over there that buskers were beggars and explained how hard it is to get a licence.'

Josh's eyes furrowed a little as he wondered why that was an issue, and then he realised I meant the busker currently preparing to perform and his eyes went wide. 'You didn't!'

'Not on purpose!'

'He probably knew you didn't mean it.'

'I hope so.' I could feel my cheeks warming to the temperature of the wine.

Josh led me to the steps near the tree. 'Come on, the snow's starting soon. We'll watch his show – you should really, after your terrible comments.'

I grumbled, but Josh dragged me along, and we sat as the crowd began to form around the busker.

'One minute until the snow,' Josh added, looking at his watch as the busker began to talk to his audience. I didn't hear his introduction, so I missed his name. But what would I have done with it, had I heard? Stalk him on TikTok? Tag him in a video?

I got my phone out and began to record.

'Get your content, girlie!' Josh slurped his mulled wine as we listened to the singer. 'He's got a good voice,' Josh commented, after the busker made a joke that caused a wave of laughter to trickle through the crowd. As ever, Josh's assessment was right: the busker's voice was rich and tuneful. He had a slightly Matthew Macfadyen-esque accent that put visions of Mr Darcy into my head, which I quickly shook away as I spun the camera around for a full view of the crowd.

The singer continued to speak to his audience: 'I know what you're all thinking, '*Oh no, here comes another Covent Garden beggar. I mean, busker.*'

Josh nearly did a spit take. I stopped recording and put my phone away as the busker's gaze found mine, his smile full of mischief.

I smiled back, mouthing a silent *sorry.*

He winked before continuing, as he pulled the leather guitar strap over his shoulder. 'But whatever money you do choose today will be donated to Crisis, a charity for the homeless.'

Josh's second attempt to drink some mulled wine went as well as the first, and he burned his tongue.

'Thank you for your kind thoughts, and Merry Christmas!'

Then, as the snow began to fall, the busker strummed the opening chords of 'Last Christmas' on his electric guitar and the song filled the square. The magic of the moment unfolded; phones went up, voices joined in, and the singer's soulful voice turned the bustling piazza into something extraordinary.

'George Michael, eat your heart out,' Josh whispered,

as the busker's voice rang out, his tone a mixture of Tom Odell and Lewis Capaldi. 'He's brilliant.'

'He is,' I agreed. But I wasn't paying attention to the snow or the song. I was too busy watching him.

Chapter 3

IT'S OFFICIAL, ALARM CLOCKS AND HANGOVERS are mortal enemies. They can never be friends.

I had no recollection of getting back to my Travelodge in St Martin-in-the-Fields. There was a hazy memory of Josh bundling me into one of those extortionately priced pedicabs in Piccadilly, the kind decked out with cheetah-print fur, blasting an odd mix of Sabrina Carpenter and Cyndi Lauper at eardrum-bursting levels while you cling on for dear life in the back; like a fever-dream nightclub on wheels. I shuddered at the thought and groped blindly for my phone, which was screeching its 6.30 a.m. alarm.

Eventually – painfully – I silenced it, collapsing back against the pillow. A message from Josh stared back at me, sent at 3.00 a.m.

Josh: *Did you get in okay?*

I'd had three hours of sleep. Not great, not terrible. I could probably survive the day on that.

'Why?' I said into my pillow, my disgustingly acidic breath making me want to gag. It would have been a much calmer evening if I had just had that one cup of mulled wine with Josh, as we said we would. But then one turned into two, as my embarrassment over insulting the busker overcame me. And then, open to suggestion through the headiness of alcohol, I was convinced by Josh to go to Heaven after all. Needless to say, my Friday night was not spent clipping my nails in my hotel, but singing 'What Makes You Beautiful' with two drag queens and a BDSM enthusiast. The chains were great for percussion.

Groaning, I peeled myself off the bed. Last night's clothes clung to me like a bad decision, and I desperately needed a shower and any kind of hydration. Shrugging off the straps of my dress, I shuffled around the room collecting my washbag and a slightly damp towel from the back of a chair, waiting for my dress to fall before I reached the bathroom. I still had tights on and, with a hangover-induced lack of care, I hooked a finger into an already trashy ladder and ripped them off me Hulk-style. If this were a romance novel, it might've seemed sexy, but in reality – panda eyes down to my chin – it was nothing short of vulgar.

The shower lasted longer than usual – I needed it – but, by the time I stepped out, I felt marginally human again. By 7.30, I was dressed in a classic Evie Frost ensemble: black jeans with flower patches hand-sewn onto the back pockets, an extra-fluffy jumper that shed like a nervous cat, and for a festive – if unprofessional – touch, a Santa hat with diamante sparkles. You couldn't miss me in a crowd, even in Christmas-mobbed Leicester Square.

I grabbed my phone, holding it up in selfie mode.

'Good morning, my lovelies! Today is a very exciting day – it's the first of many tech rehearsals,' I said, channelling my inner Anna from *Frozen*. 'I've got a great feeling about today, and I can't wait to take you along with me. So, without further ado, let's get going!' I saved the video, popped the phone into my bag, and promptly downed a bottle of water, two paracetamol, and rubbed a liberal dose of menthol headache balm onto my forehead.

'Good morning!' The hotel receptionist greeted me at the front desk as I came downstairs with my oversized handbag and my gaze deep in my phone, looking at today's itinerary.

'Morning, Andy!'

'Busy day ahead?'

'Yes. Lots more guests arriving for the holidays today.'

I paused at the exit to face him. 'Good luck! I hope they're not humbug.'

He chuckled. 'I hope so too.'

I stepped out of the automatic doors and emerged onto the street. London in the early morning had a specific kind of magic. It was too early for the masses to have descended into the city centre, but there was an air of anticipation. Porters and security guards were setting up signs outside the National Gallery, artisans and chefs were arranging their festive stalls in nearby Trafalgar Square, and a street sweeper was whistling 'Step into Christmas' as he picked up crisp packets and beer cans with his grabber on the corner of the road.

'Morning!' I shouted, as I pulled out my headphones – which also acted as earmuffs – and walked past, taking a quick video of my surroundings. The sweeper looked up, startled by my cheer.

As I made my way from St Martin's Lane towards the Strand, I slipped on my headphones and hit 'Play' on my signature Christmas playlist. Wham!, Mariah Carey, the Ronettes, and Brenda Lee crooned into my ears as I hummed down the street.

I had plenty of tasks to tackle before meeting Pim at

the Savoy at 9.00. First, her dry-cleaning, then breakfast, followed by a quick trip to the newsagent's for her essential reading material, as she can't eat breakfast without the latest news from gossip magazines, despite me showing her time and time again how to use Instagram.

The dry cleaners weren't technically open for another two hours, but years of working for someone like Pim had taught me to make inconvenience feel worthwhile. And I found a genuine smile, an easy-to-deal-with attitude, and a generous tip was more than enough to make people feel comfortable doing the odd favour for a relatively well-known figure, even if they were really just dealing with me. I might have seemed to pop up out of nowhere, but being polite, grateful, and mindful of people's time went a long way, and I genuinely enjoyed getting to know them.

As I approached the shop, the dry-cleaner was already outside, cigarette in hand, smoke curling into the frosty air.

'Aha! You're late,' he said, glancing at his watch. It was 8.05.

'I was letting you have a lie-in,' I replied, following him into the shop, where his perpetually bored teenage daughter perched on the counter with three large dry-cleaning bags draped over her lap.

'Here you are,' he said, sweeping the bags off her knees and gesturing to her to get down. She rolled her eyes and slouched into the chair behind the counter.

'You're a dream,' I said, juggling the weighty bags while fumbling to open my phone's card function to tap his machine.

'When should I expect the next lot?'

'Probably the day after tomorrow. She's going shopping

and she hates wearing clothes others might have tried on until they've been properly cleaned.'

He tore the receipt from the machine and handed it to me with a bemused shake of his head. 'You know what we call that kind of person? A diva.'

'I thought you had heard of Pim Hardcastle.'

He smirked, pausing to hold the door open for me. 'Until the day after tomorrow then.'

'You can catch up on some sleep in the meantime,' I said, shifting the bags.

'Me? How about you?'

'Wouldn't that be nice.' I waved awkwardly and made my way further down the Strand to a tiny bistro tucked into a side street. Its front was dark and uninviting, the *closed* sign still firmly in place, so I slipped round the back. Like the dry cleaners, I had spent some time coaxing my way into the kitchen of a well-rated, family-run restaurant, reliant on light-hearted humour and easy-going discussions about my time in Greece to make the owners feel excited about cooking for the one and only Pim Hardcastle.

A goods-in door was open. Over my headphones, I caught snatches of a Greek rock band blasting from within the kitchen.

'Michalis!' I called out. 'Michalis!'

The sous-chef looked up mid-grill, spatula in hand.

'Sorry, sorry,' he said, flipping the halloumi expertly. 'You here for breakfast?'

'For Pim's breakfast. She said what she had last time was…' I hesitated, translating Pim's *passable and filling* into something more complimentary. 'Delicious. The cheese pie with nuts and honey?'

'Sfakianopita.'

'That's the one.' I hoped it was the one. I may have spent three sunny months living in a hostel with a fantastic view of the Acropolis, but I had never mastered the basics of the beautiful Greek language.

'Fifteen minutes,' he said, turning back to the stove.

'Fabulous. I'll grab her coffee and come back.'

'Got it.' He reached for the volume knob, already tuning me out. Michalis wasn't the chatty type, but he did love a compliment. After discovering his restaurant during a Pim-mandated quest for the best Greek food in London, I'd charmed my way into early-morning kitchen privileges with lavish praise and hefty tips. It turns out money and flattery really can open doors.

Pim's coffee order was mercifully easy to fetch: a blisteringly hot, skinny caramel macchiato with an extra shot of espresso from Starbucks. The line was non-existent at this early hour on a weekend, sparing me the usual commuter chaos.

On the way back to the restaurant, with the coffee in one hand, dry-cleaning draped over my arm, and my oversized handbag balanced precariously on my shoulder, I ducked into a newsagent's to gather the necessary literature that Pim expected every morning. Somehow, I managed to stack them onto my already overflowing load. There was no way to record this portion of my morning with all the items in my hands.

Back at Achilles & Sons, Michalis was waiting with a Styrofoam box in one hand and the card reader in the other.

'Thank you so much.' I tapped my well-worn phone and added the breakfast to my tower of burdens.

Balancing everything, I headed down the Strand towards the Savoy. Thankfully, the walk wasn't as far as, say, crossing Central Park or the Opéra district in Paris. The familiar sight of the hotel was like a finish line, and I practically collapsed through the revolving doors, greeted by the ever-efficient bellman, who immediately relieved me of my load.

'Morning, Miss Frost,' Tony, the doorman, said with a nod, echoed by Charles, the concierge.

'Good morning!' I said breathlessly, handing over everything but the coffee to the bellman. 'Charles, did the plate and cutlery make it to Pim's room?' Even with a hangover, I had a good feeling about today and no amount of hard work was going to dampen my spirits.

'They'll be on a trolley outside the room.'

'Wonderful, and would it be possible to book a taxi for 9.40? We need to get to the Southbank Centre at 10.00 on the dot.'

'I'll organise that for you now,' Charles said, reaching for the phone.

'Amazing, and can you…'

'I will call up to Miss Hardcastle's room at 9.20 to say the car has arrived,' he finished smoothly, cutting me off with a knowing smile.

'Brilliant, you're a gem.' Pim never left her room on time, *ever.*

'Thank you, Miss Frost.' His eyes flicked to my sweater, his expression warming. 'Fantastic jumper.'

'Thank you, I made it.'

'Really?' His face lit up. It really was a joyful jumper. 'I'll have to get the pattern off you. My girlfriend enjoys a bit of knitting.'

'It's a great hobby when passing the time in airports and green rooms,' I said, smiling as I reached for my phone. 'Want to be in a TikTok again?'

Charles scoffed but couldn't hide his grin as he stood from his desk. 'Only if I don't have to dance this time.'

'How about a wave and that dazzling smile?' I lifted my phone to frame him. 'Cheese!' Charles added a playful hip bop for good measure, making me laugh. 'I appreciate you, Charles,' I told him, before gesturing to the coffee in my hand. 'But I'd better get this upstairs.'

'Of course. Have a good day, Miss Frost!' He exchanged a wink with Tony, who was smirking in the doorway.

'It will be your turn next, Tony!' I called over my shoulder.

I distinctly heard Tony mutter, 'Not bloody likely.' As I skipped past the floral display in the foyer, where two florists were meticulously replacing wilting blooms with fresh arrangements. The busboy was patiently waiting by the lift, holding open the door.

'Onwards and upwards,' I narrated as I entered.

Pim's suite was on one of the Savoy's most exclusive floors, in a room that practically doubled as a luxury flat, with its own living room and a grand wardrobe, which Pim had made a point of filling so it would barely close. She didn't have a permanent home, preferring instead to rent storage units in various cities and multiple countries to be able to make a home wherever she landed. 'A nomad isn't a nomad if she can't make a hotel room feel like home,' she often said.

I opened the door to her suite with my keycard – Pim didn't answer her own doors, especially this early. I asked the busboy to hand me the bags, rather than following me just in case he glimpsed Pim without her make-up and hair done – a firing offence if ever there was one – before handing him a £20 note and wishing him a Merry Christmas as I wheeled the plate and cutlery inside.

'And to you, Miss.'

I shut the door. The air was infused with the faint scent of Chanel perfume, and it triggered the return of my hangover. I had to keep those symptoms at bay as long as possible, and the best way to get over a hangover is to get on with it.

Without pause, I pulled open the curtains and hastened to add Pim's breakfast onto a proper plate.

I moved into her bedroom. She was awake, propped against her mountain of pillows like a queen awaiting an audience. Her raven-black hair was coiffed to perfection, not a strand out of place. She wasn't wearing make-up, but her skin gleamed with the dewy sheen of a £300 toner and gold-infused moisturiser, which made me think she had had a shower and blow-dried her hair, before she got back into her nightdress and robe.

She was a beautiful woman, not even for her age but just in general. A cross between Jackie Collins and Kristin Scott Thomas. Buxom, petite, and perfectly symmetrical, with large eyes that could pierce you. Eyes that were staring at me with benign frustration.

'You're late,' she announced.

'Am I?' I glanced at the clock. 8.45. I was exactly on time. 'Apologies,' I said lightly, bringing her tray to the bed. Don't ever disagree with Pim Hardcastle, at least not directly, a lesson I had learned early on in my career. 'I've brought you your breakfast.' I laid the tray across her legs, and she looked over it for a moment before shrugging in a defeatist *if I must* way and began to eat.

'My coffee?' she asked mid-bite.

I placed the Starbucks cup on a waiting coaster on the side table. She insisted on drinking it straight from the branded cup, a quirk I found amusing. I tidied the room while she sipped her coffee, flipping through the magazines I'd placed at her bedside.

'What's on the itinerary today?' she asked eventually.

'We have the tech rehearsal at the Southbank in about an hour.'

'My dry-cleaning?'

'Hanging up in the dressing room,' I said, having just finished that task. 'Would you prefer to wear flats or heels?'

'Heels, but pack flats. My ankles may revolt.'

I hastily pulled a pair of black ballet flats, which probably cost more than my monthly salary, from the shoe rack and placed them in my bag so I wouldn't forget. 'After the rehearsal, you're having lunch with the BBC producer.'

She complained theatrically. 'He's such a bore.'

'A bore organising the televising of *Pim's O'Clock*.' The name of her one-night event.

'Who is going to pay for tickets to a one-night event if it's just going to air on TV?' she said tetchily, launching into a well-worn debate.

'It's more lucrative, and it lets all your fans, more than just the thousand in attendance, be part of it.'

'Just a thousand,' she scoffed. 'One thousand dedicated, obsessive, and intelligent fans. It's not a small thing.'

'No, it's not, but you have a lot more than one thousand dedicated, obsessive, and intelligent fans,' I reminded her. 'They'll love to hear you speak.'

'They can hear me speak whenever they like. It's not like I'm a recluse; I'm on TV more than the King of England.'

'Yes, but not like this. Ninety minutes, just you and your wonderful stories. They're going to love it,' I said, leaning into my role as personal cheerleader. Ego stroking should be a LinkedIn skill choice.

Pim waved dismissively and pushed her tray aside in favour of drinking her super-strong coffee. 'You know I don't like to talk about myself.'

Here we go. Time to pander to the queen of reality TV who makes her money by talking about herself.

'I know, but your fans adore you. They want to be a part of your world. They look up to you,' I said, settling into the chintz armchair by the window. Pim needed a healthy dose of ego stroking before she'd even consider getting out of bed. 'I love hearing your stories.'

'Well, you're in a privileged position. Sworn to secrecy,' she remarked, her beautiful eyes bulging with the reminder that what happened in her world stayed there. 'Not that it matters to you any more. You probably don't even mean it when you say you enjoy my stories.'

I smiled dolefully, lowering my phone with her itinerary into my lap.

'I'm not leaving because I don't enjoy my job. I've been with you for eight years,' I reminded her.

'I practically raised you,' she replied, her tone laced with bitterness.

'You were pivotal in my formative years as an adult,' I said, my reassurance almost theatrical now. I truly liked Pim – I did – but, as much as she was a role model to me (once I got past the falsehood and flounces), she was also my boss. Career loyalty could only stretch so far. 'I'll never be able to repay you for everything you've given me.'

'Repay me?' she scoffed, pushing the tray off her lap

with dramatic flair. 'Darling, you couldn't afford me.' She flung off the duvet in an exaggerated gesture. 'Right, let's get to work.'

'Sounds like a plan,' I said, guiding her towards the dressing room, where her outfits awaited her.

'After the lunch with the ghastly producer, what's next?'

'Facialist at three, manicurist at four, dinner with the Foxes at five, and a gathering with the Greys afterwards.'

'Why am I so popular?' she griped, her back to me as she began to disrobe. I returned to the living area, getting her bag and items for the day in order.

'Because it's Christmas, and everyone wants to see you. It's been years since you last spent Christmas in London.'

'I was here two summers ago.'

'But not Christmas.'

Pim scoffed. 'So they're all trying to fit me into their festive calendars. Christ, it's not like I'm *dying*, and they need to say their goodbyes.'

'It will be lovely to catch up with so many friendly faces.'

'*Friendly?* More like Botoxed faces.' As if she hadn't had Botox – I know she had, I booked the appointment. 'What about the other task, the assistant hunt?'

I exhaled with relief; thank Christ she had brought it up herself! Any mention of it on my part and she would usually give me the silent treatment for a good hour before asking me to pass her jade roller or feed Gerald the Chow Chow.

'The ad is live. I'll meet the candidates next week.'

'An ad? Ugh. Back in my day, assistants threw themselves at me.'

'I must've been the cheapest,' I quipped brazenly, earning a pointed glare before apologising, as Pim disappeared back behind the wardrobe door. 'How are you doing in there?' I called after a moment. She stepped out, a cloud of Chanel announcing her presence, dressed immaculately with red lipstick applied with the precision of a painter.

'Doing? I'm doing fine,' she sighed in a bored kind of way. 'What time is the taxi?' She looked at the clock on the wall: 9.15 now.

'Not long. I've packed your bag.'

'Did you pack my mints? Last time you forgot the mints.' I hadn't forgotten actually; they were just inside the zip pocket.

'I triple-checked and they're in there. The car is due at 9.20, so shall we head down shortly?' Instead of moving to get her shoes or jacket on, she perched on the sofa, scrolling absently on her phone.

'How was your night out?' she asked.

'It was great. I got to see my friend, Josh, and my sister, Megan. They've made me a Christmas bucket list before I move to Toronto. I'm shooting it for my Assistmas series on TikTok. We're going to go ice skating, mulled wine, the works.'

'How… fun,' she said, her tone distracted. 'I think they're serving mulled wine at the event.'

'Surely it's Pimm's?' Suddenly panicking that the Southbank Centre hadn't got the full plan from the producer and checking my emails. 'Yes. See, it's a free Pimm's – or non-alcoholic version – upon entry.' I tried to show Pim the phone, but she waved it away.

'Well, they should serve mulled wine. It *is* Christmas, after all.'

'It's Christmas Eve,' I whispered. The event was happening the day before Christmas, in three weeks' time, when most of the city would be fleeing to the countryside to spend the holidays with family. Pim, of course, was staying at the Savoy, along with a small number of high-profile guests. I made a mental note to pick up some thank-you gifts for the staff on Pim's behalf. They'd be working through the holidays, and I knew how hard that could be.

Despite having no blood family to spend the holidays with, it still wasn't easy being away from Megan, Josh, Denise, and Bob on Christmas Day every year. There was always a moment – often more than one – where I would picture myself sipping prosecco, nibbling on turkey sandwiches, and laughing through game after game of Pictionary and Monopoly with them. But, invariably, every year I would push down the feeling and get on with my day, as if it were any other day. And with Pim, it always was the same day.

The phone began to ring on the dresser. 'That'll be Charles saying the car has arrived,' I said, reaching for the phone.

'Leave it. Let's go!' Pim huffed, suddenly grabbing my shoulder for support as she stepped into her heels before jolting for the door as if she had been the one to suggest it. 'What are you waiting for?' she called back.

I smiled and picked up her bag. 'Nothing at all, Pim.' Only a few more weeks, I reminded myself. Then I'd be my own boss again.

Chapter 4

LATER THAT AFTERNOON, AFTER DROPPING PIM off for a Michelin-starred dinner with the Fox family dynasty, I headed to Holborn for a much cheaper meal with Josh.

Josh was an extravagant Londoner, who considered kitchens purely decorative. Whether from laziness or lack of culinary skill, I could never truly tell. Either way, he was great company, and since my palate had barely scratched the surface of London's food scene, I was more than happy to indulge.

I arrived at the restaurant early, a habit I'd picked up from managing Pim's schedule. Producers, directors, and casting agents despised tardiness, so my running early often ensured she was on time. At the restaurant, the hostess informed me, 'Your table will be ready in twenty minutes,' and gestured towards a plush sofa in the bar. Sitting down with my enormous bag, I pulled out my trusty iPad to review the CVs sent over by a recruitment agency.

So far, the calibre for the 'new me' wasn't inspiring hope. There were a few too many PAs jumping from client to client, clearly unable to handle big personalities – an instant no when hiring for Pim. Then there were the few promising ones I knew she'd detest: a West End ensemble actress-turned-assistant, a veteran PA no doubt set in the ways of an old client after twenty years of service, and the aimless university graduates treating this job as a stepping stone. I'd started in the latter way, but my no-strings lifestyle and bulletproof ego had made me surprisingly well suited to wrangling a dramatic, jet-setting performer with an ego the size of Sheffield and a bank balance to match.

Basically, I needed to find someone like me: low-maintenance, low-fear, and low on attachments. Not easy.

'What're you reading?' Josh's voice startled me as he appeared behind me.

I yelped, clutching the iPad to my chest.

'Ha! Gotcha!' he said, kissing my cheek before sliding onto the sofa beside me. He glanced around, frowning slightly. 'This isn't where we're eating, is it?'

'No, our table's being prepared,' I said, hastily stuffing the iPad back into my bag.

'What are you hiding away?' He peered curiously at my bag.

'I was trying to find the "new me",' I said, using air quotes.

Josh scoffed. 'There'll never be another you. Just hire someone who can get the job done, bail, and then leave the mess behind.'

'I'm not doing that,' I replied, quietly appalled at the thought of leaving Pim stranded. She wasn't a friend, but she deserved better than that.

'She's a tyrant,' Josh added.

'She's an ageing star; she's earned a little tyranny.'

'She acts like Katharine Hepburn on-screen, but off-? She's more Katharine "Kay" Francis.'

'Who?'

'Exactly.'

Josh flagged down a passing waiter, who stopped instantly, drawn to Josh's chiselled jaw and dark, smouldering eyes. With his thick stubble and unruly hair, Josh was the quintessential tall, dark, and handsome cliché. Once, he was mistaken for Oscar Isaac and didn't know whether he should be delighted to be associated with such an attractive man or aghast that someone thought him fifteen years older than he was. I told him to take the compliment.

'I'll have a Peroni,' Josh said with a flirtatious smile. 'No rush; we're enjoying the ambience.'

Josh might as well have been alone. The waiter barely acknowledged me as I added, 'I'll have a Peroni too.'

As soon as the waiter had left, still pausing to glance back for a few lingering seconds to stare at Josh, I hummed Mendelssohn's 'Wedding March' under my breath.

'Stop it,' Josh said, sitting back. 'He's nice to look at, but there's nothing behind the eyes.'

'Really? How can you tell? I say ask for his number.'

Josh rolled his eyes and smiled as if he had been waiting for a comment like this so he could say, 'Darling, I'm spoken for.'

I sat bolt upright – not easy on this kind of loaf-like sofa. 'You're *what*? Since when?'

'Since last month,' he said, beaming. 'It's been blink-and-you'd-miss-it kind of quick.'

'Clearly! Last month, you were crying over the lack of decent Grindr dates. Now you've found someone?'

'Maybe *the* one,' he said, his eyes sparkling.

I bit my tongue, resisting the urge to remind him that all his last six boyfriends had been 'the one' at some point. 'Exciting! Who is he?'

'His name's Zach. He's an accountant.'

'Please tell me he looks like Richard Armitage circa *Vicar of Dibley*?'

'I wish. He's not quite *that* good-looking, but close.'

'Tell me everything.' I scooted closer, eager for details.

'We met trying to get into the same taxi at Charing Cross. I said he could have it – being polite and all – and he said he hadn't realised I was waiting, so it was mine. In the end, we just decided to share it.'

'Oh, my God, that's such a sweet meet-cute,' I said, feeling a warm glow spread through me. 'It's so Hallmark movie, I love it.' The only meet-cute I'd ever had was when I ended up going on a date with a man who accidentally trapped my wrist in a sliding door at a butcher's in Italy. It was more *meat*-cute than meet-cute, but he did introduce me to tiramisu gelato as a way of apology, and as a date, before getting distracted by another woman's extremely long legs as we walked across the Ponte Vecchio. I ended up making out with the gelato rather than the man.

'It really was,' Josh continued. 'Anyway, we were both heading to Piccadilly, not far, I know, but it was raining, and you *know* I'm a martyr to my hair.'

I nodded solemnly, resisting the urge to pat his head.

'So we're in the cab, chatting and flirting, and by the time we got to Eros's statue, we'd exchanged numbers. The taxi driver even joked, "*When's the wedding?*"'

We laughed as the waiter returned, placing our drinks on separate napkins on a side table. I thought it was odd – beer bottles on napkins? – until I noticed a phone number scribbled on Josh's.

'Oh, poor guy,' I said, watching the waiter walk away with a hopeful glance back. 'And to think I encouraged it.'

'It's fine,' Josh said, pocketing the napkin casually. 'Just because I've already ordered doesn't mean I can't look at the menu.'

We clinked bottles and relaxed. Josh took a small sip before diving into a rhapsody about his new boyfriend.

'The symmetry of his face is ridiculous. And the way he smells; like nutmeg cookies mixed with mulled wine.'

I raised an eyebrow. 'He smells like Christmas?'

'Christmas with a hint of cherry vape and a touch of Tom Ford.' Josh grinned. 'And the sex, Evie. The *sex*!'

'This I don't need details for,' I laughed, taking a long draught of my beer to give myself the time to do the mental maths on when I'd last had sex. Three years? Maybe more. The longest dry spell of my life; nothing worthy of an existential crisis. As a graysexual, my interest in sex was more of a polite curiosity, like wondering how the stock market's doing while rarely investing. Occasionally I'd reap a reward, but it had been a while.

'You're getting the details anyway.' Josh leaned in conspiratorially. 'It's vulgar, I know, but *my God*! I never thought sex could be so quick and yet still be A+, spot on, would come again.'

'Quick?' I asked, blinking. 'Are we talking... premature enthusiasm or—'

'Oh, it's all him,' Josh interrupted, a little too defensively. 'But not in a bad way. He just – he can't wait for the pleasure, skips right to the good stuff. It's magical.'

'Is it, though?' I asked, doubtful. Josh had never been one to equate brevity with brilliance before. I knew his preference was long and slow, more a marathon than a sprint.

'We're both busy! It's on-the-move sex, not gymnastic

stay-at-home sex,' he explained, as if this clarified everything.

'Okay,' I said, thinking that was more my speed than Josh's, but people can change. Although it felt... off. But this was Josh, and his taste in men had always been unconventional: from the Mancunian circus performer who set up a pole in Josh's living room (and left it!) to the Latvian rock guitarist who enjoyed strumming his guitar during fellatio or the architect who designed prison cells and would do anything sexual, so long as they did it outside.

'So when do I get to meet him?' I asked.

Josh flushed, looking suddenly uncomfortable. Oh wow, was it *that* serious?

'Come on,' I urged. 'I want to meet him.'

'It's not that I don't want you to. It's just... complicated.'

'Complicated how? Does he work abroad? Not into exclusivity? Are *you* keeping it casual?'

'None of the above,' Josh said firmly. 'I want it to be serious. But... it's complicated.'

'Why? Spit it out. Or don't.' I shook my head quickly. 'I don't want to push.'

Josh hesitated, then sighed. 'Maybe I *do* need to talk about it. I can't tell Megan, though.'

'Why not? She wouldn't tell anyone.'

'She'd judge.'

'Doesn't everyone? Secretly anyway.'

'Now you're making me doubt telling you,' he said, retreating slightly.

'You *know* I don't judge.' I gave his shoulder a reassuring squeeze. 'As long as you're happy and not hurting anyone, I'll support you.'

Josh went quiet.

'Oh God, what?' I asked, my chest tightening as scenarios flooded my mind. His bitter smile only confirmed my worst theory. 'No. He's married, isn't he?'

Josh's eyes scrunched shut as though bracing for a blow.

'Josh…' I whispered, leaning closer. 'You can't date a married man.'

'He's not happy,' Josh said, almost whining.

'That doesn't matter. If he's separated, fine. But if he's *married* married, then no. You've got to end it.'

'But he doesn't love him,' Josh insisted.

'Josh, you can't be the other person.'

'I'm not! I'm *his* person,' he said stubbornly.

'And his *husband* might disagree when he finds out. Which he will. Think about what happens then.'

Josh shook his head as if to dismiss my warning. 'This is why I shouldn't have told you.'

'I'm not judging you; I'm warning you,' I said firmly. The disaster waiting to happen played out vividly in my mind. Zach's husband finding out, Megan finding out, Josh's workplace finding out. Adultery is never a good look, especially if you knew and stayed. 'Babe, there's someone out there for you. But if Zach's taken, you need to move on.'

'What if this is one of those tests God sends?'

I cringed. Josh only referenced religion when he knew he was in the wrong. But I also knew better than to argue theology with someone who was brought up as a Jehovah's Witness. Josh's relationship with religion and homosexuality was a complicated one, even he hadn't dissected it yet.

'Just think about what I've said.' I held up my hands in a gesture of peace. 'Our table will be ready soon.'

'I really like him, Evie,' Josh said softly, a rare vulnerability in his voice.

'I know.' My heart was aching for him. 'I just wish that it wasn't so complicated.' Or *uncomplicated*, as to me there was really only one option when it came to sleeping with someone else's husband.

'Me too,' he admitted, but I could tell he sensed my judgement, though I tried hard to maintain a lid on it. With a sudden slap of his thigh, he pushed the conversation aside. 'Let's see if our table's ready.'

'They'll call us.' But Josh was already standing and grabbing his beer.

'Oh, screw that! I'm starving. Excuse me!' he shouted, weaving through the crowd to the hostess, who was already picking up the menus.

Chapter 5

LIFE WITH PIM WAS NEVER BORING, and certainly never quiet.

After numerous tech rehearsals, dress fittings, and hair trials, Pim still couldn't make a single decision about her upcoming show without doubling back at least three or four times. I was always there to smooth the waters: reassuring the producers, comforting the stylists, and bolstering egos wherever needed. My job was to make sure Pim didn't cause too much damage as she perfected her prima-donna routine.

Four times that week, I'd worked late into the evening, wining and dining various frustrated set producers and lighting technicians after a bad day. I let them vent, complain, and curse until we found a solution that satisfied everyone.

On rare afternoons away from set, I would visit museums and markets and walk around the Thames admiring the Christmas lights as they went up all around London. I'd always message Megan or Josh to see if they were free, but Josh was right in the thick of his Christmas takeover of Harrods and Megan had started to reply to texts with voice notes at midnight, saying she was still at the office.

'Sorry, love. I'll be free for lunch soon. I just have this one client who's a nightmare and I need to get the project over the finish line so I get paid before Christmas. And then Alex is being a right arseho— He's, erm, been off work this week with Alfie, who's got chickenpox. His nursery will be ground zero for the plague that turns us all into zombies, I swear! So I'll probably be working from home through to the weekend as Alex needs a break... Do you fancy dinner round ours soon actually, once Alfie's not contagious? Alex would probably like that. Adult company and all. Anyway, I've just got one more email to send, then I'll be heading home. I'll speak to you tomorrow. Love you lots!'

She was back at the office by the time I texted her the following morning at 8.00.

I didn't know whether it was time to worry or not yet. She and I were both 'workaholics' but, out of the two of us, I always thought Megan had the work-life balance under her belt. She had a husband, a toddler, and an active gym membership; you don't maintain those by working every hour.

I had to admit, to myself if not out loud, that it was frustrating to not be seeing them much. They had busy lives, and I worked odd hours, but it was my last Christmas in London, for a while at least. And it had been so long since I had spent this much time in the UK, but neither of them seemed to be putting much effort into seeing me. It was lonely spending every evening in my Travelodge watching *Gladiators* on ITV while eating yet another Pret sandwich – their Christmas range was on point this year.

Instead, for the days that the two of them were out of commission, and I was free from work, I made tons of videos for my TikTok to keep me occupied and my viewers sated. Energetic day-in-the-life clips, voice-over food reviews, everything brimming with festive cheer. I kept it light and positive; after nearly a decade in TV, I knew how quickly negativity could destroy a career and I was terrified all my hard work with Pim would be wasted by one stupid decision online. But what's safer or more joyful than Christmas content?

I was like a child in Hamleys in every video, eyes wide and glowing with excitement as I shared my festive solo adventures. My followers seemed to be enjoying it:

It's my dream to spend Christmas in London. But a bit pricey to fly from Melbourne! Love seeing all the sights on your channel.

Loving this new content. Can't wait to see more! 🎄🎄

What's the TV industry like at Christmas? Are the shows filmed live, or are they all pre-recorded in August? Would love to see what brand of decorations they use. Have you decorated for Christmas yet?

My thumb would hover over the screen, fluttering through the queries and requests, gaining new content ideas as I went. Most companies were happy for me to include some elements of behind-the-scenes, if it promoted the show, but some preferred the only cameras to be the ones shooting the actual show.

I always tried to get as much Christmas content as possible – as we did film it in the summer – well in advance, to capture the cheer, the fairy lights and snowscape. The actual Christmas period was usually much emptier, filled with gaps between jobs, airports, and hotel rooms dressed with napkins and paper chains.

No viewer wants to see that and I didn't want to film it. Yet this Christmas, my engagement rate had risen by five per cent – my largest jump yet. Filming live content, editing it, *and* ushering Pim around the city, had largely kept me busy in early December. It was a useful distraction from Josh's revelation about Zach.

He'd been a bit distant after telling me about him, but things had finally begun to settle into our old rhythms. He hadn't offered any further details about his relationship when we met up, and I didn't press for them, though I could tell he was itching to talk.

I wasn't judging him, not exactly. Zach was the one truly in the wrong, as far as I was concerned. But I couldn't bring myself to support Josh's role in the affair. It wasn't my business, but adultery was hard to condone, no matter how much I loved my friend and wanted to see him happy. In my mind, this situation was never going to end well.

Still, December was racing on, and my work had to be my focus.

'Pim, tell us, how are the preparations for your one-night show going?' The radio presenter's voice crackled through my headphones as I stood just outside the booth watching as Pim was quizzed on a BBC radio show.

'Oh, it's going so well! We've just announced that Emily Heston is chairing the event, which is so brilliant. She's fantastic.'

'Emily is wonderful. We've had her on the show a few times.'

'She's such a talent in the industry,' Pim interjected. 'I'm always so sad to hear that the community still alienates homosexuals. Emily is married to a delightful woman, and she told me the negative impact coming out had on her initial career. Well, not today, Satan! She can chair a show with me any day of the week.'

The radio presenter laughed heartily, completely unaware that I had fed Pim details on Emily, using flash cards, in the taxi to the studio that morning.

'Pim Hardcastle, everyone! As ever, an utter delight to have you on the show.'

'Thank you so much.' Pim beamed, looking radiant in an orange two-piece with her striking black hair in a perfectly styled messy bun.

'Tickets for *Pim's O'Clock* are on sale now, but they're going fast! Get yours soon, folks!'

'Today, preferably,' Pim added, laughing in a slight falsetto tone that I could tell meant that she was almost done with the charade. 'If I may be so cheeky.'

'Indeed you may. Pim Hardcastle, everybody! Stay tuned for the latest news from Alexandra Holmes and an update on the weather from Steven Ainsley! For now, I'm Thomasina Michaels and this is BBC Five Live.'

'And we're out,' the producer said from behind the door. I saw Pim and Thomasina removing their headphones from inside the booth.

The door opened.

'No, thank *you*!' Pim was wringing Thomasina's hand as the producer barged past and began re-setting the room with new scripts, papers, and talking points.

'Always wonderful to see you.' Thomasina smiled but her attention for Pim was waning.

'And you.' Pim let the assistant begin to direct us out of the building. The BBC offices do enjoy shepherding you in and out like you're a bomb about to explode.

'You were great,' I told Pim, offering her a water bottle and removing her printed talking points before she simply dropped them.

'What are they saying online?' she asked, her voice deepening back into her normal voice rather than the one she used for radio. I opened my phone and searched the relevant platforms.

'All good things,' I said cheerfully, scrolling through the comments that had come in so far.

'Read me some.'

I opened my phone as we entered a lift. 'Okay, one says *I have tickets to the show and I couldn't wait, now hearing Pim on Five Live I'm dying to hear her talk in person. Hurry up, Christmas!*'

'Not bad.' Pim nodded, clearly not yet sated with praise.

'Then someone called Sophia said *My heart can't take it! Pim Hardcastle gives me all the Miriam Margolyes vibes without the vulgarity. I just want to hug her.*'

'That's unfair on Miriam. She's hilarious.' Pim chuckled darkly. 'But I'll take the compliment.'

'I mean all of them are like that, everyone loves you, they can't wait for the show and there's been a lot of great feedback since the news of Emily chairing dropped.'

'She's a bit of a prat though,' Pim said, and I quickly cleared my throat as the assistant was still in earshot. We reached the doors to the reception, next to a Tardis just casually located beside the security doors, and I stepped in front of her.

'I think we can take it from here, thank you so much!' The assistant nodded without much interest, walking off with the kind of detached professionalism I recognised from years of managing celebrities – or, simply, Pim.

'Where to next?' Pim slammed her water bottle into my chest as I handed our security passes back to the team of threatening-looking door staff.

The car was waiting, just as planned. Pim slid into the back seat without hesitation, leaving me to dash around to the other side – it was one way to ensure I got my steps in.

'Next up is dinner,' I said simply, barely getting the door shut before the driver was already pulling away. There were times I wondered if I had developed the power of invisibility.

Pim glanced up from her phone. 'That little Thai spot behind King's Cross?'

'No, the Italian place in Chinatown.'

She went quiet, her gaze dropping back to her screen. She didn't have active social media accounts but, despite being a self-declared sceptic, she did love to know what I was posting on my TikTok and occasionally logged into Facebook just to play Candy Crush.

With a little trepidation I set my bag between my legs and reached inside.

'If you want,' I began, 'we can start to look through some of the CVs from the job ad. The agency has sent more, and some of them look promising.'

Pim didn't even glance up. 'Why would you open an Italian restaurant in Chinatown?'

I pressed on, undeterred by her avoidance of my question. 'There are four candidates I would like to invite for interview.' I swiped on the iPad to try and show her the details. 'Perhaps next week we could…'

'Italian food is so heavy on the stomach. Don't you realise I'm going to be on stage in front of thousands in a few weeks.' Her tone never wavered, making her sound surprisingly menacing.

'One serving of gnocchi – your favourite – is not going

to hurt,' I said, waiting for the inevitable *if-I-must* eye roll. It didn't come. She didn't even look at me. Her thumb kept tapping the screen of her phone, eyes locked on whatever was flashing in front of her.

Defeated, I put the cover on my iPad and put it back in my bag, the rustling of my over-filled bag pockets filling the silence between us.

Almost as soon as I pulled the zipper on my bag closed, Pim dropped her phone in her lap.

'I suppose one always puts weight on at Christmas time,' she remarked, staring out of the window as we stopped in the inevitable traffic of Regent's Street. It would be quicker to walk, but God forbid I ever mention walking to Pim. Public streets are for the public, not for household names. I wondered if she knew that she was only a household name because Pimm's was such a popular beverage in summer, or if she truly thought her acting career rivalled that of Judi Dench?

'I certainly plan to,' I said, letting the words settle between us. Food, I realised, had always been the one constant of Christmas I could rely on no matter where I ended up with Pim.

In Malta, I had devoured entire Maltese chocolate logs, my teeth sinking into cherries as I lounged about in bed, rewatching *The Grinch* for the hundredth time. In Australia, we feasted on so many seafood barbecues on the beach that I had half expected to grow gills. In Dubai, I had practically lived at the all-you-can-eat hotel buffet, drowning in turkey, mince pies, and every festive beverage under the sun. And in New York, I'd learned that the city truly never sleeps… and neither did the chefs.

'Christmas Day,' she began, still not looking at me.

'I'm thinking lunch at the Savoy and then dinner with the Redgraves?'

'They're away in Majorca.' My head ached from remembering the schedules of all Britain's most prominent acting families. 'The Foxes have extended an invite.'

'I just had dinner with them.'

'Well, they said that you were more than welcome to join them this Christmas if you find yourself…' I trailed off, but I didn't need to finish the sentence. She'd caught the drift.

Her neck stiffened and she flinched. 'Well, you and I will make do with the Savoy then. Maybe Gordon will cook it.'

'Gordon's with his family,' I blinked. 'And… and…'

'And what? Spit it out!' she said, as she picked up her phone again.

I took a deep breath. 'I'm planning on spending Christmas with my friends this year.'

Technically, Christmas was a mandated bank holiday, but I'd never taken it off before. There was always the stress of flights, baggage reclaim, the impersonal rush of travel. But this year? I was finally home. I could hop on a train with Megan and head down to Kent to Denise and Bob's, no hassle, no flight, just… home.

Pim didn't say anything at first, the only sound between us was the tap of her fingers on her phone screen. We passed the familiar shops of Chinatown, the vibrant signs blurring in my peripheral vision.

'I'll be an orphan on my own this year,' she said finally, her face unreadable.

The guilt landed instantly. Part of me hated how quickly it came, how easily my excitement shifted into something that felt selfish. Immediately I felt myself opening my mouth to say that I could maybe spend the morning with her first… but, before it came out, she added, 'You can accept the Foxes' invitation on my behalf, but only for the evening. I quite like the sound of the Savoy lunch. And I'll need to buy them gifts.'

I nodded, mentally adding it to the ever-growing list. 'Of course.'

I felt my excitement rise again; she hadn't even tried to get me to cancel my plans.

We sat in silence for a few moments, the car slowing as we neared our destination. I began to say, 'You'd be more than welcome to…' But Pim had already opened the door, the car barely stopped outside the restaurant.

'Finally, we're here,' she said, a smile developing on her face like two strings were being pulled at the ends of her lips. 'How lovely!'

Chapter 6

I HAD NEVER WALKED DOWN CARNABY STREET before – at least, not at Christmas. Given how busy it was when Megan and I turned down it to admire the lights, I doubted I ever would walk down it – or squeeze down it – again.

'I didn't expect it to be so busy,' Megan shouted over the droning voices of tourists, spectators, and shop workers.

'The lights are pretty, though,' I remarked, looking up at the striking neon signs and Christmas fairy lights dangling across the street. The theme was 'Iconic', with lights in the shapes of iconic phrases *'Here's looking at you, kid'* and *'Is it still raining? I hadn't noticed'*, alongside depictions of notable pop culture like Geri Halliwell's Union Jack dress and Freddie Mercury's white-and-yellow suit.

Megan had arrived straight from work, looking sharp in a tailored coat and immaculate heels. I, meanwhile, was my usual colourful self in a red dress, blue tights, and a hat with an oversized bobble that jingled when I moved.

'I won't lose you in this crowd,' she told me, eyeing my outfit with amusement when we met at the top of the street.

'Look!' I dodged a passing tourist wielding a vape like a weapon, invading my personal space. 'I see an opening!' There was a vacant alcove by one of the only stores closed in the street.

Megan made a beeline for it, somehow finding me in the throng of bodies and pulling me with her.

'Jeez!' she said, exhaling dramatically. 'Finally enough room to breathe. Whose idea was this again?'

'Yours,' I reminded her. 'But look at it, it was worth the chaos, right?' It was a visual influencer's dream: every corner was a burst of colour and nostalgia. It was perfect TikTok fodder for my channel, and I took my chance to quickly snap a few stylised shots from above various shoppers' heads and around Megan's tiny waist.

'Be sure you get my good side.' She struck a pose and pointed to the *'What a sad little life, Jane'* sign above our heads, but the shot was ruined by my hands shaking so much from laughing.

'This is brilliant.'

'Well, you're easily pleased.' Megan relaxed her pose and leaned against the door frame, first checking to make sure there was no gum or lingering hazards that could jeopardise her Chanel coat. 'And energetic. My feet are killing me.'

Nothing could quell my energy. 'It's Christmas!'

'How many coffees have you had today?'

'Too many,' I admitted. It had been another long day of Pim rehearsals and put-downs, with the occasional light-hearted thanks and the odd joke from a lighting technician or the director to get me through.

'You'll be glad when it's over.'

'When I hand in my notice, you mean.'

Megan rubbed her ankle. 'You said it, not me.'

I shrugged as I offered her my arm to rest on when she replaced her shoe. 'I'm not good at looking forward. I never have been. Not since… well, you know.' Not since my mum got diagnosed. Fear of the unknown was a childhood trait I never truly overcame or even embraced. I kept moving forward but I didn't stop, you'd think I was rushing towards the future, but I was more afraid I'd get stuck and never push on if I paused for a moment.

'Sometimes I wish I could stop looking back.' Megan's expression softened as she released my arm. She smiled at me briefly; she was never very good at holding a smile even when she meant it.

She pulled her phone from her pocket and began scrolling mindlessly.

I watched her for a moment. There was a weight hanging on her, the kind that wasn't just about a long day at work.

'Are you taking care of yourself?' I asked.

Her doomscrolling paused for a second in surprise. 'Of course I am. I'm a fricking monk. Did I tell you I was thinking of going palaeo?' That wasn't what I meant and she knew it, and I knew *she* knew.

I nodded politely as she talked to me about palaeo vs keto diets, and eventually she trailed off, her jaw tightening. There was a weariness about her that I hadn't noticed at the pub with Josh; I couldn't put my finger on what was different and I didn't want to pry, so instead I reached out and gave her arm a gentle squeeze. She tensed, then shrugged it off. Megan had never been one for overt displays of emotion, even with me.

'I know, I know, you don't care about diets.'

'Not in the *dieting* kind of way. I don't have the time to be that disciplined.' Or spending time locating Whole Foods and organic takeaway meals. I spent enough of my life locating escabeche and nut-free nut roasts for Pim. I didn't want to add my tastes into the mix.

I exhaled softly, feeling my energy start to match hers as

I rested my chin atop her shoulder and stared at her screen blindly. 'This coat is really soft,' I said, burrowing my head into the shoulder pad of her jacket.

'You can't have it,' she was quick to respond. 'At least not yet.'

'I always appreciate your hand-me-downs,' I said but she continued to scroll. I caught seconds of #CleanTok footage and various parenting influencers, the occasional marital therapist, and news reels. It was typical TikTok fodder.

Trying to lighten the mood and spotting a lull in the crowds, I rushed out into the street and struck a pose under Sherlock Holmes's deerstalker hat. 'What do you think? Could this outfit one day become an iconic neon sign?'

Megan looked up and laughed at my pose, as I proactively lifted my leg and hugged a door frame. 'I've never felt so sexy.'

She snorted so hard she almost blew her own phone away, nearly dropping it on the damp wintry pavement.

I laughed and wrapped an arm around her shoulder. 'Right!' she declared, back into Christmas mode. 'I need to get to Doc Martens. Are you willing to join me in the mosh pit?' She referenced the growing crowd again.

'If I don't make it, tell Josh I died well.'

'There would be no better way than this, in his mind anyway.' Megan agreed, pushing forward.

Once we got past Timberland, we were able to breathe again. The crowds mostly gathered at the entrance to the street and less people walked the whole street, though it was still a relative squeeze.

The smells and sounds of Christmas were more apparent here. I lifted my nose into the air to catch the strong scent of roasted chestnuts, and I gravitated towards the singer playing 'Stop the Cavalry' by Jona Lewie, a highly underrated Christmas song.

'I'm going to pop in here,' Megan said as we reached the store she wanted. 'Do you want to come in?'

'You go ahead; I want to listen to the music.'

She murmured in assent and carried on with her shopping task, as I gravitated towards the singer, a man by the sound of his voice.

A crowd had gathered around him, blocking him from view; people were hovering with Styrofoam cups of mulled wine and hot bags of chestnuts. It was a perfect Christmas gathering.

I joined the throng just as the singer sang the last notes of 'Stop the Cavalry' and the crowd began to dissipate. To keep their attention, he struck up his next song quickly: 'Sweet Caroline'. Not quite a Christmas classic, but a banger nevertheless.

Ducking under the arms of retreating listeners, I found a spot as the inevitable fist-raising dum-dum-der moments began. And that's when I saw him.

It was the busker from Covent Garden.

He looked remarkably similar to the last time I'd seen him, even wearing the same kind of outfit in front of the same microphone stand. This time, he was playing a blue-ice-coloured guitar.

I watched for a few moments, mouthing along to 'Sweet Caroline' as the crowds ignored him and wandered past, only involving themselves in the song's famous chorus with fist-pumps and mouthed singalongs.

As he came to a close, I reached into my pocket and found my trusty purse I'd had since childhood, and you could tell – it had diamonds stuck on the purple velvet in the shape of the word *Diva* – and pulled out a £10 note. Stepping forward I dropped it into his upturned hat on the ground.

'For charity,' I said with a wide smile.

It took him a moment to place me. When he did, his eyes widened. 'Covent Garden girl.'

I sucked my teeth in amused embarrassment. 'The very same. Although I'm surprised my moniker isn't "beggar girl" or "insulting cow".' We both laughed. 'Sorry about that, by the way.'

'You said that... before, I mean.'

'I did, didn't I?' I nodded and felt suddenly like my arms were very out of place at my sides. 'Oh, well! *That* was really good,' I said, gesturing to his guitar.

'Thanks!' I waited for him to carry on, to say anything, but he just stood smiling confidently. It was mildly infuriating.

'You're a man of few words.'

He made an agreeable 'hmm' sound and rubbed the back of his neck; whether self-consciously or just because he was cold without a scarf I couldn't tell.

'I can be.'

'Don't tell me you're one of those singers that *lets the songs speak for me*,' I mocked and realised I had gone right back to insulting him. Shaking my head and scrunching up my eyes, I almost shouted. 'Sorry! That was rude too.'

'Mocking, not rude,' he laughed. 'And it was funny.'

'I'm not normally so insulting.'

'That's what they all say.' He was still smiling as he leaned down to pick up some loose change that had fallen short of his upturned hat.

'No, truly.' I leaned down to help him. 'Most people tell me I'm too nice for my own good.'

'I'd say giving a tenner to a busker is pretty nice, so maybe they're right,' he said, lifting the hat so I could drop the collection of five- and twenty-pence pieces back into it.

'Well, it's for charity,' I pointed out, groaning much louder than a twenty-nine-year-old should as I pushed myself back up to standing again. He didn't groan at all, the bastard.

'*Actually…*' he began playfully, his lips tilting into a lopsided smile that I often associated with charming bartenders and waiters looking for a tip.

'Aha, so this time it *is* for you.'

He shrugged. 'Man's got to earn a living.'

'Indeed he has,' I said, crossing my arms but still smiling. 'I won't begrudge you for that. You may keep the £10 note.'

'You couldn't get it back now if you tried.'

'And why not? Technically I gave it to you due to false advertising.'

He looked around him dramatically for a moment.

'What advertising?' Oh, the cheeky bugger!

'I meant from last time,' I said, dragging the word *last* a little too long.

'So you *assumed* it was for charity. That's not false advertising then, is it? That's just a mistaken assumption and, if you were to attempt to take the money back now, that would be stealing?'

'Stealing!' I said, smiling at this humorous conversation that was slightly darker than I expected and much, much longer than I had intended. Although I wasn't complaining.

'Yeah,' he said, his grin widening. 'If you were to take

this £10 note back, it would be like stealing change from a wishing fountain.'

'Except those are for charity, which you've just stressed this isn't.'

He opened his mouth but shut it almost instantly.

'Hmm. Want to keep digging your hole?'

'Fine.' He held his hand up. 'I'm no master of wits.'

'You're not bad,' I said, uncrossing my arms and placing my chilled hands in my pockets instead. 'What's next on the set-list then?'

He tilted his head in consideration. 'Whatever I fancy.'

'I noticed that you weren't sticking to a purely festive theme.'

'"Sweet Caroline" is a classic, all year round. And very suitable for this street, I would say.'

'You know your audience; I'll give you that,' I agreed, and he nodded in assent.

Suddenly I heard my name being called: *'Evie!'* Megan reappeared in the distance, lugging a massive Doc Martens bag at her side. I waved her over and she walloped my leg with the bag.

'Sorry.'

'Some early Christmas presents for yourself?' I remarked, rubbing my calf – not realising at first that I was using the busker's guitar to steady me; he put a steadying hand behind it for my sake, but I noticed his eye twitch as if in pain – Megan smiled innocently.

'Hello,' she said to the busker, in surprise and eager flirtation. Her impressed tone and the way she glanced between me and him felt very quick off the mark. 'I'm Megan,' she said to the busker, and that's when I realised, he and I had never even exchanged names, even though we'd met twice and already sparred verbally both times, however unexpectedly.

'I'm Simon,' he said, offering her his hand as I released my own from his guitar.

'Evie.'

Simon's lip twitched upwards in amusement. Megan jabbed me in the ribs. 'Were you making a request?' she asked.

'More like...' I didn't know how to explain, but Simon saved me.

'Exactly that,' he said smoothly.

Megan grinned. 'Fab. What did you choose?'

I looked back to Simon, who raised the guitar strap over his head and licked his lip in one smooth motion that sucked every thought from inside my brain. I couldn't remember a single song, even though cheesy Christmas songs were my absolute favourite.

After a moment I opened my mouth to speak but nothing came out. Simon rescued me again, mouthing 'Merry Christmas Everyone'.

Thank Christ for Shakin' Stevens!

'I asked if he knew "Merry Christmas Everyone".'

'And I was just saying,' he began immediately. 'Who doesn't know Shakin' Stevens?'

'One of my favourites,' Megan agreed, perhaps a bit too earnestly.

'I'll just get set up,' Simon said, pointing back to his amp and moving away.

'Get you!' Megan whispered. 'And get *in*!'

'Oh, ssh!' I said, poking her in the side as Simon turned and adjusted his microphone before swiftly bringing his guitar in front and hitting a pedal on the floor which triggered the opening jingles and backing singer vocals.

'*Snow is fallin', all around me, children playing, having fun…*' he began, and Megan bobbed from side to side until the drum section kicked in, and then she was full-on dancing. It was pleasant to see her letting her hair down, especially when she'd seemed so off colour earlier; soon I couldn't help myself either, I was swaying with her, bobbing to the beat and trying not to blush too heavily as Simon grinned in our direction and tapped his foot on the floor.

A fresh crowd began to gather and soon we were not the only ones dancing awkwardly. Simon stepped back to enjoy the scene.

I thought he kept looking at me, but it was probably just the glare of the neon lights in my eyeline. Everything was distorted, a magical hue settling over a perfect Christmas moment – that or I was bobbing around too much and my jingle-bell hat was starting to give me a migraine.

'Come on!' I said breathlessly to Megan as Simon got to the bridge. 'We've got more shopping to do.'

'Are you sure?' she asked, still dancing. 'It's not every day you get attracted to someone.'

I tried not to roll my eyes. 'I'm graysexual, not a unicorn.'

The truth was, it *was* rare for me to catch feelings, even a few. And that flicker of feelings I felt, noticing him, being *noticed* back, surprised me more than I wanted to admit. I wasn't used to that spark, and certainly not when I was supposed to be packing up my life and moving to another country.

Megan wolf-whistled Simon, and I cringed. 'Come on, let's go.' Hooking my arm through hers, I led us back up the street.

But I couldn't help myself; just before we turned the corner, I glanced back over my shoulder to Simon.

He was fully immersed in the crowd, but he caught my eye and winked.

Chapter 7

'It's Pim Hardcastle, everybody!' The host, an energetic thirty-something who recently came second on a popular TV dance show, was welcoming Pim onto the morning TV show with more excitement than was normal. It made my insides squirm, but the early-morning TV viewers loved it, apparently.

Pim stepped onto the set, confidence radiating from her as she waved and then gave a subtle tug to her bright fuchsia-pink suit jacket. No one would have known that twenty minutes before she was having a mini-meltdown from stage fright, which only I – and Gerald, her supportive Chow Chow – could pull her out of. But here she was now, undoing her jacket button and sitting down with elegant ease.

The cameras adored her, and she knew exactly how to give them what they wanted.

I hovered near the edge of the set, stealing glances at the assistant producer's clipboard. He stood tall, his tailored suit fitting like a second skin, exuding an effortless authority that made him look as if he'd stepped out of a *GQ* photoshoot. One day, I promised myself, I'd match his easy confidence. For now, I focused on imitating his air of competence, my eyes flicking between his paperwork and the camera angles.

With my job change imminent, I'd found myself shadowing every producer I could, learning the rhythm and chaos of live TV from behind the camera instead of from the green room. I loved the immediacy of it, the way the decisions were made on the fly and the quiet authority of people who knew exactly what they were doing and how to do it well. But the more I watched, the more my chest tightened with anxiety.

This was nothing like the cushioned chaos at Salient when I worked with Pim behind-the-scenes on one of her many guest spots on cookery shows. Maybe British TV was more cut-throat. Or maybe I'd never really paid attention, too busy finding the exact brand of tuna Pim liked in her sandwiches or making reservations at three restaurants in case she changed her mind over where she wanted to go for dinner.

When I undertook my new role at Salient, there'd be no buffer or famous name to hide behind. It would be my own crises I was dealing with, not someone else's.

The thought was terrifying and thrilling in equal measure.

Whenever the nerves threatened to take over, I clung to that idea. Of having my name on call sheets and of being trusted to make decisions that mattered. Not the idea that I would be alone to handle it all myself. Besides, thinking too far ahead made everything feel too overwhelming. I'd never been good at looking forward anyway; the possibilities were what frightened me.

TikToks were great for looking back, a digital diary of all my experiences and learnings.

I produced a lot of videos while in the UK studios, but I didn't dare pull out my phone to take any sneaky videos on set now. Not with this eagle-eyed AP with sexy gravitas standing next to me.

Pim was in full flow, talking about the upcoming charity screening of *Wuthering Heights* and her exclusive in conversation after the screening. She hadn't been on stage live, even to host an event, for years. It was going to be quite the event for her fans, of which there were surprisingly many. 'It's so exciting that so many people are still eager to discuss and review *Wuthering Heights* forty years down the line. I'm…' She clapped her hands together, her rings catching the studio lights. 'I'm blown away. Absolutely blown away.' She sounded so sincere, but I'd heard her earlier, bemoaning to a make-up artist, how frustrating it was to be pigeonholed by her past.

'Tickets are selling out fast, I hear, and a portion of the proceeds will go to charity,' the presenter said. Pim nodded enthusiastically.

'Absolutely! It's happening on Christmas Eve! The time for giving and helping others,' she said with a tinkle of a laugh that the presenter mirrored. 'And as an LGBT+ production of *Wuthering Heights*, it only seemed right to donate to LGBT+ charities. Though I'm only an ally, as a she/her heterosexual, as someone who was part of this ground-breaking movie, helping others within the community has always been a big part of my life.'

I released a breath I hadn't realised I was holding. Last night, she'd railed against the whole 'ally' narrative. '*I don't care if you're diagonal and purple, but why do I have to spell out the alphabet backwards!*' she'd snapped, arms crossed, chin jutting out stubbornly. It had taken an hour and two glasses of wine to convince her that showing solidarity mattered.

I could see the assistant producer and presenter were impressed. They exchanged approving glances as Pim hit every talking point perfectly. A surge of confidence rushed through me, straightening my spine and lowering my shoulders, which had slowly reached my ears.

I gripped my phone in my pocket, wanting to shoot my shot.

'Sorry,' I whispered to the AP as they cut to an advert break. 'Do you mind if I take some photos for social media?'

He barely looked up from his clipboard, waving his hand. 'Sure, go ahead.'

I stepped around the massive TV camera, capturing clips of Pim and the presenter having their make-up retouched, adjusting their jackets on the vibrant orange sofa. Pim looked regal, commanding attention even when the cameras were offline; she was in full-on performance mode, refusing to let nerves get the better of her. Put me in front of one of those cameras and I would go weak at the knees and forget the entire English language, but Pim was a professional faker. She knew how to appear confident – even if the reality was she'd had to use several CBD oils and listen to a calming meditation, as she clung to Gerald and me during the taxi ride over.

I took a few video clips, zooming in and out expertly, imagining the edit in my mind. The transitions and the music, down to the caption. It was strategic but as easy as breathing sometimes.

Feeling as if I had prime content for my TikTok, I pocketed my phone and gave Pim an excitable thumbs-up as they called for silence on set and began to count down back to the interview.

Just as the red light of filming came on, my phone began to buzz in my pocket, with what I assumed was an incoming WhatsApp message.

Wanting to avoid the telling-off for having my phone out behind the live camera, I stepped backwards to exit the studio. The door to the green room was off to the side and I hurried over, tiptoeing as quietly as I could, as Pim and the presenter picked up their conversation effortlessly.

Once inside, I pulled out my phone but, before I could even unlock the screen, someone crashed into me. A man in a navy pinstripe suit barrelled through the door, nearly knocking my phone from my hand.

'For Christ's sake!' he barked, just as the soundproof door clicked shut behind me. 'Why don't you watch where you're going?' He shook his shirt sleeve and droplets of coffee splattered across the fabric.

'S-sorry,' I stammered, even though it wasn't my fault. I'd been coming out of the studio; he'd been charging towards the door without looking, like a boulder shoved by Sisyphus.

'You should be.' He glared, eyes narrowing, then stomped towards the green-room kitchenette, muttering under his breath. A runner rushed up, taking the man's mostly empty coffee cup, whispering about keeping the noise down during recording.

'Get off my coffee, and make yourself useful, you imbecile,' the man growled. 'Get me a new jacket.'

The runner, a young man no doubt straight out of a media-studies course at university, paled, his hands trembling. He nodded and dashed off. My chest tightened as I watched the man curse under his breath, shaking out his sleeve as if the coffee was toxic.

I started towards him, rage igniting in my gut like a

struck match, but I stopped myself. He wasn't worth the trouble. No point risking a reprimand over this odious man. Instead, with a quick breath, I sat down on the sofa and unlocked my phone.

Josh had sent over costume ideas for the Great Christmas Pudding Race. One was a screenshot of Miss Piggy in *A Christmas Carol*. Yeah, that needed shutting down immediately. But, before I could respond, the runner returned with a black pinstripe jacket, and instinct made me look up.

The man's face had gone scarlet.

'Black? I'm in fucking blue, you idiot!' he bellowed. 'Is this your first day? Are you colour-blind? How are you this useless?'

The runner flinched, his shoulders curling inwards as the man snatched the jacket from his hands and hurled it across the room.

'That is enough,' I said before I could stop myself. The man turned, eyes narrowing, surprised to still find me there. I stood firm, summoning every ounce of courage. 'You don't speak to people like that. Not at work. Not anywhere. A mistake was made – you can cope.'

His eyes widened. 'Do you know who I am?'

That tired line. It never worked, especially not in this industry. I crossed my arms and arched an eyebrow, letting a hint of dry humour slip through. 'I don't care.'

The runner's lips twitched, the ghost of a smile, before he hurried off with the discarded jacket. The man's face contorted, mouth opening and closing like a fish gasping for air. He looked ready to explode when a woman from hair and make-up breezed in through the side door. 'All righty, are you ready, Michael?'

Michael. The name echoed in my head and flashes of news anchors shuffling papers and making sombre announcements appeared. This was Michael Holland.

A critic-turned-news-anchor-turned-presenter – and an all-round ass-hat.

Michael Holland's smug face had haunted Pim more times than she cared to admit. For years, even while abroad, she couldn't flip through channels without stumbling upon him standing on some windswept mountaintop in Asia, salt-and-pepper hair artfully tousled, staring earnestly into the camera, as if dispensing wisdom from on high.

To Pim, he was more than just an irritant – he was her nemesis. He'd barely been interested in theatre when he seemingly destroyed her career, his lack of interest evident from his quick escape from the Arts and Culture section to what he clearly believed was more meaningful journalism. And yet, his words had the power to dismantle everything Pim had built for herself. Because of him, she had retreated from acting, abandoning a promising career despite her success in *Wuthering Heights*.

He'd been a critic for the *Evening Standard* during her last performance on the West End – a daring turn as Hedda Gabler at the Fortune Theatre. His review had been nothing short of savage: '*An actress whose ego could fill the auditorium, but whose performance leaves countless seats empty come the second act.*' It was a line that had branded itself into her memory. She still carried that review, tucked inside an old powder case, even now, nearly twenty years later. It seemed unnecessarily cruel.

But, seeing Michael Holland in the flesh, I could tell that cruelty came relatively naturally to him, and that no one ever stood up to him.

He swallowed and nodded at the make-up artist who was so focused on finding the right utensil in her toolkit strapped around her waist that she hadn't even realised there was tension in the room. Michael pushed open the studio door, and a burst of noise spilled out – cameras shutting down, crew members resetting the stage.

'… so wonderful! Thank you so much!'

'No, my goodness, thank you!' Pim was hugging the presenter, her smile taut, lips stretched like they were hooked by fishing lines – a clear sign she was done with pleasantries and in dire need of a glass of Merlot.

I held the door open, my heart pounding. Pim was finishing up her small talk when her eyes landed on Holland waiting in the wings. Immediately her expression faltered, her jaw tightened, the smile vanished with her interest in the presenter, who stuttered hopelessly before walking away dejected.

Michael's posture relaxed, his smug smirk flashing across his aged but still interesting face as he folded his arms. 'Well, well! Pim Hardcastle. I heard you were here, clinging to the same old glory.'

Pim fixed her expression, her eyes like ice. 'Michael! Still trying to turn bitterness into a career, I see.'

He tilted his head, feigning pity. 'I'm just heading into make-up. You should join me – Taylor could do wonders for those eye bags. Must be exhausting pretending you're still relevant?'

A muscle twitched in Pim's jaw as she prepared her serve in the insult tennis match the two of them had begun. I was impressed by the speed with which both entered into it; no British apologies here, this was all-out warfare. I was both exhilarated and terrified just witnessing it. 'Oh,

I didn't realise you were relevant. I thought you just narrated travelogues now. Tell me, do you get a discount on all those beige trousers you typically wear on-screen?'

Michael let out a mock laugh, taking a step closer. 'I wouldn't expect you to understand my documentaries. You were never one for substance.'

'And yet here you are, still obsessed with me. Honestly, Michael, I've had stalkers with more originality.' She patted his chest in the most patronising fashion. Game, set, and match.

Michael's jaw tightened, a flicker of irritation breaking through his carefully maintained nonchalance. 'Funny, I thought you'd retired from acting.'

Her eyes narrowed, but her voice remained steady. 'I know you wished I would. Tell me, what was it that bothered you so much? Were you threatened? Frustrated? Or were you just upset that someone was actually watching me, unlike your programmes?'

Pim let out a slow breath, her shoulders dropping just a fraction, not in defeat but in genuine exhaustion. This was not a fight Pim was interested in carrying on. Her gaze softened as she looked at me. 'Are we leaving?'

'Yes.' I cleared my throat as Michael's eyes flicked to me, his sneer returning. 'You've got…' I thought fast, unable to keep up with the two of them. 'You've got another appointment.'

'I do!' Pim said vivaciously. 'I'm terribly busy today.'

'Michael!'

A sharp voice cut through the tension – it was the GQ-lookalike producer. 'We're ready for you on camera. What happened to your sleeve? *Ivan*! Michael needs a new shirt!' He slapped his clipboard, already turning away.

Michael didn't say a word, no witty retort, no cutting comeback. He just spun on his heel, face tight, and stalked off towards the wardrobe department.

Pim sagged against my shoulder, her smile collapsing the moment he was out of sight. 'Michael Holland… what a grade-A arsehole.'

'Pim!' I hissed, glancing around. We were still within earshot of half a dozen producers and crew members. The last thing we needed was for their spat to become public gossip. It was bad enough that I'd snapped at him in the green room, there was no need to throw fuel on the fire. 'You handled yourself very well.'

'Well, thank you, darling.' I couldn't tell if her tone was mocking or genuine, but she did seem to smile. 'He gets under my skin. Painful and unnecessary little man, he's like Botox.' Except she loved Botox.

I faked a laugh as my phone buzzed again. I glanced down at the screen. It was Megan's reply to Josh's message about the Great Christmas Pudding Race: '*Fuck right off. Not going to happen.*'

My laughter became authentic and Pim raised an eyebrow. 'What?'

I showed her the screen and, for the first time since Michael appeared, she smiled. 'I don't understand the context, but at least someone's standing their ground today.'

For a split second, watching her like this – relaxed, amused, leaning into me like a friend instead of a celebrity demanding something – I felt a familiar tug of doubt and anxiety. I was leaving her soon; these moments would disappear overnight and I would miss them, even if I wouldn't miss the dramatics that often came with them.

Pim had been my boss and *almost* friend for eight years.

I knew everything about her. I was practically responsible for keeping her alive. I was a combination of parent, child, therapist, employee, and friend. Sitting there with her, on the same page for once, I couldn't help wondering if I was walking away from something safe. Or if that was precisely the reason *to* walk away?

I slipped my phone back into my pocket, pushing the doubts away.

'Yeah. Let's get out of here. I think you deserve a Merlot.'

'A large one. With a straw.' She yawned widely as we headed for the exit, leaving Michael Holland and his poisonous attitude behind.

Chapter 8

'As Edgar, the John Lewis dragon discovered, I can't fight this feeling any more,' Josh belted dramatically from his kitchen, exploding forth from the entrance, wearing a tinsel crown of his own making. He deposited a scorching tray of freshly baked mince pies on the coffee table, narrowly missing a tangled mess of Christmas lights.

'Niche. Not everyone knows about the John Lewis Christmas ads.' I knew that first hand from my many years abroad, trying to get access to YouTube via dodgy data connections.

Josh ignored me, of course; nothing was getting between him and his beloved cultural references.

I was curled up on his sofa in my fluffiest Christmas jumper – complete with a squirrel, because every Christmas jumper needs a squirrel – scanning his extensive collection of holiday DVDs for tonight's Moviethon winner.

'It has to be *Scrooge the Musical*,' he announced, throwing down his *Ya Filthy Animal* oven gloves and collapsing onto his IKEA sofa with such force that I nearly bounced out of my seat. 'Best. Christmas. Musical. Ever.'

'But not the best Christmas movie?' I asked, still trying to decipher how we had got onto the careful delineation of

Christmas movie sub-categories this early in the evening. We hadn't even opened the prosecco yet.

'That is and will always be *The Holiday,*' he declared, flinging his hands up as if it were the most obvious thing in the world. 'Jack Black is my ideal husband.'

'A surprise to us all,' I agreed. 'What about *Love Actually*?'

He groaned. 'It hasn't aged well, and I'm not just talking about the political incorrectness. The storylines are… bizarre. Did we really need Martin Freeman discussing traffic while faking sex acts? Or Keira Knightley getting married at eighteen?'

'It's still on the list.' I held up the DVD case.

'Well, duh! We can't *not* watch it. It's a Christmas classic.'

'Just an ageing one.'

'There is the gorgeous Liam Neeson storyline.'

'*We need Kate, and we need Leo, and we need them now*,' I quoted effortlessly.

Josh grinned.

'Okay,' I began again. 'But why are we watching DVDs as if it's 2005? Haven't you heard of streaming?'

He looked at me as if I'd suggested setting fire to his Christmas tree. 'You try to find *The Grinch* on a streaming platform at Christmas. Or *Miracle on 34th Street*; the classic or the Richard Attenborough one! You're more likely to find Santa's workshop before Christmas Day than those masterpieces.'

'Ooh, *The Santa Clause*,' I said, holding up the nineties classic DVD. 'Another that hasn't aged well.'

'It's doing better than *The Santa Clause 3*, at least.' His nose wrinkled in disgust.

'We don't speak of *The Santa Clause 3*.' I threw Josh the DVD case.

Josh pushed himself up, humming 'We Wish You a Merry Christmas' as he did so, and went to his ancient DVD player to set it up.

I glanced around at the explosion of tinsel, paper chains, and snowflakes dangling precariously from the ceiling, courtesy of an illegal amount of Blu-tack. Tinsel draped every window, mirror, and frame, and the Christmas trees – there were multiple – were each decorated in a different colour scheme. His flat looked like Santa's Grotto had thrown up on it.

'I see you opted for fake trees over real this year.'

'I can't be dealing with hoovering every five minutes,' Josh protested. 'I love the smell, but I can get artificial candles and diffusers for that.'

'And here was me thinking you were all about the authentic Christmas.'

'Darling, I work in retail – we go for sparkle and shine far more than authenticity,' he laughed darkly. 'If I wanted authenticity, this,' he gestured grandly at the Christmas chaos, 'would be replaced by nativity scenes, praying, and bloody misery. Now, eat a mince pie.'

Laughing, I grabbed two, ignoring the plates entirely.

Together we sat back down on the sofa, and he began the route through old trailers for early noughties Disney films and the enforced '*You wouldn't steal a handbag*' piracy video.

'So how goes the hunt for your replacement?' Josh asked, settling in to watch the anti-piracy trailer with his mug of home-brewed mulled wine. He was right, his house did smell just like Christmas, with or without a tree.

'As well as can be expected.'

'So not going well at all.'

'Pretty much,' I laughed. 'Every time I try to talk to Pim about it, she shuts me down or changes the subject.'

'Is it that she's averse to change or is she simply ignoring the fact that you're leaving?'

'Both. Neither. Who knows with Pim? All I know is that I have to find my replacement before I leave, otherwise Pim Hardcastle is going to fall apart.'

'That's on her. She's a grown-ass woman, let her live in the real world for a change.'

'Excuse me, don't you have an assistant?'

Josh rolled his eyes. 'I have three. But they don't work for me, they're my co-workers, not my slaves.'

'Your minions, basically.'

'I prefer Christmas elves.'

'Of course you do,' I said, snuggling into a blanket as Josh pressed 'Play' on the screen selection and the movie began.

'I think I'm just going to have to ignore Pim—'

'Like she ignores you,' Josh cut in.

'And just interview the applicants myself. I've got a few lined up this week.'

'Good plan. Take the initiative and screw Pim! Or, better yet, hire someone truly awful as the ultimate revenge of a disgruntled employee.'

'But I'm not disgruntled,' I corrected. 'I'm only leaving because a great job opportunity has come up.'

He rolled his eyes again, and pressed 'Pause' before Tim Allen had finished giving his terrible speech at the Christmas party.

'Look, if you're not disgruntled, you should be. She took you away from your family.'

The word '*family*' stung, pulling at the ever-present

ache of being an orphan. I fought to keep my expression neutral.

Josh noticed. 'Okay, she took you away from your friends, then – who are *like* family. She underpays you, never praises you *at all*, and then treats you like you have two brain cells when really you're the brains of her whole operation.'

'Hardly. She has that freelance publicist sometimes.'

'Whom *you* deal with, not her.'

It was true – I did most of the talking on Pim's behalf. After eight years of handling her schedule, her bills, and even her well-being, from her laundry to her prescriptions, I knew her better than she knew herself.

'She'll fall apart when you leave, no matter who you hire,' Josh said. I opened my mouth to protest, but he held up a hand. 'And not because you'd sabotage her. You're too decent for that – I'd do it, but you wouldn't. The irony is she won't realise what she's lost until you're gone. Funny how people never appreciate what they have until it's gone.'

'A bit like Scott Calvin in *The Santa Clause 3*.'

'I thought we agreed never to acknowledge *The Santa Clause 3*.'

'I know, I know. But the lesson was so perfect it had to be brought out for that moment.'

'C'est vrai,' Josh said, glancing at me with an almost mischievous smile.

'Oh, you speak French now, do you?'

'Didn't I tell you Zach's learning French?'

I hesitated, unsure if I wanted to get into a discussion about his life with a married man.

'No, you didn't.' I kept my tone flat, not encouraging any more details.

'Well, he is,' Josh said quietly, pressing 'Play' on the movie again.

We fell into a comfortable silence for a time, watching Scott Calvin's antics: burning the turkey, taking his son to Denny's, failing miserably at bedtime stories, and then the loud clatter.

'What would you do if you heard Santa on your roof at night?' Josh asked, casually brushing mince-pie crumbs off his trousers onto the floor.

'Probably call the hotel manager,' I replied, making him laugh as he remembered my transient living situation.

'You nomad!'

'Santa doesn't visit hotels. I know this because, when I wake up on Christmas Day, there are never any presents at the end of my bed.'

'What does Pim do about Christmas?' he asked as I nestled deeper into his sofa.

'Not much. She says she's too old for sitting and unwrapping presents so *I* typically give her one and then all the other gifts – which she buys herself – she just leaves me to hide and then hand them over on Christmas Day.'

'What a delightful day you both have.' he said dryly. 'Tell me she gets you something.'

I focused on the screen, watching Scott Calvin squeeze down a chimney with the help of nineties bad CGI. 'She gives me a hundred of whatever currency the country we're staying in has and tells me to go wild. I got some fantastic perfume one year, and a year's Amazon Prime subscription the next.'

Josh's silence spoke volumes.

'She's never been one for the personalised, handmade

effort, Josh,' I added, my voice softer. 'Nor is she particularly good at shopping for anyone but herself.'

'I just don't know what you see in her.'

'She's my boss, not my life partner.'

'Hmm!' Josh gave me a judgy side-eye. 'You've never even been in with a chance of getting a life partner since you've been with her. Another catastrophe, as the men of the world have been missing out on pursuing you.'

'I have dated while working with Pim.'

'And how many times do you go on second dates with the people you've "dated"?' He lifted his fingers in quotation marks. 'I'm guessing none.'

The challenge in his voice was unmistakable.

It wasn't as if I'd sworn off relationships, I just hadn't made room for them. That felt different. Practical, owing to the way I lived, sensible, even.

But hearing Josh frame it so plainly made me feel uncomfortable. He wasn't being cruel; he was stating a fact. The fact that he'd noticed that this was how my life looked from the outside unsettled me more than I wanted to admit. 'There is hardly a chance, what with work and moving on so quickly.'

Josh didn't seem to think this was a valid argument, but that was hardly surprising, given the furthest he had travelled for work was Lapland on a trip for 'inspiration'. Even then he had managed to shack up with a pilot and a husky handler – at the same time. Respect.

But not wanting to discuss my non-existent dating life, or my desire to finally have one, I cleared my throat.

'I'm not happy,' I began, leaning forward to hand out the last two mince pies to each of us. '… with the fact that we've still not found our Christmas costumes for the Great

British Pudding Race,' I said, shoving the last mince pie in my mouth all in one with no shame.

Josh sat up then, immediately animated by Christmas planning.

'I've found the perfect Grinch costume for Alex and, of course, I'm set for my *Die Hard* re-enactment; I even have a semi-bald cap, I'm that dedicated to my performance,' Josh shared. 'I'm just struggling to find the perfect Cindy Lou Who and a Jovie costume.'

'Well, for me, I'll just go full-Elf costume and then add some typical Jovie touches.'

'You're just going to sing "Santa Claus Is Comin' to Town" everywhere you go?'

'Pretty much, yep! And we'll add copious amounts of blusher and highlighter to Megan's nose to make her look like a proper Who of Whoville.'

'We got this,' Josh said, lifting his hand to high-five me and I returned it. 'And if we don't, I have the perfect two-person reindeer costume on standby.'

'Never,' I said.

Chapter 9

To hold the interviews for my replacement, Megan had kindly offered her office space on 11 December.

'Thanks for letting me do this,' I said, filling a jug of water at the sink in the shared kitchenette. Megan was busy with her own work but had a separate room for taking meetings, away from her desk. She shrugged, adding a heaping spoonful of sugar to her decaf coffee – a surprising choice, given how much she normally relied on caffeine.

'It's no problem. I hate being in the office by myself, but there's no way I'm working from home again. I need the boundaries.'

'The never-ending work-life balance challenge,' I said, leaning against the counter.

'It's not even about balance. It's about space. Alex and I were in each other's pockets every day when I worked from home. It was… suffocating.' Her shoulders tightened as she stirred her coffee a little too vigorously, the casual tone at odds with the tension in her. 'I didn't realise how much I needed my own space.'

I glanced at her, trying to gauge how much she wanted to share. 'I thought you two were good at giving each other space. You used to brag about how you could spend whole weekends in separate rooms and still feel connected.'

She let out a brittle laugh. 'Yeah, well… things change.' Her fingers tightened around the mug before she took a long sip, as if to stop herself from saying more.

I hesitated, then ventured, 'Everything okay?'

'Oh, sure,' she replied too quickly. 'It's just… different now. He's at home all the time with Alfie, and I'm here or at meetings. We barely see each other during the day and when I get home, it's like we've run out of things to say.' Her eyes flicked to the floor, her voice dropping. 'He used to ask about my day. Now he just… hands me Alfie and goes to his laptop or the gym or wherever he can get a break.'

The word *break* lingered for a moment. I wondered silently what, exactly, Alex needed one from. The baby? Megan? Or the version of their life that no longer resembled the one they – or *he* – imagined?

I kept the thought to myself. I could tell Megan was trying to sound nonchalant, but the tightness in her jaw gave her away.

'Maybe he just needs some adult conversation after a day with a toddler. It's a different world.'

'I get that,' she admitted. 'I really do. I just… I thought we'd still be us, you know? But it's like we're roommates who swap childcare shifts. We never talk about anything and the sex…' She gulped some of her coffee and shuddered. 'It's like going through the motions or acting like we're not doing anything when we're doing it. No fun whatsoever, just in out, in out, done.'

'The kind of sex where you're thinking about whether you got the bread out of the freezer and if you locked the back door?'

'Precisely,' she said. And I nodded, thinking that that basically described most of the sex that I had had in my life, and I'd had sex in hotel rooms with views of the Eiffel Tower. Yet on that occasion all I was thinking about was whether or not I could manage the 674 steps up the tower or whether I should skip it and go ahead with visiting Shakespeare & Co instead.

She shook her head, forcing a smile. 'Listen to me, getting all melodramatic. It's fine. We're fine. The sex will *be* fine.'

'Maybe introduce a toy or something.'

'The only toys I could produce are a Paw Patrol car or a lightsaber.'

I went to speak but her hand shot up so fast she knocked her coffee cup. 'Don't you dare ruin lightsabers for me.' So I closed my mouth.

She straightened, brushing an invisible crumb off her sleeve. 'Anyway. Enough about me. How many applicants are you seeing today?'

'Four. I narrowed it down from the twenty-two who applied.'

Her eyebrows shot up in surprise. 'Twenty-two? I didn't realise being a personal assistant was so sought after.'

'Neither did I,' I laughed. 'But I guess people see the travel perks and think it's glamorous.'

'If only they knew.' Megan's smile was genuine this time, a flicker of the old her. 'I still don't know how you did it for so long. I can barely handle a business trip to Manchester without losing my mind.'

'That's because you like routine,' I teased. 'You always have. Even when we were kids, you planned our sneaky midnight feasts down to the minute.'

She laughed, but it was a little hollow. 'Yeah, well, routines are safer. You know where you stand. And you don't get caught raiding the chocolate cupboard at 11.45 p.m.' She shook her shoulders to loosen herself up. 'Anyway, I should get back to it. I've got back-to-back calls all afternoon. But let me know if you need anything.'

'Will do. Thanks again.'

She waved it off with a casual flick of her hand. I watched her go, a knot forming in my stomach. Something was definitely wrong but, if Megan wasn't ready to talk, I'd have to wait. She never did like admitting when things were falling apart. If she admitted to feeling anything less than perfect, she'd see it as failing. She'd always been like that – even in school, she couldn't admit to a bad grade without laughing it off as a fluke due to a bad period or a mistake by the teacher.

The buzzer from reception downstairs wailed suddenly.

'I think your first interviewee is here,' Megan called from behind her standing desk in a sing-song voice before accepting the call and instructing the receptionist to hold them downstairs so I could go and fetch them. 'I'm not even here.' Megan lowered her desk in dramatic fashion. It whirred and we both stood there waiting for it to finish.

'*No*,' I said sarcastically. 'You blend right in.' She threw a paper ball at my head as I left to fetch the first applicant.

To say the interviews were terrible would be an understatement.

The first applicant, a man dressed more for a day in Camden Town than an interview, clearly only wanted the job to get access to people who could help him with his acting career. Halfway through answering a question about time management, he launched into a prepared monologue from *Angels in America*, and that monologue is flipping long. Megan's head popped up over the alcove we were sitting behind, and she mouthed '*what the fuck*' as he was doing it. I bit my lip to keep from giggling, nodding politely until he was finished.

Needless to say, I escorted him out with a typical casting-director 'we'll call you' smile.

The second applicant was memorable for all the wrong reasons. She showed up smartly dressed, with eyeliner so heavy it looked like war paint. As she arrived, she handed me a list of airlines that she had been blacklisted from for previous inappropriate behaviour – apparently, she'd glued herself to a jet plane to protest against the environmental impact of aviation fuel.

'I know the role involves travel,' she said briskly, as if anticipating my confusion. 'But I believe in changing systems from the inside.'

The list was alarmingly long, and the interview became less of an interview and more of a rant from her on climate-change activism. A worthy cause, but not ideal for an interview regarding a job that requires constant air travel with a celebrity.

The third applicant was a straightforward no. A fresh-out-of-school young woman, who opened with '*I think Pim Hardcastle is overrated*.' Apparently, she'd only applied for the job as there was travel involved and her parents wouldn't fund her gap year.

Megan actually ended that interview for me, marching the girl out, muttering under her breath something that sounded suspiciously like 'My child would never…'

'How many more?' she asked, as I made us both another round of coffees.

'Just one.'

'One more to go,' Megan echoed, looking as dispirited as I felt.

I fetched the last applicant from reception with low hopes and even lower expectations but was pleasantly surprised.

Alison was a thirty-something woman wearing a sensible dress and a three-quarter-length blazer and actually looked like she had prepared for an interview – neither overdressed for a corporate gig nor too casual for a coffee date.

She shook my hand with a firm grip, smiled warmly, and said, 'Lovely to meet you.' It's true what you're told in school, the first minute of an interview is the most important. I was judging her so much – down to the dark academia book she had been reading while waiting – but so far everything was a tick from me. Walking up the stairs, she asked about the role, rather than prying into celebrity gossip. She seemed relaxed yet in control and perfectly pleasant to be around.

'Would you like some water?' I asked, as we sat in the alcove. I could see Megan peering over the top of the screen and nodding approvingly.

'That would be great, thanks,' Alison said. 'How long have you been a personal assistant?' She caught me off guard in a good way.

'About eight years,' I told her, offering her the glass. 'Although it feels like less some days, more on others.'

'I get that.' She nodded, taking a sip of her water. 'I've been an administrator at various companies over the years, and some weeks can fly by, but others drag as if for months.'

'The ever-changing highs and lows of working life.'

'Indeed,' she said. 'But that's kind of why I'm after a change.' I loved how she was answering my questions without me even needing to ask them. This was becoming less of a formal interview and more of a chat, and that's precisely what being a personal assistant was like most of the time: anticipating needs, reading the room, and keeping things moving.

'So I'm aware the job description didn't give much away with regard to the client, but this role is actually as a personal assistant for Pim Hardcastle, the actress and TV personality.' I watched her carefully for a reaction, but she just nodded, perfectly composed. 'She's a bit of a jet-setter; she rarely stays in one place for more than a month.'

'Got it.' Alison continued to nod. Still no sign of star-struck curiosity.

'The role is a bit hard to describe as well. There are weeks where you'll be handling your standard schedules, meetings, minuting, organising travel, and general administration, but there is also a lot of personal administration involved as well. Dry-cleaning clothes to return to stylists, fetching food, holding bags, that kind of work. Would that be a problem?'

'Not at all,' Alison said, relaxed as ever. 'I was a PA for a fashion director once. It wasn't an always-on role like this one, but it was a lot of "personal administration", as you politely called it.' She smiled knowingly. 'As long as it's not inappropriate, it's fine by me.'

I couldn't help but grin. I liked her already.

'A lot of people would class it as scut-work,' I admitted, and Megan cleared her throat from behind her desk. She was definitely one of those people.

Alison laughed. 'Well, it is and it isn't. Particularly, I imagine, when it comes to a celebrity client.'

More ticks were appearing in my eyes.

'How do you feel about the travel element? It would mean having to give up any kind of long-term lease, probably furniture, and any semblance of a social life, if I'm being entirely honest.' Another cough from Megan.

Alison shifted in her seat. 'London is out-pricing me anyway, all my furniture is second-hand, and, as for family and friends, I hardly see them as it is.'

'You would see them even less.' I had the urge to be entirely truthful with Alison, not in an attempt to scare her off, but to give her the full picture. 'I've worked for Pim for eight years and in that time my "time off" was limited and usually spent exploring for a day or two in whatever city we found ourselves in. I've never been able to leave her for longer than three days without phone calls, emails, and disasters occurring. She's incredibly needy, and I say that with affection as well as honesty. She *needs* an assistant full-time. Someone that isn't going to go on holiday or return home without her.'

Alison took a moment, processing everything I'd said. 'That sounds manageable to me.'

'Does it?' I said, sitting back in my chair and laughing a little. 'It's a lot. You have to put her before everyone else.'

Alison's gaze was steady. 'Can I be honest?'

'Of course.'

'I've been in a relationship with someone for the last five years and it recently ended.'

I blinked, caught off guard by the sudden intimacy. Up until that moment, Alison had been impeccably professional, her answers polished and precise. And yet something about her level of comfort and confidence felt familiar in a way that made me smile.

'I'm sorry to hear that.'

'It should have ended years ago.' Alison swatted my apologies away. 'I stayed because I thrive on taking care of people, but I don't need anyone to take care of me. I think that's what makes me a good assistant. However, I do speak my mind, I am no-nonsense, and I know what I want. I want to travel; I want to work, and I don't want to be tied down to anything.'

'You'll be tied to Pim,' I pointed out.

She clicked her teeth, a spark of humour in her eyes. 'Well, I suppose each of us needs a weight to keep us grounded, otherwise we'd never get anything done.'

I laughed. 'Have you even heard of Pim Hardcastle before?'

Alison opened her mouth and then closed it, before finally saying, 'You know what? No.'

I grinned and looked over to Megan, who was nodding with an impressed look on her face. It was refreshing. Alison wasn't dazzled by fame, she was candid, and she wanted the job, not the gossip.

'Well, if you think London office jobs pay badly, you might be surprised by this pay cheque. But the benefit of this role is that all the travel, accommodation, and food is paid for. All the money you get is for you and you alone. No bills, no tax, no rent.'

'No time to spend it either, I imagine.'

I couldn't stop the grin expanding on my face and, as I looked at Megan's, I could see she was smiling too.

Clearing my throat, I extended my hand. 'Alison, how would you like to be Pim Hardcastle's new assistant?'

Chapter 10

'THIS SHELLFISH IS DELIGHTFUL!' PIM CRIED, as she dug into a poached oyster in the Savoy restaurant. Of course, it was the most expensive starter on the menu, but it did sound and smell delicious. 'You must try this,' Pim said to me, offering one of the oysters for me to try. I took the shell and tilted my head back. She was right, of course. It was utterly divine.

'Good God, that's amazing,' I said. My starter of steak tartare was also delicious, but now I regretted not pulling a Pim and going full-on decadent.

It was fairly typical for us to dine together at least once a week and go over her upcoming schedule. Although it had been a while since our last dinner; Pim had had so many evenings out with old friends and co-stars from way-back-when as a result of rarely being in London for the past eight years. I don't think she had realised how happy it would make her to be amongst her old friends again, but I could tell how pleased she was to have so many invitations. These days she was usually up and out of bed when I arrived with her coffee and breakfast in the morning, bustling with energy, waiting for the day to begin. And more and more she was asking me to organise taxis to collect her from parties and dinners later than normal, as she knew she was going to want to stay and enjoy herself. It was pleasant to see her having fun – and giving me extra time to spend by myself, in my favourite city.

Especially when it meant running into handsome buskers and enjoying a little harmless flirtation.

I shook my head, reminding myself that I would probably never see Simon ever again.

With indecent haste, I finished off the last of my tartare. 'How was the latest tech run?' I asked Pim, who was making a dramatic effort to make her starter last for as long as possible, pulling different orgasmic faces with each new taste. I looked around for any fellow diners taking sneaky photos. This was not a moment I thought she would want captured and shared online.

'Perfect,' she spoke with unexpected jollity. 'The lighting is superb. I had someone sit in for me so I could see for myself what every viewer would see from each seat in the theatre.' I bet the lighting designer and producers loved that, I thought sarcastically. 'Even those in the balconies at the back will be able to see me clearly.'

'Well, that sounds good,' I said. 'And the microphone issue was sorted.'

'Oh yes, I'm just going to hold the microphone. None of those clip-on things. I don't want to have to plan my outfit based on that, I want to plan my outfit based on my mood and my hair.'

'And the lighting.'

She agreed, nodding as she took the last bite of her starter.

'Utter perfection,' she said, placing down her napkin with a flourish. Within seconds the waiter had returned and cleared our plates. 'Tell the chef that that was the best dish I've ever eaten,' she told the young man, before quickly taking up her compact and pressing powder across her nose. 'Maybe the chef will come to the table,' she explained.

I smiled at her, realising what she was up to now. She had spotted the chef earlier when he had left the kitchen to visit at another table; one look at him and she was licking her lips. It was as much him she was hungry for as the oysters.

Since she was in such a good mood, I placed down the papers with her schedule for the rest of the week, thinking now was as good as any time to tell her about Alison.

'I have some good news for you,' I said, and she smiled, leaning forward a little. 'I think I've found your new assistant.'

Pim rolled her eyes and sat back, adjusting her hair and replacing her compact in her clutch with a sharp snap of the clasp. I'd hoped for curiosity, maybe even relief, but instead it felt like I'd said something mildly tedious rather than quietly life-altering.

'Her name is Alison, and I would love to add a quick meeting into your schedule for next week…'

'Oh, Evie, why don't you have an evening off tonight?'

'Sorry?'

I kept my tone light, professional, even as something in my chest tightened. Pim's refusal to engage wasn't new, but moments like this made leaving feel harder, not easier. It was difficult to step away from someone who refused to acknowledge the gap you were about to leave behind.

'No work. Let's just catch up. You haven't told me anything of what you've been doing lately.'

'Well, I was looking for my replacement,' I said, trying hard not to sound sarcastic or bitter.

'I meant in your personal life. Has it been nice being home?'

I didn't say that I didn't have a home, as that felt a bit too dramatic – even for Pim; instead I nodded. 'It's been wonderful being back in London and seeing friends.' And meeting buskers.

'Good! Now what have you been doing? Going to the theatre? Eating out? Going to parties?'

She had never shown this much interest in my personal life before but I thought, why not embrace it? I placed the papers back into my bag on the floor and went to speak, when suddenly she interrupted.

'Oh, speaking of eating out… guess who I saw at The Wolseley the other night?'

Oh, right. I guess we're not going to talk about me then after all.

I took a sip of my wine and tried not to let my frustration show about being swindled out of discussing my replacement… again. 'Who? Someone you hate, I suppose,' I guessed, because I knew Pim well enough to sense when a villain was about to be introduced.

'Michael Holland! That slimy, two-faced, smug little—' She exhaled through her nose dramatically. 'He's like a bad penny. Ever since we ran into him at the BBC, he just keeps showing up.' I failed to recognise the coincidence, given that they were both circling the drain of the TV industry these days, so no doubt both of them ran in the same circles. 'He's been swanning around with his posh toffs lot, acting like he's some kind of broadcasting legend just because he's managed to churn out a few documentaries.'

'They've done quite well, though, haven't they?' I

ventured cautiously. 'People seem to like them.' The ratings were mixed but the reviews were good.

'People like Pot Noodles too, Evie. It doesn't mean they're any good for you.' Pim waved her hand dismissively. 'He's such a fraud. Smiling at me like we're old friends when we're in public. I wanted to knock his block off, but the weight of it hitting the floor would probably make the earth implode.'

'Did you say anything to him?' My heart hammered at the drama that could ensue if her feelings towards this wannabe national treasure ever got out.

Pim's eyes glinted with mischief. 'Oh, I was the picture of charm. I looked him dead in the eye and said, "Michael, how wonderful to see you again! I had no idea the BBC let interns dine at The Wolseley." Then I turned back to my dessert like he didn't exist.'

I rolled my lips together, trying not to laugh. 'That's quite, erm, *petty,*' I dared to say, though truly I was delighted. I didn't like the man either.

'No.' She swirled her wine glass again with a satisfied smile. 'That is justice.'

She took a long, triumphant sip, clearly pleased with herself. 'Honestly, the nerve of him. Smarming his way through the industry, acting like he's some authority just because he does *documentaries*.' Her voice became long and drawn out, mimicking an old Etonian's.

Ah, I thought, she wants to do documentaries but now they're tainted because Michael Holland does them too. There goes Pim's dream of being the next Mary Beard.

'Well, I suppose he does have a certain… presence,' I admitted. 'People find him charismatic.'

'Oh, he's good-looking,' Pim agreed begrudgingly. 'A

right silver fox. And single, to boot. But that's the most dangerous type, isn't it? The ones who get away with murder just because they've got a nice set of teeth and a decent jawline.' She stabbed at her fish, clearly imagining it was Michael's face.

I smirked. 'It sounds like he's got under your skin.'

'Not at all.' Pim sniffed, lifting her chin. 'I'm just warning you, Evie. Watch out for people like him. They pretend to be charming, but they're as slippery as snakes. I wouldn't trust him as far as I could throw him.'

'Duly noted,' I said, making a mental note to avoid watching any Michael Holland documentaries while in Pim's employ from now on.

Satisfied that she'd made her point, Pim's mood lightened. 'Now, where were we? Ah, yes. You.'

'Me?'

'Yes, *you*.' She rolled her eyes. 'What have you been up to?'

My eyes could have popped. She was serious, she did want to know about my life. 'Erm, well, I…' I cleared my throat. 'I've been completing a Christmas bucket list. Or trying to, at least.'

'Oh, really? What's on the list?'

'Erm, well, drink mulled wine in Covent Garden,' I recited, counting the items on my fingers. 'Walk down Carnaby Street to see all the lights.'

'Carnaby Street? Really?'

'The Christmas lights are famous.'

'Famously tacky,' she sighed. 'What else?' The waiter returned with our mains. A mushroom linguine for me and Dover sole for Pim. 'Me and my friends are taking part in the Great Christmas Pudding Race tomorrow to raise money for charity.' Pim's knife and fork froze above her fish.

'The Great Christmas what?'

I finished my first mouthful of linguine, which was, of course, delicious.

'The Great Christmas Pudding Race. It's a relay race in Seven Dials, where you dress up and run through an obstacle course… while holding a Christmas pudding,' I finished lamely.

'It's not flaming, is it?' she asked seriously, and I shook my head imagining Father Christmas in an extremely flammable costume running with a lit Christmas pudding.

'No, just your standard Christmas pudding. It sounds silly, but it's fun. And it's for charity.'

'Which charity?' she asked, delicately adding some capers and cucumbers to her forkful of Dover sole.

'Cancer Research.'

'Oh,' she said, her expression flickering for just a moment before her mask of indifference slipped back into place. 'That must be an important charity for you.'

I looked down at my plate, running my finger around the delicate pattern on the rim. 'I'm running for friends as well as for the charity. But it is important.' My voice was softer than I intended but I didn't want to get into a discussion on my dead mum if I could help it.

Pim knew my mum had died. She knew the timeline, the age I'd been, the touchstone details. What she didn't know was how it still surfaced unexpectedly, particularly at this time of year.

Over the years, before I even began working with Pim, I'd learned to keep that part of myself carefully folded away. But *especially* when I was with her. Grief didn't fit neatly into filming, flight schedules, or dressing rooms, and Pim had always had enough of her own to manage.

I didn't want to open the door now. So I stayed where it was safe, talking about the run, about the cause, and not about the real reason behind it.

Pim didn't say anything right away but carried on chewing thoughtfully. 'How much are you trying to raise?'

'I haven't had much chance to fund-raise.' My neck flushed with embarrassment. I hadn't even started to fund-raise. 'You have to be able to raise £100 minimum to run,' I told her, thinking that I would probably need to pay up that £100 myself, which wouldn't be a problem.

I did feel bad for not doing more, though. I was sure Josh had probably put up some massive collection pot at Harrods, telling everyone about his epic run for charity. Even Megan would have done something, like adding a 'donate' button to her email signature so major CEOs and corporations would see it every time she responded about their appraisal strategies, or whatever it was she did. Even Alex had probably got his football league to donate the cost of a pint.

I hadn't even so much as mentioned it to anyone. Not even Pim until now.

'£100 will hardly cure cancer,' Pim scoffed, her signature bite returning.

I blinked, half expecting her to be joking, but she looked deadly serious. 'You're right,' I said quietly, the back of my neck beginning to burn. 'But every little helps, I guess.'

'Can I donate?' Pim asked softly, not looking at me as she ate more of her meal. This was probably a good thing, as I nearly dropped my fork at the question.

'If you'd like to,' I said, eventually, upon recovering myself. 'I have a form you can fill in.'

'Oh pft,' she said, taking a sip of her white wine. 'Just fill it in for me. Put me down for…' She thought for a moment and then shrugged. 'It's Christmas, let's say £1,000.'

I did drop my fork then.

'A thousand,' I repeated, expecting her to laugh and take it back like it was some sort of exaggeration. 'Are… are you sure?'

She arched an eyebrow. 'Why wouldn't I be? It's for charity.'

'Wow, Pim, that's… wow.' I felt a lump rising in my throat. This was the first time Pim had done anything like this for me, and it was for something as silly as running in a costume around Covent Garden. I'd had influenza in Greece and she hadn't so much as sent an order of room service to my door, but she did send me the menu for her flight back to Canada and asked me to order the duck. 'Thanks, Pim.'

She smiled with tight lips before looking back at her plate.

'Make sure to use my name as well. None of this anonymous donor malarkey.'

Ah! 'You know that the donations aren't shared publicly, the amount is but not who gave what.'

She paused mid-bite, her eyes narrowing. 'I don't need people to know, Evie. Donating is enough. Besides, think of it as your Christmas bonus.'

There's the Pim I knew.

'Thank you,' I said warmly. She didn't have to donate after all, and she could have taken it back since there was no credit. And sure, I wasn't getting a genuine Christmas bonus for my last Christmas with her, but to give £1,000 for me to run a race in costume with a pudding was still a nice thing to do.

With a shake of her shoulders, Pim straightened up, her familiar imperiousness returning. 'Anyway, this Dover sole is atrocious,' she declared, pushing her plate away with a loud clatter. 'I don't know why I keep ordering it here. What did I get for dessert again?'

'The banana and salted caramel tart.'

'Hmm… do you think they'd swap that for another plate of oysters? They really were delicious. And an aphrodisiac too.' Her eyes sparkled wickedly. 'I wonder where that chef has got to.'

Chapter 11

RESTING MY PHONE AGAINST THE STEPS of St Martin-in-the-Fields, I did the standard influencer twirl on the spot in time to 'Step into Christmas'. I had recorded a clip earlier that morning in my hotel room while in my regular clothes and, with a little light editing, I could piece the two together to reveal my outfit for the Great Christmas Pudding Race in my next TikTok video.

As planned, Josh had found a green Elf costume for me and I had spent the better part of my Friday evening, after dinner with Pim, hot-gluing extra tinsel and jingle bells to it.

I wore red block-heeled boots – a decision I would probably come to regret when running through inflatables with a Christmas pudding – and a hat with an extra-large bell on the end. I couldn't say I felt sexy, but I definitely felt Christmassy.

'You're going to be late,' Andy, the concierge at the Travelodge said, walking past me twirling by the steps with his favourite Starbucks iced coffee, a brave choice for December. I looked at my watch.

'Damn!' I said, gathering my things quickly. 'Thanks, Andy!' He raised his hand in a swift thumbs-up before heading back inside the Travelodge.

It was 10.30 in the morning, and despite being fairly quiet, I still got plenty of funny looks as I walked up Monmouth Street into Covent Garden. Still, it was nice to walk through the piazza in the morning before the throngs of tourists descended. They were gathering but it was nowhere near as busy as it would be by lunch time or once night fell, but it was still packed enough that groups of shoppers parted ways to look and let me pass, and buskers had pulled crowds around them.

Without meaning to, I looked around for Simon at his previous busking spot and there he was.

He was singing into a microphone, a backing tune of 'What Christmas Means to Me' by Stevie Wonder. Before I realised it, my feet had altered my direction and I found myself headed towards him. He was like gravity, pulling me in.

For a while, he didn't seem to notice me. I'd have thought I was pretty hard to miss in my Elf costume, jingling with every step among the sea of puffer jackets and Christmas jumpers. But he was lost in his element, his eyes crinkling at the corners as he belted out the lyrics, his energy infectious. I couldn't help but smile, watching him charm the crowd.

'Thank you!' he called as he hit the last note, the crowd erupting into applause. Coins clinked into his upturned hat and he gave a little bow, his face alight with genuine joy. I manoeuvred my way to the front, the bells on my skirt chiming softly, and called out, 'Who are you raising money for today?'

He turned, his eyes widening as they landed on me, taking in my sparkly boots, the jingly skirt, and the ridiculous green hat perched on my head. For a second he just stared, his mouth twitching as if he were trying to hold back a laugh. Then his eyes met mine, dancing with that familiar mischief.

'Crisis,' he answered into the microphone, his voice warm. 'Which, judging by that outfit, you might be in.' The crowd laughed, and his grin grew wider, his gaze never leaving mine. He held up a finger to me, mouthing 'One minute' before handing the microphone to another busker and making his way over to me.

As he moved closer, his eyes did another slow sweep of my costume, lingering just a second too long before locking with my eyes again. 'Nice outfit,' he said, his voice lower, softer.

'I'm Jovie from *Elf*,' I replied, giving my skirt a playful twirl and jutting my leg out to show off my sparkly boots. 'I'm about to run the Great Christmas Pudding Race.'

'Yeah, I heard that was happening today.' His gaze dropped to my boots again, his mouth curving into an amused smile. 'You're actually running in those?'

'Don't sound so surprised,' I said, feigning offence. 'I'm more coordinated than I look.'

'I don't doubt it,' he murmured, his voice teasing.

I cleared my throat, desperate to break the sudden electrifying tension before I did something stupid, like stare at his mouth. 'So is that why you're busking so early? To get away before the madness descends?'

He cleared his throat, turning and running his hand through his hair. I got a good look at his biceps from the gesture and my stomach stiffened; he had muscles. 'That and it was the only slot available,' he admitted, looking back and leaning in conspiratorially. 'It gets pretty cut-throat around here this time of year.'

'You make it sound like *Game of Thrones* or something.'

'It kind of is.' He laughed at his own joke pre-emptively. 'Winter Wonderland is coming.'

I moaned. 'I walked right into that one.'

'I regretted it as soon as I said it.'

'No, you didn't.'

We stood there chuckling and for a moment his face softened, his gaze turning to me thoughtfully. 'Right,' he said finally. 'I need to get back. I've got ten more minutes to fill. And you.' He pointed to my feet. 'Try not to fall flat on your face in those shoes.'

I laughed, taking a step back. 'No promises.' I gave another short twirl. 'Go back to your adoring fans. Have a good show.'

'Cheers,' he said, stepping back already.

As I walked away, the first notes of 'Santa Claus Is Comin' to Town' floated through the air, his voice wrapping around me like a hug. I glanced back, just once, to see him watching me, his smile soft, his eyes warm.

Seven Dials seemed less of a place and more like one large crowd. All the streets were blocked, either by characters in an array of familiar costumes or race organisers in red outfits and Christmas hats, wearing large badges and waving hands and clipboards above their heads like exhausted parents hosting a children's party. My body seemed to relax as I saw them. It was not unlike the behind-the-scenes of one of Pim's many TV appearances.

I looked about, trying to spot Josh, Alex, and Megan and seeing multiple Grinches, Santa Clauses, the occasional Buddy the Elf and Muppets character, but no John McClanes or Cindy Lou Whos.

But suddenly I heard someone scream, 'Evie!' from behind me. And it was a scream, not a shout.

Josh was running towards me wearing a muscle suit and holding his unflattering bald cap. He grabbed both my arms, his eyes wide and almost bloodshot.

'We have a disaster,' he said, turning and pulling me into the throngs of reindeer and Kris Kringles.

'Where are we going? Where's Megan and Alex?'

I heard Josh repeat 'Alex' in a very frustrated tone.

'Josh?' I asked, as he pulled me into an alcove where Megan was pacing on the phone. She looked so cute in her little pink Cindy Lou Who costume – even if she was about two feet taller than the actual Cindy Lou Who.

'Megan?' I asked but she shook her head, looking very worried. 'He's not answering,' she told Josh more than me.

'That *Ebeneezer*,' he hissed.

'What is going on?' I asked, holding my hands up to stop both of them, only noticing as I did so the green Grinch costume over Megan's arm. 'Where's Alex?'

'He's ill,' she said, unsympathetically.

'That's no excuse,' Josh said, throwing his hands up dramatically. Megan sighed, her voice cracking as if she might cry.

'Now he's not answering his phone,' she said.

'Wait, what?'

'This morning he said he was unwell and wasn't going to make it. He wouldn't get out of bed; he's got this cold that's been going around.'

'Tell him to man up!' Josh shouted, and I stopped myself from pointing out the sexism in that statement, since he was slowly turning as red as one of his Santa suit swatches.

'He's going to be in costume. No one will see the snot pouring down his face.'

'Gross,' I said. 'So we're down a team member.'

'He said he'd get his mate Billy to do it,' Megan said, pressing 'Dial' on her phone again. 'But I can't get hold of Billy and now Alex isn't answering his phone. What if he's doing a *Love Actually*?' she asked suddenly.

'A what?' I said.

'You know – when Colin Firth goes to the wedding and leaves his girlfriend at home as she has a cold, but she's actually fucking his brother.'

'Well, in this scenario that would surely mean Alex is fucking me, which I can swear by Mary, Joseph, and the wee donkey he is not,' I pointed out.

'But he's not answering,' Megan practically wailed.

'And we're a team member down!' Josh also wailed.

'Okay, calm down,' I said and both of them glared at me, since when has anyone ever calmed down because they were told to? 'He's probably not answering as he's downed too much NyQuil and is sleeping it off and besides, this is Alex, he can't prepare a takeaway order let alone a coordinated cheating moment. And we can run just the three of us.'

'The minimum team is four,' Josh pointed out. 'If we don't have a fourth, we have to forfeit our place.'

'Surely we can speak to someone,' I suggested calmly – putting my practice with Pim to good use – and looked for one of the Santa hats with a clipboard. 'There must be a few spare runners who couldn't get a team together on the sidelines, or someone we can just pinch from the crowd.'

'What about the costume?' Josh shouted, flinging his arms in the air. How many espressos had he had this morning? 'We need a man to fit the costume and we need them *now*.'

My heart skipped a beat.

Call it a lightbulb moment or a ton of bricks, but I knew exactly what to do. He was going to hate me. But it was for charity. And deep down, I knew he'd do it. At least, I hoped he would.

'I know who we can ask.'

Before Josh or Megan could question me, I bolted out into the crowd. If I didn't get to him before he wrapped up his set, I'd lose him to the sea of people flooding the streets.

'Excuse me!' I shouted, pushing past racers and the growing crowds of viewers, all of whom took double takes when they spotted – or heard – my wildly jingly costume. 'Christmas emergency!' I added for good measure, feeling my role overtaking my personality. It was remarkable how many people seemed to stop and pull children and their handbags out of the way at that declaration. Suddenly it was as if I was an ambulance, and crowds were respectful enough to pause and pull into gaps. 'I'm trying to save Christmas!' I shouted again for effect, and once again the crowds parted, and I found myself back in the open-air market of Covent Garden.

Looking around to find my bearings, scanning the festive chaos, I spotted the Christmas tree and ran towards it. A police officer shouted, 'Slow down, love!' but I simply waved energetically and carried on running.

Simon was still there.

He was reaching the crescendo of 'I Wish It Could Be Christmas Every Day', his voice soaring above the crowd, his arms flung wide, his body moving to the beat, and the onlookers were completely enthralled, clapping, and singing along. I pushed through them, earning a few glares but mostly laughter as my jingling skirt swished around me. I stopped just short of tackling him.

His eyebrows shot up when he spotted me. For a second his voice faltered, his eyes widening as if he couldn't quite believe I was back so soon. His mouth curled into a half-smile as he continued to sing, his voice unwavering even as his expression clearly asked, 'What are you doing?'

Awkwardly I bobbed along, looking to one of the observers that I had just pushed past with an apologetic '*I'm just excited*' smile, before turning back to Simon. My heart was racing, anticipation bubbling in my chest. Waiting for him to finish was excruciating. I couldn't help it – I started making subtle hand gestures, mouthing *hurry up*, which only earned me a confused head tilt and a playful eye roll.

Finally the song ended and he stepped back from the microphone, slightly breathless but grinning, as he called, 'Thank you so much! Merry Christmas!' Coins clinked into his hat as people came forward, and I took my chance, ducking around them to reach him.

Simon immediately made room for me with a very confused and amused: 'What's up with you?'

'I'm *so* sorry, but I need a favour,' I blurted out, trying to keep the urgency out of my voice, but failing miserably.

'A favour?' He turned every few seconds, nodding and thanking the crowd as they dropped coins into his hat. 'Couldn't it wait?'

'Well, it's kind of time-sensitive,' I said, feeling my phone buzz repeatedly in my bag. Clearly Josh was losing his mind. 'I need you… now. Like, right now.'

'Now? I've got to clear up, I'm…'

'I know! And I swear I wouldn't ask unless it was life or death.' I hesitated, then amended, 'Okay, maybe not *death*, but definitely Christmas.'

His eyes softened, his posture relaxing just a fraction. 'Christmas, huh?'

'Yes! We need a fourth for the Great Christmas Pudding Race.'

His head swerved and his eyes bulged in a way I could easily translate as 'No fucking way!'

'Oh please! Alex – Megan's husband – is ill and we don't have a fourth, and we need a fourth or we lose our spot, and it's for charity. You love charity!'

His face fell for a split second before he caught himself. 'Evie…' His voice was softer now, less guarded. 'I – I do but…'

'It's for a *really* good charity,' I interrupted furiously. 'It's Cancer Research, who, you know, do really great stuff and cure cancer – or *try* – and I'd really like them to *keep* trying so no one else gets cancer like Mum and die…' Ooft! Straight for the sympathy jugular.

Simon visibly flinched, his body stiffening as his gaze snapped back to me, his eyes wide and glassy. His mouth parted, but no sound came out at first. 'I…' His voice was a whisper. 'I'm so—'

I panicked, throwing my hands over his mouth. 'Don't say you're sorry. Just say you'll save Christmas and run the race.'

His eyes widened in surprise, but I felt his mouth curve into a smile beneath my palms. I dropped my hands, suddenly aware of how close we were, the space between us charged once again, as if my body had just been plugged into the mains.

He didn't attempt to say anything, but I hadn't realised how loud I'd been speaking, or how close to his microphone I had said it.

'Oh, go on, lad!' one of the bystanders said. 'Do it for the girl!'

'Do it for Christmas!' another woman said, smiling in a mischievous way that made me feel as if I was in the middle of a Hallmark movie.

'You should listen to them,' I said, lowering my hands slowly from his mouth.

'Yeah, listen to us, mate! Go on, eh!' another man, in a backwards cap and a large red puffer jacket said, walking past. I don't think he had a clue what was going on, but it seemed to have the desired effect. I saw Simon's misgivings disappear.

He looked at me intensely, his gaze flicking over my Elf costume once more, lingering for just a beat longer than necessary. I watched his resolve crumble, his shoulders dropping in defeat. 'When?' he asked.

'Kind of right now,' I said, pointing over my shoulder awkwardly. 'We've got the costume waiting and everything.'

He groaned, his head dropping back as he looked up at the sky, his Adam's apple bobbing as he swallowed. 'You're impossible, you know that?'

I grinned, feeling a wave of relief and something else – something warmer – flood my chest. 'It's part of my charm.' I jolted my hip on purpose, to get the bells to ring.

He shook his head, his smile softening as his eyes met mine. 'Yeah. It really is.'

His voice was low, almost vulnerable, and I felt a shiver race down my spine. I cleared my throat, trying to break the tension. 'So… is that a yes?'

'Yeah,' he said, his shoulders relaxing as he bent down to gather his things. 'It's Christmas after all.'

'Amazing!' I did a little leap. 'We just need to hurry up and get you in your costume.'

Simon had bent down to gather some of his belongings, but he stopped midway to his toes at the reminder of the 'costume'.

'It's very tasteful!' I said immediately, trying to placate him. 'Josh, one of the other runners, is a professional.'

'A professional what?' he asked, returning to his task, but still glancing back at me and my jingly costume, probably trying hard not to imagine what kind of outfit we had in mind for him.

'A professional Christmas organiser,' I said, rushing to pick up some of the money and his flat cap to try to help. It felt slightly odd gathering someone else's money for them, but time was of the essence.

'That's a job?' he said, pulling his microphone off the stand and quickly dismantling it as the next busker entered the cordoned off-stage area to set up his own equipment.

'It is.' My phone buzzed again in my bag, and I awkwardly pulled it out as I placed Simon's cap of money on top of his full arms with the microphone and stand. 'Hold on.' I placed the phone against my ear. 'I'm coming! I've got someone to join us.'

'Well, hurry the fuck up!' Josh shouted down the phone, although the relief in his voice was apparent. 'The race starts in ten minutes. They're doing the warm-up.'

'We'll be there. Warm up for me!' I hung up quickly. 'We have to get going now, like *right* now.'

Simon, who usually appeared so calm when performing to crowds of hundreds suddenly exhaled in a panic-stricken way. 'Okay, okay.' Looking at his many boxes and wires and up at me again, his eyes flickered over my shoulder. 'Ethan,' he called, walking past me to the next busker setting up. 'Sorry to be a pain, mate, but can you watch my stuff? I need to get off to this charity race.'

'The Pudding Race?' Ethan said, stopping organising his circus-trick apparatus to turn and grin. 'You?'

'Yes, me. I'm helping a friend.'

I'm officially a friend?

I felt a warm glow in my chest. 'Can you just look after it until I get back?'

Ethan looked at the boxes and then nodded. 'Sure thing. I might even come and watch if I'm done with my set in time.'

'But who would watch my stuff?' Simon froze.

Ethan laughed mischievously. 'I'd have no shortage of volunteers to help me bring it over, don't you worry.'

'Don't you dare tell anyone about this,' Simon said, clapping him on the back in reluctant thanks.

Ethan smiled and turned his head slowly in the direction of his microphone as I grabbed Simon by the wrist and quickly pulled him away.

'Okay, fine. I won't tell the other buskers that Simon's running in the Great Christmas Pudding Race,' Ethan's voice reverberated out of his speakers and almost immediately the buskers patiently waiting for their sessions under the cover of St Paul's Church began to jeer. Their cheering followed us as they shouted, '*Go for it, Simon!*'

'Thank you,' I said quickly, to distract Simon from the echoing jeers of his fellow buskers, brushing his hand with my fingers as I handed him a few last coins.

His hand closed around mine for a second, his thumb

grazing my knuckles, before he pocketed the coins. 'You owe me for this one.'

I laughed, the sound breathier than I intended. 'I know. And I'll make it up to you. Promise.'

'Good,' he said, his voice lower now, his eyes locked on mine. 'I'm counting on it.'

His words hung between us, and for a second, I forgot how to breathe.

I grabbed his hand properly, giving it a playful tug to break the moment. 'Come on – Christmas isn't going to save itself.'

His fingers curled around mine, holding on just a little tighter than necessary. 'Lead the way, Jovie.'

Chapter 12

'It's a little snug, but it will have to do,' Josh said, pulling up the hood of the Grinch costume on Simon's head. 'Right.' He clapped his hands managerially. 'Are we ready?'

Other teams around were gathering and were equally energetic in their pep talks.

'Almost,' I said, taking the green face paint from Megan's waiting hand and dampening the sponge in a little tub of water in the other.

'What is that?' Simon asked, looking from me to the neon-lime face paint.

'I will personally donate £100 to Crisis,' I said, rubbing the sponge in the paint before he could object, and slathering it on his chin. He went silent at once and noticeably pouted, which was actually quite helpful in the paint application.

'What's our team name, Josh?' I asked Josh over Simon's shoulder, as I ignored his playful glare.

Josh turned from speaking to one of the Santa organisers and, with a dramatic arm flourish, announced he had registered us as Fab-YULE-Us.

'I had nothing to do with it,' Megan pointed out, looking

at her phone once more, willing for a message from her husband that had still yet to arrive.

'What? It's perfect,' Josh exclaimed. 'Much better than the others.'

'What are the others?' Simon asked curiously, as a race marshal came by asking for us to get into position as the celebrity of the day – a winner of the recent *Celebrity MasterChef UK* – was about to come on stage to start the race.

I hastily dropped the face paint into a Tesco Bag For Life, not remembering that my crossbody bag was stashed inside until it was too late, and prepared to get in line to get a tray and a Christmas pudding.

'Well,' Josh began as Megan, Simon, and I hastened to get to the start of the race. 'There's the Jingle Belles, an all-girl team with a seventy-plus-year-old, so we've got them beat. Then the Parumpapumpums, who I think we'll need to watch out for.'

'Yeah,' Megan interjected as we were jostled towards the starting line. 'They were shouting Christmas slurs like "I will deck your halls!"'

'And the ever-so-imaginative "We will sleigh you!"' Josh added, rolling his eyes in horror – forgetting that he had named our group the Fab-YULE-Us. We were not innocent of pun murder.

'Sounds dreadful,' Simon said, trying to hide his smile as he rubbed his eye, smudging the badly applied face paint.

'What's dreadful is the make-up. I'm so sorry,' I added, patting his now furry green arm apologetically.

'At least this costume is warm. I don't have to worry so much about scarves and hats.'

'Wait until we start running,' I pointed out. 'You might not be so thankful for that costume then.'

At that moment the marshals began calling for teams to come forward.

'That's us!' Josh cried, moving immediately to get to the front of the starting line for his tray and Christmas pudding, with the three of us following, leaving our stuff at the side of the street. Thankfully, being a team within the race meant that we got to stand behind a security barrier and could leave our items safely.

'So what actually happens?' Simon asked me and Megan, as the two of us began pushing through the other groups to get in line.

'It's an obstacle course,' Megan shouted over the rising din of competitive voices. 'We each get a tray with a Christmas pudding on it.'

'I got that part,' Simon mumbled, grumpy that a Hans Gruber had pushed him aside to join his other collective Grubers.

'There are obstacles we have to climb over and through, like that inflatable slide.' I pointed to it for Simon's benefit. 'Oh, and the race marshals spray you with foam before you go on the slalom.'

'And we've all got to decorate a Christmas tree and dress a snowman at the end as well.' Megan grinned – of course, her favourite bit would be the home décor portion. 'With Josh on our team, that will be a piece of cake.'

'The winning teams battle it out in a Grand Final,' I said finally as I was passed my tray and pudding, which was surprisingly heavy. 'Oh, and don't drop your pudding.'

Simon mouthed 'Okay' in that adorably bewildered way of his, and I couldn't help but laugh.

'£200 for Crisis,' I muttered to him, raising an eyebrow. He glanced at me, his lips curling into a slow, easy smile.

'At this rate, you're going to raise more money for Crisis than you are Cancer Research.' His voice was teasing, but there was something warm in the way he said it.

'We'll raise money for both, no jingle off my bells.'

His laugh was deep and unrestrained, a sound that sent a little thrill through me. We almost missed the *MasterChef* winner's opening instructions, but we certainly didn't miss the '*Ready, get set, go!*' that followed.

The horn blared, and suddenly we were swept up in a wave of runners – shoved forward by reindeer, elves, fat Santas, bad Santas, and more. Megan let out a shriek, her sensible shoes propelling her forward with surprising speed, while I nearly slipped in mine. Simon, either suddenly possessed by competitive fire or eager to finish, jolted ahead.

I caught up with them as we all tried to climb the inflatable slide, our trays and puddings swaying dangerously. It was chaos, and not the good kind.

'Give me a boost!' Simon shouted and without hesitating Megan and I had one hand on either side of his backside and were pushing his furry green bottom up and over.

'The gentlemanly thing would have been to help us!' Megan pointed out, half-giggling, half out of breath, but there was no time for further complaints; Simon's head suddenly reappeared at the top of the slide. I heard the commentator laughingly pointing out that 'The Grinch appears to be saving Cindy Lou Who!'

Somehow, Simon managed to hold onto both his tray and the slide, pulling Megan up with him. She yelped as she rolled down the slide, and I heard Simon's voice ring out, 'Your turn now.'

Trying my hardest not to lose my slippery footing as I laughed, I lurched forward to grab him and squashed the Christmas pudding into my chest.

'Oh, fuck!' I exclaimed and I heard one of the Jingle Belles shout, '*Language!*' at the top of her lungs. 'So sorry!' I screeched, as I toppled over and landed on top of Simon and we both fell down the slide together. Now two Christmas puddings pressed into our chests.

'I hope these costumes weren't rentals,' Simon murmured, his breath warm against my cheek as we tried to right ourselves.

'Knowing Josh…' I said, groaning as I got to my knees and offered him a hand as I precariously peeled most of the Christmas pudding back onto the plate, '… they're not.'

'Come on,' Simon exhaled with a huff but his face glowed with a rosy pink tint, the laughter and exertion painting him in a charming light. 'We can still win this,' he said, that infectious grin spreading across his face.

We had all made good time through the obstacle course, even if our puddings were a little more squashed than they had been at the start. Simon and I found Josh and Megan already expertly adding details to the Christmas tree as we arrived, and we were instructed to start work on the snowman.

'What shall we call him?' Simon asked, clearly getting into the spirit of things, as he wrapped a red scarf around the snowman. His focus on the task only seemed to make him more endearing.

'Not Jack Frost,' I said, my mind struggling for something clever as I began to place a hat on the snowman's head.

'I was going to stick to the pun theme,' Simon suggested. 'Something like Michael Snow or Cold Porter.'

'Snowen Wilson?' I recommended.

'Meltin' John,' Simon suggested with a grin so contagious I almost fell over, trying to stop myself snorting.

I clutched my ribs, gasping for air as my laughter took over. 'Stop it! I can't breathe.'

Simon covered the snowman's hat dramatically, a mischievous glint in his eye. 'Ssh! You'll upset Snowprah Winfrey. They've never breathed, you know.'

I threw one of the baubles from the props table at Simon as Josh pronounced his tree was 'Perfect!' And it was. Even with cheap Amazon-buy props, Josh had managed to make our Christmas tree look like something out of a John Lewis catalogue.

'Last bit! Go, go, go!' Josh urged, snapping us back into the race. It looked like we were only behind one team, we still had the opportunity to win this.

'Go!' I instructed, grabbing my slightly dented Christmas pudding and racing for the finish. We had to pass through waiting strangers who had silly string at the ready as crowds cheered on.

'Come on, Simon!'

'Go on, my son!' I heard the recognisable sounds of Simon's fellow buskers, all harmonising in their supportive cheer. Turning over my shoulder, I saw Simon give them a swift middle finger before grinning like a mischievous schoolboy as he surged ahead.

'£300!' I shouted to him, catching up just as we neared the final inflatables.

'I'll forget you owe me anything if we win this,' Simon called back, practically charging ahead, only a step behind Josh, who was sprinting as if the finish line led to an early Boxing Day sale in Zara.

'Come on, Megan,' I said, grabbing her hand as she panted over the last inflatable. 'We've got this.'

'Woo!' Megan cheered lazily, raising her pudding above her head in a mock *Chariots of Fire* finish.

Josh and Simon both beat us to the red ribbon but we finally made it. And collapsed in a heap of Christmas cheer and exhaustion.

'That was bloody hard work,' Megan said, sitting up with her Christmas pudding – still perfect – in her lap.

Simon rested his hand against a scaffolding pole that was holding up the finish-line sign. 'I definitely got my steps in,' he said, his eyes twinkling. Josh was correcting his costume, ensuring his bald cap was perfectly lined up and none of his muscles had gone in the opposite direction from his body.

'Well done, team,' he said matter-of-factly, like a manager at the end of a forced team-building exercise.

'That was hilarious,' I added for good measure, my ribs still twingeing with a stitch brought on by laughter.

'Congratulations, all!' a race marshal said, coming up to move us away from the finish line as another group approached. 'You've made it to the final race.'

'Who beat us?' Josh asked, immediately competitive again.

'The Parumpapumpums were first,' the marshal said with a tiny amount of sympathy.

'The humbuggers,' Josh said, and I saw the race marshal flush in surprise.

'There's still the Grand Final to go,' he said, and I gently pulled his trouser leg from where I sat on the floor, so he turned to look at me.

'And what does the Grand Final entail?' I asked.

'Exactly the same again, except instead of the tree and snowman, you just need to deliver a present to Santa.'

'But still carrying a Christmas pudding, I presume?' Simon asked calmly.

'Yes, indeed. Wouldn't be the Great Christmas Pudding Race without one.' The marshal smiled and moved away to the next group to offer commiserations.

'Right, this is it, team.' Josh moved in, pulling Megan over by her padded shoulder. 'The finale, our curtain call, the big one.'

'Josh,' I said, still sitting on the floor beneath this pep-talk huddle. 'It's just a bit of fun.'

'Do you think the Parumpapumpums are classing this as a bit of fun?' Josh said, sarcastically. 'I think not. They are hard-and-fast fighters, and we must beat them.'

'Josh took great offence at their punny takedowns,' Megan reminded me.

'*Sleigh me*,' Josh repeated, breaking the circle. 'Like they could ever.'

I looked up at Simon, who was grinning and clearly enjoying Josh's over-the-topness.'

'£400?' I said, offering my hand so that he would help me off the floor. He did so with a not-so-polite groan; I'm not that heavy.

'I told you, if we win, I'll clear the whole debt.' He looked at his squashed Christmas pudding and took pains to make it presentable.

'I think we get new ones,' I pointed out, correcting the holly atop his pudding, since I was still wearing my elfish gloves.

'I'm good, I've grown very attached to my pudding,' he teased.

'Don't tell me you've named this one as well.'

'Not yet. But how about…' He thought for a moment, sticking out and biting his tongue as he examined his squashed cake. 'Puddington Bear.'

Laughing, I moved away towards the race marshal, who was waving his arm to gather us Fab-YULE-Us and the Parumpapumpums together.

To think the first race was competitive. Now that it was only down to two teams, it was like the crowd had become larger, the cheering had become louder, and Josh's pep talk had got much more aggressive.

The Parumpapumpums continued with their Christmas slurs, all in good jest, of course, but that meant nothing to Josh, who seemed to be in the business of using Christmas puns to genuinely insult others.

'This is snow laughing matter, we're going to win!' one of the Parumpapumpums shouted, to get a cheer from the crowd. These were a group of full-grown, forty-plus men dressed as the three wise men – though there were four of them, which was pissing Josh off even more, as aesthetically they were incorrect.

'Yeah, get the Elf out of here!' another called.

Suddenly Simon, who had been quiet after he saw more of his fellow buskers lining up at the sidelines to cheer him on, piped up with 'We'll snow you!'

Megan's and my head turned towards him, like the spinning heads of *The Exorcist*.

'He was a good find,' Megan said to me.

Simon shrugged, once again blushing under his face paint, which had mostly sweated off anyway. I told him he would regret saying he liked his costume.

'Racers, are you ready?' the *MasterChef* winner shouted from their podium to get cheers from the growing crowd. 'This is for the Christmas crown. On your marks, get set, go!'

Once again, the race began and Josh and Simon shot off, while Megan and I lingered behind all the men. By the time we got to the inflatable slide, it was like the scene of *World War Z* when all the zombies are climbing up over each other.

I was all for waiting but Megan was in it for the win.

'Hold my pudding,' she said, slamming her tray into me as she stepped over the men and clambered up the side of the slide. She made it to the top with ease.

'Now your turn,' she said, over the din of the men shoving each other out of the way. I followed suit, handing up the trays before stepping on more than one person's hand and gracefully falling down the slide with Megan.

I couldn't see Simon's lurid green costume in the pile-up, so assumed he got ahead.

'Let's go!' I cried, as the cheering of the crowd spurred me on. We raced around the slalom through the crazy string road and down to a wall of numbers or, as the race marshal shouted at us, 'Presents!'

We each grabbed a numbered piece of paper from the wall and ran down the street until we saw a man dressed as Santa sitting in the middle of the road with a waiting bag. Each of us plunged the numbered paper inside and ran off, grabbing hold of each other's hand as we raced to the finish line.

Simon was waiting, cheering, and waving his arms. 'Come on, girls!' he shouted. 'We've got this!'

Then, suddenly, Josh appeared from behind me and Megan.

'For Christmas!' he shouted, pushing through Megan's and my linked arms to reach the finish line first, followed swiftly by the two of us. All four of us landed in a pile, puddings forgotten, hugging with screams of joy.

'We won!' Simon announced, as we heard groans from the fast-approaching Parumpapumpums, who had clearly just realised it was all over.

We had won the Great Christmas Pudding Race.

Chapter 13

'I'M SO SORRY I FORGOT THE make-up wipes.'

While Simon was out of his Grinch costume, now sweaty and stuffed to the bottom of the Bag For Life, he was still covered in lingering green face paint as we sat in a crowded pub.

He rubbed his finger across his chin and then laughed. 'It was worth it.'

We were alone, waiting for Josh to return from ordering our drinks and Megan from phoning Alex outside.

After receiving our Christmas pudding trophies on stage, it felt like such a downer to suddenly all head back to our respective homes and hotels. Instead, Josh made the fantastic suggestion of grabbing a celebratory drink on him, since it was he that almost lost us the race getting caught up in the Parumpapumpums' mosh pit at the inflatable slide.

'Why not?' Simon said, asking for a few minutes to get his things – and endure some light teasing – from his fellow buskers.

'I'm glad you had fun.' I nudged Simon in the shoulder. 'Especially since it was all so last-minute, and not your usual cuppa by the sound of it.'

He shook his head in agreement. 'It really wasn't, but it was fun. I don't mind admitting it.'

'Will your busker friends ever let you forget it?'

'Absolutely not,' he said, playing with one of the paper-thin beer mats on the table. 'Particularly since I plan on bringing this trophy with me wherever I go from now on.' He lifted his glass trophy, engraved with the details of the day and encasing a fake Christmas pudding.

'That is a prestigious trophy,' I agreed, holding mine up as well. 'Not many people have one of these.'

'I will treasure it always, although I feel kind of guilty. I did none of the fundraising.'

'Trust me,' I said, using one of the napkins to polish the engraving of my trophy; there was a little bit of silly string still on it. 'You did plenty with helping us out. Besides, Megan, Josh, and I raised about £2,000 between us. So you're covered.'

'Oh, good, otherwise I'll have to start bringing two caps with me to my sets to gather money for both Crisis and Cancer Research.'

'Alternative sets maybe?'

He paused for a moment, putting his trophy down again. 'I really was sorry to hear about your mum,' he said. I pfted and gestured with my hand to forget it, but he carried on. 'My mum also had cancer.'

'Oh, I'm…' I stopped myself before I fell into my own most hated trap of saying sorry.

It wasn't that I wasn't sympathetic or appreciative of people's care but saying 'I'm sorry' always sparked a fear of pity in me. Maybe it was because I was an orphan and I hated the idea of people seeing me just as that, a helpless orphan. Or maybe it was because half the time people said 'I'm sorry' because they felt they had to and they felt awkward. When they did that, suddenly I had to care for them and make sure that they were okay after feeling awkward about something horrible that happened to me.

There was no win in it for anybody.

'It's fucking awful,' I said finally, forcing a smile that felt very awkward, given the topic.

Simon nodded. 'Yeah, it was, but she would have loved this.'

I swallowed. 'Would,' I repeated and he nodded.

'When I was eighteen,' he clarified, and I felt awful for asking. He wasn't that much older than I was when my mum passed. Sure, he was technically an 'adult' but you're always a child when you lose a parent, no matter your age.

I went to reach for his hand, an instinct that had never hit me before, but he had moved his hand away from the table so it looked like I was suddenly very interested in the salt and pepper pots. They were shaped like Santas and snowmen, so it wasn't inconceivable.

'I was ten,' I said quietly, feeling the dormant lump of grief beginning to rise in my throat. 'But you're right, she – *they* – would have loved this,' I said brightly, setting the salt and pepper pots down again when I realised he had noticed.

What surprised me wasn't the emotion that sprung up in me, but how safe it felt to let it show. Simon hadn't rushed to fill the silence or tried to fix anything. He'd simply understood, and somehow that made the moment feel lighter instead of heavier.

'Thanks again. That's another item of my Christmas bucket list sorted for this year.'

He smiled quizzically. 'I'm sorry, your what?'

I looked over my shoulder at Josh. who was pointing to a list of cocktails and discussing the tweaks he would like made to them. He was a regular Sally from *When Harry Met Sally* when it came to his cocktails.

'It's my first Christmas in London, and kind of my last…' I mumbled the end of my sentence and cleared my throat. 'And Megan, Josh and I kind of have this plan – it's sort of all the things we've said we'd always do if I was ever in London – one of them was the Christmas Pudding Race.'

'And the others?' Simon asked, clearly curious as he leaned forward on his arms.

'Drink mulled wine in Covent Garden.' I smirked.

'Ah, well, I know you did that already.'

'Yep. Others include eating dinner in an igloo.'

'An igloo?' he repeated.

'Apparently it's a thing.' I shrugged. 'That was one of Josh's ideas.'

'Okay, that I understand. Any others?'

'Buy something Christmassy from a market, go ice skating.'

Simon nodded, still smiling. 'No light shows?'

'We saw the lights at Carnaby Street,' Megan said, suddenly appearing at the table. 'What did I miss?'

'Nothing much,' I said, leaning back and making sure she had plenty of room. 'I was just telling Simon all about my Christmas bucket list.'

'Ahh, yes, the famous list of things that we always said we would do if Evie spent a Christmas in London,' Megan laughed. Clearly her husband had finally answered the phone.

'Is Alex okay?' I asked quickly.

'He sounds like he's at death's door.' She grinned. Obviously, Alex sounded realistically ill still and therefore unlikely to have been having a secret shag with a neighbour or one of Megan's relatives.

Simon's brow furrowed in confusion over Megan's oddly assigned glee.

'It's a long story,' I said, and he shrugged as if this was a fair enough explanation.

'So how are you two friends?'

'I feel like I should be asking you two that,' Megan said, winking between me and Simon. 'You never really told me how you two knew each other the first time we met.' Megan pointed between herself and Simon.

'I did tell you.' I blushed. 'I bumped into him and then bumped into him again.'

Now was not the time to say that I was really quite happy to be bumping into him again and again. In fact, I was thinking of making it a habit over Christmas.

'Sounds like the opening of *Bewitched*,' Megan said, not pacified. 'I need details!'

'She did bump into me.' Simon laughed. 'Clearly, Evie is not known for her coordination. Today's Christmas pudding was the victim today.'

'Don't judge my Christmas pudding!' I lightly threw one of the beer mats at him.

'What about you two? You're best friends, I assume?' Simon pressed.

'She's practically my sister.'

'Practically?' Megan repeated, mock-offended. 'I *am* your sister. We lived together for over ten years after all.'

I rolled my eyes, thinking I might as well tell Simon the whole story, if abridged, to avoid the sympathy-scene repeat.

'After my mum passed away, I went to live with Megan

and her family. I was still at school, but we met when we were at nursery, so I've known her my whole life. At least, as far back as I can remember.'

Simon nodded, smiling at what sounded like a sweet story once you've removed all the chemotherapy, funerals, and therapy that preceded and followed the initial move.

'And then we met Josh at university and we all lived together while we studied, or rather Megan studied. Josh and I weren't the best students,' I admitted with a laugh.

'Eight years ago.' Megan shuddered. 'How can it have been so long since we graduated?' She went back to looking at her phone to check her WhatsApp for messages from her husband.

I shrugged and played with the beer mats, just as Simon had been doing. 'It probably feels like a long time ago for you since you've actually lived a life since then. I've just travelled.'

'Travelled?' Simon repeated. 'I don't actually think I've asked you yet, what you do?'

'Oh, I'm...' I began but Josh interjected, fanning himself with the cocktail menu as he returned from the bar.

'She *was* a fabulous personal assistant to a world-famous celebrity, but now she's moving to Toronto to become a world-famous TV producer in her own right.' He took his seat with a balletic flourish.

My eyes flickered to Simon. He hadn't known about the move to Toronto and since this friendship – he had called me his friend after all – was so new, it seemed like a bit of news that he might seem a bit surprised by.

If he was, though, he hid it very well.

'Wow...' he said after a moment, looking from Josh to me. 'That sounds like a really exciting career.'

'It's not bad.' I shrugged. 'I get to travel a lot, which is why I haven't been able to do most of the things on our list.' I was really wishing my negroni was here so I could take a sip of it to fill the space I suddenly felt between me and Simon.

'You should check out her TikTok!' Josh said, suddenly pulling his phone out of his back pocket.

'No!' I said, lurching across the table to get it. But he was too quick, and I heard my voice suddenly reverberating around our booth. Simon leaned over Josh's shoulder to watch, an intrigued smile on his face.

Josh opened the app to a video of me at one of Pim's guest appearances in New York. I had walked past Radio City at 2.00 a.m., after a night shoot in Central Park, and had chosen to dance and record a voice-over later about the event. It was a good night.

But witnessing Simon watching it made my stomach curl into a knot.

'Wow, that's so cool,' Simon muttered quietly, but sincerely.

'Stop it,' I groaned, shrinking into the table.

'Check this one out.' Josh flicked to another video. One of the first that had received over 800,000 views. It was when Pim had a photoshoot for a celebrity show set in the jungle and I had to travel with her on a private yacht to the set along the coast of Australia. I had never seen such blue water in my life. You could see the stingrays swimming beneath the boat as if you were looking at a lit rockpool in the London Aquarium.

'Geez, that's awesome,' Simon said, taking the phone and flicking through a few more of the generic videos of me hanging out in hotel rooms while Pim got her hair done for the Emmys. Or on the back of a TV set as Pim did an interview on daytime TV.

I reached for the phone, but Josh pushed my arms away.

'Our Evie is a starlet,' he said, glowing with pride, while Megan made an 'uh-huh' noise, still looking at her phone.

'And you're leaving all this behind?' Simon said, pointing to the screen. I shrugged.

'It's not all glamour and greasepaint. Most of the time it's long hours, non-stop days, and so much effort.' I sighed as if exhausted, which in truth I was. 'And after eight years I could do with a bit of stability.'

Simon nodded again, doing one last final flick over my TikToks before handing Josh his phone back.

'What about you?' I found myself asking. 'Is busking your future?'

Simon's lip twitched knowingly. 'Well, it wasn't always the plan, if that's what you really want to know.'

'Oh, she does.' Josh smirked. 'Look at her! She's digging for details into your past, darling.' He pointed it out as if Simon didn't already know, and I rolled my eyes. Josh was not adept at subtlety.

'My past,' Simon repeated, nodding as if preparing himself.

'I don't know anything about you,' I pointed out. 'And I've just told you an awful lot about me. Or, actually, Josh did.'

'Fair is fair,' Josh agreed, and Megan once again made an 'uh-huh' noise without looking up from her phone.

'Couldn't I call that favour you owe me?' Simon joked and Josh countered by saying *he* would simply ask again, so he had no choice.

Admitting defeat, Simon inhaled and sat up.

'My mum passed away when I was eighteen,' Simon began and immediately Josh flushed in embarrassment, which Simon was quick to remedy. 'As I told you earlier,' he said to me. 'So, I was raised by Dad, who wasn't a natural single parent, or parent in general. He's always working. He works in media too, actually, so I kind of know what you mean about the long hours.' He smiled bitterly. 'I was sent to boarding school at thirteen, when I became a bit too teenager-y for him. School wasn't bad but as you can guess of any highly paid education system, they valued academic subjects over creative ones, and I've never been interested in maths and English. Not in the way I was with music anyway.'

'I feel like I see where this is going,' Josh said, his ears pricking up.

'Probably.' Simon laughed darkly. 'After mum passed, I told my dad I wanted to go to music college, and he downright refused to support me. Obviously, I did it anyway, but when I graduated at twenty-one, without a job and not much interest in getting one, he cut me off.'

'And you've been busking ever since?' Josh asked, surprised that that could sustain a person for so long.

Simon leaned back and ran his fingers through his hair, appearing surprised when a sudden cloud of glitter seemed to fall out of it. I brushed it off his shoulder for him.

'The busking is relatively new. I mostly do it for charity.'

'Mostly,' I joked. Simon shrugged with his hands up in a mock 'don't shoot' manner.

'Sometimes I run a little short of cash, normally just before payday. But my actual job is in advertising.'

'Advertising?' I repeated in surprise. 'You?'

'Me,' Simon said. 'Why? Are you surprised?'

'Very.' I took on some of Josh's non-subtlety. 'Feels a bit too much like a job for *the man*. Too corporate for a musician.'

'Well, you might be surprised…' He seemed to be trying to stop himself from laughing.

'What?' I asked. 'What is it?'

'If I tell you my job title, you'll laugh.'

'Oh, no!' I was unable to hold my anticipatory smile in.

'Now you have to tell us,' Josh said, leaning in and resting his chin on his shoulder.

Simon sighed, defeatedly. 'I am my company's Chief Jingle Writer.'

Josh and I fell to bits, we laughed into the table so much that Megan finally looked up from her phone and had to ask Simon to repeat himself, from which she joined me and Josh in our laughter.

The waitress that brought over our cocktails had to hand them all to Simon, since he was the only one capable of holding them steady.

'Chief *Jingle* Writer,' I repeated.

'Yep, get it out.' Simon smiled in good humour despite our overreaction.

'It just seems like…' I tried to catch my breath. 'Not the job for you.'

'It pays the bills.' Simon lifted his beer to his lips. He was not a cocktail kind of guy.

'You're a… a…' Josh couldn't contain himself. 'A jingler!'

'Jingle writer,' Simon corrected, a bit more sternly, although only in jest. He clearly understood that his job title was hilarious.

'Oh, honey!' Josh was wiping a tear from his eye and

picking up his sex on the beach. 'You and I should talk. Do you freelance?'

'Josh designs retail Christmas displays,' I explained quickly.

'I do actually,' Simon said to Josh, who immediately began to talk his ear off about a *Gingerbread House* display he wanted to make in the children's department of Harrods that wasn't too scary but not too sweet either.

'I like this man,' Megan suddenly whispered, leaning into my shoulder and acting as if she were still deeply concentrating on her non-existent WhatsApp messages.

'I can tell,' I said under my breath, before leaning closer to her. 'Me too!'

The look of joy that passed over her face was gone in an instant, but something inside me seemed to light up upon admitting it. I really liked Simon. Not just because he was really good-looking, with his sort of rough-and-tumble blond locks and sandy facial hair I had a strong urge to run my fingers over, but because he was kind and humorous. He was everything you could want in a really good friend or, in my imagination, a really good boyfriend.

But it was impossible. I was leaving.

I'd spent years telling myself that relationships were almost an inconvenient thing, something I didn't have time or space for. Now that I finally did have, I was on the verge of uprooting my entire life again.

Starting something now felt reckless: a recipe for heartbreak built from temptation. Wanting Simon was easy. Staying long enough to find out what that might mean was not.

So I did what I always did when my thoughts edged too close to something real: I folded them away and focused on what was right in front of me.

I played with the cocktail umbrella in my negroni as Josh and Simon spoke about a few of the adverts that Simon had scored – Josh had to deny himself from saying 'jingled' – and the kind of work Simon could do with him.

'I see a beautiful partnership developing,' Megan interjected after ten minutes, clearly bored of their work talk. 'Are we eating as well? I might order some nachos.' She stepped down from the booth. 'Josh, come and help me.'

Subtle, Megan, real subtle.

I glared at her from behind my negroni as she pulled at Josh's sleeve. Josh, looking very confused, followed her and couldn't turn back even if he wanted to, as Megan had her arm around his shoulders in a sort of headlock as she dragged him back to the bar.

'She wants a lot of nachos,' I said to Simon, my heart leaping as we were suddenly alone again.

He smiled. 'So when do you start this new job of yours?' There was something about the immediacy of his asking soon after the others had left that made me wonder if he had been wanting to ask this question for a while.

'In the New Year.'

'In Toronto.' He swilled his beer around gently.

I nodded. 'Yeah. It's at this studio that I know really well from working with Pim – she's the actress I work for – she was on a show of theirs for a while, so I met a lot of people backstage.'

He nodded now, continuously and with a forced smile.

'What sort of work will you be doing?'

I laughed breathily, unsure how to talk about a job I had such impostor syndrome from. 'Well, it's an assistant TV producer role.' I flushed. 'Josh and Megan like to drop the *assistant* as I've been an assistant for eight years.'

Simon smiled encouragingly but said nothing.

'I'll be supporting the main team of producers initially,' I said, playing with the umbrella in my drink again. 'And helping produce ideas for the shows that they have. Mostly they produce game shows with celebrities and the like. The kind of thing you might watch on daytime TV when you're ill or if you've got a hangover.' I stopped myself degrading the studio with an awkward laugh.

I didn't know why I was talking down about the job. It was a great job, one I was barely qualified to do and mostly got because of nepotism and recruitment laziness. Salient had wanted someone that knew the team, who would fit in and know how to handle the celebrities. All things they knew I could do from my time with Pim on their many shows.

Everything else I needed to know I would learn on the job and maybe I would work my way up. That was how most people did it, start from the bottom and work their way up. After all, there was no ladder with Pim, only a car door to open and shut. This job would give me the opportunities to grow, to develop new skills and earn more money, and, more importantly, give me roots in a new city. The roots I've always wanted.

'I move in January. It's going to be great.'

'Sounds it.' Simon had some more of his beer before suddenly asking, 'Weren't there any jobs in the UK you wanted?' I hadn't even applied for any, I hardly looked. Every time I opened a vacancies page my mind would roll through all the scenarios of getting an interview, only to be rejected for some nepo baby fresh out of university. The disappointment seemed far more potent than applying out of the country. 'Seems a long way to go for a job.'

I fell silent, slightly stunned.

I considered him for a moment, before forcing myself to answer.

'It's quite a competitive area. There aren't many Broadcast Production Assistant jobs in the UK.'

'Surely Pim would have given you an in?'

'I don't want to be a nepo baby,' I joked, though that wasn't the full truth either.

I wasn't aware of many studios in the UK that Pim had connections with; we were hardly ever in the UK for work. Any connections she did have were probably out of date. I had never dared to ask her for help, not directly at least. Not only because of the nepotism, but because it felt disrespectful to ask: *I know I'm your assistant but could you help me get another job using your connections?*

Besides, I was used to fighting for others, not for myself.

I moved hair out of my eyes. 'That being said, I think I mostly got this new job because I got the chance to work with the company during one of Pim's TV stints, so who am I to say I hate nepotism?'

'That's not nepotism, that's networking.'

'Sure,' I mumbled. 'That's just the industry, I guess.'

He nodded, saying nothing more for a moment. And then he smiled again, his lovely warm, slightly lopsided smile. 'I'm happy for you.' He lifted his beer in the air. 'To you and your new job!'

I felt the light in me flicker as I remembered my new job. My new home come the New Year. The new start I was really looking forward to. The do-over I needed for my life to really begin. It was in Toronto, not London. No relationship could last, so I shouldn't be cruel and let it begin.

Forcing a placating smile, I lifted my glass to his bottle with a light chink.

'And to you, for your first Great Christmas Pudding victory. I hope this will become an annual thing?'

'Once will be enough.'

Chapter 14

'I AM GOING TO COMPLAIN.' PIM STORMED out of the BBC building, her heels clicking aggressively against the pavement. I had to half-jog to keep up, which wasn't ideal given my questionable choice of shoes – a pair of newly broken-in (or almost broken-in) Doc Martens I had treated myself to when I realised my usual Vans and slip-ons hardly suited the London climate.

'What now?' I asked, attempting to balance a takeaway coffee in one hand and the leash of Gerald in the other. He barked like a prince but acted like the court jester.

'The call sheet, Evie! The bloody call sheet!' she seethed, waving a crumpled piece of paper in my face. 'They spelt my name as *Pimm*. Like the drink. As if I am some sort of novelty alcoholic beverage rather than a serious actress.' She rolled her r's on actress, which hardly helped her cause in my opinion.

'Well,' I started, unable to help myself, 'you are refreshing on a hot day.'

Pim shot me a look that could curdle milk. 'Don't.'

I rolled my lips together nervously. 'I'm sure it was just a typo.'

'A typo that completely undermines my entire existence.

This is a national broadcaster. They wouldn't call Olivia Colman *Olive* Colman, would they?'

'Maybe if she was starring in a very specific cooking show.'

'Evie.' Her eyes thinned.

'Right. Not the time.'

Before I could attempt any more damage control, Gerald – who had the strength of a small bear despite looking like an overgrown teddy – suddenly yanked the leash from my hand and took off down the pavement, his tiny legs moving at lightning speed.

'Gerald, NO!' I shrieked as Pim growled aloud, her hands rising like Evita in damnation at the way her day was going. I was the one being flung around the BBC office entrance.

Suddenly, Gerald spotted his target, a pigeon pecking the ground in blissful ignorance, and the prized pup barrelled towards it, only to completely miss and instead – in strikingly ironic fashion – barrel into the legs of a very well-dressed man stepping around the corner with a cup of takeaway coffee.

Everything happened in slow motion.

One moment the man was upright, dignified, clearly important. The next he was flailing, his long coat billowing around him like a disgruntled bat, coffee spilled all down his front. He landed in a completely ungraceful heap on the pavement.

'Oh, for *God's* sake!' he snapped, propping himself up on his elbows and brushing at his soiled coat, his voice rich with disgust. I recognised him with horror as I battled to keep Gerald within my grasp. It was Michael Holland.

'I am *so* sorry…' I began, but Gerald tugged me away,

forcing me to give a strangled cry of 'Stop! No! *Gerald*.'

Michael Holland lifted his head, fixing me and now Pim with a look that was both affronted and incredulous. 'Honestly! You're a danger to society, Pim Hardcastle.'

Pim, still in full fury over the BBC's inability to spell her name, folded her arms with a suddenly amused smile. Had this encounter really just brightened her day? 'Well, maybe watch where you're going next time.'

'Excuse me?' Michael threw his cup away and began to push himself up from the damp ground.

I was still chasing after Gerald, who was gleefully zigzagging between BBC workers who were gathering around the mess he had just created, while he remained adorably ignorant of the chaos he'd just caused.

'You heard me,' Pim continued, brushing imaginary lint from her coat and not bothering to assist Michael, though she was less than a foot from him. 'If you were paying proper attention, maybe you wouldn't have been completely taken down by a ten-kilo ball of fluff.'

Michael's nostrils flared. 'I was paying attention. I was minding my own business until your rat in a fur coat launched an attack on my legs!'

'I beg your pardon?' Pim gasped, scandalised. 'Did you just call Gerald a rat?'

'A rat would be better than what you've called it? *Gerald*? Ridiculous.'

'He's a Chow Chow, you imbecile.'

I tuned them out, pissed off now that Pim had failed to notice that I was still desperately trying to maintain control of the little rat, *dog* even. He had just decided to dart across the pavement towards a delivery cyclist. 'Gerald, STOP—'

As I ran, my phone buzzed in my bag.

One buzz. Then two.

I wrapped the leash around my wrist and tugged until Gerald gave way, finally allowing me to scoop him up, hair plastered to my face in the sudden sweat that effort had caused, and I fished out my phone from my bag. Breathlessly I answered without checking the screen.

'Hello?' I failed to keep the annoyance out of my voice.

At first, all I heard was a sharp intake of breath.

'Can I help you? Who is this?'

'Evie—' Megan's voice was unsteady, thick with emotion, but entirely recognisable to me. 'He's gone.'

My stomach dropped. 'Wait… what? Who's gone?'

'Alex.'

The noise of the street faded into the background as Gerald nipped at my fingers with his long, scratchy tongue.

'What do you mean, gone?' The world had seemingly frozen as I suddenly thought all the worst things: Alex is dead. Megan's a widow. Alfie's without a father. Oh, God. I felt sick.

'I mean, gone, Evie. As in, left. He's left me.'

I stopped and breathed. Relief flooding me, followed quickly by a horror that I was relieved in the first place. 'Wait – what? When? *Why?*'

'I don't – I don't know. He just—' She sniffed loudly, gasping in between sobs. 'He packed a bag and said he couldn't do it any more and now he's just gone.' Her words were followed by a wail that was utterly unlike anything Megan ever did.

My head spun. Megan and Alex had been together for years, since they were teenagers. Sure, they bickered, and Megan sometimes called him '*an idiot in a nice coat*', but they loved each other. They had had a child together and spent anniversaries holidaying in Mexico, drinking margaritas on beaches and turning their phones onto airplane mode during sex.

Didn't they?

'I don't understand,' I said. 'Did he say anything? At all?'

'I—' She made a small, broken noise. 'I don't even know what I'm saying. I just – I thought maybe you could come over.'

'Of course,' I said instantly; she didn't even need to ask. I was already walking back towards Pim. 'I'll be there as soon as I—'

A loud '*Oh, grow up, you pretentious git*' rang out from behind me.

I looked up just in time to see Pim and Michael still locked in a furious standoff, entirely oblivious to the fact that someone – a man in a dark coat, phone held high – was recording them from the street in front of the office. A small party of BBC employees returning from various lunch breaks hovered in the corners, their phones out too, all held high in an act that was definitely recording.

My stomach twisted.

'Megan, I'll call you back. I'm coming to you,' I said quickly, then hung up before she could respond, the guilt returning, but I knew what I had to do right now and it wasn't bolting for the Tube.

By the time I reached Pim's side, hurriedly whispering, '*We need to go*,' she was mid-sentence. '—which clearly explains your desperate need to police other people's pets, considering you have the personality of a wet sock.'

Michael let out a short, cold laugh, crossing his arms over the brown stain across his white shirt. 'You do realise that the only reason people tolerate you is because you say things loudly and with an affected accent, right? No one actually cares what you have to say.'

Pim recoiled as if he'd slapped her and, by the way her hand was flexing at her side, I could sense she was planning to slap him.

My gut lurched. 'Okay, that's enough,' I said, stepping between them before Pim could either a) throttle Michael or b) eviscerate him with a single sentence – or another sentence, given I had probably missed a few verbal rallies. Glancing at the phone crowd, I wondered how soon it would be before I saw it all online anyway.

'That's enough,' I said steadily, though Gerald barked for good measure as I handed him to Pim, hoping to use him as an emotional support dog and keep her hands for something other than throttling Michael Holland in the street. 'I think it best we leave.'

Turning back to Michael, I noted he had taken a step back and was now straightening his coat with a tight-lipped expression. 'I wish I could say it was a pleasure,' he muttered, 'but it never is.' Brushing past us, he walked into the BBC building without another glance.

Pim let out a sound of pure indignation, squeezing Gerald to her chest. 'That man—'

'We have a bigger problem,' I cut in, my voice urgent. I nodded towards one of the men still standing a few feet away, who quickly lowered his phone and stuffed it into his pocket, turning and walking off with a little too much nonchalance.

Pim frowned. 'Who was that?'

'I don't know,' I admitted, 'but he was filming you two.'

Her expression flickered, uncertainty replacing her outrage. 'Filming us?'

'Yes. And I think—' My stomach twisted. 'I think he wasn't the only one.'

Pim's face paled.

Gerald, oblivious to the potential PR disaster unfolding, chose that moment to lick Pim's made-up face affectionately, his tongue lolling in triumph.

'Oh, fantastic timing, Gerald,' Pim muttered, shaking her head. 'Perfection.'

I rubbed my temples, heart still racing from Megan's call. Between Pim's potentially viral argument and my best friend's world falling apart, I had no idea which crisis to deal with first.

'Right,' I exhaled. 'I think I need to get you back to the hotel.'

'I think I need a lawyer.' Pim blinked and lowered Gerald to the ground – the little dick stayed still and well-behaved for her.

And with that, we turned on our heels and marched away, Gerald happily trotting at our side, completely unaware of the shitstorm he'd just unleashed.

Chapter 15

JOSH PLACED A BOTTLE OF RED wine on the kitchen counter. 'First bottle here, another coming.'

I'd arrived at Megan's, after leaving Pim at the hotel, trading one kind of emotional firefighting for another.

Josh and I had already spent hours trying to comfort Megan – takeaway, taxi offers, even Googling how to change the locks. Nothing helped. She didn't know what she wanted: Alex or no Alex. Us or to be alone.

She wasn't just upset with Alex; she was furious with herself. And I had no idea how to fix that. Wine was the only thing she hadn't rejected outright.

Josh, ever the overcompensator, poured Megan a goblet full of Shiraz, then himself one just as generous. There wasn't any left for me, which was probably for the best. Someone had to stay clear-headed. And I was currently cradling Alfie, who had fallen asleep on me after all the upset.

His warm little self, spread-eagled over my chest, made me feel like I was only half-listening, half-preoccupied with keeping him from stirring. I felt pinned to the seat, but I wasn't complaining. I had hardly seen Alfie since he was born, and it was nice to think he trusted me enough from those few and far-between meetings and FaceTimes to fall dead asleep on me while his mother sat wailing in the corner about wanting to enter her husband in *Squid Game*.

Megan took a gulp, sniffling noisily.

Josh cleared his throat. 'First of all, you're a queen. Alex is an idiot. Full stop.'

She gave a thin, wet laugh.

'He doesn't realise how lucky he is. But he will. They always come crawling back.' Josh was confident in the extreme, to the point of sounding bored, as he repeated the sentiment he and I had been pushing for the better part of two hours.

'If he comes back,' Megan muttered, more to herself than to us.

'We love you, no matter what,' I said. 'And he hasn't gone far.' I'd checked the wardrobe for Alex's things when Josh arrived and took over the hugging duties of Megan. I had quickly surmised that Alex had merely whipped around the flat for some clean underwear and shirts before he left. His passport, car keys, Xbox and Nintendo Switch were still in the house and, knowing Alex, the latter two would have been the first items packed if he had truly *left* Megan.

What might have been the mother of all arguments was not going to lead to divorce, not yet anyway.

'He adores you, Megan,' I said, smoothing some of Alfie's tufty brown locks with my chin. 'Both of you.'

Megan gave the briefest of smiles before falling into fits of tears again. 'He loves Alfie more than…' she sobbed. 'I mean, he's been different since I got pregnant.'

'Megan…' I began with no train of thought; this was out of my territory. I wasn't a mum, or a wife – I hadn't even been a *girlfriend*. How did I offer advice and support in this situation?

'He *does* love you. Although…' Josh caught my hesitancy and looked puzzled – or was it boredom? 'Do *you* love him?'

Megan stiffened as if the question physically hurt her. 'He just… he gave up on us. He said he's done.'

I noticed how neatly she'd sidestepped the question, how she'd turned it back onto him instead. I didn't push. Some answers needed more time than a kitchen conversation could give.

Josh, however, was far less inclined to let it slide. His eye roll could have caused him a medical emergency, it was so dramatic. 'Honestly, some of the guys I've dated barely put in any effort, so I get it.'

Where was he going with this?

'Why is it always one person? For Christ's sake, Zach is always so sensitive, but then I think that's because his husband has all this moon energy, so Zach has to be macho all the time at home to make it work; when really, he just wants to be emotionally cared for now and then. *You* get it.' He lifted his empty glass at Megan, completely oblivious to the minefield he had just stepped into.

Megan's brow furrowed. 'His husband?' Oh, no.

I shot him a severe warning look, but he was too deep in his own tangent to stop.

'Speaking of relationships, I was talking to Zach about all this—' He burped.

He hadn't noticed that Megan was staring at him. 'Who's Zach?'

Josh grinned at the change of subject and I internally cringed. This could only go badly.

'This guy I'm seeing.' He blushed like a regency bride.

'Should I put Alfie down?' I interjected, trying to distract Megan from the car crash I was foreseeing. But Megan barely acknowledged me, eyes locked on Josh like a predator scenting blood. 'Megan, it's fine. Ignore him, we're here for *you*.' I spoke to Josh more than Megan, my eyes widening at him.

'Just because *you* don't like him,' he said, his voice unnecessarily petulant. 'You've never even met him; we should organise something, then you'd see.'

'Josh…' I began to lift Alfie from my chest, and his hands starfished as he startled at my sudden lunge.

'Who is *Zach*?' Megan repeated, which for Megan was never a good sign.

Josh was still blissfully unaware. 'I told you; he's this guy I'm seeing.'

'You're seeing a guy with a *husband*?' she said, this time slower, louder, impossible to ignore.

Josh's expression froze for half a second too long.

Megan's knuckles whitened around her wine glass, as her words dropped like a guillotine. 'You're screwing a married man?'

Josh twisted his head, having realised he had mentioned Zach's husband, not ex-husband but *husband*. The 'oh-shit' expression that passed over his face, spread to mine as Megan pounced.

'It's not as simple as that!' Josh said, his voice rising just as Megan walked around the sofa.

'How the hell is it not? He's married, or isn't he?' Megan's rage was like a living thing; she spoke with such venom. I was surprised Josh didn't run and duck for cover. I certainly wanted to but, with Alfie in my arms, it was hard to get between the two of them.

I shifted him higher on my chest, my heart thudding, torn between stepping in and instinctively staying quiet, as if conflict was something you could survive by keeping your head down.

'Where's the crib, Megan?' I asked, hating how small my voice sounded, how absurd it felt to be worrying about a baby while everything burned around me.

'I was just trying to distract you,' Josh looked at me for backup, but this train was a runaway now.

'Oh, is that what this is? And why would you bring it up now?' Megan stepped closer. 'You're disgusting. You think it's fine because it's messy and complicated and whatever excuses you tell yourself.'

Josh paled, blindsided. 'Megan, stop. You're being unfair—'

'Oh, I'm unfair?' Megan barked a hollow laugh. 'God forbid someone around here actually has *standards*!'

Josh opened his mouth, but Megan barrelled on. 'Do you even know what it's like to stand at the edge of ruining your life and *choose* not to?' She hurled the words at him, her chest heaving. 'To make the right call even when it feels like you're drowning?'

Josh looked utterly confused. So did I. I felt everything unravelling around me; this argument had slipped its original shape and become about something else entirely.

'Megan, maybe we should go for a walk,' I said softly, realising there was more here than she was letting on – way more. I awkwardly laid Alfie on the sofa, hoping he would soon release my necklace so I could do so without choking myself. 'I know it's late, but we could go to the pub for dinner.'

'No!' she snapped. 'You don't get this, Evie, you don't

even have sex. You're always *too* busy for anything and anyone!' I went still. Not because of what she said – I've heard worse – but because she used it like a weapon. Like my life choices disqualified me from understanding desire, or choice, or consequence.

'Woah.'

'Megan!' Josh looked aghast. 'Really? Low blow.'

'Oh, you care about defending her schedule but *not* someone's marriage.'

My insides tightened as if I was being strangled by a vice. I'd spent years trying to be useful, accommodating to others, always the calm and practical one, but I hadn't realised how easily that could be mistaken for indifference.

'That's not fair,' I said quietly, steadying my voice. 'Just because I don't have sex often – or at all sometimes – doesn't mean I haven't made hard choices. I still know what it's like to want something and say no.'

But Megan wasn't hearing me. She wasn't even looking at me – I don't think she could. She was staring at Josh, trembling with fury.

'Neither of you *get* it! And you don't get to stand there and brag about adultery like it's nothing. Like there'll be no wreckage because of it!' she choked out. 'There always is.'

Josh shook his head defensively. 'For God's sake, Megan. You don't get to use your imploding marriage as a moral high ground. You've clearly made questionable decisions in the past, otherwise this wouldn't be your pity party we're attending.'

The shift in him was instant – prey to predator in a blink. It was the same edge I'd seen when he'd told me about Zach, trying to paint infidelity as some complicated, modern relationship instead of what it really was: selfishness dressed up as romance.

'Josh,' I tried to be stern, but it was almost impossible while trying to be quiet around a toddler. 'Megan's allowed to be in her feelings.'

'With Megan, everything's a drama,' he returned bitterly.

'Okay, get out!' Megan thundered, grabbing his coat and shoving it at him as I prised Alfie's hands from my necklace.

'What? You're insane!' Josh shouted. 'This isn't even about me!'

The splash of Megan's remaining wine over his head made me turn back.

I watched him wiping his eyes rapidly, the red wine dripping from his hairline and staining his collar.

'You crazy bitch!'

'Get out!' Megan thundered again.

'Bloody hell! Both of you, stop!' Alfie woke up and began crying loudly.

Both Megan and Josh continued to ignore both of us.

Josh shook his head; his face twisted in anger. 'Unbelievable. You act like the world owes you something.'

Megan forced him back towards the door. Josh stumbled but caught himself, his eyes flicking to me. 'Evie?'

It was in moments like these I wished I had more than two best friends. I was stuck between them, having to make a choice and in my mind the choice was shockingly clear: Megan needed me more.

'Josh, just go.' My voice was barely a whisper.

His face hardened. He turned on his heel and slammed the door behind him.

I barely had time to exhale before Megan spun on me.

'You should go too.' She was scooping Alfie off the sofa, holding him close to her like a shield.

'Megan…' I started, confused.

'You knew, didn't you?'

I opened my mouth, closed it.

'You didn't say anything,' she went on, as if narrating it to herself.

'Please, Megan.' I wiped away my tears. 'I didn't think Josh would bring up Zach tonight, nor do I think what he's doing is right. But it's his life.'

'But you said nothing. You didn't say anything to me, and you've known since… when? When you got back?' I didn't respond and she knew it was true. 'Weeks, Evie. And you could tell things were bad between me and Alex!'

'It wasn't my business.' I hated how defensive I sounded – though I wasn't sure any more if that was because I was wrong or because I was being cornered.

She let out a short, sharp laugh. 'Not your business?'

I stepped forward instinctively, but she flinched almost violently…

'You stood there and watched me make a fool of myself?' Her voice cracked.

'I didn't think—' I started helplessly, stopping to regain my composure. It wouldn't help if I lost it in this situation, even if Megan's inability to see my side was aggravating. 'Megan, I didn't tell you because it wasn't my secret to tell. And if it had been the other way around – if you had trusted me with something like this – I would have protected you too.' Megan said nothing and refused to look my way.

'I know you're hurt,' I said softly. 'And I know this is about more than Josh. But please don't make me the stand-in for everything that's gone wrong.'

Her chest was heaving in fury, but I wasn't even sure if she heard me at all.

'I didn't know things were this bad with you and Alex,' I said, softer now. 'You've never really talked about it.'

Her head snapped up, eyes blazing. 'Oh, so it's my fault I didn't send out a newsletter or hand signals or bloody semaphore about how miserable I've been.'

'Was Alex cheating?' I asked before I could stop myself.

She barked a bitter, humourless laugh. 'I don't know. Maybe. Probably.' She shifted Alfie to her other shoulder, blinking fast. 'No, I *know* he did. I guess he just had the guts to do what I didn't.'

The words seemed to rip out of her, unplanned. She caught herself, breathing hard.

'Megan…' I began stepping towards her.

'Don't,' she snapped.

Alfie started to cry again, unsettled by the tension. Megan swayed slightly, trying to calm him.

'I kissed someone,' she spoke calmly, with painful frustration. 'Someone else, before Alfie was born. One stupid kiss. I stopped before anything else happened. I thought that meant something. I thought it made me *better*.' She laughed again, a broken, hollow sound. 'Turns out it just made me a bigger idiot.'

My heart squeezed painfully.

'I stayed.' Tears began to stream down her red cheeks. 'I stayed and I worked at it with Alex; I put him first. And he just walked away and found his happiness elsewhere. He didn't fight for me.'

She finally looked at me, her face ravaged.

'You could've told me.'

She shook her head, furious now. 'Told you? When? On one of your quick visits home between flights?'

'I didn't know how bad things were,' I said quietly. 'You didn't tell me, not really. We've both been holding things back, Megan. Me because I didn't think it was my place. You because you didn't want to admit it.'

Megan had no argument, but tears fell freely down her cheeks.

'I'm here now.'

'Right. Just in time for New Year's Eve, before you head off to Canada for that shiny new job,' she scoffed. 'You're always leaving, Evie. You're not here for me like a sister should be. It's as if you don't even try any more.'

The words landed heavier than anything else she'd said that night.

This wasn't about Josh. Or Alex. This was the unspoken fear that had been trailing me for years, finally given a voice by the person whose voice would cut me the most.

I felt myself recoil; it was so strong I thought I might be sick.

I'd spent so long believing I could be dependable from a distance, that love didn't require constant presence. Yet hearing it laid out like this made me wonder when that had stopped being true.

Or what I could do about it now, as I was preparing to jet off to the other side of the world.

'I'm allowed to have a life too.' My voice was cracking now.

'Yeah. You are. And I'm allowed to stop expecting you to show up.'

I stood there, the weight of her words sinking in fast and heavy.

'It's not that I don't care,' I said desperately. 'I care *so* much—'

'You care,' she repeated hollowly. 'You just don't *stay.*'

The floor felt like it tilted under me. I opened my mouth to defend myself – but nothing came out. Because she was right.

I hadn't stayed. Not when it really mattered.

The silence between us swelled, thick with everything we weren't saying.

Megan shifted Alfie on her hip, her eyes glistening but cold.

'I think you should go as well.'

I stumbled over my words. 'I'm just trying—'

'I know.' She looked away, heading towards her staircase. 'But it's too late.'

I nodded once, then walked out, carrying the weight of everything we hadn't managed to say with me into the cold.

Chapter 16

ALL THE WAY TO THE TRAIN station I kept replaying Megan's words over and over in my head.

'You care, but you don't stay.'

Was she right? I wanted to argue, to defend myself, to say I had reasons: Pim, work commitments, a life that kept pulling me away. But all the reasons felt paper-thin now, pathetic against the ache in Megan's voice. She was right, I hadn't been there the way she needed.

I hadn't known things were so bad between her and Alex, but her eyes were red and glassy with tears; they shared more than she knew. She was used to crying, this was her normal.

And I hadn't asked, not really.

I swallowed hard, guilt rising thick and fast. I had stayed out of it, because looking too closely meant getting tangled up in things I didn't know how to fix. And maybe, deep down, I was still that ten-year-old girl who had watched her mother slip away, helpless to stop it. I learned early that love didn't always get to win. And that the best way to survive the pain was to run.

So I ran. For years, to other countries, other jobs, other lives, convincing myself I was chasing adventure, not just outrunning the grief that had long since built a home inside me. Convincing myself that living life to the fullest was what Mum would have wanted. But maybe all that running made me blind to what I was leaving behind. To who I was leaving behind.

A flash of Simon's face crossed my mind; the busker with kind eyes and hands that could make magic out of a battered guitar. There could be something there, something real, if I ever dared to stay still long enough to find out.

But Megan was right, when had I ever stayed?

I rubbed my eyes, feeling the night crash down on me, all of it.

I had wanted to argue my side; I wasn't the one who cheated after all – and me keeping Josh's secrets was hardly a demerit on me as a friend. I'd keep Megan's secrets the same way, not that she was sharing them with me these days, apparently.

As the train station came into view, my gut felt hollow. I knew it was for the best that I left the scene, no matter how much I didn't want to leave things as they were; I especially didn't want her to feel alone. She was my best friend, my sister.

But I had left her standing there, holding Alfie, both crying in the dark.

So I walked, vacantly staring ahead until I reached the train station, only realising it had begun to snow as a homeless man shook out his sleeping bag at the entrance to the platform. I gave him the change in my pocket – barely enough for a coffee in McDonald's these days – and continued to cry.

'Cheers, love, and cheer up. It's Christmas,' he mumbled in thanks.

I removed my phone to pay the Oyster charge. It buzzed, once and then again. And again.

At first, I assumed it was Megan, maybe regretting sending us all away, having come to her senses after a few minutes alone. But when I opened the screen, I was flooded with notifications.

TikTok alerts. Instagram tags. Work WhatsApps blowing up.

I clicked on one. A video. Pim and Michael Holland, mid-argument, outside the BBC studios. The caption underneath: ***Pim's O'Clock*? More like Pim and the Cock!**

My stomach sank as I tapped the 'Play' button. Holland's sneering face filled my screen, followed by Pim's unmistakable clipped tones, her retort sharp, her body language defensive.

And then, the final notification at the top of my screen. A message from Pim herself:

'WHAT THE HELL ARE YOU DOING ABOUT THIS?'

Chapter 17

I DIDN'T HEAR ANYTHING FROM EITHER JOSH or Megan the next day, despite multiple texts from me, both separately and in the group chat. But I had a text message from Denise, Megan's mum, saying Bob had driven to collect Megan and Alfie the night before, and she was at home with them in Kent.

I was relieved that Megan had had the sense to call her parents and ask for help – and unsurprisingly that they immediately offered it. Bob was the sort of father that still waited up for Megan, and me, during a night out, even though we were both nearing thirty. And I could picture Denise getting fresh bed sheets ready and making sure all of Megan's favourite meals were defrosting out of the freezer before Bob had even got his car keys.

'*We're not getting much out of her at the minute, but she just needs to sleep it off. We'll call you later this week. Don't worry about anything, she just needs some time,*' Denise had texted.

How much had Megan told her about our blow-up? About Josh, and my knowing more than I'd said, even if I'd never condoned what he was doing?

I still wasn't quite clear on why I had become her proverbial punching bag. Was it because I kept it from her, as I knew she'd have absolutely kicked off at him, or was it simply misdirected anger at Josh for bringing it up on the night we were there to comfort her about her absentee husband? We didn't even know if Alex had cheated. I didn't even fully understand what was going on in their relationship at all.

It was all one big mess.

Meanwhile, the internet had exploded.

Michael Holland and Pim's exchange outside the BBC had gone megaviral. The clip had spread like wildfire once the tabloids had got hold of it.

Pim's calm evisceration of Michael for his outdated, condescending comments, as he stood there, face increasingly puce, the unpleasantly placed shirt stain, stammering in response was hot gossip.

The comments were a mix of applause and horror:

'*Pim for PM.*'

'*Did she just verbally destroy the most feared man in TV*?'

'*Oh my God, I work at the BBC. The tea is SCORCHING – not just Holland's shirt.*'

Of course, this meant my phone would not stop buzzing. The *Pim's O'Clock* producers were demanding to know how we'd handle the PR fallout, whether we should lean into the moment or ignore it completely. The takeaway was that Pim was coming out as a voice of the people, victorious over the man who appeared to have pissed off half the UK by once saying Shakespeare was mid, at best, and that Sunday roasts were 'just an overhyped meat-and-veg pile'. The philistine.

Pim, for her part, was now delighted and was already planning to casually reference it in her next interview.

My inbox, however, was on fire.

Claire from PR was fuming that I hadn't responded

to her about an exclusive interview with Pim before Christmas, and I had eighteen separate voicemails from journalists asking for an official comment. My brain felt like an overloaded browser with too many tabs open.

And then there was Pim herself – though she was delighted by how the story had turned in her favour, she seemed oblivious to the stress it had caused.

'What is wrong with you, Evelyn?' Pim finally asked when we were back in her hotel room. She had her feet in a bubbling foot spa and her hair in rollers, looking the picture of self-indulgence, while I sat opposite, running purely on caffeine and Polo mints.

Hearing Pim use my full name, though, was a bad sign.

Evie was what Megan had christened me as children, since pronouncing *Evelyn* as a three-year-old was always going to be a challenge, particularly for the likes of Megan, who had a short attention span, and three syllables was one too many.

'Nothing,' I said, exhaling, which only made it sound more insincere.

Pim raised an eyebrow. 'I know you organise my schedule and get me from A to B – usually, anyway – but I feel like I've been doing most of the heavy lifting this week. I won't take "nothing" as an excuse for sloppiness.'

It must have been obvious to her something was up; mostly because of the stupid errors I had been making all day. I got the wrong coffee order from Starbucks – who genuinely enjoys iced teas? – forgot to book the car to take her to her last dress fitting, and I hadn't got back to Alison about meeting with Pim before Christmas.

I was usually so on it; I couldn't let it slip now. Especially not as someone leaving a job.

I was not going to work my arse off for eight years only to get a reference from Pim stating that I was unorganised and didn't care. My job was all I had truly focused on for years, even if it appeared I should have focused on a few other things more.

I braced myself for a well-earned bollocking, but Pim simply tutted and picked at her freshly manicured fingers. 'So tell me, what is bothering you?'

I hesitated. Pim wasn't exactly a shoulder-to-cry-on type, but she could read people like a book.

'Is it all this Michael Holland rubbish? He's an odious man,' she said, swishing her feet in the foamy water.

'The world is aware of what you think of him.' As is Michael Holland himself. He had remained suspiciously silent on the reaction to the video. I'd had no contact from his people about the publicity angles or how to smooth the corners of his disaster. But no one could tell me who his people were; perhaps he had scared them off as well? Or he was just waiting to catch me off guard and then spin the story his way. Who knew with the likes of him? He had been in the business four times longer than I had, he could play a master hand any second, and I would just have to roll with the punches. Just something else to look forward to this Christmas.

'I don't mind admitting I once flirted with him,' Pim carried on, ignoring me. 'Or rather, I flirted, and he rebuffed me like I was a fly and he a swatter. I can take rejection, Evie, but there is something so needlessly cruel about him.'

'That sounds awful,' I said vacantly. I didn't mean it.

Pim nodded, sipping her Starbucks. For a moment, I considered confiding in her about Megan and Josh. About how their silence was suffocating me. What did I have to lose? My job? I had already changed that.

But before I could say anything, my phone rang.

'Who's that?' Pim asked, cheeks flushing in fear. 'One of the producers?'

I checked the screen. 'It's a personal call.'

'Ugh, during work hours?' she muttered, but I ignored her, stepping out into the corridor.

'Hello?' I answered, pressing my fingers to my temple.

'Evie, it's Alex.'

My stomach clenched. 'Alex?'

'Yeah. Look, I—' he hesitated. 'I got home late last night and… Megan and Alfie weren't there.'

'She's in Kent,' I said stiffly. 'With her parents.'

There was a long pause. 'I thought so. I tried calling but no one answered.' His voice was quiet, hesitant. Denise and Bob probably didn't want to chat to him, not unkindly but for fear of setting Megan off. 'Did she tell you everything?'

I frowned. 'Honestly… no. She didn't tell me anything. Just that you left her.'

He let out a long, shaky sigh. 'I didn't mean for this to happen, Evie, really I didn't.'

'Alex,' I began unsteadily, feeling suddenly dirty, like I was the one cheating rather than Alex, or even Josh. How did Josh stand it? I wasn't even the other woman, but having this conversation without Megan's awareness or permission felt wrong. 'You know what, I can't talk to you, Alex. You need to talk to Megan.'

'Are they okay?' His voice wavered. 'Is she okay?'

I exhaled sharply. 'She's… coping. As well as can be expected.'

He let out a long, shaky sigh. 'Evie, I didn't mean for it to happen like this. I didn't plan on walking out.'

I swallowed. 'Alex, I can't do this. She's my best friend.'

'I know,' he said quickly. 'I'm not asking you to take my side. I just—' He cut himself off. 'I feel… *relieved*, and I hate that I feel that way.'

I said nothing. There was nothing to say.

'It wasn't just the last fight,' he continued, his voice thick with regret. 'You know that, right? We've been going in circles for years. I work from home, she's always in the city, and when we are together, it's like we're on different planets. We both feel it. We just don't say it.'

I shut my eyes. 'Alex, you should be saying this to Megan, not me.'

'I know.' He sniffed. 'I just… I don't know if she ever told you, but last year, she almost left me.'

My eyes snapped open. 'What?'

There was silence. 'She didn't tell you, did she?'

I hesitated. 'I was abroad.'

'She didn't tell you when you got back?' His bitter laugh was quiet. 'Jesus!'

'That's not—' I faltered. I didn't know what to say. Megan had kept that from me? Pot, meet kettle.

'Evie, I love her. I always have. But we were breaking long before I walked out that door.'

I felt my grip on the phone tighten, feeling a rage against Megan and then a shift to feeling suddenly calm. I knew my place in this situation and I wasn't risking it. 'I'm not being pulled any further into this Alex.'

'I know. And I'm not asking that. Just… please know she's not the only one hurting here.'

My throat tightened. Megan had never told me. Not

once. I thought she and I shared everything, even when I was abroad. We texted and FaceTimed, I sent presents and postcards. We always made time for each other and swore that we'd never keep anything like this from each other, and yet we had. Both of us.

'Are you going to Kent?' I asked after a beat.

'Yeah,' he murmured. 'She probably didn't take any of her things. She'll be missing her skincare routine, and she hasn't got her charger.'

The fact that he was listing off her essentials made my heart ache a little. He knew her. He loved her. But love didn't always stay the same.

'Okay.' I cleared my throat. 'If you see her, tell her I love her. And I'm always here for a chat.'

'I will.'

I hesitated. 'And maybe… don't tell her we spoke. Not yet.'

A pause. Then, 'Will do.'

The line went dead, and I was left standing there, phone in hand, unsure if I had just made everything worse, but glad I had a tiny bit more of an understanding of what Megan was going through. Her marriage was breaking down, slowly eroding, and she was afraid.

I wanted to speak to her; I was desperate to, in fact, but I knew she wouldn't answer me.

I opened my phone to text instead when I received an email alert from Elijah at Salient Studios, my future boss, with the subject line: Getting a head start.

Hey Evie,

I hope you're surviving the Pim Hardcastle chaos – what a whirlwind! Must be a relief knowing you're moving on soon. We're all so excited to have you join us in January, and I just know you'll hit the ground running. Speaking of which, I'd love to get your thoughts on a few projects ahead of your start date. I completely understand that Pim is your current priority and, of course, you'll want to enjoy the holidays, but if you could carve out a little time, it would make a huge difference. Plus, it'll give you a great jump on things before January – familiarising yourself early can only make your transition smoother! I've attached some documents. If you could review them and send over your notes by Christmas Eve, that would be ideal. Let me know if you have any questions, though I'm sure you'll find it all pretty straightforward.

Looking forward to officially having you on board! And don't forget to book that travel insurance, flights are a nightmare this time of year.

Best, Elijah

Great, I thought, putting my phone back into my back pocket. More work.

Not only did I have Pim to manage, organising the recruitment of her new assistant, and dealing with Megan, Alex, and Josh's drama/silent treatment. And now, Salient wanted me to get a 'head start'.

It wasn't just the extra tasks that made my stomach sink, it was the tone. The assumption that I'd be eager and grateful, even knowing how complicated things were with Pim – and *always* were with Pim. Maybe they believed chaos was something that didn't impact me because I'd built a reputation for handling it while working with Salient.

When I heard I had got my first job with Pim, I couldn't wait to get started. Sure, I had just graduated from university and was grateful for the job, but there was an anticipation to get started that only comes with a new job or a new opportunity.

There was no such feeling with Salient, not right now.

It didn't feel like possibility, it was starting to feel like an obligation. Like a mistake I hadn't quite admitted to yet.

Instead of anticipation and excitement, there was a low, persistent dread. It didn't feel like a door opening so much as another set of expectations snapping quietly into place. Another role where I'd be competent and agreeable and endlessly adaptable, where my ability to cope would be mistaken for enthusiasm.

The more I tried to tell myself this was what I wanted, the more it began to feel like an obligation.

I wasn't imagining a future in Toronto with any real clarity, just bracing myself for it. For being good at something without ever asking whether it was actually making me happy.

And the most unsettling part wasn't the dread itself. It was how familiar it felt.

I'd spent years of my life with Pim, moving forward without stopping to check whether the direction still made sense. Not until I applied for Salient, and even that was because I felt I had the best shot of getting a job, not a job I *really* wanted.

I hadn't let myself fully sit with that truth until now.

I heard the ding of another email arriving in my inbox. Followed by two more. Apparently, Elijah's 'few projects' were more like an avalanche.

I closed my eyes and rubbed my forehead.

Could I ever catch a break?

Chapter 18

WALKING IN LONDON AT CHRISTMAS WAS something I thought would be a nightmare. The late-night shoppers, the tourists taking photos of the city lit up in neon, and the early drunken revellers falling out of pubs from the office Christmas parties. Yet somehow, despite the chaos, I'd found it was one of my favourite ways to unwind.

There were only five days left until Christmas Eve, and Pim's event. We had officially sold out of tickets, helped in part due to the added publicity from the viral video that was slowly dying a death online, and the TV company was thrilled to finally get the go-ahead with scheduling and were making a song and dance about it in all the popular TV magazines. Pim's photoshoots increased as digital journalists and broadcast newspapers asked for features and interviews to be shared pre- and post- the event. And through my intervention – cashing in *a lot* of favours – we were able to minimise the noise on the Michael Holland debacle.

Pim's star was shining bright, yet her tunnel vision was still in full force.

'I need you to meet your new assistant,' I had insisted that afternoon, standing beside Pim in yet another make-up chair as she got primped for a Christmas photoshoot for *The Times*.

'*Possible* new assistant,' she corrected, dabbing powder off her cheeks.

I had to stop myself from snapping. Unless she wanted to hire someone herself, during Christmas Alison was her new assistant. Or she would be assistantless.

'You're going to love her,' I said, deciding to move ahead with plans for an afternoon-tea meeting between them next week.

'I need more powder,' Pim replied, calling over another make-up artist, who quickly flourished a powder puff and did as Pim instructed.

Poor Alison, I thought. Although it wasn't me being difficult, I felt like I was really messing her about. I knew what it was like to lack stability in a role, particularly at Christmas, and I wanted her to be secure in the knowledge that the job was hers, if she still wanted it. But she needed to meet Pim. There was no other way around it. And maybe I just had to stop pussyfooting around it, like I did with everything else.

With a deep breath, I stepped out of the shoot and called Megan. Straight to voicemail. Again.

'Megan, pick up,' I sighed, frustration tightening my chest.

I had left about ten messages but still she hadn't messaged me back. I had spoken to Denise and Bob multiple times, and each time they had tried to get Megan to take my call. Denise even got sharp with her; and this was the woman who couldn't bring herself to give anyone anything less than four stars on review sites, even when the service was terrible.

'Megan, it's Christmas. My last Christmas in London for a while. Are you really not going to talk to me because you're annoyed that I knew about Josh's affair and you didn't?' I hesitated, unused to letting my frustrations pour out of me. 'It wasn't for me to say anything, and I didn't want to add to your…' To her what? Worries? Stress? No one had an issue adding to mine lately.

I hung up, exhaling forcefully. Now was not the right moment to leave a message, clearly.

Instead, I took myself for a walk around London. By the time I reached Covent Garden, my go-to place lately, the tension had eased. A hot chocolate on the steps of the open market, surrounded by the hum of Christmas music and the laughter of strangers, was exactly what I needed.

Maybe I'd see Simon. To tell the truth, I was really hoping to see him.

He hadn't been on a shift – if buskers had shifts – the last few times I'd been by. But still the setting of the market brought me peace, amidst Christmas chaos.

He wasn't busking when I arrived. There was a group of female carollers at his usual spot singing 'Auld Lang Syne' at the open doors of St Paul's Church. The warm glow of the interior beckoned, twinkling lights and signs pointed to the entrance through Bedford Street, and I thought, why not? It was something new.

Following a slow but steady stream of intrigued listeners, I headed through the gates into a small courtyard, following the sound of harmonised notes and the smell of freshly brewed mulled wine.

The church was warmly lit with many yellow candles, a second group of carollers inside stood on a raised plinth near to the altar and sang a gentle rendition of 'Have

Yourself a Merry Little Christmas'. The church was not yet full, although I felt the propelling electricity in the air that was leading not just me, but also many others, into the hall, and I knew it wouldn't be long. People cuddled together on pews, while others gathered near a makeshift bar at the back of the church.

I thought of swapping my hot-chocolate order for a mulled wine when—

'Was this one from your list?'

The familiar voice sent a spark through me.

I turned to see Simon leaning casually against the wall, a flask in his gloved hands, his smile warm enough to thaw me from the inside out.

'It might have been,' I admitted, practically jumping over a church patron to lean against the wall with him. I'm nothing if not subtle. I could feel my bad mood lifting from my body immediately as soon as I spotted him laughing at me. There's something magnetic about being able to make someone laugh, even if it's at you. 'It wasn't on the cards for today, though.'

He offered me the flask and I took it without hesitation. The scent of mulled wine hit me before I even took a sip.

'Busking in the cold is fun,' he mused, crossing his arms and shivering a bit. 'But this is the real treat.'

'Caught a chill?' I asked, handing the flask back.

'Always. I don't know if you've noticed, but it gets bloody cold in December.' He smirked.

'Careful, we're in a church. Don't think you can say the B word.'

'Bollocks, bloody, or blimey?' he asked – loudly – just as the carollers reached their crescendo. Heads turned in our direction, as I blushed and nudged him in the ribs with my elbow. He grinned, utterly unrepentant.

'I haven't seen you around here in a few days,' he said eventually, as the carollers began 'O Come, All Ye Faithful'.

'I've been around,' I admitted, shrugging. 'Didn't spot you, though.'

'We must have missed each other,' he agreed.

'Well, it's not like you have a schedule. In fact, do you even have social media?'

He shook his head. 'Hate all that.'

'I got those vibes from you,' I laughed. 'Can't really see you making TikToks of your shows or making reels for fun.'

His lips twitched. 'I was tempted to download TikTok recently.'

'Oh?'

'To see what you were up to.'

I blushed and busied myself with another sip of wine. 'Well, you would have been disappointed. I haven't posted much lately.'

'No? Not even our success at the Great Christmas Pudding Race?'

I rolled my eyes. 'You're really holding on to that victory.'

'The others won't let me forget it, so I might as well bask in the glory,' he said, watching me with quiet amusement.

There was a calmness about Simon – something grounding. He didn't try to fix things, didn't offer unwanted advice. He just listened.

And right now, I needed that.

'This is good,' I said, having another mouthful of the spicy hot drink. There was a familiar comfort about mulled wine. It had the effect of warming you from the inside and making you feel like everything was going to be all right just because it was Christmas. To me, this was the drink that the Ghost of Christmas Present offered to Ebenezer Scrooge. The drink of good cheer. 'I needed this.'

'Mulled wine?' Simon asked, though his expression was softer now, less teasing.

'Work's a bit much,' I said. 'And Megan and Josh had a falling-out,' I carried on. 'And now neither are talking to me as I didn't take sides, but they seem annoyed that I didn't take theirs or share their secrets or… I don't know.' I took a breath, and he didn't interrupt, surprisingly. 'Plus, my new job got in touch and want me to do some work early, over Christmas. I've not really had a break. Or a real Christmas.'

I let out a breath, surprised at how easily it all came tumbling out.

He just nodded. I offered the flask, but he didn't take it back. There was a definite understatement of *you need that more than I do* about his actions, which made me smile.

The fact he didn't often express an opinion made him that much easier to open up to, though it was frustrating when I wanted to know more about him. This mystery man who I felt magnetised towards.

I nodded with a sigh but said nothing else as I returned to listening to the perfectly harmonised choir for a moment more.

We just stood there, side by side, letting the music settle around us.

He leaned down a little as the pews began to fill and we were pushed further into the wall by new viewers and excited families.

Then, Simon leaned in, his voice low, just for me. 'Want to get out of here?'

I turned my head slightly, catching the glint of mischief in his eyes. 'And do what?'

'I have an idea.' He offered me his hand but didn't elaborate. He just held out his hand, an invitation wrapped in warmth and quiet adventure.

I hesitated for less than a second before slipping my fingers into his.

'Lead the way.'

Even when we stepped outside into the crisp December air, he didn't let go. His fingers were freezing, but I could feel the ridges left by his guitar strings, the evidence of his music imprinted into his skin.

I squeezed his hand slightly, just to see if he'd squeeze back.

He did.

'Where's your stuff?' I asked as we ducked down a side street, the market glow fading behind us as we reached the Strand.

'I lent it to another busker for the evening,' Simon said, glancing over his shoulder. 'We take turns with amps and guitars so we don't have to lug everything back and forth. I brought it down this morning, he's taking it home tonight.'

'So next time he'll bring it and you'll take it back.'

'Exactly. I only have that arrangement over Christmas, though. The rest of the year I hibernate.'

'Hibernate?' I laughed.

'Like a bear.'

'You? A bear?' I almost snorted and I noticed he squeezed my hand this time and my stomach dropped to my knees. I was walking hand in hand, in my favourite city at Christmas with a man I – I'll admit – was *obsessively* attracted to. This was a new feeling. I was not used to anything romantic, and this definitely entered that category. 'I was thinking of you more like a squirrel – always darting around, playing music, charming unsuspecting strangers.'

'I feel there's a nut analogy coming, and I'm not sure I'm going to like it.'

I snorted noisily and the jolt made us both stop, crashing into others as we laughed.

'I'm so sorry,' Simon explained in charming fashion to unsuspecting strangers who laughed, somehow knowingly. He retook my hand and pulled me back into the street.

'Have you guessed where we're going yet?' he chuckled, shaking his head as we stopped at a zebra crossing. 'It's unlike you not to interrogate me.'

'Oh, isn't it?' I teased, acutely aware that we were still holding hands. Were we just… not addressing this? Did handholding come with mulled wine and moonlit strolls, like some unspoken festive rule? Was this normal? How was I supposed to know? The last people I'd held hands with for this long were Josh and Megan – and only because, when drunk, I tended to fall over without physical intervention. 'I feel like a surprise,' I replied as he crossed the road and headed towards the North Bank.

'How much of that mulled wine did you have?' he asked, pointing with his spare hand to the flask I was still holding.

'Not as much as I wanted,' I admitted.

'Well, hold off on drinking any more.' His smirk grew wider. 'You won't want to be unsteady on your feet where we're headed.'

'You do remember how we met,' I pointed out. 'I'm not steady on my feet when I'm stone-cold sober, let alone with a quart of mulled wine in me.'

He shrugged. 'I've got you.' He gave my fingers another squeeze, sending my heart somersaulting into my ribcage. Everything in me seemed to become cinched and my breath caught in my chest. What was this feeling? *Bloody gorgeous* was what it was.

Suddenly, he stopped, and I – being my usual graceful self – crashed straight into him.

'See?' I yelped, giggling but feeling like I had just proved my own point by bruising my nose against his shoulder. 'Exhibit A.'

'Look up,' he replied simply.

'Here?' At a crossroads and traffic junction.

'Well, almost. That building in front of us.' He pointed and I looked up. Somerset House.

'Oh.' My breath hitched in realisation.

'What was one of the things on your list again?' he asked knowingly.

'Ice skating!' I squeaked. 'We're going ice skating!'

He nodded as the green pedestrian light flickered on, and we dashed towards the entrance like kids on Christmas morning.

The gates were open, and a few shoppers and viewers strolled out, arm in arm or laden with shopping bags from the mini Christmas market inside. The ice rink shimmered under the glow of fairy lights, a few last-minute skaters gliding across the near-empty surface.

I was tempted to get my phone and start TikToking for my Assistmas series, but I didn't want Simon's surprise to fill a slot on my social channels. I wanted it to be something that he and I did. Together, and unshared.

'Don't you have to book?' I asked Simon as we got closer. The ticket booth appeared to be shut. Clearly, they were wrapping down for the night. Maybe this wasn't going to be the perfect surprise after all.

'Wait here,' Simon said, releasing my hand and walking away. The sudden feeling of cool night air over my previously warm palm shocked me back to my senses. A late-night stroll with Simon after carols and mulled wine was still a decent evening, even if a surprise skate would have just made this the most perfect of moments. Possibly *the* perfect moment.

I wrapped my arms around myself and my sparkly jumper with an embroidered snowflake in the centre. One of my own creations from my last Christmas with Pim, in Malta. I had been craving snow and a little bit of magic, and a hand-sewn snowflake was as close as I could get.

'Evie!' Simon called from the nearby booth. He was talking to a man in an oversized black puffer jacket and baseball cap. I wandered over, still hugging my arms around myself. 'We're in! We've got thirty minutes.'

'What?' I gasped, as the man in the puffer jacket offered me a pair of skates.

'Guessing you're a five?' he said, handing them to me.

'Four, but I've got super-thick socks on.'

'Give 'em a go,' he said with a wink and headed back into the booth, where the tell-tale smell of burning dust made me think he had a contraband floor heater.

'How did you manage that?' I asked Simon, after we entered the purpose-built changing room, pulling on the hefty plastic boots, unable to contain my grin. Simon was hopping from foot to foot awkwardly, trying to balance on the skates on the primary-school blue carpet.

'I told you the busking community was small,' he explained. 'We help each other out.'

'That guy's a busker?'

Simon nodded. 'He plays the drums on the underground.'

This was blowing my mind – and I loved it. I pushed myself up from the bench and nearly toppled over.

'This is bonkers!' I said, wobbling slightly as I stood, grabbing hold of Simon's arms to steady myself, although that wasn't helpful since he could barely stand upright himself.

'You're telling me,' he muttered, hopping awkwardly towards the rink entrance. 'Come on.'

The safety marshals offered us each an arm to step on the ice. 'Do a lap along the rail, then let go,' one of them advised with a knowing smile.

'Good plan.' Simon nodded, gripping the side for dear life as he pushed off.

'I think you're supposed to *glide*,' I said, testing my own balance. Surprisingly, I felt… kind of stable? Maybe it was because ice skates were actually meant for ice – unlike, say, solid ground and cheap carpeting.

'Bend your knees,' I suggested, finding that that helped my balance.

Simon squinted at me. 'Since when did you become the expert?' He was still gripping the side.

'Since watching one tutorial on YouTube last Christmas.'

I dared myself to let go and skate around him. With a shriek I made it, and he threw out his arm to protect me, though I managed to skate ahead.

'Let go,' I encouraged. He shook his head.

'I'm *fine.*'

'Are you?' I smirked, effortlessly – or comparatively effortlessly – skating around him.

His jaw dropped. 'You traitor. You pretended to be bad at this!'

'No, no, I *am* bad at this,' I reassured him. 'You're just worse.'

He sighed dramatically. 'This is humiliating.'

'I thought you had done this before. Given that the ticket guy is your mate.'

Simon shook his head again. 'I don't often call in favours.'

'Yet for me you've called in two.'

'Two?'

'The other buskers looked after your things when you ran the race.'

Simon smiled in recognition. 'That was only a small favour.'

'What did you have to give your friend in return for this?' I skated backwards, tentatively releasing the side of the rink every now and then to test my limits. Poor Simon was hunched over like an arthritic, hardly able to move.

'Give me your hand,' I said, offering the one not holding the rink. At least this way I could bring him with me as I skated away.

'Crikey, you're fast,' he said. Although, looking around the rink, we were moving slower than the two-year-old sitting on a skate aid, chasing their older sibling.

'Go on then. What did this cost you?'

'Nothing much,' he said vaguely.

I narrowed my eyes. 'Simon.'

He opened his mouth and closed it a few times, before

finally saying, 'I gave up my New Year's Eve busking slot.'

My jaw dropped.

'I was going to perform in front of the church again about one o'clock – you know, when all the bargain hunting shoppers are going mad, and they're starting the New Year celebrations a little early so everyone's a little extra-generous.'

'That sounds like a good slot.' A seed of guilt was developing in me.

'It is,' he admitted. 'But there will be others about the city. I'll book a new one.'

'What about raising money for charity?' I asked, stopping for a rest as we made it halfway around the rink. Simon sighed with relief and gripped the side fully, finally standing straight.

He paused and looked away. 'I've been busking nearly every day this Christmas, after work and before work, so it's not like I haven't raised a ton of money for charity already. In fact, I've raised nearly triple what I made last year.'

'Really?' I asked, surprised to find that people were feeling that generous, even at Christmas.

'Well, it used to be that I only busked at the weekends, and maybe one afternoon in the week. But now I…' He stopped again and laughed, a little embarrassed.

'Why have you been busking every day then? Particularly if you've got work as well.'

He hesitated. And then – very slowly – he looked at me. It was a look of a thousand words, though it took only a few seconds for me to translate it.

Finally I got it.

He'd been busking… to see *me*.

My breath caught in my chest and my mouth went dry, not uncomfortably so, just enough to stop me from speaking and putting my foot in it.

I took his hand again. 'Come on,' I said confidently, not sure what else to say. 'You've got to let go this time.'

'The marshal said one full round and *then* let go,' he argued petulantly.

'I dare you,' I said cheekily, gently tugging him from the wall. 'You've got this. And I've got you.'

He took a second and then slowly lifted his hand an inch above the side of the rink, grabbing it again almost immediately, before letting go fully.

'There you go!' I cheered.

'Don't you *dare* let go of my hand!'

'*Let it gooo, let it gooo*,' I began to sing wickedly, lifting my fingers from where they rested on his wrist.

'No!' He lunged for the wall, overbalanced and…

Whump!

We both hit the ice in a tangled heap.

'Oh my God!' I gasped, half-laughing, half-gasping for breath. 'That was so bad.'

'It's not funny,' he groaned.

'Oh, it *is*,' I said, neatly lifting myself up as Simon's legs rolled from under him. If I wasn't distracted by laughing at, and with, him, I would have been amazed by the discovery of my natural centre of gravity.

'You're the worst.' His face was still half buried in his scarf.

'Happy to oblige.' I beamed as Simon continued to flail around like a turtle on its back.

'Having you suck at skating is making me feel so

confident in my own ability,' I admitted, offering him my arm to help him up. He took it hesitantly, fearful I would let him go again.

'Happy to oblige,' he repeated my words sarcastically, finally righting himself. With a large exhalation he huffed, 'Right,' finally getting to his feet. 'Bend the knees—'

And then – like some ice-skating prodigy – he took off.

'What the—' I gawked. 'Where did that come from?'

'Your lack of faith in me gave me a second wind,' he called over his shoulder.

Sure, his arms were thrown out and he was waving them like a baby bird just out from the nest, but he was skating.

I chased after him, the two of us moving faster now, cackling as we weaved around the near empty rink.

It wasn't long before the marshal raised a large sign that said '*Five minutes left*' on it, just as 'Only You' by the Flying Pickets came over the speakers.

'May I have this dance?' Simon asked, offering his hand now both of us were less fearful because we had already fallen over.

We skated into the centre and I took his hands, feeling steadier immediately.

'You may.'

He paused for a moment and released one hand to grip my back. My chest pressed into his and I felt his breath on my chin.

We swayed, gliding in slow, lazy circles as the other skaters departed around us.

'This has been incredible,' I said.

'A nice surprise?'

'The best.' I meant it. Every second of this night had felt like something plucked straight from a Christmas movie, the kind with just the right balance of charm and absurdity.

'Would it be even better with hot chocolate after?'

I grinned. 'Can you read my mind or something?'

His smirk grew wider. 'Maybe.'

And then – under the glow of fairy lights, with the ice glistening beneath us – he kissed me.

It was our first kiss and, by all reasonable standards, it would have been acceptable to be bad or awkward or completely misjudged. We could have bumped noses, miscalculated angles, or, given our shared lack of skating skills, toppled over in a heap of crushed dignity, just as we had before.

But no. This was just disgustingly perfect.

The meet-cute of a million Christmas romances perfect.

The Richard Curtis kiss of dreams. Except I'm not American and he's not called Bernard. Thank God.

His lips were warm, tinted red by the mulled wine, and when I pressed my tongue against them – just a hint of invitation – he deepened the kiss.

'Only You' reached its crescendo and, balance be damned, I leaned into my toe pick, lifted my arm from his, and wrapped it around his neck, pulling him in closer.

His cologne – spiced apples, cloves, and vanilla – wrapped around me like the cosiest Christmas sweater and the light scrape of his sandy stubble against my cheek sent a shiver down my spine.

His hand drifted down my shoulder to my lower back, lingering just enough to make my pulse race as I pressed into him further.

'*Times up!*' a voice called off the ice and instinct pulled us apart.

For a long second, we just stared at each other, the world around us fading to a blur of twinkling lights and laughter.

Simon said nothing, his chest rising in shallow breaths as we stared at one another.

'That,' Simon finally said, voice a little husky, 'was pretty spectacular.'

My lips curled. 'Not bad at all.'

But we both knew it was so much more than that.

Chapter 19

After shuffling off the ice – awkwardly assisted by the marshals, since neither of us could quite remember how to walk, as a result of the kiss or the ice I couldn't tell – we made our way to the carpeted changing rooms in silence, smiling dorkily at each other, and we unlaced our boots, neither of us quite knowing what to say to the other.

'You ready?' Simon asked as I handed over my boots to the bemused-looking cloakroom agent and nodded.

He offered me his hand.

I took it after a beat.

We made our way to the nearby Christmas café. It was open later than the rink, thankfully; it was the kind of place that permanently smelled like a gingerbread house.

'I haven't been skating since I was a kid,' I said as we sat down, cradling a hot chocolate Simon had treated me to. It was drowning in whipped cream and marshmallows. 'I forgot how much fun it was.'

'And how hard,' he added, tipping half a container of cinnamon on top of the cream on his drink before attacking it with a spoon. 'My mum took me skating once. I was about as useless as I was tonight.'

'You got the hang of it,' I reminded him.

He shook his head. 'She and I gave up after about

twenty minutes. Just sat, drank hot chocolate, and watched everyone else fall over instead. It was one of my favourite days with her.'

There was something in his tone – warm but also fragile, as if the memory was holding him together and breaking him at the same time.

I smiled. 'That sounds lovely.'

I licked my lips to clear the cream off my chin but missed a spot. Simon leaned forward without thinking, his thumb brushing just below my lip. He licked the residue off his finger, completely unfazed.

I cleared my throat, suddenly unable to hold his gaze.

His expression became playfully amused. 'What about you?'

'I have memories like that with my mum, but I don't tend to think about them much.'

Simon didn't push. He just nodded, the way someone does when they understand something too well.

'I think about memories more at Christmas,' he admitted. 'She's still such a big part of the holiday season, though it's been more than ten years since I spent Christmas with her.' He took a breath as if wanting to saying more, but he stopped himself.

'You love Christmas, don't you?' he asked instead. 'Even with… everything?'

I nodded slowly at first and then quite passionately. He laughed.

'I can't help it. It's the season that just lifts my mood. Everything seems hopeful, or possible. The year's coming to a close, fresh beginnings are going to happen.'

He nodded slowly now too, running his finger around the top of his hot chocolate.

'I do get that,' he said. 'But I suppose it's just a weird time for me. I seem to remember a lot of stuff at this time of year, especially about my mum. And, usually, the small things more than the big ones; like the way she would only use a particular bowl or spoon to bake the Christmas pudding, or how she used to hum when she was thinking.'

Simon's gaze flicked up to mine, sharp with recognition.

'People always talk about grief like it's this big dramatic thing,' I said. 'But mostly, it's the little things that catch you off guard, isn't it? A smell, a song, a stupid movie you watched together once.'

'Yeah,' he murmured.

For a second, we just sat there, both of us orbiting the same kind of loss.

It felt strange to have someone understand such a large part of me, without even the need to truly explain it. It lifted a weight off my shoulders I hadn't even realised I was carrying. I wasn't used to that ease. It shifted something in me, the way I saw him, the way the space between us felt less like distance and more like a tether.

After a moment, I allowed myself to smile. 'It was Denise, Megan's mum, who was the one that took me ice skating the first time,' I continued, chasing away the heaviness. 'With Megan, of course. Megan was convinced she'd be a figure-skating prodigy, and I was more interested in being a hockey player.'

'Violent, you mean?' Simon teased.

I shook my head passionately. 'I was obsessed with *The Mighty Ducks*, actually. But one disastrous attempt at skating with a stick led to some bruised knees and a very bruised ego, so I let the dream go pretty quickly.'

Simon laughed and, as he leaned back in his chair, his

shirt rode up slightly. My gaze dropped, catching a glimpse of a trail of hair under his belly button – and the faint outline of an ab. A real, defined ab.

A shiver ran up my spine, and for the first time in a long time, I felt… well, something stirring. Like a tornado in my midriff.

'So was personal assistant the next grand ambition or were there others in between?'

I rubbed the back of my neck and lifted my gaze to his face, trying to remember how to form words. 'I had plenty of dreams,' I admitted. 'Vet, Oscar-winning actress. I wanted to own a launderette at one point. There was even a phase where I was convinced I'd be a time traveller.'

'Did *Doctor Who* inspire that dream?'

'Nope. *Bill and Ted's Excellent Adventure*.'

That got a proper laugh out of him. 'Clearly TV and film were a pivotal part of your childhood.'

'Oh, massively.'

'And now you're off to be a producer,' he pointed out, a flicker of emotion – disappointment? – lurking beneath his words. 'Success incoming.'

I swallowed. Could he hear the same hesitation in my voice that I heard in his?

'They've sent me some work to do, actually.'

'The new job?' he confirmed, and I nodded. 'Over Christmas?'

I nodded again. 'I haven't opened the email – *emails* – yet. I've got too much on with Pim and her show. Plus Megan and Josh, and all that.'

Simon tilted his head slightly. 'What's going on with them?'

While I'd been refusing to talk about what had happened with everyone, from Pim to Denise, for some reason with Simon I felt I could share anything, and it would be safe to do so. In this moment, sitting in this Christmas-themed café bedecked with garlands of holly and tinsel, with aromas of cinnamon, orange, and hot chocolate, and as countless lights softened our expressions, I thought I could hand him my soul and he would take care of it.

So, I told him everything.

From Megan and Alex's split, Josh's situation with a married man, Pim's show, her new assistant, and the weight of my guilt over leaving her. And the strangest part? The job I'd spent years dreaming about, the one that should have felt like a golden ticket, which just... didn't.

'It's one of the best studios I've ever worked at, and I'm ridiculously underqualified for the role, but they offered it to me anyway. I should be thrilled, right? I just can't seem to focus enough on it to care about it.'

Simon considered me for a moment. 'Fear perhaps?'

His hot chocolate was now completely gone, while mine was practically untouched, the cream had folded into the delicious molten chocolate while I had been explaining everything.

'It's not easy changing jobs, especially after a long period of time in another. And eight years in the same job without a promotion or pay rise is a long time.'

I laughed bitterly, thinking about the scripts in my inbox and the dread. 'I never thought I was a procrastinator before. Or that I was afraid of change.'

'Most people don't,' he said, leaning forward on his elbows. 'But big change is terrifying. Even good change.

And if you make the wrong decision, you can regret it.'

'Is that how you live your life?' I asked, blowing on my long-cold hot chocolate out of habit.

He smiled, glancing up and down at me and my cup. I felt like I was being X-rayed.

'Mostly,' he began. 'I feel for you, though. It sounds as if everyone around you is going through something right now, and it's bleeding into your own life.'

I considered for a moment, not having thought of it that way.

'It's odd to think that, when I was living abroad, I felt closer to everyone than I am now.'

Simon reached across the table, his hand resting on my arm briefly before pulling away. 'They'll come round.'

'It's Christmas,' I reminded him and myself. 'Every movie, book, and song tells me that they'll come around, so it must be true. Right?'

'The odds are in your favour.'

'I just wish one of them would answer their phone,' I said, pulling my phone out of my pocket to check for messages. There were none, not even from Pim.

My stomach clenched at the emptiness of the screen, the reminder that the people I cared about were keeping me at a distance. Simon glanced at the screen.

'What about your TikTok? You said you haven't been posting much.'

I shrugged. 'I enjoyed making TikToks when I had things to share. My glamorous life, so to speak, and it hadn't felt very glamorous of late. It's weird to share TikToks that your friends watch when your friends aren't speaking to you.'

He frowned. 'You're worried they'll be angry if it

looks as if you're having a good time while they're falling apart?'

I hesitated. Hearing it put like that made me feel small. Ridiculous, even. But it was true. I nodded, tracing my thumb along the edge of my phone.

'I know I'm only hearing one side,' Simon continued carefully. 'But, to me, it sounds as if it's Josh and Megan that have issues to sort out, and neither of their issues are with you but, for some reason, you're bearing the brunt of their drama. If I'm being honest, I think they're being a tad selfish, Evie.'

'They're not…' I started, the automatic response slipping from my lips. But something stopped me. A knife-in-the-gut realisation that I had been making excuses for them, that I was angry. Not just hurt but properly pissed off that my so-called best friends had taken their stress out on me. 'I'm the fixer,' I told Simon, my voice quieter now. 'I've always been the people-pleasing, happy-to-help fixer in life.'

'Why?'

The question landed heavily between us.

I narrowed my eyes. 'Are you my therapist now?'

Simon held up his hands in surrender. 'I don't mean to dig. I just know what it's like to be the person that takes on other people's problems.' He paused for a moment and played with his collar. 'It's a way of avoiding your own.'

That hit harder than I cared to admit.

'Look, I'm not trying to shame you or anything, I've only known you for a few weeks – Christ, I don't even have your number – but I just…' He stopped and cleared his throat quickly. 'I just care about you, in a way I've never really cared about someone before, certainly not so quickly.' He paused again, not making eye contact but appearing to tremble.

My breath caught in my throat.

No one ever said things like that to me. I never gave them the opportunity.

I'd spent years being useful and caring for others, even from a distance. Being cared *about* – openly, without expectation – felt unfamiliar, almost destabilising.

Simon looked away as his voice became gentle. 'I know what it's like,' he said hesitantly. 'When my mum died, I thought if I stayed busy enough, distracted enough, I wouldn't have to feel it. Wouldn't have to stand still long enough for the grief to catch up with me. But it does, Evie. It always does.'

I looked away, my throat tightening.

'I think you're doing the same thing,' he said, more quietly still. 'Running. Running so fast you don't even know what you're running from any more.'

I swallowed hard, wishing he would just stop.

'I mean, what happens if you stay?' His voice was almost a whisper now. 'If you stop fixing, stop people-pleasing, stop running. What's left?'

I hated how much the question shook me, and that I didn't know the answer.

'You think you're living life to the full,' he said, a little more direct now. 'With your friend's Christmas list and your fun runs, I see someone who's scared to live her own life, or rather follow *her* dreams.'

A hot flare of anger rose in me, defensive, protective. What the hell did he know? We'd only known each other a few weeks. He didn't get to dig into my life, into the cracks

I kept hidden even from myself. And yet he wasn't wrong, which was the worst part.

'You're allowed to want something for yourself, you know.'

I looked away, suddenly feeling too seen, too raw. His words sank into me, thick and uncomfortable, like swallowing a large marshmallow whole.

'I should get going,' I said abruptly, the lump in my throat making my voice tighter than I intended as I slipped from my chair.

Simon's expression shifted, concern flashing across his face. 'Evie, I—'

'No, it's fine,' I cut in, forcing a small smile. 'I have an early start with Pim tomorrow. The show's only a few days away.'

'Evie, I'm so—' He seemed to growl at himself, as if he had realised his own mistake. 'Can we walk to the station?'

'I'm getting a bus,' I lied.

St Martin-in-the-Fields was only a short walk away but Simon was standing and, despite the wonderful evening, I suddenly really wanted to be alone.

I had spent all evening confiding in him and now I regretted it. I felt as if I'd said too much, and just one comment from him had made me feel more unsteady than I had felt on the ice.

Simon hesitated, as if he wanted to say more, but wary of saying something wrong – or *more* wrong – and I wasn't ready for whatever it was he could say. So, instead, I leaned in and pressed a soft kiss to his cheek. That shut him up.

'Thank you for tonight,' I murmured, my lips grazing

the light stubble on his jaw. 'It was really wonderful.'

Before he could react, or before I could change my mind, I turned and left.

Chapter 20

I barely slept that night. Simon's words had embedded themselves in my brain like an irritating jingle. Was I really burying my own problems by dealing with everyone else's? Running, not for adventure but from fear? It was easier to help others, to stay in motion, than to face the stillness of wanting something for myself – and risking losing it, as I lost Mum when I was ten.

For years I told myself I was chasing life, squeezing every moment dry because it might end too soon. But that was a lie. I wasn't chasing anything, I was hiding. From loss, or from needing too much.

Somewhere in the chaos, the version of me who had dreams got lost. I'd become a professional helper, jumping into other people's fires while mine quietly smouldered.

I was living day by day, not dream by dream, but I was sure I had had dreams once.

Simon's voice echoed in my head: *You're allowed to want something for yourself, you know.*

I hated that he saw it so clearly when I couldn't. If he had figured it out after just a few weeks, how long had I been pretending?

No matter how many times I turned it over in my head, I couldn't find a fault in his logic. He had seen right through me, in a way that made my stomach twist with resentment at him, at myself, at the truth of it all. Because he wasn't wrong. And that was the worst part. He knew. He had lived it. And if he could see it in me so easily, then how long had I been fooling myself into believing I was fine?

By 5 a.m. I gave up on sleep. My body was exhausted but my mind wouldn't stop. I took an extra-long shower, letting the hot water scald my skin as if it could burn away the unease curling inside me.

Megan and Josh hadn't messaged me in nearly a week. Not a single check-in, not a meme, not even a passive-aggressive '*I'm fine*' text. Nothing. And they were supposed to be my best friends. The people who knew me better than anyone.

My thumb hovered over my phone more than once, to call them or to reach out on the group chat. I could smooth it over – probably easily if I apologised for things I hadn't done, or if I offered myself up as the bridge back to normality.

But I also knew that, if I did, it would be me bending again. Me absorbing the discomfort so that everyone else could stay where they were.

And I hadn't even done anything wrong.

This couldn't go on.

I had lied to Simon about having an early morning: in fact, it was the opposite. Pim had gone out to a Christmas party with an old friend, so it was best not to let her surface until well after noon to give her a chance to sleep off the after-effects of the champagne.

I had a different plan for this morning.

After my shower, I pulled on my jeans and a sparkly green jumper and I got on the Tube with one thing in mind: Josh.

I took the Tube across the city, gripping the cold metal pole in the carriage with gloved hands, my mind racing with all the things I wanted to say.

By the time I reached Josh's building, I was shivering with nervous energy. I banged on his door and pressed the buzzer repeatedly, determined to get an answer. It took a few seconds before the intercom crackled to life.

'What the fuck are you doing?' he shouted, groggy and irritated.

'Open the door, Josh,' I said into the intercom, my voice steady but firm.

There was a beat of silence. Then, 'Evie?' His tone was suddenly higher, confused.

The buzzer sounded, granting me entry.

He was waiting at his door like the Ghost of Christmas Regret, in a pair of fluffy white pyjama bottoms and a Christmas T-shirt with a gingerbread man and the words '*Let's Get Baked*' stretched across his chest.

'We need to talk,' I said, brushing past him before he could form an excuse.

'It's not even seven,' he moaned, shutting the door behind me.

'You've disturbed my sleep for days by pissing me off, so I thought I would return the favour and disturb yours,' I snapped, throwing my bag on the sofa and going to his kitchen to turn on the kettle. 'I've had enough of the silent treatment. You and I are going to talk.'

He groaned and fell flat on his face atop his sofa. He clearly wasn't that annoyed with me or he'd have launched into a tirade of cutting wit.

'Kettle's on.' I returned, sinking into the blanket-covered armchair. 'So can we talk?'

'Do I have a choice?' His voice was muffled by the sofa cushion.

'Nope. It's been a week, Josh,' I said. 'Why the hell haven't you messaged me back?'

He might've shrugged, but with the way his body was curled into the sofa, it was hard to tell.

'I didn't want to,' he said finally.

'Why? Because I so greatly wronged you? What did I even do?'

Another shrug. This time more obvious, as he shifted into a more comfortable position.

'You just automatically took Megan's side.'

I blinked. '*What?*'

'And then she threw a drink on me and you just let her chuck me out.'

I chewed my lip for a moment before finding my resilience again. 'We were there to help her, Josh. And as much as you're my best friend, *she's* my sister. She needed me. If the roles were reversed and we were there for you, I would have stayed with you too.'

'Wow! What a comfort.' His voice was laced with sarcasm as he rubbed his eyes, which I now noticed were red-rimmed. His face was blotchy and he had the general air of someone who hadn't slept properly in days.

I decided to take a different tack.

I shoved his legs out of the way and hugged one of his many cushions to my chest to match his petulant energy.

'If it helps, she's ignoring me as well.'

'It doesn't. I'm not trying to screw up your relationship with Megan. I was just pissed in the moment. And pissed in general. I *really* shouldn't have opened that second bottle of wine.'

'Y'think?'

We blinked at each other for a moment. 'Coffee?'

'I'd love one.'

'Do you want to have a shower?' I added, pottering about in his kitchen and trying to sound casual. The Shiraz still seemed to be clinging to his skin.

He laughed but said nothing. I returned with his coffee, black no sugar.

'So why,' I began, 'if you recognised you were drunk, did you remain annoyed at me? For days, I might add.'

'I didn't...'

'Go on.'

He stared into his coffee as if it might suddenly offer him wisdom. 'I didn't mean to drop you in the shit.'

'Well, you did,' I shot back. 'I understand why you were mad at me in the moment, but a whole *week*, Josh? I thought we weren't those kinds of friends.'

His eyes flicked up, guilt flashing through them before he masked it with an eye roll.

'Guessing you haven't spoken to Megan either?'

He shook his head.

'Same. She won't take my calls, but she's back in Kent with Denise and Bob.'

'Not with Alex?' His concern broke through his apparent exhaustion. 'Do we even know what happened yet?'

'No.' I didn't want to admit my conversation with Alex to anyone but Megan. 'I don't think they'll be getting back together, though.'

'Oh, fucking fabulous!' He threw his head back. 'That's going to make her even more pleasant.'

'Josh, really?'

'What? She threw a drink on me—'

'And you spoke about your affair with a married man when we were supposed to be comforting her after her husband had left. I mean, *come on*. Pick your timing next time.'

He went to speak but I cut him off. This was my time to be angry, not his.

'And you dropped me in the shit, for good measure. Why did you choose that moment? Drunk or not: why?'

'I was just…' He stopped and exhaled. 'I don't know.'

'And me? Why did you ignore me?'

He threw his head back and I felt the familiar feeling of wanting to let it go. To say 'No worries' as I usually did, to let the moment pass and be done with it.

But it was about time someone else did some work for a change.

'Well?' I pressed.

'I don't know. I was… embarrassed? Frustrated? I just didn't want to deal with it.'

'Great! Love that for me. Especially when I only have two weeks left in London.'

He winced. A direct hit.

'Yeah, I know,' he whispered, shifting to sit properly on the sofa instead of curling into it. 'I was being a dick. I shouldn't have ignored you. And I shouldn't have let my own shit make things worse.'

'Thank you,' I said, quieter now. Sincere and relieved that it wasn't in my head.

Josh sighed again, rubbing his temples. 'I do stand by the fact that Megan overreacted—'

'Josh.'

'No, hear me out. I get why she was upset. And I get that my timing was abysmal.'

'Apocalyptic,' I corrected.

'But she went nuclear on me. She chucked wine on me, chucked me out, and then cut both of us off. That's not exactly fair, Evie.'

I chewed my lip, knowing he had a point. Megan had always been quick to react, especially when emotions were running high.

'I think she's spiralling,' I theorised aloud. 'She's hurting, and you were an easy target. But, Josh, you have to admit that what you are doing isn't right.'

He hesitated, then nodded. 'I know. I just—' He exhaled. 'I think I was so caught up in being pissed at her for throwing the drink and you not defending me that I didn't want to admit that maybe she had a point.'

'She did?' I was surprised he'd admit it.

'It was my timing that pissed her off more than the subject matter.'

'I think you sleeping with a married man still annoyed her. You know how paranoid she's been, thinking that Alex is cheating.'

'But that's just it, it's *paranoia*!' Josh's voice rose in volume. 'And it's not like you or I can do anything about it. She needs to sort herself and her house out.'

'And *you* need to talk to her,' I insisted. He pulled a face of disgust, but I was deadly serious. I reached over and nudged his knee. 'It's not too late to fix things, you know. You don't have to be best friends again overnight, but you should at least try before this stain sets in.'

He pulled another face. 'I threw away that shirt.'

'I'll buy you a new one.'

He laughed and immediately acquiesced. 'Fine, I'll try. Eventually.'

'Soon.'

He squinted at me. 'Define *soon.*'

'Before I leave for Canada.'

Josh rolled his eyes, but I caught the small twitch of a smile. 'Fine. But if I get another drink thrown at me, you're paying for my dry-cleaning.'

'Deal.'

It wasn't a perfect resolution, but it was a start.

Josh looked at his mug, then quietly said, 'Truth is, Evie, I don't really see Megan unless you're around. You're the glue. Without you, we just… drift.'

That made sense. In fact, I had long suspected that that was the truth. Megan was my sister and Josh was my friend from university. The fact was we had become a trio was because I connected the two of them. But that didn't mean it wasn't a good friendship, or that it didn't deserve a little TLC to maintain.

Softly, because he needed to hear it, I said, 'You know when I go… she's going to be the only one here who really knows you like I do.'

He glanced at me, something shifting in his eyes.

'Don't throw that away too, okay?'

He didn't say anything for a moment, then casually, 'It's Canada, not the moon. You'll visit. Or I'll visit. Or we'll both learn how to text.'

I smiled, but it caught at the edges. 'Sure.'

Josh nudged my foot with his. 'Don't get all weepy on me now.'

'I'm not,' I lied. 'You are.'

'You're gonna leave, and Megan's gonna throw drinks at

me, and I'm going to have no one to split movie marathons with. It's tragic, really.'

'It is,' I said, letting the quiet settle around us again. 'But I'll miss you.'

'Yeah,' he said quietly. 'Me too.'

And, just like that, the joke faded – but the truth stayed.

I didn't want to dampen the mood, though. 'If you can make it up with Megan by Christmas Day, so I can spend Christmas with Denise and Bob without the risk of someone launching a roast potato at your head, that would be even better actually.'

'She wouldn't throw a roast potato; she'd throw the scalding hot fat.'

'Dark.'

'It's Megan. She's ruthless.'

'But she's *our* Megan.'

His eyes narrowed. 'Okay, you're laying it on thick now.'

'Sorry.'

We settled into a comfortable silence and I enjoyed the feeling of having the weight lifted off my chest. That was one friend back in my contacts. I'll sort Megan next, but first I wanted to savour the relief.

'I haven't asked.' I yawned, feeling my own tiredness now the moment was beginning to pass. 'What are you doing for Christmas?'

Josh didn't move at first. He slurped his drink noisily, suddenly becoming very interested in getting his toe to rest neatly into a crevice of his coffee table.

'I dunno,' he mumbled eventually. 'It's kind of depressing really, to be the self-proclaimed King of Christmas – or *Queen* – and not have anywhere to go on the actual day.'

He gave a mock regal wave and swatted it away.

'I've certainly made up for all those missed years of festivities growing up as a Jehovah's Witness. At least in my career. My personal life.' He waved his hand in the air and made a 'meh' sound as if giving it a five out of ten on some judging score.

'What about Zach? No trip to Paris to practise your French?'

Josh let out a short, humourless laugh. 'Ah, that! Well, *that* is over and done with. There's nothing quite like walking in on the man you're seeing having sex with his husband to really drive home that *you're* the problem.'

I winced. 'Shit!'

'No, it's fine. I mean, how *dare* they not pause mid-thrust to consider my feelings, right?'

I tried not to laugh. It wasn't funny... but it kind of was. That's one way to learn your lesson, I supposed. But I wasn't telling Josh that.

'There's really no way to be the wronged party in a situation like that. I had no right to be angry, no real claim to be hurt. Just a front-row seat to my own terrible life choices.'

I reached for his hand, giving it a squeeze. 'That sounds brutal.'

He shook out his shoulders, as if releasing the 'ick' from the situation. 'Yeah, well. Being the mistress in a romcom really makes you question everything. A lot. And it turns out the answer is: I was an idiot.'

'You're not,' I began, but he cut me off with a shake of his head.

'Oh, I *am* the idiot. His husband was *hot*! I completely picked the wrong man.'

I couldn't help but laugh. His delivery was sometimes so spot on, but it didn't mean I missed the way his smile didn't quite reach his eyes. There was a shine to them that hadn't been there a minute ago.

'I'm really sorry that he wasn't your happily-ever-after.'

'I'll be fine.' He shrugged, sucking his teeth noisily. 'Besides, I was hardly going to get to spend Christmas Day with Zach, since he had to keep up the façade with his family. So no harm done, really.'

'Oh, babe.' The guilt of not clocking that earlier was like a kick in the stomach.

Josh waved it off with a tilt of his head. 'It's fine. It'll be just like when I was younger: no Christmas, no presents, no midnight mass. Just me, a fry-up, and a lot of Christmas TV.'

His words were hollow, but his voice was light. It was a well-practised speech, and that hurt like a cut across the throat. I'd spent my entire life terrified of being alone, of waking up one day and realising I had no one left – it was why I had pushed people away, why I acted as if I was fine when I wasn't. Because the thought of needing someone and then losing them was unbearable.

Josh, on the other hand, had spent his entire childhood already knowing what it felt like to be alone. He'd spent most of his childhood without any kind of celebration at all. Now in adulthood he had even less; being gay wasn't exactly welcome within his family's community.

And now, as much as he tried to fill that void with baubles and fairy lights, there was still a part of him that believed, deep down, that he didn't deserve it.

'*Or...*' I began, an idea forming. 'You could come back to Kent with me?'

'What?'

'Why not?' I said, suddenly excited. 'Come with me to Pim's show on Christmas Eve, and we'll travel down together that evening.'

'Really? Are you serious?'

'Of course I bloody am. I'm not leaving you alone on Christmas Day.'

'What about...' He trailed off, clearly thinking of Megan.

'Leave Megan to me. Denise and Bob will love having you. They've got pillows, blankets, and the air mattress.'

He whimpered. 'Maybe a hotel?'

'Good luck finding a hotel room this close to Christmas!' I pointed out. 'Come on, come down to Kent and rough it with me in my teenage bedroom.'

'Still, what about...'

'Megan will be fine. She's a grown-ass woman and, since she was the one that was insistent that I make the most of my last Christmas in London, this is what I want. All my loved ones, my family, in a room with me at Christmas.'

Josh swallowed, wiping his stubbly face again – probably realising how unkempt he had become in the days since discovering Zach going at it with his husband.

'I love you, you know.'

'Then never give me the silent treatment again.'

'I'll just call you when I know it's 3 a.m. in Canada, get my own back.'

'You're never going to forget I woke you up, are you?'

'Never.' He pulled me in for a long and smothering hug. 'One day, when you're least expecting it, I will get my revenge, Evie Frost. Just you wait.'

Chapter 21

One down, one to go, I thought as I left Josh's flat about five hours and two Christmas movies later.

Heading to the Savoy to get Pim ready for the afternoon ahead, mostly shopping and eating out to distract her from the show – and bitching about Michael Holland – I debated calling Megan again. But if the past week had taught me anything, it was that she wasn't going to pick up.

My phone had been buzzing non-stop all morning – as was now the standard – with messages from Pim cancelling her morning coffee order and requesting a lie-in, emails from journalists and publicists wanting a quote about the Michael Holland dispute, all of which I replied to with a very blank 'no comment' response and, in addition, near-constant reminders and notifications about the week ahead.

But nothing from Megan.

'Afternoon, Miss Frost,' Tony, the doorman, greeted as I approached.

'Hey, Tony. How busy is the bar today?' I asked, thinking that a little privacy wouldn't be a bad thing.

'Neither are open just yet.'

'Ah, of course.' Just as I had hoped. 'Would anyone mind if I took a quick call from the American Bar? I'd rather not do it in Pim's suite.'

Tony shook his head. 'Francesco's on today. You know he won't mind.'

Francesco was the bartender responsible for making Pim's wicked highballs whenever she needed a sensory-depriving nightcap to help her sleep. That worked in my favour.

'Perfect! Thanks, Tony!' I said, pulling out my phone as I slipped inside the world-famous bar. The space was dimly lit, cosy even when empty, and the mirrored walls reflected the quiet grandeur of it all. The door was unlocked, and I entered, spotting Francesco at once.

'Tony gave me the heads-up,' he said from behind the bar, motioning to the walkie-talkie in his apron. 'Go ahead and take your phone call.'

I grinned. 'You're a gem.'

Settling in, I took a seat near the door, to avoid disrupting Francesco's set-up for the day. Finding my phone under my many wintry layers, I pulled up FaceTime and tapped on Denise's name.

It rang twice before Bob's face appeared on the screen.

'Evie, my girl!' he bellowed, his voice booming through the bar.

'Bob! I was calling Denise – I didn't expect you to pick up?'

'She's currently lying under the Christmas tree.'

He was so matter-of-fact it threw me off my train of thought.

'Lying *under* it?'

He nodded, completely unfazed. 'She wanted to get to the radiator but reckoned the tree was too heavy to move, so she crawled under it instead.'

'Isn't that going to make the clothes more crumpled?'

Bob's mouth opened, ready to agree, but Denise's slightly strained voice rang out in the background. 'It'll be fine!'

Bob rolled his eyes. 'What's up, love? What can we do for you?'

I hesitated, my thumb tracing the edge of my phone.

'How's Megan?'

Bob's expression softened. 'She's all right. She's back in London now.'

That made me pause. 'Oh!' I'd assumed she'd stay in Kent through Christmas, maybe even to avoid me. But now she was back in the city? Did that mean she'd decided to cut me off completely?

Bob must have seen the worry flash across my face, because he quickly added, 'Don't panic – she went back with Alex.'

I sat up straighter. 'Wait. So… they're back together?' That didn't seem to marry up with what Alex was saying to me on the phone.

'Don't ask me, love. I know nothing,' Bob said, shaking his head cluelessly. Or at least, pretending to be clueless. He gave the distinct impression of a man trying to bury his head in the sand.

'Okay, okay,' Denise's voice got louder with each word. 'I'm done. Give it here.'

'I was talking to Evie!' Bob whined in mock protest.

'Away with you. That tea won't make itself.' Denise smiled as she came into view, her cheeks puffy and red from exertion. 'Hello, love.'

'Oh, so now I'm just a tea boy?' Bob grumbled.

'Yes,' Denise and I answered in unison.

She settled onto the sofa, eyes twinkling. 'So Alex and

Megan are *not* back together. But they are *together*, if you catch my drift.'

'Sort of.' That sounded more realistic. 'So are they talking again?'

'I'd hope so. He drove her back, so I imagine that would have been one long drive on the M20 if they weren't.'

I could already picture Megan sitting in the back seat with Alfie, her headphones on, listening to some TedTalk from a guru that didn't like to be described as a motivational speaker – but was exactly that.

'Well, so long as they're not arguing, I suppose.'

'He apologised for how he'd behaved,' Denise said, stretching with a yawn. 'I need a nap. She didn't apologise for how she'd behaved, though, but then she is stubborn. She gets that from her father.'

She said it as if it explained everything. As if stubbornness was some kind of cute family trait. But it wasn't cute. It was the thing that made Megan leave without a word and made me feel like an outsider for worrying.

A distant, muffled 'I heard that!' came from the kitchen.

Denise blinked and softened. 'Look, you know our Megan. She's a drama queen, bless her, and sometimes she needs a bit of parental TLC to reset. Now she's calmer, she and Alex can chat things through like adults and come to a decision. Whatever decision that is, mind, we'll support her no matter what. I think she's feeling a little neglected, but then so's he. So who knows!' She exhaled sharply as if bored with the conversation – which she probably was if Megan had been staying with her for a few days. 'Anyway, you're welcome to some TLC too, you know, whenever you want it.'

She meant it with warmth, but it landed oddly, like

being offered a jumper you didn't ask for. It didn't quite fit, and I wasn't sure it ever would.

I forced a smile, even as my face ached from the effort.

Denise studied me for a beat too long. 'How are you? How's Pim?'

'Pim's…' I trailed off, my mind still on Megan and Alex. I didn't really want to change the subject just yet, I wanted to know how Megan was, how the drive with Alex went and what's happened since she got back to Catford – without informing me she was back. Was she okay? Was it over between her and Alex? Did I need to set fire to his belongings? Or help her move out? A dozen questions fought for space in my head, making it hard to focus on Denise or notice the concern creeping into her expression. 'Erm, she's fine. It's been busy, though. *Really* busy.'

'You're worrying,' she said. Not a question – just a fact. There was a finality to the statement that felt close to the bone.

'Yeah.' I shrugged. 'I guess. This whole event is quite a big undertaking, and what with the new job and now this big Michael Holland blow-up…' I heard a guffaw in the background and Denise turned around and tutted.

'Honestly.' She slapped something off-screen, probably Bob's thigh.

'He had it coming. The tosser.' Bob continued to laugh.

'What have you got against Michael Holland?' I asked the body off-screen and suddenly Bob's face appeared at the corner of the screen, upside down, looking comically like a Minion from *Despicable Me* with only one eye visible.

'He said there was no difference between Manchester United and Man City on one of his old morning programmes. I'll never forgive him.'

'Christ, do you have to make every conversation about *football*!' Denise batted him out of frame, and he continued to chuckle to himself. 'I'm guessing the publicity fallout wasn't the most fun experience for you.'

I shook my head, but it wasn't worth going into detail over. 'Just tabloid fodder; I think we're over the worst. And it least the event sold out as a result.'

'No such thing as bad publicity,' Denise said warmly.

I cleared my throat. 'Actually, apart from checking in on Megan – which I guess I need to do by calling her, *if* she'll answer me—'

'I'll tell her to answer you,' Denise interrupted.

'We'll see.' I wasn't convinced her mum telling her to do anything was going to be enough to get Megan to answer my call in this situation. I'd have to figure out another way of getting to her. 'I was actually calling to ask a bit of a favour.'

'The answer's yes!' I heard Bob call from off-screen. Denise smirked at him.

'Well, I hope so,' I laughed. 'I spoke to Josh today.'

'How is he?' Denise asked.

'Does he still support Tottenham?' Bob shouted again. 'If so, I revoke my answer.'

'Oh, Bob!' Denise scolded. '*Really?*'

I tittered. 'I think he generally just supports whatever football, cricket, or rugby team his latest boyfriend supports.' I think the last team was Millwall, which was quite a comedown from Tottenham Hotspurs 'But, regardless, he's had a bit of a break-up.'

'Did he break up with that married man?' Denise asked, leaning me – or rather, the phone – against a stack of coasters on the coffee table so that she could return to her previous task of folding laundry that was evidently on the floor of her living room.

'So Megan filled you in?' I queried, to which she nodded. 'He knows it was wrong, and he's sorted it all out now—' I didn't bother adding that he had caught his boyfriend sleeping with his husband; that was a little too messy for my liking. 'We all make mistakes.'

'That we do,' she said. 'And if you're about to ask if he can come over for Christmas, the answer is and always will be yes.'

'Even though he and Megan had a bust-up. *And* he got with a married man and, y'know, *you're* married.'

Denise laughed abruptly. 'I doubt he'll be on the prowl for Bob, love.'

'Eww! No!' I cried as Denise chortled and Bob paraded into view doing his best *Kinky Boots* kind of walk that only made him look like a penguin. 'Oh, God, stop! Please. I beg you!'

'He's welcome to him,' Denise added, and Bob leaned down to give her the sloppiest of kisses he could muster.

One day I'd love a relationship like theirs, I thought, it's so much fun and silly, but there was also an implicit trust that felt wholesome and rare.

But I wasn't sure what that kind of love might look like for me. Not as a graysexual woman with limited experience and even less time.

It was not something I ever raised with Denise and Bob, though. Partly because they'd never quite understood my sexuality – or perhaps hadn't known how to – and partly because I hadn't known how to explain it myself. They'd nodded along, made all the right noises, but deep down I think they just thought I was picky or scared.

They didn't see that it was more than that, *or* that I was comfortable with my lack of interest until they made me feel otherwise.

But it was hard for them to know that, when I never raised it with them.

The truth was, I'd never felt entitled to take up that kind of space with them. They'd already given me so much when my mum died: a home, stability, love. I didn't want to add confusion or disappointment to the list, or risk being misunderstood when I was still working it out myself.

And without my mum, there had never been anyone it felt natural to talk it through with first.

Josh knew, in the loose, unexamined way LGBT+ friends sometimes do. Megan and I had tried to speak to about it, but she was so focused on her own explorations and her relationship with Alex, that I never let her examine it further. Brushing it off whenever she brought it up, making a joke and changing the subject. It was easier to be the low-maintenance one, and I preferred being the truth bearer, not the truth sharer.

It wasn't that I was picky or didn't want love – that couldn't be further from the truth. I *did* want it; I wanted what they had. But what if my love life looked and felt different?

I hoped it wouldn't.

'Look, Josh is always welcome here.' Denise's cheery planning pulled me from my introspection. 'Even when Megan's furious with him, he hasn't hurt her, he just made some erm…' She considered for a moment. '*Questionable* life choices. Besides, I don't think she is mad with Josh at all now.'

'Really?' I said, my eyebrows creasing in confusion. 'Then why isn't she replying to his messages? Or mine, for that matter?'

Denise continued to fold the laundry.

'I think she's a little embarrassed about how she behaved. And about how little she's shared. I'm her mother, I can tell when things are wrong with her – and with you.' I swallowed again but said nothing. 'She's not been entirely honest with anybody in this situation. *But…*' she stopped herself and threw some single socks across the room. 'It's not for me to talk about. I'm sure she'll call.'

'Really? By Christmas?'

Denise scoffed. 'Well, even if she doesn't, you'll certainly see her at Christmas. She's coming here with Alfie. And you'll be here with Josh.'

I didn't even want to picture what Christmas would look like if Megan still wasn't talking to us. Josh's prediction about flying roast potatoes may well come true. Although I suspected it was more likely Megan would be more underhand than that and would serve me more roast parsnips than potatoes, as she knows the true betrayal of biting into a parsnip thinking it's a potato. It's a soggy disappointment, unmatched by much else in life.

'Okay…' I said, elongating the vowels. 'But just to be clear, Josh is welcome?' I confirmed, and Denise nodded vigorously.

'He can sleep on the sofa. Unless he wants the air bed.'

'He can have my room,' I said, with a knowing smile. 'Save him complaining. I'll take the air mattress.'

Denise didn't even try to protest. 'So will no one *else* be joining?' she asked, with a hint of anticipation.

'No?' I pondered, surprised she would ask. 'Pim definitely won't be joining us.'

The idea of Pim, the woman who lived in the Savoy,

ate chef-cooked meals every evening and thought cocktails were acceptable as dessert choices, coming to eat burned turkey, sausage-meat stuffing, and bottled Buck's Fizz in Kent was laughable.

'I meant a young man.'

'What?' I grinned because usually the idea was laughable – and laughing was my go-to reaction whenever Denise or Bob mentioned my love life.

But maybe this year there *was*, or had been, a chance of bringing someone home.

Simon.

'I'm not bringing anyone else,' I said, with a tone of finality that I hoped Denise would catch.

She didn't say anything right away. Just gave me that look – soft around the edges, like she was trying not to push too hard. But there was something behind it too. A quiet hope perhaps. Or just parental worry.

'All right, love,' she said eventually. 'We always have room if there is anyone.'

'She means the air bed, not *your* room,' Bob shouted from the other room.

'*Bob!*' Denise and I both said, her sharply and me with embarrassment.

'There's no one,' I said again.

'Fine,' Denise said, nodding into the camera as she folded the last of what looked like tablecloths and tea towels. She held my gaze for a moment longer than before, as if checking something beneath the words.

'You know you don't have to wait until things make sense before you talk to me,' she added gently. 'You never have. Even if it's just to say you're tired, or there's something wrong and you don't know why yet.'

My throat tightened at that, the way she offered it without fuss or expectation. I nodded, grateful and a little undone by how mothering it was.

'I know,' I said quietly. She nodded again but said nothing further as she picked up the pile of tea towels and pushed them off-screen.

'How's the last few weeks of the job going? Aside from the Michael Holland thing?' she asked, changing the subject and her tone smoothly.

'Oh, fine,' I said, happy by the easy change of subject. 'Busy, but there's only a few more days and it will be done.'

'Have you managed to find your replacement?' Denise pressed, slight concern in her voice as she dropped the last of the folding and placed her hand on a hip to have a rest. She looked as if she'd earned it, still wearing a flush from over-exertion.

'I think so. Her name's Alison, she's great, but I'm having a hard time finding an opportunity for her and Pim to meet.'

'You'll manage it, just bring her in when Pim least expects it.'

'Like just before the show?' I asked and Denise frowned.

'Maybe not just then, she might not appreciate it at that moment, but the party after?'

'I'm going to try and introduce them to each other tomorrow, I think. Pim's got a lone afternoon tea so it seems like a good moment.'

Denise nodded supportively. 'You know best. Trust your instincts and you'll be fine. Not long until you can have a break and then start your new job.'

'Well, funny you should say that,' I muttered, rubbing

the bridge of my nose as I felt a pressure headache building, when I remembered I had still not opened the email attachments from Elijah at Salient Studios.

'They've sent you work, haven't they?' Bob stood next to Denise to chat.

'How did you know?' I asked, with a low attempt at laughter.

'I don't understand companies that do this, it's a blatant disregard of your contract.' Bob, a retired HR executive for an advertising agency, had strong opinions when it came to recruitment and team management. I could never tell him anything about my contract with Pim for fear he would travel across the world to collect me and bring me home. He was protective in that way. 'You know you're not obliged in any way to complete that work before your start date.'

'I know,' I said. 'But it's good form…'

'Don't give me *good form*, give me mental-health awareness and boundaries.' He lifted the phone from the table and walked me to the kitchen. Denise followed behind, protesting.

'What he means is that you shouldn't burn yourself out before you begin,' she said, translating her irate husband, who only had my best interests at heart, as Bob rested the phone against the microwave and moved over to the kitchen sink to wash some dishes. Denise placed her hands on her hips and grumbled. 'I was speaking to her in there – *anyway*.' She sighed and let his sudden move to the kitchen go. 'Christmas is a time for loved ones, and to have a break. You need to enjoy it, Evie.'

I did need to enjoy it and, more importantly, I *wanted* to enjoy it. But it hadn't been easy the past few weeks.

'That's what everyone keeps telling me, and I keep telling myself.'

'Then you know what you've got to do, you just need to stick to your guns and do it,' Denise insisted as Bob muttered 'yes' every few words in the background. 'You've got to remember that the first few months of a new job are always stressful, prepared or otherwise. Throw in a move across the world and it's doubly stressful. You need this time, Evelyn. You need to have a break.'

Ah, the first-name usage returns.

Denise tutted slightly. 'You need to learn how to switch off, you know. It's like you don't know how to relax unless someone gives you permission.'

'I'll have a break.'

'Promise me,' Denise replied, crossing her arms. Even Bob's head reappeared back on-screen, floating halfway up the side of my phone with a tea towel wrapped around his shoulder like a cape.

'I promise.'

'Good,' Denise said, patting Bob's back like it was a drum, for no other reason than that she could. It was typical Mum-and-Dad behaviour, but they weren't my mum and dad. They never adopted me, out of respect for my mum, who had loved me fiercely and deserved to keep her place in my life. I'd understood that, even at ten years old. What I hadn't reckoned, at the time that decision was made, was how it would leave me feeling untethered, as if I belonged everywhere and nowhere at the same time.

Growing up in foster care, even in a familial and loving home, I was always aware that eighteen wasn't so much a birthday as a line in the sand. I was on my own from then on, no matter how much love Denise and Bob may offer.

They weren't my mum and dad and legally they weren't able to offer much beyond an unfunded roof over my head.

That alone made me feel guilty, as if I offered nothing in return for their kindness. And fear that it would all be taken away. Just like it had been with Mum.

They were my guardians, my caregivers, and occasional life coaches. But in this moment over FaceTime, for the first time I recognised that they were simply two people that loved me.

I sniffled and adjusted my seat, feeling the familiar lump return. 'Why is it,' I began, chuckling lightly to reset my emotions, 'that just as I'm about to start this exciting new job, in this fantastic new country, that I suddenly find myself with opportunities in the city I'm about to leave behind?'

Denise laughed knowingly off-camera. 'This doesn't happen to involve the man that *doesn't* exist, does it?' Bob's head returned at the side of my phone before Denise's did.

I rolled my lips together. 'Maybe?'

'Bob,' Denise said, still grinning and patting his back. 'I *think* you should plan on blowing up that air bed.'

'Oh, I don't think we're there yet,' I said over Bob's rising voice about not enough room – there was always enough room.

'Why not?' Denise pressed, her grin widening as she closed in on the screen.

'Because I'm leaving in January,' I reminded her, as if saying it aloud could hammer the fact into my own brain as much as hers. It had been mere seconds since we had discussed it. Surely she couldn't think starting a relationship less than *two weeks* out from leaving for a permanent job on the other side of the world was the best idea? Even for a romantic – however practical – as Denise.

She pfted at me. 'Darling, it's Christmas. Have some fun.'

I swallowed, my heart tightening in my chest. Simon had told me – no, scolded me – for never putting myself first. For always choosing the practical option, the safer route, the one that didn't leave me open to getting hurt. And he wasn't wrong. I could still hear his voice, direct but earnest, cutting through my usual self-preservation: *It seems like you're maybe making decisions based on what's easiest, instead of what you actually want.*

I didn't want to leave London and regret it.

I didn't want to go to Canada and think of him.

I didn't want to change my life for a man who hadn't even asked me out.

And yet… he had kissed me. Kissed me so passionately, so perfectly, that I had felt it down to my toes. That had to mean something. Didn't it?

'I don't want to hurt anyone,' I said finally, my voice quieter.

'And is it serious enough that you could?' she asked, her tone changing subtly as Bob's head reappeared, but this time attached to his body. He wrapped his arm around Denise's waist.

The two of them on-screen were everything you saw when you thought of a happily married couple of thirty-odd years. Content, comfortable, and joyful. It was the perfect picture, which I had never realised I wanted or could picture for myself. Until now.

'It could,' I admitted. My heart did a double flutter inside me as I acknowledged it, not just to them but to myself. I'd never talked about my feelings like this before; it felt strange and slightly exposing. But it also felt safe.

Denise and Bob weren't leaning in or bracing for impact, they were just listening. They were treating it as something worth hearing rather than a problem to solve. 'Well, then…' Denise said, kissing Bob on the cheek and clamping his mouth shut with her hand. 'The air mattress will be ready, and we will be there for you no matter what.'

In one sentence, my whole future – the one I had so meticulously planned out and committed to – felt both completely untethered and yet, at the same time, more secure than ever.

Chapter 22

'THANK YOU SO MUCH,' I SAID to the waiter who brought a third chair to the table for my afternoon tea with Pim. Pim had yet to descend from her suite upstairs, mostly because she and her dog, Gerald, were catching up on the *Love is Blind* reunion and were not going to turn it off for anything, not even for me.

It was probably a good thing, since I still had to set up for Alison's arrival for our secret rendezvous and introduction. Alison was aware that Pim did not know about her being there, but she didn't seem flustered at all on the phone.

'If you think this is the best way, then I'll follow your lead,' she said, and I appreciated her so much in that moment that I didn't hesitate further.

This was the best, and only, way to get Pim to sit down and accept that I was leaving, and Alison was taking over.

For the third time I re-arranged the cutlery on the table, adjusting it just a millimetre this way and a millimetre that. Disrupting the perfection that the staff had already achieved hours before. My hands continued to fidget, itching for something to do to alleviate the anxiety of waiting. Eventually I gave in to it, reaching for my phone and opening my TikTok app to continue editing some drafts of short videos I had made, introducing my followers to the team at the Savoy and some of the staff backstage at the Southbank. I added some music from *Encanto* – the song about the grandkids' round-up – and began to adjust the clips to fit the timing. But still my anxiety continued to rise.

I was sure that something was going to go wrong. Pim was going to hate Alison or Alison was going to think this job was too much and I would have to spend Christmas hunting out yet another assistant, nowhere near capable. I couldn't start my new job having left Pim at a loss, even if it was due to her actions. I needed this Christmas miracle to pay off.

'Evie?' Alison's voice stood out for being unwavering, with no anxiety. I looked up and quickly replaced my phone face-down on the table.

Alison was dressed casually but smartly, with a chunky necklace that naturally drew the eye. Her smile was her second-biggest feature and immediately put me at ease.

'Alison! How are you?' I stood to greet her, enveloping her slightly unusually in a tight hug, grateful for her appearance.

'I'm good. How about you? How are you feeling?' she asked, releasing me but still holding my arms, her expression clearly showing that she had sensed my nervousness. 'Is Pim coming down?'

'Yeah, she'll be down soon,' I laughed, exhaling and pulling out her chair for her. 'She just wanted to finish something off.'

'Good, gives us a chance to catch up,' she said, sitting down with a comfortable sigh.

I wanted to get straight down to business, especially before Pim sat down.

'I'm assuming you've heard about the drama with Pim and Michael Holland?'

Alison sucked her teeth. 'I did see it. I was surprised the BBC ran an article about it, given they've hired the two stars.'

'No such thing as bad publicity,' I parroted Denise and Bob. 'It's done wonders for her sales.'

'And his documentaries?' Alison queried, but I shrugged. I didn't know, but I would assume the viewing figures would be up. He did seem to be appearing on my television a lot more than he had done weeks prior, but perhaps that was purely due to my sudden focus on him.

'It's been a bit of a week. But it's starting to die down.'

'Typical news churn,' she agreed. 'How is Pim with it all?'

'Delighted,' I said honestly. 'She got to say her piece and now she's famous again. It's been a real boost for her.'

Alison smiled. 'I'm relieved for you. That wouldn't have been easy to deal with had it gone another way, but I'm glad.' I smiled appreciatively, glad that she recognised my discomfort before she lifted her menu to peruse the many tea options available. 'What's good?'

'Oh, everything,' I said, taking my seat. 'I don't think I've had a bad meal here, and everyone's so lovely and caring. Though a tip every now and then does help.'

'I bet!' Alison said with a light chuckle. 'I'm guilty, or rather not guilty but very happy, to offer tips to grease the skids to get a job done.'

'It certainly helps to cut corners every now and then, especially when clients aren't known for their patience.'

'And staff need a bit of…' She paused and chewed her lip. 'How to put this politely… a bit of compensation?'

I began to laugh – she got it.

'All things we can discuss together, but not with our clients,' I said, a light-hearted warning in my tone, though she was definitely accurate.

'Oh, of course,' she agreed, tapping my wrist lightly. 'I would never.'

We both took a moment to review the menu, my eyes glazed over the flavours I preferred for the ones Pim would usually request, unable to switch off from putting her needs first. Though this meeting was partly for me, a chance to turn off my Pim mode and focus on myself and my wants.

My phone buzzed on the table, an email alert flashing.

'Excuse me,' I said, putting down the menu and reviewing the message.

It was from Elijah.

'Hey, Evelyn,' it began. *'I just wanted to check if you received the treatments we sent over for the new shows. Any feedback or ideas? Eager to hear your thoughts. E.'*

Well, that was a chase if ever I read one. And on 22 December!

I put my phone face-down on the table without replying.

Leaning on my elbows, I decided to focus on Alison.

'How are things with you? Have you finished your notice period?'

She nodded happily. 'Yes, last week. I can't believe I get a break this Christmas, that's the first in a while.'

'I'm glad. I'll be honest, you won't get much of a break with Pim next Christmas.'

She shrugged. 'It's not all it's made out to be. It's nice to do something different as, for the last however many years, I've just been stuck in the same office over the festive period and getting Christmas and Boxing Day off to spend with my partner's siblings and their family. My family are all spread out. If I get to spend Christmas in Nepal one year and then Christmas in Sydney the next, it will be brilliant. I just want something different.'

I smiled. 'It certainly is that. We don't realise how pigeonholed we are in the UK, we forget how amazing Christmases can be in different cultures, and sometimes not even Christmas, just winter.'

Alison grinned, her eyes glazing over with imaginings about her future. A future I used to find so exciting but now find draining.

'Be sure to find time for you, though. Have a break and enjoy what each location has to offer. Pim's pretty good at allocating time for me, I mean you, to experience the culture. It gives her a chance to enjoy herself with friends or just on her own.'

'She doesn't want you to live in her pocket.'

'Maybe on occasion, but mostly she wants you to get her from A to B without her needing to think about any of it.'

Alison nodded, taking it all in.

It felt stranger than I'd expected, talking through the role – my life – like this. My stomach felt knotted but as if it were unravelling, even if it was a little painful. I didn't realise how much of my life was reading the room and staying one step ahead at all times until I was passing the baton and sitting still for the first time in years.

I wasn't walking away from something important; I was choosing to stop and reflect. It was nostalgic to realise how much I was the person who others relied on before they even knew it. But that pressure was gone.

It was Alison's turn to hold the baton now.

She reached for her bag and pulled out a brand-new

notebook and stylish fountain pen. She waved it between her fingers.

'A leaving gift,' she sniggered. 'You'd think after twelve years they would have monogrammed it. But I think that would mean remembering how to spell my surname.'

I tutted on her behalf. 'I doubt I'll get anything as fine from Pim,' I said, but Alison shook her head.

'Yes, you will. I'll probably be buying it.' She winked.

Suddenly, from behind us, I heard the yapping of a familiar dog and the clicking of two high heels on the black-and-white marble floors.

'Would you mind?' Pim's voice rang out grandly, not for the sake of the person she was talking to but so everyone else in the Savoy restaurant heard her coming. 'He prefers bottled water. Thank you.'

'Here she comes,' I muttered to Alison as I rose from my seat, butterflies fluttering in my stomach as I moved to head Pim off before she spotted Alison and me together. Alison didn't even shuffle in her seat, she was so calm and confident. I fed off her energy.

'Pim!' I waved my arm so that she spotted me and began to walk towards me. 'We have someone joining us today.'

Pim frowned. 'Who? I didn't ask you to invite anyone?'

'Her name is Alison, and she's interviewing to be your new assistant.'

Pim froze as she reached me, less than five metres from the table. She said nothing. I could see her tongue working its way across her teeth in consideration while she stared me hard in the eyes with her own owl-like gaze.

'Alison?' she repeated quietly. Tasting each syllable.

'Alison.'

Another pause.

Without warning, she clicked her cheeks and sighed, walking around me to the table, and speaking a hundred miles an hour as she did so.

'Do they have that jasmine tea I ordered last time? I would like that again, but not in that cup they used before. It was too close to a mug. No, I'd like a teacup and saucer, preferably china. And no biscuits, too many crumbs. They get in my pleats and then Gerald sniffs them out and it's most unbecoming to have a dog sniffing around your lady garden. So unrefined. You're Alison?' Pim sat down without extending a hand and Alison nodded politely.

'Lovely to meet you, Pim.'

'So,' Pim began, putting her small clutch, which only contained her phone and a single tissue, heavily on the table. 'Evie tells me you're going to be my new assistant.'

'If you think I'm a suitable match.' Yes, Alison! She knew exactly how to pander to Pim, reminding her it's *her* decision, not mine. I retook my seat, my heart still pounding heavily in my chest.

Pim made a hmm sound and picked up her menu.

'Have you seen many of my films?' she asked.

'I recently caught *Wuthering Heights* on the BBC. They were playing it ahead of your show.'

Pim pursed her lips. 'And what did you think?'

'You made a powerful Heathcliff.' Alison carried on confidently, placing down her menu and leaning interestedly on her elbows. 'An inspired choice of casting, especially given the times.'

Pim nodded, still not looking up from her menu, though her eyes remained focused on one spot, so she clearly wasn't browsing through it.

'It was. The director was initially quite insulting, saying

I cut a boyish figure, but I showed him. Having masculine and feminine energy is no bad thing; in fact, it helps to get things done.' She dropped her menu and lifted her hand in the air to gain the attention of a waiter who had previously served us and knew to be ready to fly to Pim the moment she walked in the door.

'I'd like the jasmine tea and a scone. No fruit. And you?' She turned to Alison, completely ignoring me. So far so good.

'Any recommendations?' Alison asked Pim, who rolled her eyes, so Alison requested an Earl Grey. 'And would it be possible to have all three drinks served in china teacups? With saucers?' she added for good measure.

I smiled, but covered my mouth to hide it, before finishing with my order. 'I'll have a decaf coffee,' I said to the waiter, who nodded and walked away.

'It's an afternoon *tea*, dear,' Pim pointed out, never once acknowledging Alison's memory.

'I have a lot to do this afternoon,' I replied.

'Though you ordered decaf?' Alison said.

'And then I need to sleep,' I finished with a light laugh. 'Tomorrow's going to be even busier. We have a packed schedule ahead of the show.'

'I'm very much looking forward to it,' Alison said, as the waiter returned at lightning speed with our requested drinks.

'Oh, you're coming, are you?' Pim asked Alison, but looked at me as if I had planned it.

'I bought tickets,' Alison explained. 'After meeting with Evie a few weeks ago.'

'I could have got you complimentary ones,' I began but Pim flicked her hand.

'Get her to come backstage,' Pim suggested, trying to appear blasé. 'You might as well get the full experience. Have you ever seen an "in conversation" live? Or a theatre show come to that?'

'I've attended the opera and the ballet, but I will admit that theatre was never my favourite,' Alison said, never once slipping into being sheepish as she stirred her Earl Grey. I poured out Pim's jasmine tea, filling the cup to the brim as per her preference, before nudging over the saucer to the edge of the table. Alison's eyes were keen and watching everything. I saw her make a quick shorthand note in her notebook as Pim sipped the boiling tea.

'I'm surprised you would want this job,' Pim began shortly after. 'Not having been to the theatre. Never seeing a production of mine until recently.'

Here we go. The first of probably many nit-picking complaints of Pim's against Alison.

'I thought it better to hire a person who would perform the role of your PA without pandering to your…' I stopped myself short of saying 'ego'. 'Past successes. We all know – you especially – that you're a wonderful actress, Pim, but that doesn't mean the production value is always of the highest quality. Alison here can ensure that level of quality.'

Alison beamed at me. Pim took another sip of tea.

'What are your credentials?'

'I've been in personal administration for over twelve years, across multiple firms dealing with high-end, white-collar clients across the media and advertising sectors.' Alison was fluent in speaking 'impressive'.

Pim still refused to even look at Alison as she stared ahead at a lovely display of winter roses. 'Any firms I'd be aware of?'

'Plenty. I worked for a CEO of a media agency that handled VOD advertising and worked very closely with a recent client of yours to produce the trailers of your latest show.'

Pim said nothing. 'And you handled their diaries, travel arrangements, and finances?' I added instead.

'Anything that they needed me to handle,' Alison finished expertly, sipping her Earl Grey calmly as I held my breath.

'Hmm,' Pim said, finally looking away from the display. 'Where is my scone?'

'Alison is very qualified and very discreet,' I said, glancing at Alison, who nodded. 'Not to mention, a fast learner.'

'I like to think so.' Alison laughed.

Pim said nothing but tapped her ring-adorned finger against the handle of her teacup. For one moment she looked at me, holding my gaze for a few seconds before sighing with defeat.

Placing down her teacup, she turned to face Alison.

'I'm thinking of spending January in New Mexico. What do you think about that?'

Alison took a second to pull back her grin. 'Which airline would you like to fly? I'll book a first-class ticket for you and economy for me.'

With urgency Pim shook her head and placed her hand warmly over Alison's.

'No dear, two first-class flights.'

Knowingly, I looked to Alison to see the confusion and slight excitement appear.

Wait for it, I thought.

'I need a seat for Gerald,' Pim finished.

Chapter 23

THE HOTEL WAS QUIET, SAVE FOR the low hum of the TV and the occasional crinkle of wrapping paper, as I folded and taped the last of my Christmas presents.

For once everything felt... still. My to-do list was getting shorter – Pim had met and liked Alison, which meant I could mentally tick that off. Josh and I were speaking again. Actually, *speaking* was an understatement, he wouldn't stop sending me photos of outfits for Christmas Day, asking for my opinion on everything from ties to socks, like we were suddenly the kind of siblings who coordinated wardrobes.

It was nice, though.

I glanced at my phone, absently tapping the screen. My TikTok was still going strong – over *120,000 views* now. A little montage of my time in London, set to a soft, nostalgic track. Shots of the Thames at sunset, the Christmas lights on Regent Street, steaming cups of coffee in tiny cafés, the ice rink at Somerset House...

The ice rink. Simon's and my hands linked as we skated – or fell, in his case – his cheeks flushed from the cold as mine flushed with more.

The kiss.

'Only You' scoring the moment I would never have even dreamed of; it was too perfect.

The mere memory made my chest ache with wordless longing as the feelings washed over me – the cold air, the soft glow of the rink lights, the way his hands had settled at my waist, sure and steady. The way he had kissed me like he *meant* it. Like he *felt* something.

I should have stayed. I should have said *something*, rather than bristle and run when he said something I didn't want to hear. But instead, I had run, because that's what I did. Because I was scared. Because I didn't know how to want something and not immediately talk myself out of it.

I glanced at the time. After 21.00. Too late to go to Covent Garden. The busking would be over. And we'd never exchanged numbers – he had pointed it out himself, half amused, half exasperated.

And now I regretted it.

I *missed* him. That's why I had returned to the rink, only once after, to find the magic again – and hoping to run into him and reclaim that perfect evening, to correct its ending – but he wasn't there. And the magic wasn't the same without him. Though viewers had commented about how dazzling it looked, how they wanted to visit, how they could *feel* the love I had for this city. Maybe more than the city?

And I did. I really did. I set my phone aside and picked up the next gift to distract myself. Megan's gift. A beautiful leather journal, embossed with her initials. Josh was getting a ridiculous cookbook I'd found in a second-hand shop, called *Meals Men Can't Mess Up* – he'd either laugh or be deeply offended. Possibly both. For Pim, a thick, cable-knit scarf in a deep forest green. She always complained about the cold but refused to wear anything practical. Denise and Bob were getting a beautiful, framed print of a London street at Christmas, the kind that felt warm and nostalgic, like a memory you weren't sure was yours.

I placed the last gift in the pile, stretching my legs out in front of me as I turned my attention back to the documentary playing in the background. Michael Holland was standing on a wind-battered cliff, hair messy from the sea breeze, speaking passionately about the history of smugglers along the Cornish coast.

He was good. Really good. Even if he came across as a bit of a dick sometimes.

There was a sharpness to him, a slight arrogance in the way he spoke. But he knew how to hold an audience, how to make you care. And he *cared*, that much was obvious. His enthusiasm bled through the screen, making history feel alive, instead of something buried in textbooks.

Curious, I picked up my phone again, fingers idly typing his name into Google.

Michael Holland.

It was there, in one of the first articles. His wife had died of cancer in her early fifties. I frowned, scrolling further. He had a son. No name, no details, just a passing mention.

I sat back, chewing my lip.

It was strange the way we only ever saw fragments of people's lives. On-screen, he was confident, opinionated, larger than life. Off-screen, he was a man who had lost his wife too young, he was a father raising a son. It made him more human, I supposed.

I dropped my phone onto the bed sheets, my thoughts drifting somewhere else entirely. But almost immediately, my phone buzzed.

I picked it up, expecting another outfit update from

Josh. Instead, it was another email from Elijah, chasing me for a reply.

I stared at it for a moment before locking my phone and tossing it onto the coffee table.

It could wait.

Everything could wait.

For now, I just wanted to close my eyes and pretend I was still on the ice, with Simon's hands on my waist and the world slowing down around us.

Tomorrow, I'd figure everything else out.

Chapter 24

As expected, the day of Pim's event was hectic.

Pim had been in a near-constant state of a nervous breakdown since the moment I arrived. The grand suite, which had once felt spacious, now seemed impossibly small – crammed with stylists, make-up artists, assistants, and various hangers-on, who all seemed to be talking over each other.

'What if I forget everything I prepared?' she kept asking, pacing about the room barefoot on the plush carpet, as the stylists tried desperately to get her to stand still long enough to finish her contour or zip up her gown.

We were still a few hours away from the show, but with the travel and time it took to get Pim ready, it was better to get her initial make-up and dressing done now before she got to the theatre.

'You've got all your notes and Emily won't let you slip.' Emily was currently sitting in her own suite going over talking points with her publicist, like a true pro. She was calm, professional, and, unlike Pim, not currently causing a make-up artist to silently beg the heavens for patience. 'Both of you have rehearsed this to the nines. It'll be great.'

'It's just muscle memory,' a stylist said, somewhat desperately, as she held onto Pim by a zip, trying not to let it slip so that Pim was left standing in only her knickers and nipple covers.

'I'm too old for this sort of dress,' Pim said suddenly, batting at the stylist, so that I had to step in.

'You look amazing,' I said, standing in front of her so she had nowhere to go, and the stylist could finally zip her up and stand straight again. We all heard her back crack under the strain. 'Just like a star.'

'Not like a Met Gala freakazoid?' she said. 'I don't want to look like I'm attending Heidi Klum's Halloween party.'

'You look like you're going to Elton John's Oscar after-party,' I countered, gently pulling up the sleeveless gown at the sides so that it hugged in all the right places.

She looked amazing, and not just 'for her age', as the press would no doubt say, but just in general. Her reflection in the full-length mirror was a study in elegance: navy silk clung to her curves, silver embroidery along the seams catching the morning light, making her look almost ethereal. But Pim wasn't seeing that.

'I look like Delia Smith.'

'More like Nigella, if we're going down the chef comparisons.'

'So long as it's not Jamie Oliver, I suppose it will do,' Pim said, somewhat dejected, as she slumped back into her make-up chair and allowed the make-up artist to finish off her contouring as the stylist quickly whipped over a cape to protect the dress.

Taking a rare moment to myself, I stepped back, leaning against the cool marble wall, listening to the room as it hummed on; steam rising from a curling iron, the quiet snip of scissors, as someone made final adjustments to a hem, the spray of perfume and calls to 'blot' as Pim's lipstick was applied.

A manicurist, waiting for her turn with Pim, joined me.

'What are we going to do without you?' she said kindly. 'We wouldn't even get a quarter of the way through the prep work if not for you.'

I smiled. 'Oh, Alison will do a great job.'

'Maybe *eventually*, but I don't envy her the first few weeks.'

I crossed my arms, getting comfortable. 'It's something you pick up quickly, when you're thrown in at the deep end. You either sink or swim.'

The manicurist hummed knowingly. 'I doubt Pim was throwing many lifelines your way?'

I released a quiet laugh. 'She's not too bad when it's just day-to-day. It's only at events like these when she's a bit tougher to handle. The trick is to be prepared for *anything*.'

As if summoned by my words, Pim suddenly cried out, 'Evie!' She was lifting her arm to wave me over, even though I was barely a cushion's throw away.

'I'm here,' I said, appearing automatically at her side.

'Is my bag packed?'

'For the show?' I asked. She nodded, irritated that I had to ask. 'Yes. I've got your clutch for the stage, so you'll have everything you need with you.'

'What's in it?'

'A tissue, a breath strip, a soluble paracetamol, a nail file, all your notecards.'

'Right, right,' she said, clearly straining through her memory in case I missed anything. 'And for after the show?'

'Your larger clutch with room for your lipstick, extra tissues, hand sanitiser, chewing gum, standard paracetamol, blister plasters, foldable flats, a jade roller, and a small can of espresso martini.'

'Right, right,' she repeated, this time shutting her eyes and rubbing the space between them. Her make-up artist barely suppressed a groan as she undid twenty minutes of work with that one thoughtless gesture.

Then, to my surprise, Pim reached for my hand.

The room, sensing the shift in mood, instinctively scattered. Assistants busied themselves elsewhere, the manicurist pretended to be absorbed in her polish selection, and the stylists found clothes bags that suddenly needed attention.

'You'll be backstage?' Pim asked quietly.

Her grip on my hand was firmer than I had expected, but I noticed the slight tremor, and squeezed it gently.

'Of course,' I replied.

She exhaled sharply, staring out of the window. 'I feel like something is going to go wrong.' Her voice was softer now, almost vulnerable, wound with nerves that were unlike any I'd seen Pim experience before. Usually she'd be over-energetic, practically bouncing, unable to sit still. But she was quiet and whispering, as if she didn't want her nerves to know she was nervous. She only wanted me to know.

'Nothing is going to go wrong,' I said, desperately trying to reassure her as I stroked her knuckles with my thumb. This wasn't about tripping up on stage or missing a cue, it was about wanting it to matter. *She* wanted to matter again. And I wanted her to know that she did matter, especially to me. And that made me really want to make her smile. 'The only thing that *can* go wrong is if I don't get you to the theatre on time.'

Pim's lips quivered in an almost smile.

'That's still your job, for now, I suppose.'

I paused, still stroking her hand as I felt the tremors subside. I moved to stand in front of Pim's chair.

'I'm very pleased to do it,' I told her sincerely. 'You know, my leaving is not because I was unhappy, Pim.'

She rolled her eyes. 'You know every employee who leaves says that but never means it.'

Screw it, I thought. What have I got to lose in this moment.

'You drive me crazy,' I told her. 'You're incredibly bossy, entitled, sometimes irritatingly particular – but you never made me unhappy.'

I did my best to ignore the widening eyes and shocked glances from the make-up artists and manicurist as I continued.

'I do wish I could get more sleep and didn't have to clean up your dog's poop or sneak in snacks to night shoots because production won't allow assistants to eat at craft services. I sometimes get annoyed at ordering three things from a menu for you to try, only to eat cold takeaway for my dinner. And I'd be lying if I said it didn't bug me that after a long-haul flight, you get whisked straight into a taxi while I'm left waiting for the luggage and cramming it all onto a bus.'

I let out a sarcastic laugh at the memory.

'But… I love that you include me on set and ask for my opinion when no one else even acknowledges me. I love your runaway commentary of TV shows and having afternoon tea and dinners with you all over the world. I love that you have a wicked sense of humour and an adventurous streak – and that you always drag me along for the ride.'

I paused, feeling a warmth spread through me as I realised just how much these past years had meant.

'Most of all, I'm grateful for all the opportunities you've given me over the last eight years.'

By the time I finished, I realised I was beaming – lost in the memories, in all the chaos, the frustrations, and the unexpected joy.

'It's time for me to move on and settle down,' I said finally. 'But I've never been unhappy.'

There was a gaping pause as I stood up, straightening my back, still smiling at Pim, who seemed frozen in one spot. 'You're going to do great tonight,' I added, trying to bring her back round to herself.

She started to nod minutely, and then more actively.

'Yes, I am,' she said, looking around briefly. 'Am I *ever* going to get my nails done, though?'

And just like that, the make-up artist, stylist, and manicurist flew back into action.

I wasn't surprised that she hadn't verbalised a response, or even so much as acknowledged my monologue of thanks. That was hardly the Pim way. But, as the room filled with movement again, I found myself feeling a euphoric release. I had said my piece, and somehow it seemed to have settled her, and me at the same time.

She now knew how I felt, even if she didn't mark the moment in words. She didn't need to.

The relief came quickly, settling physically somewhere near my diaphragm, as I watched her refocus on the task at hand. Whatever happened next, I could release any guilt I held for leaving my job – as it was a job – but in the knowledge that Pim could be my friend as well.

Even though I knew she'd never say it aloud. Or text me. Ever.

I'd know that deep down she cared that *I* cared, and that was more than enough.

Straightening as the feeling in my chest deepened, I said, 'I've got a few errands to run' to the team, though no one was really paying me that much attention now. 'But I'll see you at the venue.'

'Are you not coming with us?' a stylist asked suddenly, slightly out of desperation.

'I won't fit in the car,' I pointed out, since all three of them would likely travel with Pim to the venue for final touches. 'I'll see you there.'

'Don't forget to drop off my bags!' Pim cried from her chair, my little outburst about my time with her already forgotten.

'One of my errands!' I called back, gathering the large travel bag I had already packed for the venue. The other errands were of a more personal nature.

Chapter 25

THE STAFF AT THE THEATRE WERE all in a tizzy when I arrived, and I had to put out a few fires about not enough programmes being printed, confirming which guests would need the red-carpet arrivals, and ensuring the box seat attendees each had their complimentary Pimm's upon entry.

I left all Pim's belongings in her dressing room, removed all the drooping red roses and loose leaves from the bouquets sent with well-wishes from admirers and friends, and then checked my watch. I had three hours until the show began. Just enough time to get ready and sort out one pressing issue.

Exiting Covent Garden Tube station on Christmas Eve was tantamount to completing a second obstacle course. I ducked under and jumped over gift bags, nursing several bruises on my elbows and legs from the remaining bags I missed. It was the retail version of a game of Sardines until I reached St Paul's Church.

I looked around the buskers, who seemed to have multiplied, given the day, but I couldn't see Simon anywhere. He wasn't skulking by the Christmas tree, enjoying a show, nor in the church, people watching.

Glancing at my watch and realising I needed to hurry, I found an off-duty busker packing up his knife-throwing props.

'Hey! Excuse me!' I said, approaching him. He looked up, his bobble hat jingling. 'Great hat.'

'Thanks,' he said, giving his head an extra vigorous shake for effect.

'Do you know Simon?'

'Oh, aye,' he said with a strong Scottish brogue.

'Is he performing today?'

The busker looked suspicious. 'How d'y'know Simon?'

I opened my mouth to reply but didn't have a ready-made answer, so stuttered for a moment as the busker's eyes narrowed.

'I'm… uh… I'm – we ran the Pudding Race together!' Given that Ethan, Simon's other busker friend, had built a crowd around the race to specifically watch Simon in full Grinch mode run while carrying a Christmas pudding, I made an educated guess that another busker who also knew Simon would be well aware of the anecdote. 'I was dressed as Jovie, he was the Grinch.'

He immediately started to laugh, and my body relaxed slightly.

'Ah, you're the lass that persuaded him to give up his dignity.'

'And he did me proud – but do you know where he is? I really need to speak to him.'

The busker shook his head. 'Not today, love,' he smiled, still laughing. 'He never performs on Christmas Eve.'

'Oh? Really?'

The busker's bobble-hatted head jingled jauntily. 'No,

it's the anniversary of his mum's passing. He must have told you.' He clearly assumed I knew more about Simon than I actually did. 'He works on Christmas Day, but not today. I think it's the only day he takes off *all* Christmas. Glutton for punishment, our Simon.'

'His mum?'

The busker nodded. 'Aye, love.'

A chill that had nothing to do with the December air settled over me. I knew Simon had lost his mum, but I had never realised how close to Christmas it had been. He'd never said as much. And now, suddenly, it made sense why he threw himself into busking for charity in December and only December, why he worked relentlessly through the season, barely stopping to breathe.

Christmas wasn't just Christmas for him. It was the time of year his world had changed forever.

Now it all felt glaringly obvious.

Throwing himself into the noise and chaos as if trying to drown something out. The way he had brushed off conversations about Christmas traditions with a joke or a change of subject.

The way, just last week, when we had been in Covent Garden watching the carols, he had turned to me and said, *'You love Christmas, don't you?'* in a voice that had been both wistful and something else, something I hadn't recognised at the time.

Grief.

I swallowed hard, my mouth dry. 'Right.'

The busker must have noticed something shift in my expression because his voice softened. 'He'll be at the graveyard. Don't know which one, mind. But he told me once that it's the one day he and his dad get together to lay flowers on the grave. A kind of Christmas ceasefire.'

I shook out my shoulders, trying to get the feeling to return to them. *So that was it.* I had seen the strain on Simon's face whenever he mentioned his father in passing, a quiet resentment, usually followed by a brief but sharp-edged silence.

'Yeah,' I murmured, my thoughts spinning. 'He said they didn't get on.'

The busker scoffed. 'No one seems to get on with Michael Holland, though, do they?'

He returned to packing up his bag, unaware he had just dropped a weight in my stomach; I suddenly felt as if I had just missed the bottom step and was about to fall flat on my face.

My pulse drummed in my ears. 'Wait! *Michael Holland*?'

'Yeah, the documentary guy. I was surprised too when Simon mentioned it.'

'Michael Holland is his dad?'

The busker nodded, though I didn't see it, I just heard it.

'Nothing like Christmas to reunite family, aye,' he said, zipping up the last of his goods, unaware I'd stopped listening.

Michael Holland was Simon's *dad*?

The arse of a man who had ripped into that poor runner for bringing him the wrong shirt. The pretentious, sneering man who Pim Hardcastle had torn to shreds in the viral video for something he wrote twenty-odd years ago.

How was *he* Simon's father?

I thought back to when I had first met Simon in Covent Garden, busking with that easy smile and his blue guitar, doing crowd work between songs with ease and charm. A man who wrote jingles for a living. Who gave every spare coin he earned from music to charity – well, mostly. Who was *good*.

How had *this man* come from *that man*?

Holland was a common enough name. It had never occurred to me that Simon, with his easy laugh and warm brown eyes, could be related to a man who seemed incapable of joy.

But Michael Holland had a son. I had read it online. A wife who had died of cancer several years prior. And one son.

And Simon had said he'd been raised by a dad who worked in media and cut him off. *That* sounded like Michael Holland.

I felt light-headed.

'You all right, love?' the busker asked. Apparently, he'd just asked me a question, and I had missed it.

'Oh sorry,' I said. 'Away with the fairies.'

He chuckled. 'Happens to the best of us.'

I nodded, but my thoughts were already elsewhere.

Michael Holland. Simon's dad.

I had so many questions.

'I was just saying Simon'll be back on Boxing Day. He's doing an early show for the bargain-hunters – he'd normally have a break between Christmas and New Year, but I heard he gave up his New Year slot for some reason. But you probably know more about that than me.'

He winked and I flushed, because I *did* know the reason. But it wasn't the reason he was thinking. Mostly.

'I've got to get to Kent this evening,' I said after a moment, thinking about how I had promised Denise and Bob, and I needed to get Josh down there too. And make up things with

Megan, if she was even talking to me, that was. I reached into my pocket hurriedly. 'Do you have his number?'

The busker shook his head, this time disappointed. 'I don't.'

I growled. 'What about Ethan? Is he here?'

'Ethan'll be round later. He's on not long after me this afternoon.'

My stomach did a somersault of nerves as I prayed this would work. 'Could you give this to Ethan and tell him to give it to Simon?' I asked, feeling like this was the most ridiculous plan I'd ever come up with, as I handed over a receipt from one of Pim's Starbucks runs. I'd scribbled my number on the back. Sure, I couldn't expense it any more, but who knew when Simon would be performing again after Christmas? And who knew if I'd even catch him before I had to jet off to Canada. I only had a few days between Christmas and New Year, and I was intending on spending the majority with Megan, Denise, and Bob, and even with Pim post-show craziness.

But I wanted to see him. And this mad plan might be my only chance to let him know.

Why had we not exchanged numbers before! God, I felt like an idiot.

There had been something thrilling about the mystery between us, but now it just felt dumb.

'Sure, I can ask Ethan later,' the busker said. 'If I see him. We might miss each other, but I'll try.'

'If you can, I'd be *really* grateful,' I said, starting to back away and thinking that I needed to get ready soon, otherwise I was going to be late for the show. 'Just tell Ethan that Evie was here and *really* needs to get a message to Simon.'

'Aye,' the busker repeated, a little shell-shocked by how serious I was, swinging his bag over his shoulder. 'Evie was here and needs to get a message to Simon,' he repeated.

'Thank you!' I shouted, turning on the spot and running as quickly as I could through the crowds. 'And merry Christmas!'

Chapter 26

'I'M LATE! I'M LATE!' I CRIED, running through the entrance to the theatre. Flurries of ticket holders were pushing through, heading to the merch stand for a programme and a commemorative pin badge, and to the bar for their complimentary Pimm's.

I ducked and weaved through the chaos, muttering apologies as I reached the side entrance and flashed my ID to the usher. He barely glanced at it before waving me through to backstage.

Josh was waiting backstage, looking effortlessly sharp in a dark emerald suit, an ID pass hanging from his neck. He was standing stiffly, radiating the energy of someone who very much did not belong.

'I'm so sorry!' I gasped, clutching my side as I came to a halt. 'I'm late.'

'Evie!' he breathed, throwing his arms open. 'Jeez, I thought you were going to miss it.'

I checked my phone, still fifteen minutes until curtain up.

'Have you seen Pim?' I asked, still panting.

Josh shook his head. 'No. She's guarded like the crown jewels. Though I think I met your replacement. Alison?'

'Replacement sounds so harsh,' I said, shoving my clutch

and jacket into his hands so that I could finally reveal my outfit.

We had to be dressed befitting the red carpet so that, when we escorted Pim out of the venue and on to the after-party, we were properly attired. I had gone for a burgundy, waterfall capped sleeves, ballerina-length dress with a simple silver chain and my hair loose across one shoulder. It had taken me longer than I thought to get ready, and then I couldn't get an Uber to save my life. I had to run across to Charing Cross to join the taxi rank, looking like a harried wedding guest.

Josh took my accessories without protest and gave me an approving once-over. 'You look stunning.'

I poked my cheeks. 'My face doesn't match my dress, does it?'

'Not at all.' Josh smiled warmly. 'I'm very proud to call you my date for the evening.'

I scoffed but then sighed with relief. Josh would tell me if I looked like a beast, he was never one to hold back about appearances. If a hair was out of place, he'd be moving it, framing me in his mind's eye until perfect.

'He's right. You really do look stunning,' said a small voice from behind me, and I noticed that Josh had started to turn the colour of my dress.

I turned around, pulse stuttering. It was Megan.

She was also sporting a backstage pass; one that I had had sent to her weeks ago when she and I were still talking. She was standing, slightly tear-stained but upright and confident in a light blue two-piece.

'Hey,' I said, suddenly breathless for an entirely different reason.

'Hi,' she said.

'I didn't think you'd come.'

'I wanted to support you.' She looked from me to Josh. 'And to see you both. I didn't think you'd come to my place if I called.'

'We would have,' Josh said, a little harsher than he probably intended. Then, grimacing, he sighed. 'I was a complete cun—'

'Josh!' Megan and I cried in unison.

'What?' he asked, genuinely baffled. But it broke the tension, and Megan and I started laughing.

'Not in the workplace,' Megan teased, waving a hand at the pristine backstage corridor.

'Well, I was… one of *those*,' Josh said. 'I was so mind-blowingly self-centred I thought the word apt.'

Megan let out a small breath of laughter, but there was something tentative about it, something hesitant. She shifted on her feet, tucking a strand of hair behind her ear.

'I was selfish too,' she admitted, her voice quieter now. 'I should have reached out sooner. I should have—' She stopped, shaking her head. 'I should have been a better friend. To both of you.'

Josh, who had been bracing for an argument, blinked in surprise.

'It's been a hell of a few weeks,' she went on, swallowing hard and trying to laugh through it, but she was struggling. 'And I know I've been… absent. I just…' She exhaled sharply and looked me in the eye. 'I'm really sorry, Evie.'

The sincerity in her voice hit me like a gust of wind, catching me off guard.

For two weeks, I'd gone over and over what I'd say to her when we finally spoke. I'd imagined angry words, sharp retorts, long explanations. But now, standing in front of her, I realised none of that mattered any more.

'I missed you.'

Her face crumpled. 'I missed you too.'

And just like that, the dam broke.

I closed the distance between us and wrapped my arms around her. Megan clung to me just as tightly and for a long moment we stood there, the noise of the theatre around us fading into nothing.

When we pulled apart, she gave me a wobbly smile. 'I should have told you everything from the start. About Alex, about how things were, even before Alfie. I wasn't honest with you – or with myself.'

I tilted my head, waiting.

'We were broken before we even became parents. But when I found out I was pregnant, and…' She trailed off, looking away for a moment. 'We tried. We really *tried*. But we gave up on each other. We stopped being a couple a long time ago, and I… I don't want to try any more. I should have just been honest with him. And you.'

I nodded, processing her words. Allowing her to let it all out without interruption.

'We're separated now,' she continued. 'We're co-parenting, and it's… well, it's not perfect, but it's peaceful – or it *will* be peaceful.' She hesitated, but I said nothing as I got the sense she was talking to herself more than me anyway. 'I trust him. And I do love him. Just not in the same way.' Her voice cracked at the edges, something inside her finally giving way. 'Not in the way I did when we were first married. We're just friends – I hope.'

I reached for her, rubbing her shoulders gently. 'That's all Alfie needs.'

Megan nodded but her lips wobbled as she tried desperately to maintain her composure.

'Two parents who love him, even if they're not together.'

Megan gave me a small, grateful smile. 'Yeah.'

Josh let out a loud exhale, throwing his hands up. 'God, it is so *refreshing* when people act like adults about break-ups. I feel like I should record this conversation and play it for half my exes.'

Megan chuckled, appreciating his age-old levity.

'Well, I can't take full credit,' Megan began. 'I had a minor breakdown and hired a life coach.'

'It's been, what, a fortnight?' I pointed out, unsure whether to laugh at her efficiency or be jealous of it.

'Don't be impressed, I think I've been paying him to have someone to talk to about *The Traitors* more than my own issues.'

Josh gasped. '*UK* or *US* version?'

'Both.'

'You are *forgiven*.'

We all laughed, and for the first time in weeks, things felt normal.

But Josh began fidgeting with the edges of his sleeve. Then cleared his throat, louder than necessary.

'Well, since we're all being honest… I ended it with Zach.'

There was no dramatic pause, just a flat statement dropped like a stone in the middle of our reunion.

He had to say it. Of course he did. Josh couldn't resist turning a heartfelt moment into an overshare. It didn't stop my insides from cringing.

'Josh… You remember how this went last time you brought this up.'

Megan shook her head. 'It's okay, it's okay.' She didn't ask for details, just took his hand. 'I'm sorry.'

Josh blinked down at their hands as if he didn't quite believe they were real.

'I really am too. For being such a—'

'Josh!' Megan and I repeated, instantly silencing him.

For a moment, we all stood there in silence, letting the weight of everything settle and slide right off.

'God, I've been so *me-me-me*,' Megan said, releasing my hand to wipe under her eyes.

I went to immediately say 'It's okay' but Simon's words at the ice rink repeated over and over again in my brain; I didn't need to say it was okay or make her feel better in this moment. It was okay to be frustrated with my friends, and for them to be frustrated with me.

But Josh didn't have Simon in his life.

'Yeah, something was going around,' he said, repeating the ever-often-repeated winter-flu phrase.

'I hope I didn't catch it,' I said, and both shook their heads.

'Out of all of us, I think you were the least self-centred, and typically this was the year that you had licence to be,' Megan joked.

'Thanks?'

'I only meant that this Christmas we had planned to make it all about you, and instead we made it all about us.' She pointed between Josh and her.

'This Christmas hasn't gone to plan…' I paused, inhaling slowly. 'I'm going to be honest, I had really wanted to spend it with my friends, and instead I found myself slightly, as ever, on my own, dealing with other people's shit and putting everyone else first.' Both Josh and Megan said nothing but began chewing their lips nervously, glancing between each other again like siblings caught stealing sweets. 'I don't want to fight,' I added quickly, trying to placate their nerves and dull the undercurrent of frustration still inside me. 'Today is going to go well – it *has* to — but I don't want Christmas to be full of tensions and arguments. I just want to enjoy it.'

'And we're going to.' Megan nodded, squeezing my hand warmly. 'I *promise*. No more drama. No more fighting.'

'I swear on my Gucci handbag.' Josh lifted his bag theatrically and Megan slapped her own hand atop his and then I placed my own.

Josh, never one to handle deep emotions for too long, studied me for a moment and then straightened abruptly. 'Well, ladies, as much as I'd *love* to dive deeper into the rich tapestry of our collective trauma, I've just spotted a rather exquisite specimen of a man loitering by the lighting rig, and I feel morally obliged to introduce myself.'

Megan rolled her eyes. 'You are *so* predictable.'

'I take that as a compliment,' he said, smoothing down his emerald suit and adjusting his posture as if he was about to strut down a catwalk. He turned to me. 'Are you going to be okay?'

'I'll be fine.'

Josh studied me for a moment longer, then nodded. 'Good. Now, if you'll excuse me, I have to go and see if that man has a boyfriend, or if he just looks that smug naturally.'

'If he has a boyfriend, what are you…'

'Too soon.' He winked and disappeared down the corridor, leaving Megan and me alone in the relative quiet of backstage.

For a moment, neither of us spoke. The sounds of last-minute stage preparations buzzed around us, the crackle of radios, the distant hum of the orchestra warming up, the nervous energy in the air. I checked my watch. I had exactly eight minutes before I needed to be back in Pim's dressing room.

'I meant what I said earlier,' Megan said suddenly, pulling me from my thoughts. 'About you.'

I sighed. 'Megan—'

'No, just listen,' she interrupted, stepping closer. 'I know you're in work mode, and I get it, you don't have time to think about anything else because you have to get Pim on stage and then deal with whatever comes next. But when do you actually stop? When do you actually sit down and ask yourself what *you* want?'

I looked away.

'Evie… I did the same thing,' she continued, her voice calmer now. 'I buried myself in work when things with Alex started falling apart. It was easier to be busy than to deal with what was actually happening. Easier to say I was too stressed, too occupied to face reality. And I kept telling myself I was doing it for us, for Alfie, for our future, until one day, I woke up and realised I didn't even recognise my own life any more. Or want it, for that matter.'

She took a breath.

'And you know what? The second I stopped running from it, the second I actually looked at what mattered, when I was at Mum and Dad's, it was the easiest decision in the world. I knew I needed to make a change. Work was always going to be there, but my life? My relationships? They were slipping away.'

Her words hit me somewhere deep in my chest, but I tried to shake them off. 'It's not the same thing.'

'Isn't it?' she countered. 'You're running too. Maybe not from a failing marriage, but from something. You keep throwing yourself into work, into other people's problems, into Pim's world, because it's easier than stopping and figuring out what *you* want.'

I swallowed.

'And I don't think you want this job in Canada,' she added gently.

I flinched. 'Of course I do,' I said too quickly, the words tumbling out in a perfected routine. 'It's a great opportunity.' Everything inside me dropped as I considered the *opportunity* and failed to translate what that even meant to me any more.

'Is it?' She tilted her head. 'Or is it just another thing that keeps you moving so you don't have to think about your life? About everything you want? About your mum?'

I couldn't argue with her, not really. Not when the truth was already burning in my chest. I didn't want the job. I hadn't told anyone that – I had barely admitted it to myself – but the moment she said it, I felt the weight of it settle on me like one of Pim's heavy faux-fur coats.

'Evie, I love you,' she said, reaching for my hand. 'And I know you. You need to stop. You need to take a breath and choose what comes next, instead of just letting it happen to you.'

I squeezed her hand, hard. My throat ached, too full to speak. She was right, and I hated how right she was. I didn't want the new job. I was just running away again.

'Five minutes, this is your five-minute call,' a voice sounded over the Tannoy.

'Oh, shit!' I exclaimed, releasing Megan extra-gently. 'I have to get to Pim,' I said.

Megan nodded, but she didn't let go of my hand just yet.

'Just… think about it, okay?' she said. 'Really think about it.'

I gave her a small, shaky smile.

'Go, go!' Megan said, shuffling me away with all my things as we wiped our tears and widened our smiles.

'You've got this!' she called. 'We'll be cheering from the seats.'

At the sound of the three-minute call, I began to panic. After all the promises I made to Pim, I was going to miss her entrance. Oh, fuck!

Chapter 27

'I'M HERE!' I SHOUTED, BOUNDING INTO the dressing room. Only one hair stylist remained, tying up the cord of a pair of straighteners, a look of pure terror on her face. Gosh, what had Pim said to her?

Releasing the door, I ran for the stage entrance, dropping all my things on a random chair and lifting my skirt to move as fast as possible.

The overture was ending. Emily Heston was walking on to do her short introduction and to invite Pim on stage.

I could see the wings and Pim's bouffant hair just ahead of me. I was nearly there.

'Welcome, Pim Hardcastle!'

Oh, hell! I missed it.

Pim went on stage with a rapturous applause just as I reached the black-winged entrance. She was practically gliding, elegantly holding her navy dress up slightly at the slit so that she didn't slip, and the guests all got an eyeful of her 1940s pin-up legs.

She waved with the other hand; her clutch already on stage at a table just behind her seat so the audience couldn't see. At least the stage manager had sorted that for me.

'Welcome, Pim! What an entrance!' Emily was saying as

Pim took her seat, crossing her legs and once again giving the audience an eyeful. Wolf-whistles and cheers continued as Emily opened the show with an explanation of why we were all there, to celebrate Pim and her shattering performance as the first female Heathcliff.

'She looks amazing,' a voice said from behind me.

'Alison!' I exclaimed opening my arms, and giving her a quick hug.

She was zipping up a small bag of cosmetics as we whispered.

'We got her on in the end,' she muttered knowingly, with a smile.

'You helped her?'

'I got your text about running late,' she said, showing me Pim's phone and my many messages updating her on my progress. Clearly Pim hadn't been paying any attention to her phone while I was panicking trying to get to her. 'I thought I'd step in and help out a little earlier.'

The relief was like someone had pumped me full of morphine. Every inch of my body relaxed.

'Oh, thank you!' I said, so heartily a stage assistant had to ssh me. 'Thank you!' I whispered again. She shrugged as if it was nothing, but it wasn't nothing. 'You're not even on the payroll yet,' I pointed out, guiltily.

She shrugged again. 'It was useful to see her at her worst,' she said, and my mind's eye exploded with fears about what Pim had been up to and what she had said, my mind returning to the terrified-looking stylist in the dressing room.

'Was she awful?' I asked, placing a hand on Alison's hand apologetically. She shook her head.

'She was scared,' she said. 'Stage fright.'

I nodded. 'She has it quite badly,' I muttered. 'I thought we had done the prep work for her to have a handle on it this time, though.'

Alison smiled at me. 'You did. Yes, she snapped and cursed every now and then, but really, she knew exactly where she needed to be, who with and when. Even with me there to fetch and carry, you really set the groundwork for this event to run like clockwork.'

It was Alison's time to pat me on the shoulder. I grabbed her hand and squeezed. It really meant a lot to see the event come together, especially after so much work and effort. The phone calls to the venues, caterers, and the staff, getting all the timings down to a T, the lighting perfect, the staging immaculate. Everything to Pim's exacting standards, so there was nothing for her to blame in order to cut and run. It had all come together, and now I could just enjoy it.

'What a brilliant story!' Emily said as Pim finished an anecdote about each of her co-stars, whom she no longer spoke to because of said anecdote. Pim's laugh chimed across the stage, and you could hear a pin drop from the audience – they were so mesmerised by her.

'So, tell us, Pim, you were never meant to be an actress, were you?'

'Oh no, Emily, not at all.' She laughed again. 'I was the daughter of a working-class couple from Lincoln. My mother was a seamstress for a tiny local theatre and my father worked as an electrician. After school, I would sit with my mother in the dressing rooms of these little-known actresses, the vaudevillians of the day, and listen to them run lines and do vocal warm-ups. You know, and all the rest. And I grew to mimic them.'

Emily grinned. 'So you were a mimic from a young age. Seems like you were always destined for storytelling. Speaking of stories, you've had quite the week, haven't you? Your name has been all over TikTok.'

A ripple of anticipation moved through the audience. Pim arched a delicate brow. 'Oh, Emily, you make it sound as though I've taken up viral dancing.'

Emily tittered. 'Not quite, but your, shall we say, spirited discussion with Michael Holland certainly had its moments.'

Pim tilted her head, exuding effortless composure. 'Ah, yes. Well, you know how it is, Emily. A harmless conversation morphed into a news moment. I simply suggested that not everything needs to be narrated in a voice that sounds as if it's trying to summon a ghost.'

Laughter rolled through the audience.

Pim continued, smoothing an imaginary crease in her dress, 'But Michael Holland is just one of the many men who I've butted heads with, however innocently, in this industry. One of the first men…' She began another anecdote, moving on from the moment with ease and professionalism.

'One night, when I was about thirteen or so, I finally plucked up the courage to ask the stage manager, Mr Flowers his name was, if I could sit and watch the show from the wings. He said yes, so long as I didn't move and didn't get in anyone's way. And that evening I fell in love.' The timbre of Pim's voice changed, softening to a low hum as she took us all back to that moment of her childhood.

'I begged my mother to allow me the chance to audition for the theatre company, for any role, I didn't care. Bit-parts, ensemble, non-speaking roles, I just wanted to be on the stage. And eventually, after a year or so, my mother allowed it. But, as you all might be able to guess – though I did get the bit-parts and the ensemble, non-speaking roles – I didn't stick to those roles. On the night I'd improvise, I'd add a flourish here or a delayed gasp there. On occasion I'd find a way to add in a line or throw in a speaking part, just to draw the audience's eyes to me. Oh, I got into so much trouble with the cast and crew.'

Everyone laughed at her mischievous grin.

'When I was sixteen and performing at another theatre, as my mother's local wouldn't have me any more for all my rule-breaking, a casting agent finally saw me and did the one thing I always hoped one would. They offered me representation.'

She paused for a moment and corrected her posture. Emily didn't interrupt or add in any vocal cues. This was Pim's show and Pim's moment to shine.

'I ran away,' she said eventually, to a slight gasp of the audience. 'My family would never have allowed me to move so far away to work, so I made the decision and did it myself. I ran away to London like a modern-day Dick Whittington to audition for a company, and I made it. I got a job with a radio company, performing as a voice actress in all the childish roles. I had a much lighter voice then, you see, before all the cigarettes of the late twentieth century ruined it for me.'

The audience laughed.

'I had that job and a few other parts for a few years before I started to make the transition to film and TV. I had a proper agent by then and I started meeting just about anyone that would allow me in the room, and even some that wouldn't allow me.' She paused and scratched her nose, looking out to the wings for just half a glance and I smiled at her, as encouragingly as I could. She looked away.

'You know, Emily,' she began, 'this industry is a hard one, back then and now, and the difficulties haven't increased or decreased. They've just remained the same – hard. And the solution for getting through it is the same as well. You need help,' she said simply. 'I've had a lot of help throughout my career. Those vaudevillians who let me watch their warm-ups, that first stage manager, Mr Flowers, the casting agent, the radio company, the many actors and actresses I met along the way.' She paused for a moment and smiled widely. 'To even now, my darling assistant, Evie, who gets me from pillar to post.'

Alison's grip around my hand tightened and I felt the tears from earlier returning.

'I love working with Evie,' Pim said with a laugh, surprising me so much I think I forgot to breathe. 'She never lets her inner saboteur get a speaking role in her life, and she tells me exactly how it is, even when I'm being a right pain in the behind,' Pim joked, and the audience laughed too, allowing me a chance to release a sob of shock and gratefulness from inside me. 'I never got a chance to say thank you to many of the people that helped me,' Pim continued. 'But I can say thank you to Evie. So…' She turned to the wings and nodded in my direction. 'Thank you, Evie.'

A round of applause began from the audience, started no doubt by Megan and Josh, and soon the whole auditorium was clapping as well, alongside Emily and Pim, who joined in. Alison released my hand for a moment to clap, and I couldn't do anything but stand there and sob, grinning from ear to ear, my heartbeat thumping in my ears to the beat of the applause.

It only lasted a few seconds, but it was probably the best moment of my life.

Alison wrapped her arm around my shoulder, and I tried desperately to pull myself together.

'Right, now back to me,' Pim said wickedly, before quickly laughing and adding with dramatic flair, 'I'm just kidding,' so that the audience knew to laugh with her.

Chapter 28

THE HOURS AFTER THE SHOW WERE a blur of prosecco, Pimm's, and clinking of glasses. Pim was a rip-roaring success, with so much praise and calls for her time that I barely got a few minutes with her before Josh and Megan bundled me into a taxi to Megan's flat to meet Bob, who had arrived earlier to babysit Alfie, and who had volunteered to drive us all down to Kent after the event.

It was Christmas Eve, after all; there were no trains running this late.

'First pay the car tax,' Bob demanded, when we arrived, opening his arms as Josh attempted to fit his suitcase of just Christmas jumpers into Bob's twenty-year-old Mazda.

'That's not going to fit,' Megan insisted, watching on with disinterest as she strapped Alfie into his car seat.

'How are you? How'd the event go?' Bob asked, never once letting me actually answer before he asked the next question. 'Do you want the heating on? I've just installed a CD player. Do you want me to put on Band Aid?'

It was a bit of a squeeze in the back, with Alfie in the baby seat and Josh and me pressed together like sardines – of course Megan had bagged the front seat – but we made it to Kent eventually, with only a few bruises from speed bumps and one tiny kerb crawl.

'Your mum will be asleep,' Bob said, taking one look at the mess of suitcases and squashed overnight bags in his boot before heading inside without offering to help. 'She's getting up at five to baste the turkey.'

'What time's lunch?' Josh asked.

'Two,' Megan and I said in unison, and the first ounce of Christmas Eve excitement began to glow in my midriff.

Christmas Eve could be the most magical day of the year, I decided. Christmas Day's wonderful – or so I'd heard – but the possibility you feel on Christmas Eve is overwhelming. Especially when surrounded by loved ones.

'I'm going to bed as well,' I told Josh and Megan, who looked surprised that I didn't want to stay up for yet another toast to my successful event with Pim. But I wanted to get tucked up in the Christmas pyjamas I knew Denise would have laid out on my bed, with a hot water bottle and a stupidly sugary hot chocolate from Bob, knowing that the presents would be pulled from the garage by Denise at 6.00 a.m. – after she basted the turkey – and would be arranged under the tree by Bob before we rose the following morning.

Despite years of feeling an unspoken sense of anxiety around Christmas, around being the foster daughter in a happy family, who should always strive to be a good girl and not an inconvenience, I realised that I was *never* made to feel that way. I kept those feelings alive, while Denise and Bob only ever kept the traditions. Traditions *I* was and, still was, a part of.

I knew why that still felt complicated, and letting myself enjoy it felt a bit like tempting fate, or betraying a younger version of myself who was trying to keep her mother's memory alive. But loving Denise and Bob would never take that away, it never had. Because, however old we got, the traditions of a family Christmas lived on, because they *were* my family. I just had to let go of *how* they became my family, and trust that they were.

They'd never let me down yet. And I doubted they ever would.

Especially as I reached for my laid-out pyjamas, thinking about what was waiting for all of us the next day.

I didn't want to rush through it or keep myself at arm's length any more. I wanted Christmas to come as quickly as possible. Not because I was afraid it might disappear, but because I finally felt ready to be part of it.

'Merry Christmas!' Denise, Bob, Megan, Josh, and I chorused around the dinner table the following day.

As expected, the anticipation had been worth it. Christmas morning was perfect, and then some.

Josh had woken Megan and me up at 6.00 a.m. by landing on my air mattress and practically launching me into Megan's bed, as he declared it was Christmas like he was a member of Wizzard – but with much better hair.

He had been infectiously jolly all morning, cracking jokes and making us all ache with laughter as we hugged and kissed, wishing all the tidings of the season like a picture-perfect postcard. I noticed Josh's jokes increased when we were opening presents. Megan had become subdued as she helped Alfie open presents from her and Alex, every one of them labelled with 'Love from Mum & Dad'.

'Have him open mine,' Josh said, handing Megan a packet of wrapping paper, which bemused us all greatly.

'Uhh, Josh?' I didn't even need to ask before he went off into an explanation.

'Everyone knows that a child of Alfie's age doesn't give two hoots about Christmas presents, they just love the wrapping. So that's what I got him.'

The fact that it was Harrods wrapping, perfectly packaged in cellophane, and not just regular ripped-up wrapping, was lost on Josh. But we had all eaten our words when later Alfie was screaming in delight, rolling and ripping up the expensive paper.

'You may now call me Uncle G.O.A.T.'

'Huh?' Bob looked confused.

'Uncle Greatest. Of. All. Time.' Josh grinned.

Now we all wore ill-fitting Christmas crowns in a multitude of colours. Mine was yellow, while Megan and Josh both sported pink ones. Alfie's child-form-fitting blue crown matched his Chelsea-themed Christmas jumper – which Bob ignored with little grace – while Denise had had trouble getting her crown over her light-up Christmas antlers. Bob's crown slipped off his bald head with no hair to statically attach it to, but he kept replacing it without fail.

'Cheers, my dears!' Denise said jovially, reaching across the table as the tumble for the gravy boats and sauces began.

'Who has the horseradish spoon?'

'Don't pass the salt! It's bad luck.'

'Don't scrimp on the gravy, there's more in the kitchen.'

And then the food swap and eyeing up took over.

'Don't you touch my Yorkshire!'

'Josh has one more roast potato than me.'

'No, he doesn't. You each have four big ones.'

'I always forget how much I like roast parsnips.'

'Do you want mine?'

'Swap you a stuffing ball?'

It wasn't long before the food was devoured: a rogue stuffing ball, splashes of gravy on the Christmas-themed table cover, and six very full people lolling back in their chairs, the only sign that it had happened in the first place.

'I can't eat another morsel,' Megan said, placing down her glass of fizz and rubbing her belly with satisfaction, as we all groaned in agreement.

I stayed standing, checking my phone which kept buzzing. At first, I thought it was Christmas well wishes, but glancing down I saw notifications from Elijah.

Groaning, I put my phone back in my pocket.

'We do have some homemade trifle, if anyone wants it,' Bob said after a beat, leaning back in his chair, bouncing Alfie on his lap. 'My speciality.' There was a momentary stillness, broken only by Alfie's gurgling ah-ah-ah, as Bob bounced him even more.

'I suppose a spoonful wouldn't hurt?' Denise said, already standing and grabbing her pudding spoon.

'Somebody go with her before she eats the whole thing,' Bob suggested, looking to me as the person closest to the door. I stood with an unbecoming groan, pausing only to come back for my own spoon playfully.

I found Denise, as Bob predicted, shovelling a mouthful of trifle straight from the decorative serving bowl into her mouth.

'Save some for me.' I helped myself, scooping up a white chocolate Malteser from the cream for good measure.

'Why does trifle always taste better at Christmas?' Denise asked, reaching for the waiting pudding bowls and proper serving spoon resting on the counter.

'It's the sherry, it's special Christmas sherry.'

'That must be it.' She handed me the first bowl so that she could scoop up the gooey trifle with one hand and protect the serving bowl with the other. 'So, are you excited for the new job?' She never once looked up from serving. 'How's the boss? Still emailing you?'

'You caught that?' I said, my voice dropping so the others wouldn't hear in the dining room. Not that they could from the way they were all chortling with laughter as the sound of Alfie ripping up Josh's wrapping paper continued in the background.

'Of course,' Denise said, stopping scooping for just a moment. 'Hard to miss the constant *dinging.* What does he want, today of all days?'

'Wishing me a merry Christmas,' I said, and with a sigh I admitted, 'And asking if I'm ready to start my new role.'

Denise sucked at her teeth. 'Has the move got you worried?'

I shrugged. 'It's not the move exactly, it's everything that goes with that.'

'The travel? The stress? The unpacking?' she suggested.

I shook my head. 'Not being here again.'

'Aha.' Denise smiled softly, putting down the spoon and taking the last bowl of trifle from my hand before positioning both of her hands on my shoulder. 'I know that what I'm about to say is going to come across all protective and mum-like, and you have my permission to completely disregard me as a silly old fart, but...' She smiled as I laughed at her jolliness – helped in part by the Christmas sherry she had no doubt been sampling earlier. 'If you don't want to go to Toronto, my darling, don't go.'

'I have a contract.'

'With a probation period?' she asked.

I thought for a moment. There was a probation period of one month.

'That's usually just a chance for them to get rid of me if they don't think I'm up to snuff.' I began to laugh. 'Do you think I should sabotage my work?'

'Oh no,' she said seriously, releasing my arms. 'That'd give you a bad reputation. No, I meant that it's just as much a probationary period for you as it is for them. You can leave without notice in that period, right?'

'I mean, probably?' I said, shrugging and picking up two of the bowls to return to the dining room and the suddenly ravenous guests. Megan was shouting, 'Where's my trifle!' despite only complaining about her fullness five minutes before.

'Double check and find out,' Denise suggested with a wink.

'I'll be without a job though,' I pointed out and she pfted.

'So? You'll find another one. In England,' she clarified. 'And until then, you can come and stay here rent-free.'

'I couldn't do that?' I protested.

'Why not? You're family.'

'Denise,' I began stiffly, and she tutted again.

'You're just as much as my little girl as Megan is, Evelyn,' she said, suddenly serious. 'To me and Bob, both.'

I didn't know what to do with that. Not because I didn't want it, but because part of me had spent years quietly believing it would be asking too much.

And here she was saying it so plainly, with no hesitation or conditions attached.

'I know I didn't give birth to you,' she said gently, as if reading my thoughts – like a mother does, 'and your mum will always be your mum. Nothing changes that.' She paused, taking a breath, I recognised was to steady her emotions which – like mine – were swimming with love. 'I want you to remember that loving you didn't come with an expiry date.'

A lump hardened in my throat, but surprisingly it wasn't painful. It was forming to stop me from making an excuse or trying to change the subject.

I needed to hear this, and Denise needed to share it. Because loving me *had* been plain to see, but I had been blind to it while I figured out who I was without a biological mother. Too afraid to lose someone that ever meant that much to me again.

'I've been your mum for a long time now,' Denise added, sniffing loudly as she carried on with her business, as if not wanting to overwhelm me. 'I'm not planning on stopping.'

I didn't trust myself to speak, not yet, so I nodded instead. Hovering by her as the intensity of her love washed over me. Reminding me that it had been there all along.

'Besides,' she laughed, 'Bob and I'd like the company again – me especially. All this football and snooker and cricket, the TV is *always* on sports. I need a conversation every now and then.' She was waffling now, but I crept up behind her and swung my arms around her waist warmly, as she patted my head and chuckled with relief.

'Thank you,' I whispered, kissing her cheek.

Denise turned and enveloped me in a full body hug. 'Oh, you always gave the best hugs.'

We laughed together, safe in each other's arms, as I felt the full feeling of being home.

She would never be Mum, but she'd always be Denise. And that meant the world to me.

But when Denise is on a roll, she doesn't stop.

'Just because this is the first job offer, that doesn't mean it will be the last,' she continued, releasing me but only enough so that she could push my hair behind my ears. 'Far from it. I bet you could speak to Pim about it. I know you're hanging up your boots with her, but surely she must have some contacts in the UK?'

I had never wanted to ask Pim. It felt too presumptuous a question, even before I handed in my notice, but especially now, given how I had handed in my notice a few weeks ago. But maybe I was judging her relevance a little too harshly, perhaps she would know somebody that could help me get a job in the UK? I just needed to ask and find out. What had I got to lose?

My stomach did an excitable somersault at the thought, not the kind it had been doing every time someone mentioned my new job in Toronto but a somersault that felt like freedom.

If I could stay in the UK, I could be near my family – even live with them again – helping Megan with Alfie and through her split, which I could tell she was dreading dealing with, no matter how brave a face she put on it.

I could see my favourite city all year round, not just at Christmas. I could really have a home, maybe even more than one: my home and my parents' home.

And then there was Simon.

He was someone I'd love to get to know properly and not in the whirlwind romance sense. Someone to laugh with, argue with, kiss with – under Christmas lights *and* summer bunting. Someone who knew how to call me out and still stick around to see if I'll ever change, and someone who would help me to if I asked him.

He didn't have to be a footnote in my *new start*, he could be part of the new start. If he wanted to be.

And my desire for that was as intoxicating as the Christmas sherry. 'Now,' Denise said suddenly, swiftly taking the two bowls of trifle from my hands and heading back to the dining room. 'Come on. It's Christmas. No more shop talk!' She entered the dining room with a dramatic bow. 'Trifle à la Bob!' she declared as she entered, and I took the brief reprieve away from my family to wipe the happy tears from my eyes.

I didn't need reminding how much my family loved me but, boy, when they did, did it make me an emotional wreck.

I sniffed and cleared my throat, before grabbing two more bowls and heading to the dining room.

'*The King's Speech* is at 3.00 p.m.,' Bob reminded everyone.

'Then we have to fight over what to watch,' Megan said. There was a lot of shouting of titles of TV shows and movies that seem to play perennially on Christmas Day.

'Whatever happened to good ol' Morecambe and Wise?' Bob lamented as he stood to enter the kitchen to get the final two bowls.

'I think they died,' Josh replied, and we all sighed.

'Cheery, Josh.'

'You don't say?'

We laughed and tucked into our desserts, all of us surreptitiously reaching to release a button on our trousers as we did so.

Chapter 29

CHRISTMAS SEEMED TO PASS IN A flash, true to the adage that time flies when you're having fun.

Christmas pudding was served as an episode of *Doctor Who* was dissected with many arguments over who was the best Doctor. I will forever be Team Tennant, but Josh and Bob were vocal fans of Tom Baker and Denise was a rogue Paul McGann fan.

'He's barely in it!'

'They did him dirty!'

I turned off my phone after the sixth email alert from Elijah. Denise was right, it could wait. I wanted to enjoy this Christmas and, boy, did I.

By the time we went to bed, all of us were waddling we were so full of food.

'I apologise in advance for what *may* occur this evening,' Megan had told me on the way up to her bedroom. She was yawning and burping simultaneously. 'I had about sixteen Brussels sprouts.'

Oh, dear God!

'Maybe I'll sleep in my old room tonight,' I told her, already dragging the air mattress from the floor of her old bedroom. 'With Josh.'

'Yay! Sleepover.' Josh clapped, and then whimpered, 'I feel like a beached whale.'

The springs of my old bed rang out as he fell onto it.

Entering my teenage bedroom was a flashback, but not a particularly detailed one.

It was hardly 'my' room at all. I never put my stamp on it, despite Denise and Bob always encouraging me to. Unlike Megan's room, which still held the evidence of multiple boy band posters, edgy floor rugs and doodles across her bedroom furniture, my room was neat and tidy with nothing on the walls except for some basic artwork Denise helped me to choose at IKEA when she took me shopping to 'find my style'. What ten-year-old has the style of 'Farmhouse' or 'Kitsch Kitchen'?

I never allowed myself to find my style, I was too concerned about behaving and not upsetting the flow of the family just because I had become part of it. Now I regretted it.

I refused to be sad about the past on Christmas Day, though, not after the wonderful day we'd had. Besides, next on the calendar was New Year's Eve, and that was a time for looking forward.

'I'll see you in the morning,' I told Josh, but he was already snoring. I forgot how loudly he snored, but was reminded at 3.00, and 4.00… and 5.00 a.m., until finally, at 6.00 a.m., I gave up and reached for my phone, turning it on for the first time since the previous day.

As predicted, a flurry of emails from Elijah buzzed on my screen, which I promptly swiped away, and then there was one text alert:

'Hey, it's Simon.'

Underneath there was another text.

'Simon Holland. The busker.'

'I got your number from Doug – he's the one who throws knives.'

'It's his job. He's a busker who throws knives. Not just a regular guy who throws knives.'

'Not that there are many of those – not regular guys at least.'

'Anyway… it's Simon Holland and I wanted to give you my number and say merry Christmas.'

A grin so large erupted on my face that for a moment I wondered if it would rip my lips. I knew I was back in my teenage room, but the giggle that escaped me was downright girlish! I was five seconds away from hugging my phone to my chest.

Checking the time, I realised I could leave him a text and say a belated merry Christmas, it wasn't *too* early.

So I did.

'Hey, it's Evie Frost. Merry Christmas to you too. I hope you had a good one.'

As soon as I pressed 'Send', a lump the size of a piece of coal landed in my stomach as I remembered about his mum, and his dislike of the Christmas season as a result of her loss.

But all fear of upsetting him was removed when my phone suddenly began to ring. Out loud. I had knocked it off 'Silent' when I was texting.

'EVIE!' Josh was vicious when he was woken up, as I knew all too well. 'What are you doing to me?'

'Sorry, sorry. It's Simon.'

'Simon who?'

'The busker.'

I've never seen Josh sit up so quickly; I was worried for his vascular health.

'Answer it!' he said, his voice steady while my hands were shaking.

'It's 6.00 a.m.'

'So? Answer it.'

'Josh, I—'

'Evie Frost, answer the goddam phone.'

'O-okay.' I pressed 'Accept'.

'Hello?'

'Hey, I didn't wake you, did I?' Simon sounded as panicked as I felt. 'I did, didn't I? Was that text from yesterday? Did it just send?'

'No, no!' Josh was bouncing up and down on my bed so loudly the springs were at risk of breaking – or waking the whole house up. I rushed to my feet and ran outside, shutting the door and clamping it shut so he couldn't escape. 'I just sent it, I'm at my… erm, my parents' house.' It felt nice to say, but also strange. 'I didn't know if I would hear from you.'

'Doug gave me your number,' he said. 'The knife-thrower.'

'Thanks, Doug.' I rubbed my eyes, feeling the flakes of mascara I'd failed to take off the night before coming off against my knuckles.

Josh was rattling my bedroom door but I retained an iron grip on the handle.

'Are you okay?' Simon asked, amusement or concern in his voice.

'Yes, sorry.' I cleared my throat so that I sounded a tiny bit more human. 'I'm trying not to wake anyone.'

'Oh, yes. I sort of saw your text and called. I didn't even look at the time.'

'You were just up at 6.00 a.m. on Boxing Day?'

'Well, I volunteered at the shelter last night.'

I laughed. 'You are after a sainthood, aren't you?'

His smile resonated through my ear – and I know it's a physical thing that can't do that, but it did! I could see it, I felt it, and it was wonderful.

'How was your Christmas?'

'It was amazing,' I admitted. 'Though my head aches a bit this morning.'

'Ah,' Simon replied knowingly. 'How's the hangover?'

'It's… it's there.' It felt like the back of my eyes were burning. 'Nothing a shower won't sort, though.'

'Fingers crossed.' He paused. 'So Ethan told me that you came by on Christmas Eve.'

'Yeah, I did.' Josh had managed to open the door a crack.

'Evie Frost, open—'

I slammed it shut again. 'I was trying to catch you before I left for Christmas.'

'Ethan mentioned you spoke to Doug; I got your number off him, but Ethan said you talked.'

I laughed. 'Yeah, it's a long story, but I was looking for you and I found Doug and he told me you were visiting your mum – your mum's grave, I mean. Sorry.'

'It's okay,' he laughed awkwardly. 'I was.'

'How was your dad?' I asked stupidly but then, with a surge of sass, I added, 'I've met your father by the way.'

'You have?' His voice practically rose an octave.

'You didn't say he was a broadcaster.' I tried to keep my tone light. 'I meet them all the time.'

'Uh-huh, I can only apologise.' We both chuckled. 'Did he interview your boss?' His voice had a touch of confusion.

'Oh, God, no!' I exclaimed, maybe a little too eagerly.

'We had more of a run-in... a few run-ins, in fact. One of which went viral.'

'Viral?'

I was unsure how to phrase it without it sounding like some ridiculous reality-show drama. 'Yes... my boss and he have, erm, *history*. And it was caught on camera and went viral. It was all over the news.'

'I don't have social media,' he reminded me.

'But... no news alerts?' I asked, still in disbelief, as Josh stopped rattling the door in the hope that I would release the door handle. He should know me better than that. 'Even about your dad?'

I could practically hear Simon's eyes rolling through the phone. 'I don't pay attention to what's trending in celebrity culture. It's just noise.'

'Well, I guess that explains why you haven't seen the video of your dad and my boss getting into it outside the BBC.'

Josh's surprise attempt to open the door failed and I heard him cry out in a high-pitched tone as he stubbed what I assumed was his toe, kicking the door.

'Hang on.' I placed my phone against my chest and opened the door to Josh. 'Stop it!'

'I'm just going to listen.'

'Fine, just... shut up!'

I shut the door again, shivering with excitement as I heard Josh pressing himself against my bedroom door. Only at the exact moment for the bedheads of Megan, Denise, and Bob to appear at their doors.

I opened my mouth to explain, but no sound came out. Instead, I walked into the bathroom and locked the door.

'Fuck!' I mouthed into the mirror silently, before sitting on the toilet seat and taking a calming breath. 'Sorry about that, the whole house is awake.'

'Oh, shit! Did I wake everyone up?'

'No, no, that was mostly my fault – and Josh's.'

'How are the terrible twosome?'

'That is not what they're called!' I laughed, enjoying the fact he had already given my friends a nickname.

'Well, I can hardly call them Cindy Lou Who and John McClane for the rest of time.'

'Yes, you can.' I grinned. 'And I'll forever call you the Grinch.'

He groaned down the phone. 'Supersexy!'

'It was.' I froze at the realisation I had said that out loud. I could take it back or cover it up. But why should I? 'Erm… I'm going to stick by that comment.'

'Really, no takebacks?'

'You sound way too proud of yourself right now.'

I could almost picture him strutting home after his saintly volunteering a sexy Grinch.

'I might just retain that moniker for the rest of my life. I'm going to put it on my tombstone. Evie Frost said I made a sexy Grinch.'

My only response was to laugh and blush.

Denise, Bob, Megan, *and* Josh's feet were gathered outside the bathroom door. They thought they were being subtle, listening in to my conversation, but it was so obvious. I threw a lazy-gift bath bomb at the door and heard them shriek in surprise, then back away.

I paused for a moment. 'Anyway, that wasn't why I wanted to speak to you on Christmas Eve: I had a question to ask you.'

'Sounds ominous.'

'It's not, I just wanted to check what your plans were for *after* Christmas?' A sudden wave of nausea hit me, partly from the hangover and Bob's trifle and partly from the sudden realisation that I may have sounded as if I'd just asked him out.

'I'm busking and volunteering…'

I interrupted. 'Oh yes, your sainthood application.'

'*But*,' he continued. 'I'm free this evening. If you're not… doing anything.'

'Tonight?' I repeated, thinking about Denise and Bob, and how I'd only spent a day with them. Not to mention *how* would I get back to London, unless Bob was to drop me off like a first date at thirteen? 'I – I…' I stumbled over my words when suddenly a piece of paper flew at me from under the door.

SAY YOU'RE FREE, it read in all caps, in Josh's handwriting.

The note was quickly followed by another.

I'M DRIVING, in Megan's handwriting.

And then there was another.

DENISE IS PACKING YOU A TO-GO BOX, in Bob's handwriting, with *P.S. REMIND HIM I OWN A SHOTGUN… OKAY I DON'T, BUT IT'S MY FATHERLY DUTY TO SAY I DO.*

'Uhh…' My mouth hung open, but then I found myself grinning. 'I'm free. What time, and where, should I meet you?'

'I cannot believe we're doing this!' Josh was shrieking from the back seat while Megan floored it on the M20.

'It's seventy miles per hour,' I pointed out, as I glanced

over at the speedometer and realised she was clearly exceeding it. 'I don't want to die before I get there.'

'It's Boxing Day.' She gestured to the completely clear roads with her chin. 'Just fix your make-up.'

'I'm not meeting him until five this evening.'

Josh was handing me eyeshadow after eyeshadow – his own, of course – and listing everything we'd need to do once we got back to Megan's.

'She can't go dressed like a piece of tinsel. Megan, do you have anything that will fit her?'

'Loads,' Megan scoffed. 'Don't fuss.'

'It's 365 days until Christmas. I *need* a new project,' Josh insisted, clapping his hands together.

I dared not think what he would do once we got back to Megan's with a full wardrobe of Zara basics and MAC make-up.

'What about Alex?' I asked.

Megan shrugged. 'He's at his parents and then he's coming to get Alfie, so he won't be there.' She cleared her throat. 'Where's he taking you?'

'He said he was going to surprise me.' I tried not to grin too hard. 'But to meet him on the South Bank, near Foyles.'

'Ooh, sexy location.' Josh winked in the rear-view mirror, before primping himself. How someone could look good with a hangover was beyond me, but he made it work. I, however, was reminded of my hangover as Megan put her foot down again.

'Oh, Jesus! Take the wheel.'

Chapter 30

THANKFULLY, MY HANGOVER WAS NOTHING A few paracetamols and a *lot* of water couldn't fix. Not to mention Josh and Megan, when they worked as a team. Josh did wonders beating my face with all the make-up at his disposal, and Megan found a pink turtleneck, skinny black jeans, and a silver pair of Doc Martens I'd once asked her to look after – when I couldn't fit them in my suitcase – which she'd never returned. I guess sisterly theft had its benefits.

To stay warm in the Christmassy weather, I borrowed a woollen hat with a signature bobble.

'The finishing touch,' Megan said, layering her prized Burberry scarf around my neck. 'Perfect. Now go. And have fun.'

'What about you two?' I suddenly realised I was leaving them alone on Boxing Day, with only a box of Denise's delicious picky bits for tea.

'Girl dinner!' Josh chorused, wrapping an arm around Megan's shoulder and Megan gripped his hand.

'Maybe a glass of Shiraz.'

Josh sucked his teeth. 'Oof! Too soon.'

*

I was prompt for my arrival at the South Bank, after getting an over-priced taxi I definitely could *not* expense.

I hadn't even checked in on Pim over Christmas, but she hadn't reached out to me, unlike Elijah, so she had at least decided to respect my boundaries over the festive period. For which I was very grateful.

Not many revellers remained in the city, now that the big day had passed.

Across the water I could see the lights of St St Paul's Cathedral still lit for all the evening services, leading up to midnight mass and carols.

The London Eye continued to circle in the sky, lit up in blues and purples as tourists and Londoners gathered for the perfect Christmas view of the city. It was a good night for it, chilly but clear. Not a cloud in sight in the night sky, only the lights of passing aeroplanes and the reflections of the city across the rolling Thames.

I found a bench to sit on, exhaling with surprise at the cold iron as I sat, playing with my sleeves while I waited.

'Watching the world go by?' Simon asked from behind me a few moments later. I didn't turn immediately, just smiled.

'I thought I would get that last Christmas memory,' I said to him, finally turning as he sat down beside me. In surprise, I laughed. He was wearing a suit, with a skinny black tie and a plain but smart black scarf. He crossed his arms playfully as I took him in. 'What are you wearing?'

He scrunched his face up in jest, acting as if his wearing a suit was completely normal.

'I thought I would go all out, seeing as it's Boxing Day.'

'Well…' I was a little lost for words. It was a bit of a shock, especially given that I was sitting in a cosy turtleneck-and-jeans combo but, God, he looked handsome. Kind of like a James-Bond-just-finished-fighting-a-guy-on-a-speedboat fantasy, with his windswept hair and slightly red face from the brisk air.

'Sorry I missed you on Christmas Eve,' he said, adjusting his scarf.

I shook my head and took his hand in mine confidently. It was surprisingly warm, as if he had just moved it from above a fire or from holding a cup of mulled wine. Maybe the flask was about to make a reappearance.

'Don't be sorry, I understand,' I said softly, hoping the weight of my words would land properly. 'I didn't realise your mum had passed so close to Christmas.'

Simon inhaled quickly, his voice a little quieter. 'Yeah,' he said, almost distantly, like he wasn't quite sure how to talk about it. 'Christmas is always a challenge after something like that.'

I nodded. It wasn't the kind of pain that could be fixed with words. Not when the holidays were supposed to be about joy and togetherness. 'After anything like that,' I muttered, trying to keep my own feelings at bay. 'I think more about my mum at Christmas than any time of year. Not her birthday, not her passing, not even my birthday.'

Simon's breath caught. 'There's something about Christmas,' he agreed, his his tone thoughtful. 'It's like… it brings everything up. Like it makes the emptiness stand out more.'

I didn't say anything, I just found myself shrugging. 'No one should be alone at Christmas.'

Simon's voice came a little stronger, though I could still hear the underlying sadness. 'And that's why I volunteer.'

He smiled, knowing that his saintliness would make me groan. I was full of admiration for him, but I did love to tease his perfection.

'You really put the rest of us to shame,' I mumbled, still holding his hand and finding myself inching closer to him on the bench.

'It's just something I like to do,' he argued playfully, leaning over to brush a loose strand of hair that had escaped from under my hat and was blowing across my face, and tucked it safely back underneath. 'It's all I know *how* to do,' he admitted, almost reluctantly. 'It helps me feel closer to my mum – she loved music as much as I do – but I don't really know how to talk about it. About her. About everything that happened after she passed away.'

I felt a strange pull in my chest, like I wanted to say something to make it easier, but I knew there were no easy words. There never were.

He exhaled slowly, as if he was preparing himself for something more. 'After my mum passed, things between my dad and me, they just… fell apart. He didn't get it. He was so caught up in work, in… everything. And I was just a teenager, trying to find my way without her. I think he expected me to go to university, as I was supposed to, but I chose music instead.'

There was a bitterness in his tone now, and I could feel how much it hurt him to say it, like opening a wound he'd kept shut for a long time. 'We've barely spoken since. It always turns into an argument. But it feels different now; as if enough time might have passed.'

'Then why not reach out to him? Ask him to dinner?'

'I'm volunteering.' He smirked. And I laughed, wrapping my arm around his. 'There's always next year.'

I felt the tug of my heart as I thought ahead to where I could be next year, in Toronto, after my first year at Salient Studios, looking back at my time in London.

Could I do that? I wondered. After the joy of this Christmas – could I still make the move to Canada?

I said nothing and inhaled the cool air.

'So where are you taking me for dinner?'

'Ah, about that,' he said with a cheeky grin that made me instantly suspicious.

'You couldn't get a booking?' I asked, knowing full-well what bookings were like on Boxing Day, having had trouble getting a dinner reservation for Pim, until I found an opening at a reputable Chinese place in Kensington.

'I did, but it's a unique one. And we have to be out of there by ten at the latest.'

'Works for me.' I thought Megan and Josh would still be waiting up for me back at Megan's at that point, ready to divulge and dissect my evening's outing within minuscule detail. It wasn't so much a rarity that I went on a date, as a blink-and-you'll-miss-it occurrence. They had missed out on these experiences with me, and now we were all going to make up for lost time.

'Right then.' Simon smirked, standing but never releasing my hand, as he helped me from the cold bench.

He directed me down the bank, past the skate park and past the Southbank Centre. Some men and women walked by in similar situations, hand-holds and smiles, admiring the view of the city on the last day of the Christmas season – before the New Year overwhelmed the South Bank with noise and fireworks.

Simon gave no indication of the name or location of the restaurant, even when I asked.

'We're not there,' he said, and I said no more, letting him revel in his surprise. 'How did you get on with your list in the end? The Christmas to-do list? Did you complete it?'

'Mostly,' I said, with pride. 'Despite the slight ups and downs, I think the only things I've got left are the New Year's Eve fireworks and dinner in an igloo, but we'll have to skip the latter. I'm not even sure how Josh or Megan would have managed that. They get booked quite early, I heard.'

'Right,' Simon said, more seriously than seemed necessary. 'I've heard that too, about the bookings.' He said no more, but a suspicion rose in my mind.

'Did you manage to book an igloo?'

'Well, not exactly,' Simon said, his cheeks flushed from the cool air and the effort of trying to remain charmingly naïve. He nodded with his chin over to his left and I turned to see where he was gesturing. There, alone, on the South Bank, was an igloo. Surrounded by security gates and bundles of other dismantled and collapsed igloos, one sat alone in the centre.

'What the hell!' I shouted excitedly, stopping in the middle of the South Bank to stare.

Inside was a small table and two picnic chairs. I could see some fleece blankets and electric candles, and a single Christmas rose in the centre of the table. 'How in the hell did you manage that?'

Simon laughed, clearly thrilled with my reaction.

'A buddy of mine is responsible for packing them all up. He's held off on packing that one up, but he said…'

'We need to be out by ten,' I repeated his words from earlier, squeezing his hand and feeling an electric-like current coursing through me. 'How did you convince the cook to stay?'

Simon's smile faltered. 'Ah, well, that little bit of the puzzle I couldn't fix.' He chuckled apologetically. 'But I have a solution.' With a gentle tug he pulled me forward.

He clambered over a security gate, before helping me clamber over as well, holding shamelessly on to my waist to place me down with as much grace as possible. His friend was nowhere to be seen, but would no doubt return to dismantle the last igloo as promised.

Close up, I could see some more of what was behind the mottled plastic sheets that acted as windows. There were sheepskin rugs across the floor, two electric heaters on at high levels so that the igloo was as warm as a fireplace. A portable speaker sat on the floor, softly crooning 'Last Christmas' at a comfortable volume. More blankets and rugs were thrown across the chairs, and our table was laid with some basic Christmas plates and cutlery from a supermarket, with a choice of mince pies, sausage rolls, cocktail sausages, the best cheeses, crackers, grapes, and a bottle of expensive red wine.

'It may look a little *Supermarket Sweep*, but I promise it will taste delicious.'

Simon's voice was light, teasing, but there was excitement there too, like he genuinely wanted me to love this, like it mattered to him.

'This is the food of my childhood,' I told him, practically salivating, as he pulled out my seat with an easy chivalry that made my stomach flutter. 'Honestly, I can't wait to dive in.'

And I did, popping a juicy grape into my mouth before Simon could take his own seat.

'There's a box of Celebrations outside as well,' Simon added, gesturing towards the heaters. 'Didn't want to keep them in here in case they melted.'

'Good thinking.' I glanced around at the scene he'd set; the festive feast laid out between us, under the twinkling stars of the South Bank. It all felt surreal, like something plucked from one of those Christmas movies where everything just works out with little to no effort, and a sprinkling of a Christmas miracle.

Simon lifted a blanket from the pile he'd moved off his chair, draping it around my shoulders before scooting in beside me. The warmth of it – of him – was instant, wrapping around me like a hug.

I snuggled in, shifting closer. 'I think this may be the best dinner date I've ever had.'

He quirked an eyebrow, a smirk playing at his lips. 'Oh, yeah?'

I shrugged, feigning nonchalance as I reached for a mini sausage roll. 'Not that you need to know my dating history.'

Simon let out a low chuckle, eyes twinkling as he poured us both a drink. 'Well, in that case, I'll just assume I'm winning.'

'Undeniably.'

A comfortable silence settled between us as we tucked into the food. The air inside the igloo smelled of pastries and warm wine, mingling with the crisp scent of winter beyond the plastic walls. It felt cosy, private, like we were in our own little snow globe while the rest of London hummed on around us.

I dived into the sausage rolls and grapes, cutting up large pieces of brie and wensleydale, so that each mouthful of cracker and cheese was more cheese and crumbs. Simon was a big fan of a cocktail sausage, and the obvious jokes that came with that.

As I sipped my drink, the conversation shifted, the way it sometimes did with Simon – effortless, natural.

'I didn't think I'd be doing this,' I admitted after a moment.

'Eating an entire tray of mini sausage rolls?' he teased, nudging my knee against his under the table.

I huffed a small laugh. 'No. Well, yes, but also… celebrating Christmas. Properly, I mean.' I stared down at my glass, watching the liquid swirl. 'I didn't really do it last year. Or the year before.'

He chewed more slowly, leaving me space to open up if I wanted to. He really could read my mind, I thought. *And if you can, I'm falling head over heels right now,* I added to myself.

I sighed, leaning back against the fleece. 'Christmas was always *our* holiday,' I said, my voice filling with emotion. 'Me and my mum. We didn't have a lot, but she made it feel like we did. She'd go all out: paper chains, John Lewis decorations, all the eighties bangers playing the moment we reached November. She'd make this ridiculous Christmas dinner with whatever we could afford – only the trimmings we liked – and we'd sit in our pyjamas all day watching movies and eating chocolate for breakfast.' I smiled at the memories, which I cherished but hid from others. They felt like a delicate things, fragile, like cupping water in my hands. What if I shared them and they disappeared. Or if I made new memories and it covered them up.

'She sounds amazing,' Simon murmured, reaching for my hand under the blankets and running his fingers over my knuckles soothingly. 'My mum was more traditional.' He bit his cheek. 'Midnight masses, Christmas carols, and volunteering. It's probably why I've always thrown myself into that side of Christmas.'

'Was she religious?' I asked and he shrugged in response.

'Not really, but she was very aware it was a religious holiday. A time for giving at the very least.'

'She sounds great too, very kind.'

He nodded and smirked as a sudden memory crept into his mind. 'She used to make all the nativity outfits at school. No other mother seemed to bother, but every year she would stitch me a new jumper or make a new tea-towel headdress.'

'Let me guess, you were Joseph.' I rolled my eyes at the vision of him, looking so proud as the brand new 'father' of Jesus, but he shook his head.

'I was a shepherd, the innkeeper, and once, ready for this, the *door*.'

'The door?'

'The door,' he repeated proudly. 'It was my finest role.'

'I can see the reviews now: *Simon Holland was effortlessly wooden*.'

We laughed. 'Go on then, were you Mary?'

I looked at him as if he had just insulted me greatly. *Mary*, of all characters. 'I was a sheep three years in a row.'

'You were typecast.' He patted my shoulder, falsely apologetic, and I pushed it off.

'At least I was always warm when we left. My mum used to spend hours hot-gluing cotton balls on old jumpers. Though, by the end of the shows, you would probably have thought I was a snow cloud, by the way they'd just fall off. I used to throw them at Megan – *she* was Mary.'

He nodded and smirked. 'Makes sense.'

'It really does, doesn't it?'

'Do you think your mum would have liked me?' he asked, cutting the last mince pie in half for us to share. It was a personal question; one I hadn't expected – to the point I almost let him have my side of the mince pie. *Almost*. 'Would she have found me charming?'

'At the rate I've dated,' I began, taking a moment to really consider what my mum would think about him, and chuckling as I realised the answer. 'She'd probably be pleased as Punch that you've got a pulse and you're breathing.'

'Wow, low bar.'

I bit into my mince pie with a smirk. 'Seriously though, she would have loved you. You're good-looking, musical, kind, and…'

'*Really* good-looking?'

I slapped his shoulder. 'Fish much?'

He pulled me forward suddenly by my chair, my knee between his legs as he rubbed some crumbs from my cheek.

'My mum would have grilled you,' he said. 'And you'd have sworn she hated you, when, in actual fact, she'd be planning our wedding and telling everyone behind our backs that she thinks you're the one.'

'Really?' He had a very clear-cut vision of his mum's opinion. But he had been older than I had been when I'd lost mine. My mum was fun and happy-go-lucky, seemingly all the time, keeping a brave face on her diagnosis for my sake. 'I do feel intimidated.'

'She'd have loved you. I imagine my dad likes you as well.'

I raised my eyebrows. 'Really? I think he *hates* me. Because of me and my boss, he went viral for all the wrong reasons.'

Simon shook his head and moved a piece of hair from my face. 'Nah, he'll have liked the attention. Besides, he's just guarded. Iron on the outside, gold on the inside.'

I pushed his hair back now, realising just how close I was to his face, more specifically his lips.

'You seem to have a high opinion of the man who earlier you said you couldn't stand.'

He clicked his teeth. 'Son's privilege. The less I see of him, the more I like him.'

'You only see him at Christmas, right?'

'On my mum's anniversary. It's so close to Christmas it feels like the right time to exchange gifts and pleasantries, in the name of her memory.'

'But not Christmas Day?'

He shook his head again. 'He's always working or away. And I volunteer. It's just the way it's become.'

I didn't say anything, giving him the space to carry on if he wanted to. But suddenly he laughed.

'Well, aren't we just the picture of festive cheer?' We nearly butted heads. 'Nothing says Christmas spirit like bonding over our dead mums.'

'It's probably not the most romantic conversation I've ever had on a date.'

'No?' His lips quirked. 'Damn. And here I thought I was really setting the mood.'

I smiled, warmth bubbling up despite the topic, and the ache in both our stories. Because it wasn't just grief. It was understanding. Connection.

Simon squeezed my hand one more time before letting go and reducing the space between us, turning quickly back to the last of the food. We soon had devoured the rest, swapping Christmas playlists and opinions on the latest John Lewis ad.

'How did you even see the ads abroad?'

'Megan was very good at keeping me up to date. Plus, with apps like TikTok, all the Christmas content is curated just for me. I never miss a thing,' I explained, pulling out my phone and opening the app just to prove my point. Immediately there was a video of a woman decorating her decadent home, using the age-old 'throw a bauble like it's a grenade effect'. 'One day I'll have a home big enough to do that video.'

'Give it 'ere,' he said, opening my profile with some difficulty, having limited experience with the platform. 'You've got over two hundred and fifty *thousand* followers!'

'I thought you saw my profile before, at the pub?' I reminded him, but his eyes were bulging.

'Your videos maybe, but not your followers. Bloody hell!'

'It's not that much,' I said, reaching for the phone, but he pulled it away.

'Not *much*? It's more than the population of Saint Lucia.'

I gave up and allowed him to flick through my content, trying my best not to blush or barf whenever he played a new video. Eventually he gave me my phone back.

'You're good. Is that the kind of thing you're going to be doing in Toronto?'

I was surprised he brought it up first but didn't let myself show it.

'Fetching coffees, you mean, and vlogging about it.' I snuggled in closer to his shoulder, listening to the lapping of the Thames and the giggles and carolling of the South Bank walkers.

'No, I mean content creation. You're *good.* And I'm not just saying that, with my upbringing I know good content when I see it.'

'You have a high opinion of yourself.'

'I am a Holland.' He blew a raspberry. 'However much I try to suppress it.'

I patted his warm chest to comfort him playfully, and he placed his hand over mine, keeping my hand in place as he ran his fingers up and down my knuckles. It was soothing, as if the lapping of waves had reached my hand.

'The content's only good because I've been in London. I was inspired.'

He grinned. 'By a certain busker.'

'Do you want me to get you a fishing pole.'

His grin widened. 'You could…' He shrugged. 'Never mind.'

'No, what?' I pushed myself up with his chest, facing him, just inches from his lips. 'What were you going to say?'

'Just that you could leverage your following, and your content. Stay in London and… stay *inspired.*'

'By you,' I finished for him, teasing him.

His smile should be illegal; it was utterly mind-melting.

All my arguments for leaving – most of which had lost a lot of potency during Pim's show and Christmas with my family – were disappearing before my eyes.

My decision to leave Pim was the right one, I knew that much. It *was* time for me to get a new job; one with progression and choices. But did I really need to move to Toronto to start again?

Originally, my intent had been to finally lay down roots, from which a family tree might spring. But this Christmas had proved I already had roots and, instead of pruning them, I just needed to let them grow.

'I could…' Simon seemed hesitant. 'I could talk to… my dad. If you want? About a job, or a contact at least.'

I sat up even more, aware that at this point I was practically lying across him.

'You'd do that? After all this time not really speaking to him? You'd introduce me, the girl who made him go viral for all the wrong reasons, and ask for his help?'

He pulled at the bobble on my hat until it fell off and my hair tumbled down my shoulder. 'I would.' He smirked as I tried to flatten my wild locks. 'Not that he's ever met any of the women I've ever… you know,' he finished lamely.

'*You know* what?' I grinned, teasing him as a pink flush developed across his nose.

'Women I've dated?' he said, unsure of himself.

'Women you've flirted with for a month. Women you've helped out, probably a bit *too* much. Women you've definitely connected with but don't want to admit it,' I suggested cheekily.

'Women I've come to really *really* fancy,' he continued on my behalf. 'And don't know how to admit it until we're snuggled up in an igloo that I had to beg my friend to borrow.'

'Oh, you begged?' I teased.

'I was on my knees,' he said, semi-seriously. 'Dignity be damned.'

'Dignity be damned,' I repeated, leaning upwards to kiss him before I even thought about it.

He met me halfway, his hand sliding into my hair, fingers threading through the loose strands as our lips pressed together, warm and certain.

It wasn't our discovery kiss, that was our first; this was deeper, lingering, as if we were both trying to make up for lost time. I felt him sigh against my mouth, his grip tightening slightly, as if he couldn't help himself. I kissed him back with just as much certainty, curling my fingers into the fabric of his suit, holding him there for a moment longer than necessary.

We parted, by an inch, when a group of men walking past began to jeer and wolf-whistle. We ignored them but our cheeks flushed as we leaned back to look at each other. Excited embarrassment, anticipation, nerves, and happiness flooded between us, crackling in the air like the fairy lights twinkling around us.

I fell into his chest, pulling my legs up so they were pressed against his. He let out a small, contented sigh before pressing a slow, lasting kiss to my forehead. His whole body relaxed, releasing a tension neither of us had previously noticed.

'Definitely worth begging,' he said suddenly.

We laughed.

I leaned upwards, already desperate for another kiss.

'Thank you!' I said, placing my hand over his cheek and stroking his warm stubble. 'I haven't said that yet. Thank you!'

'Merry Christmas!' he whispered.

'Merry bloody Christmas!' I folded into him like the ribbon that wraps around a gift.

Though we had to leave by ten so his friend didn't get into trouble, at that moment I would have been perfectly happy sleeping in his arms in that igloo all night. I had never felt so warm, safe, or loved. Not since before my mum died.

It was a Christmas gift like no other, and one I never expected.

Chapter 31

I WAS STILL TECHNICALLY EMPLOYED BY PIM until New Year's Day, but she had texted to say it was no bother if I would rather not work my notice, since I had already scheduled all her dinners and drinks until the New Year, and Alison had taken on the rest of her schedule for her New Mexico trip.

There was nothing more to do but keep her company, and she wasn't so decrepit as to need that.

At least she said she wasn't.

I was still happy enough to fulfil my role as assistant, even in a relaxed form.

Megan had returned – with all the gossip she could wring from me – back to Denise and Bob's for the remainder of Christmas. And Josh, unsurprisingly, had found a tourist on Hinge in need of a sexy tour guide.

Leaving me all the time in the world to spend with Simon. For as long as I could until the New Year, and my new job. A fact I was repressing with more and more ease with every day that passed.

'Does your phone ever stop ringing?' Simon had asked one morning, after I had watched his show outside St Paul's – prompting the crowd to cheer, sing along, and donate as much as I could, without seeming suspicious.

He was just packing up his belongings under the columns when my phone lit up and chorused with missed calls and messages.

'It's…' I didn't finish. Elijah had sent texts, voice notes, and countless emails, and was now trying to call me. I groaned. 'I don't start for another week. And all the travel is sorted and…' There was no reason for him to be contacting me. It was just too intense. 'I think this is what it's going to be like when I get there,' I lamented to Simon, the fear and anxiety settling in me like a bad cocktail. He wrapped his arm around my waist and I felt better instantly.

Kissing the top of my head, he muttered, slightly begrudgingly, 'I think it's time I called my dad.'

'No.' I don't know what it was that made me stop him, perhaps some latent feminist pride, but the idea of my yet-to-be-classified-as-more-than-friend asking his *dad* to help me get a job just gave me the instant ick. 'I have another idea.'

Pim was up, dressed and dancing when I entered her hotel room.

'Afternoon,' I said, elongating the word having realised it was after midday. Pim turned, startled by my sudden appearance. She was wearing a festive headpiece including two snowflakes that lit up like my jumper.

'We match!' I pressed the discreet button under my jumper that set the whole thing aglow. Pim rolled her eyes with a huff and removed her headpiece. Clearly, I had ruined the moment.

'What are you doing here?' she said, slightly frustrated by my presence.

I laughed. 'I take my job very seriously, as you know,' I

reminded her. 'Just because I can take the next few days off, that doesn't mean I'm going to.'

Pim exhaled heavily and sat down on the sofa. Gerald, who was fast asleep at the other end, bounced up at the surprise disruption and jumped off, back to his three-storey dog tower in the other room.

'Well, there's nothing for you to do,' she replied haughtily. 'Alison has sorted everything for New Mexico and the show's over.'

'I know.' I moved some of the newspapers containing reviews of her event – all dog-eared – onto the coffee table, so that I could sit down. 'I could sort out some sight-seeing, though? You've been in London all month and barely seen any of it.'

Pim's eyebrows rose in confusion. 'I've seen plenty. I've been to The Ivy, The Groucho, Chiltern's, Fortnum & Mason…'

'Those are restaurants and shops. I'm talking about *London*.' I added jazz-hands for effect; the moment called for it and would not be denied.

'I don't have much interest in *London*,' Pim said, repeating my jazz-hands with dripping sarcasm as she reached towards the table for a cup of coffee I'd missed.

'Not even the museums or the art galleries?'

Pim shrugged. 'It's all a load of stuff we nicked from other countries.'

'Not all of it,' I argued weakly. 'There's always the theatre?'

Pim laughed. 'And see what? *A Christmas Carol*? The pantomime?'

'There's a new Tom Stoppard production?' I suggested and Pim growled in revolt.

'Never.' She dribbled her coffee – clearly now cold – back into her cup and put it down. 'And, besides, you're not here to get me on a…' She pulled a disgusted face. '… hop-on, hop-off bus. You're after something. What is it?'

I did have to hand it to her, Pim could read me like a book when she was so inclined to take up reading anything other than the tabloids.

'I actually have a question for you. Or a request, perhaps.'

Pim's back straightened, her lips pursed, and she tilted her head to consider me for a moment.

'That's a phrase I've never heard from you before,' she said slowly, taking a long time to process my opening line.

'I know.' I wished I had some water so I could wet my mouth before asking, but I had no choice, I'd opened the can of worms, now I had to spill them. 'So my new job in Toronto, it's… it's not exciting me as much as I was hoping it would. I know that that could be down to fear, and I will still be going – contractually, I'm obliged – but I've decided, that after my probation period, I'll be coming back to the UK.' I took a breath and waited for a reaction from Pim but none came.

I felt as if I had burst a balloon, but the balloon had already been burst. There was no loud bang or surprise, from either of us. This was always meant to happen.

'I'm not coming back with my tail between my legs asking for my old job, that door has closed, and I know that Alison is going to be great at it. But I was wondering, *hoping* even, that if you knew anyone I could speak to or if you had any advice about the industry, I would love to try to find something more local. Within the UK. I just…' I took another breath and released a nervous laugh as all my anticipatory energy dispersed. 'I've really fallen back in love with London and my life here, and I don't want to let it go.'

It was a simple finish, perhaps too simple. But it was honest.

Pim made no reply. Her expression remained stoic, contemplative, as if she had only understood half of what I had said, and she was translating the rest. Or she was thinking about what she was going to order for dinner from the Savoy kitchens that evening.

She inhaled deeply and moved her head back to the centre of her spine, scanning the room around her as if looking for a misplaced item.

'I always wondered why you never just asked,' she mumbled, sighing as she couldn't find the item she was looking for and standing up from the sofa.

I was stunned into open-mouthed silence. Pim seemed to have got in the frequent habit of surprising me of late.

'I – I mean, only if you can. I wouldn't want...' I stuttered nervously and Pim made a 'pish' sound as she entered her bedroom.

'You're always putting other people first, Evie. What do you actually want in life?' she asked, reappearing moments later with a well-thumbed Filofax and a Savoy notepad. '*You*,' she said. 'No one else, you.'

'Me?' I was dumbstruck. 'I suppose... I want to stay in London.'

Pim smiled. 'Then let me make some calls.' She retook her seat and opened her Filofax with a flourish only she was capable of. 'I meant it at the show when I said I wouldn't be in this industry without help,' she said, flicking through her contacts pages. 'Let me help you for once.'

I exhaled slowly, releasing all the tension I had

unknowingly built up inside me, sinking back into the armchair, unable to resist smiling from ear to ear.

For weeks, I'd been bracing myself for polite detachment from Pim, for a clean break from my long-held role. But our relationship had changed in the last few weeks, as the detachment naturally began, and was cemented at her live show.

We moved from employer and assistant to something more mutual and respectful. The sort of relationship that doesn't need a contract. And sitting there, watching her already halfway into problem-solving mode on my behalf, I knew I was being sent off with her legitimate best wishes and not just a store-bought leaving card (that I'd already purchased *for* her).

Gerald could clearly sense glee from the other room and reappeared. His tiny tuft of a tail was wagging as he bounded over to me, his leash in his mouth, as he insisted I take him outside; his beady black eyes beaming.

'Go for a walk.' Pim appeared suddenly irritated again. 'I've got phone calls to make.'

I said nothing but stood and claimed the leash from Gerald.

'We'll talk when you get back.' Pim had a mischievous look of ambition and determination fixed across her face.

'Thank you,' I said, but immediately her expression returned to that of revulsion.

'Christ, don't thank me yet! I might stick you with an absolute – *Dick*! How are you?'

I don't care what she says, she planned that exchange.

In the nearby Victoria Embankment Park, I walked Gerald and retrieved my phone. Opening the TikTok app, I styled the camera above my head and began recording.

'Happy Assistmas, everyone!' I said into the camera cheerfully. 'I hope everyone had an amazing Christmas and isn't too hungover? I'm currently walking Gerald. Gerald, come here!' I called back the fluffy Chow Chow and he performed a little dressage trot to my side as I crouched down. 'We're going to get some fresh coffee in a minute and head back to the hotel for a little bit of post-Christmas planning.' I smiled, careful not to say too much in case Elijah was still watching my TikToks. Given his constant emailing about the late work on the treatments, I more than suspected he was.

'I know I haven't posted much over Christmas but, honestly, I have been having the *best* time. I've had amazing experiences, made incredible memories, and, best of all, I got to reconnect with the city I love best. I'm this close,' I said, creating a tiny gap between my thumb and forefinger, 'to buying an *I Heart London* T-shirt. But my dignity remains.' I smiled at the thought of Simon and his lack of dignity in attempting to date me. 'But barely.'

I winked at the camera and paused.

I could end it there. Keep it light, keep it vague. But as I watched Gerald sniff at the frosty grass beside me, I realised I didn't want to.

I hit 'Record' again.

'And you know what? I think I've changed my mind about something.' I adjusted the camera, so London's skyline framed me perfectly in the background. 'At the start of December I thought this would be my last Christmas in London. That this was a farewell tour, one final Assistmas before I moved on to whatever's next. But… maybe I was wrong. Maybe this isn't the last.'

I hesitated, saying the words felt like a spark catching fire.

'Maybe this is the first of many.'

I grinned, letting the moment breathe before ending the video. Screw Elijah, I was done making decisions based on what other people wanted.

I winked at the camera and shut it down, deciding to leave editing for later – after I saw Simon and updated him. The thought sent a rush of warmth through me. Before I could overthink it, I pulled out my phone again, my thumb hovering over Simon's name in my recent calls. I couldn't wait; I wanted to fill him in immediately.

I pressed the green 'Call' button. He answered almost instantly. 'Miss me already?'

His voice was light, teasing, but I could hear the hope underneath it.

'Actually, yes,' I admitted, pacing along the path. 'And I was wondering, would you like to go on another date?'

'Where do you want to go?' he replied. 'Name the place, I'll be there.'

I bit my lip, glancing around at the city skyline peeking through the trees. I felt giddy and confident, so I went for it. 'Your flat perhaps? New Year's Eve is coming up – let's have a night in.'

His answering chuckle sent a thrill down my spine. 'You're on. Fireworks at my place?'

Oh, there would be fireworks all right.

Chapter 32

THE WINTER AIR OUTSIDE TELEVISION CENTRE in White City was crisp, the kind that made your breath cloud in front of you but wasn't cold enough to be unpleasant.

Simon was leaning against a railing, scarf loosely wrapped around his neck, hands tucked into his coat pockets. His hair was slightly ruffled from the winter wind and he had that effortless kind of presence that made him stand out, even when he looked like he was trying not to.

He was scanning the entrance as if he didn't quite belong here. Waiting.

For me.

I felt it immediately, the awareness of him, the unmistakable pull that had been there since the moment we met. Electricity crackled between us as our eyes locked, a current strong enough to make me want to run to him.

I pulled my coat tighter around me as Simon spotted me. My mind was still catching up with the whirlwind of the last hour, so it was Simon who reached me first.

'How'd it go?' he asked, slipping his hand into mine.

'It was something.' I couldn't help grinning.

A new job. In London. The words didn't quite feel real yet.

The Head of the Studio had been polite but firm when discussing an Executive Assistant role on his social media team, I explained to Simon. It was something I knew I could do with my eyes closed, but with the added bonus of being in the thick of television production *and* social media – precisely where I wanted to be – *but* based in my favourite city.

And all because Pim had made a call. A call that I didn't think she had in her; even after eight years, Pim could surprise me. Her contacts may be older, but that just meant they had more power. There was me thinking she was irrelevant in the UK, but really it was just *her* lack of interest.

She'd reached out in such a *Pim* way too; breezy, casual, as if pulling strings in the industry was as simple as asking for an extra shot of espresso in her coffee. Not that she ever ordered her own coffee.

And the call had paid dividends for her too; she was in talks for a new baking show. A *big* one.

'Just imagine,' I said, nudging Simon. 'Pim on primetime. She'll never be able to go to the supermarket again without being mobbed by fans.'

'Not your problem,' Simon pointed out.

I skipped down the steps. 'I just can't wait to see her critiquing sponge cakes with a level of disdain usually reserved for war criminals.'

'That will be a sight to see,' Simon agreed. 'I'm glad she made the call, though. My dad *might* have been willing to help, but I doubt he's popular enough to get you anything nearly as good.'

'I don't know.' I shrugged. 'His programmes make money; he'd probably have some sway. But Pim's recommendation personally means a little bit more to me.' I smiled and Simon agreed with a reciprocal grin.

'Now, tell me,' he said suddenly, twirling me on the spot and wrapping his arms around me. 'How does it feel to be officially staying in London?'

I exhaled slowly, as if I could release all the uncertainty and fear with it. 'Good,' I admitted. 'Really, *really* good.'

And it did feel good. No more running. No more pretending I didn't want to be here. I was precisely where I wanted to be, and I was staying.

'Thank you,' I told him.

'For what?'

'For inspiring me.' I shrugged. 'For reminding me to use my content creation as leverage, for making me realise how much I love it here.'

'I wasn't the only one.'

I sucked my teeth playfully. 'Well, if I have to thank Megan, Josh, Pim, and all the others, where will it end?'

'With Christmas cards,' Simon whined.

'The horror!'

I tiptoed to reach his lips. I was all for being professional, in case someone was looking out of the window as I came out of the interview, but my body had other ideas. My breath hitched, my stomach flipped, and every single nerve ending I had lit up at once.

'Hi!' I said, keeping my voice steady.

'Hi!' he replied with a smile.

I wanted to have a lot of *Hi!* moments with Simon. I linked his fingers between my own as I tried to push myself off him and not remain close enough to smell his cologne, or I was at risk of losing my resolve entirely.

My pulse roared in my ears. He was here, real and solid

in front of me, looking at me as if I was the only thing he cared to see, and I couldn't believe it. I had never felt like this about anyone and, with being graysexual, I never thought I would. But here we were.

'Just so you know,' I said, not sure why I felt compelled to say it, but at the same time knowing I needed to. 'I'm not staying just because of you.'

Something altered in his expression, not disappointment but something almost like pride.

'Good,' he said simply. 'I don't want that. I want you to do what *you* want to do.'

'Oh, I know,' I laughed, remembering our conversation at the ice rink. 'You've made that pretty clear.'

'Hey, I'm a big believer in following your dreams. Look at me!' He gestured to himself, all easy confidence and quiet passion, the type of person who had never once wavered in what he wanted.

I stepped up and kissed him on the lips – I knew then he never would have wanted me to change my life for him. Just like I never would have done it. But the fact that my new life happened to be here, in the same city as him? That was something we could both be very, very happy about.

And I was.

'Thank you!' I said, stepping back as he rolled his lips, his eyes suddenly straying from mine to over my shoulder as his shoulders tensed.

A man cleared his throat noisily.

'Dad!'

I spun on the spot. Michael Holland, who had appeared from around the corner, his collar turned up against the cold, had frozen at the sight of us – especially Simon, who was still locked in my grasp. I failed to release him, partly due to the unpredictability of what he was going to do in this situation. This was his *father.* 'We have got to stop meeting like this,' I said, my mouth releasing the words before I had time to even think them. I shut my eyes. 'I mean, hello, Mr Holland.'

Michael only had eyes for Simon but raised an eyebrow after I spoke, clearly realising who I was.

'Well, at least you don't have a dog with you, who's going to push me into traffic this time?' He smiled, not unkindly.

'For the record, I am sorry about that,' I said, still waiting for Simon to speak.

Michael blinked. Then, after a beat, he nodded. 'Apology accepted.'

There was an awkward beat of silence before Michael's piercing gaze returned to Simon and, immediately, the air changed.

Simon's expression remained neutral, but there was a tightness in his jaw. 'Dad,' he said again. I glanced at him, and saw a mix of frustration, yearning, and uncertainty behind his eyes. He hesitated and then, as if he had steeled himself for the moment, continued, 'Evie, this is my father, Michael Holland.'

I knew. Of course, I knew. But hearing Simon say it, claim it even, felt different.

'It's nice to meet you properly,' I said to Michael, holding out my hand professionally but it was strange the moment I offered it. Michael even laughed; it was the first time I think I had seen him smile, without it being a sneer. It was the same smile as Simon's.

'I saw your Cornwall documentary,' I carried on, hating the quiet that had entered the interaction. 'It was brilliant. Passionate. You made the smuggler trade still feel alive.'

'Well, it is, in its dark ways,' Michael said fluidly, his brows lifting slightly, as if I had surprised him. 'But thank you! I enjoyed making it.'

It was a simple exchange, but the way he held himself relaxed, just slightly. He released my hand and took a step back. Simon's face was unreadable, but I knew him well enough now to see the tension beneath the surface.

Michael shifted his weight, glancing away for a second, as if debating whether to say something or just let the stillness stretch between them.

'So… how long are you in London for?' Simon's voice was steady, but I could hear the effort it took to sound casual.

Michael hesitated but cleared his throat and gestured to the building. 'A few days. I had some meetings.' He paused. 'I didn't expect to run into you here. On New Year's Eve.'

'Yeah, well,' Simon exhaled sharply, running a hand through his hair and reclaiming my hand in his; I felt his hand tremble slightly and placed my other hand on top of his to steady him. 'I've been around.'

Another silence.

'I'm here for Evie. She's had a job offer.'

Michael nodded slowly. 'Congratulations,' he said to me, though he only had eyes for his son.

'Thank you!'

'You look well.' Michael's words were awkward, halting, as if they weren't something he was used to saying.

Simon fidgeted again, his lips pressing together before he spoke. 'Thanks!' A beat passed. Then, softer, 'You too.'

It was small – barely anything – but it was something. A tentative olive branch in a sea of years where neither had reached out.

'How was your Christmas?' I asked and they seemed to turn and look at me as if to say *Why would you ask that?* 'I understand it's a difficult time for you. For you both,' I added. Simon squeezed my hand.

Michael looked at the ground for a moment but corrected himself pretty swiftly. 'It *can* be, but it was fine. Quiet, but fine.'

'Did you work?' Simon asked quickly and Michael didn't respond but, rather than letting the air between them widen, Simon continued, 'Maybe next year we can spend Christmas together.'

Michael's face remained neutral for a long moment. But then, so subtly that I almost missed it, his shoulders loosened and he smiled with his eyes. 'I'd like that.'

I seemed to be overcome by a very Pim-ish trait and stepped in. 'Maybe a lunch a bit sooner than *Christmas* next year, you plebs.'

Okay, one *final* act of helping others before myself.

'Honestly. I'll organise it, I'm great at organising lunches. *Ooh*, maybe we can get a reservation at Nobu. There's nothing like watching someone eat sushi to develop a bond quickly – or fix it, or whatever it is you two are doing besides brooding.'

I could see Simon desperately trying to hold in a laugh, and even Michael let out a breath of something that might have been amusement.

'Lunch could be arranged,' Michael said, though Nobu was out – I knew that as soon as I said it – a meal at The Ivy would do these two perfectly fine.

Simon clapped his hands together. 'This has been a rather exciting day. And Evie and I have a date to watch the fireworks.'

'A date,' Michael repeated. 'Are you Simon's, erm… girlfriend?'

The two of them paused to let me answer, but I would have hoped that was obvious.

'Uh, sure. *Girlfriend.*' I rolled the word in my mouth and liked the taste.

Michael said nothing else, just nodded and glanced at Simon and me, and then back to Simon. 'Well, I'll be in touch about that lunch,' he said, finally starting to walk away.

'Dad,' Simon began, stopping his father briefly. 'I'm looking forward to catching up properly.'

Michael nodded but said nothing else as he headed up to the TV studios entrance. I watched him go, surprised by how little it rattled me.

A few weeks ago, that silence would have felt loaded with rejection or judgement. Now it felt like opportunity, a door ajar for me and Simon to walk through at will.

Michael Holland would be unlikely to offer an effortless relationship, but with conversation and pause – specifically for Simon to take it at his own pace – I could imagine a future where the three of us met for lunch, and a time where we, or just Simon and his dad, learned how to be in each other's lives without forcing it. With *or* without me. Though I hoped beyond hope that it was with.

I waited for Michael to reach the stairs before wrapping an arm around Simon's waist and kissing him again.

'Girlfriend,' he said, our lips still pressed together.

'I like how it sounds.'

He smirked, tilting his head to kiss my cheek. 'So do I.'

Chapter 33

Simon's flat was tucked away down a quiet street in Borough, very Bridget Jones-esque of him. It wouldn't have made sense if he was *just* a busker but, when I remembered his father and his upbringing, I realised that there was no way Simon was entirely strapped for cash.

'It was my mum's,' he explained, turning the key in the lock before we headed up the narrow stairs to the top floor. It was the kind of flat you wouldn't notice unless you were looking for it. It suited him, actually, unassuming but quietly distinctive.

The space smelled of coffee, his cologne, and something faintly woody, like an old guitar case. It wasn't exactly how I pictured it – in the few seconds I had to imagine in the time it took for him to open the door – it was tidy but not overly polished, with instruments propped up in corners and hanging from bike hooks on the walls, and sheet music spread out on a small desk by the window.

The walls were plain, save for the instruments and a few framed records with silver signatures under the glass. Above the kitchen, a mezzanine led to his bedroom, the metal staircase swirling. It was a studio, or a bed-sit if you were feeling unkind, cramped but still homely.

'Do you want a drink?' he offered, already heading

towards the small fridge, whipping dirty laundry from the end of the leather sofa and shoving it into some unsuspecting cupboard, where it no doubt did not belong.

'You don't have to tidy up for me,' I laughed, throwing myself onto the lumpy sofa cushions. 'I want to see the place as you live in it, not as in a Rightmove advert.'

He giggled, slightly nervously. 'It's definitely a bachelor pad.'

'Nothing wrong with that,' I said, leaning my chin on the sofa to watch him and breathing in the heady smell of his cologne. It was potent. At least I didn't have to open the window to relieve myself of a bachelor musk; his home smelled like him and it was glorious.

For a few seconds he just stared at me, saying nothing. A small smirk at the corner of his lips.

'What?' I asked, lifting my head and poking my face as if I had something on my cheek.

'Nothing.' He turned away, reaching into the fridge for a bottle of water. 'So tell me. What's next for you?'

I frowned. 'In what way? I have the new job now, so I suppose the next thing is sorting out Salient.'

'And what do you need to do there?' He jumped over the sofa, swinging his legs around as if he often did that – when I could tell by his slightly pained expression that he didn't – before pulling my legs over his.

'You're a child!' I laughed loudly, surprised, but not appalled by his George-of-the-Jungle behaviour. It was his flat, after all, he could be himself in it. Even if this version of himself was clearly nervous and boyish. I rested my hand atop his, feeling the condensation of the water bottle soaking into my trouser leg. His fingers were still warm as I wrapped my own around them. 'I still need to go to Canada.' He groaned. 'For a short time,' I pressed on. 'Just to work out my probation so I'm not in breach of contract. The house was only a rental anyway, so it's not like I've got to unwind a load of activity. I just need to tide them over until they can re-hire – which I doubt will take three months.'

'Really?' He didn't seem convinced. 'Aren't creative industries usually the *worst* at hiring people?'

I shrugged. It wasn't my problem if that was the case. 'Probation periods are as much for the employee as for the employer. If I don't want to take the job – which I don't – they'll have no choice but to get a move on.'

He smirked again. 'You're ruthless, you know that?'

'I'm entrepreneurial and determined,' I countered playfully. 'And, for once, I'm doing precisely what I want to do.'

'With a few months in Canada before you can actually start it, though.'

It was my turn to groan now, and I instinctively pulled myself closer to him so my head was resting on his shoulder and his arm came up around me. God, it was so easy with him.

'How have I only known you for a month?' I pointed out, which set us both off.

He shrugged, lifting my head up with the movement so I was merely inches from his shaded stubble. 'Is this too early in the dating game to say *when you know, you know*?'

My stomach did a flip. 'If that's a reference to a Taylor Swift lyric, then never.' I kissed him promptly, and his grasp around my back tightened even more.

'But seriously? Too soon?'

He gave me the space to consider it for a moment, but I didn't need to.

I always imagined love being a bit like a golden orb that sits squarely in your chest and burns brightly inside you, energising you and keeping you warm. It felt like that now.

'I think it's the right time for us,' I whispered. 'Though if you had asked me six weeks ago, I would have said *definitely not*.'

His shoulder lowered and I felt his fingers finding the edge of my shirt and lifting it again, his fingers drawing patterns against the soft skin of my lower back.

'You romantic,' he teased. 'What changed then?'

'What do you mean?'

'You're a different person from the girl I met in Covent Garden a month ago.'

I laughed. 'You mean the girl who bowled you over and insulted you.'

'You did not bowl me over,' he corrected. 'But yes. You're so much more relaxed now.'

It didn't hurt that he was a calming presence for me, with his soft touch and ease.

'I think it's because I've finally found a home.' I clamped my hand over his lips and quickly added, 'Yes, I know I'm cheesy as hell but just bear with me.' I could see his eyes twinkling, wanting to laugh but waiting for me to say my piece. 'I mean I never realised I had a home. I've spent so much of my life waiting for the next thing, moving from one city to another, always ready to pack up and go. But when I thought about leaving London – actually leaving, never to return in any kind of permanence – I realised how much I would miss it.'

I released his head and he tilted it. 'London at Christmas will do that to a person.'

'Not just London at Christmas though, London all year round,' I admitted. 'I finally know I can stay,' I continued. 'That I *want* to stay. Denise and Bob have my back, Megan and I can be there for each other, and, for the first time, I don't feel like I have to accept that I belong somewhere. I can just… be.'

Simon nodded and opened his bottle of water to take a slow sip of his drink, considering me. 'And me?' he asked eventually.

I gave him a look that was both cheeky and sincere. 'I'm not staying just because of you. I've already told you that.'

'But I am a pretty big bonus,' he joked.

I laughed, shaking my head and pressing myself up against his chest so I was almost straddling him on the sofa. 'You are so fishing for a compliment.'

'It's part of my charm.' He grinned, pulling my leg further over so I *was* straddling him. This was a first for me, but it felt good. 'Go on. Admit it,' he whispered, leaning upwards so we were both sitting upright, him with his hands now running up and down my thigh while I wrapped my hand around his neck and felt the contours at the meeting of his broad shoulders.

I rolled my eyes, but my heart was hammering now, that teasing glint in his eyes making my breath catch. 'Fine. You're a *very* big bonus.'

'That's what she said,' he murmured into my ear cheekily and I couldn't help but release a giggle as suddenly he stood, holding me up with his hands under my legs. God, he was strong. Now that was a big bonus.

The air between us prickled with energy as I tried to stop giggling. He was staring at me, rolling his lips occasionally, breathing hard as he began to lower me back down onto the sofa, him now on top of me.

'Is this okay?' he whispered, and I nodded slowly, my breath catching as all the noise of outside London seemed to fade and all I could hear was his breathing and mine. My arms and legs felt suddenly leaden, as if I didn't know what their purpose was but, inside me, I knew precisely what I wanted to do. 'Stay tonight?' he asked softly, travelling down my body just a few inches to kiss my stomach as my shirt crept up again. I gasped.

'I wasn't planning on leaving.'

I felt his lips quirk slightly against my chest as they travelled, his fingers now primed at the fraying edges of my shirt, as I arched my back instinctively.

It wasn't long before his lips returned to my neck, kissing me unhurriedly, deliberately. Neither of us wanted to rush it.

His hands slid up my waist, pulling me closer as he found my lips.

My fingers threaded into his hair, tugging lightly, and he let out the quietest sound, half a sigh, half a groan, that sent heat curling through me.

His fingers skimmed the line of my jaw and wrapped around my neck lightly. 'You sure about this?' he murmured against my skin.

It was like an electric current soared through me. 'For the love of…' I didn't know I would react like I did until I did.

I pushed him up and grabbed at his shirt, kissing him heatedly and without aim. I wanted him. And I was done with working to other people's timelines.

Screw being patient! This wasn't rushing, this was a hunger. And it was insatiable.

He reacted the same, suddenly desperate for more, as if the green light had gone up after an age of amber.

'Where's… the… bedroom?' I asked messily as he pulled the shirt up and over his head with ease. To be a man without having to care about all the other layers.

His chest made me pause for a heartbeat.

I ran my fingers along his collarbone and down to the fine line of hair across his abs – I was right, they were defined – feeling him shiver in response as he leaned forward to kiss my neck again and I moaned, returning to myself and my need.

'Up the stairs,' he said into my ear. 'I'll race you.'

'No!'

We were like overgrown children, suddenly running and guffawing. Both of us charged and playful.

My legs were so heavy I didn't think I'd ever be able to make it up to the top but, with surprising speed, we landed on his bed up in the mezzanine and quickly fell about on the sheets, wasting no time in removing any additional layers between us.

In what felt like no time his body was suddenly covering mine, his hands reverent as they traced the curve of my spine and as I felt every inch of him.

His lips found mine again, like magnets, and for the first time in a long time, I wasn't thinking about what came next.

I was exactly where I wanted to be.

Chapter 34

'IT'S JUST A FEW WEEKS,' I reiterated to Simon, tugging at his collar as he held me in front of airport security. 'I'll be back before you know it and I'll text you every day.'

'You'd better.' Simon smirked. 'I don't know what I would do without your GIFs and unintelligible emojis. It's like using Duolingo but without the three-day trial.'

'Oh, shut up,' I said playfully, smoothing out the collar of his khaki jacket.

Since we officially got together, I had become even more attracted to his slightly unkempt public appearance. I even requested that he not shave for a day or two just so I could enjoy the feeling of his light stubble against my chin.

'It feels like I've got sand on my cheeks,' he had complained that morning.

'I like it,' I said, kissing him on his jawline. Since it was only for one day, before we said goodbye at the airport, he let me have my way.

He let me have my way with quite a few things, in fact.

We had barely left his flat after returning from my job interview. In fact, we nearly missed New Year entirely – it was a good thing he gave up his slot when we went ice skating, otherwise he would have had to leave the bedroom, which would have been a travesty for both of us. We found our own way of celebrating the New Year. After all, who needs the South Bank fireworks when you're making fireworks of your own?

You'd think that, after going so long without a tryst, I'd be out of practice and uncertain, but being with Simon was like finding the perfect puzzle piece. The 'excuse me's, awkward requests, and occasional recalibration of leg positions only added to the fun.

'You're actually listening to me?' I said at one point, panting through the gymnastics of Round 2 on the floor of the mezzanine. We had fallen off the bed in the first round.

I was shocked that a man was willing to let a woman take the lead and follow her instructions on exactly what she wanted from a sexual moment without any kind of criticism, suggestion, or refusal.

He laughed breathlessly, red in the face, kissed my neck – an instruction he was particularly fond of – and whispered in my ear, 'You know I can't help but do what you ask of me.'

I laughed, a sudden image of green paint and a fluffy Grinch costume coming to mind.

'You know, I think Josh would drop off that Grinch costume if I asked.'

He had kissed my neck down to my collarbone, definitely leaving a mark.

'I'd rather be John McClane,' he teased.

'Leave it a few years,' I said, turning to ruffle his light blond hair. 'And you might be.'

The evening continued in bliss and the days had been nothing but blissful ever since.

We'd found our way into every corner of his flat, breaking blinds, damaging the shower curtain, and, most noticeably, bending a chair leg. Neither of us knew how we did any of these things, our attention was solely on each other.

The New Year midnight countdown had passed us by until eventually, needfully, we had returned to spread ourselves out on his sofa after midnight, wrapped in just a blanket, watching the fireworks and revellers singing 'Auld Lang Syne' out of tune on playback on his laptop screen.

It was our way of letting the rest of the world back in.

'You were my first ever midnight kiss,' I told him.

'What did you wish for?' he asked, turning the channel to a rerun of *When Harry Met Sally*.

I hadn't told him. But standing at the airport now, holding tightly onto Simon's collar and imagining desperately what life would be like when January was over, I wanted him to know.

'I wish I didn't have to leave.'

'It's just a few weeks,' he reiterated, and I snuggled into his neck, feeling secure in his grip as he wrapped his arms around me.

'Will you be here when I get back?'

'Four hours early,' he said. 'Just in case. I might even get a busking slot in for an excuse.'

I could see the cogs turning as he planned.

'Knowing me, I'll be four hours late, but I appreciate the anticipation.' I grinned.

'I'd find something to do,' he insisted. 'Maybe write a jingle or two?'

'Maybe not perform those.'

He scoffed. 'They pay the bills.'

'Well, I can always help with that.' I quickly pulled away, the sensible Evie coming out. 'Much later. When we move in, *if* we move in! We don't have to move in. Unless you want to. Maybe?'

It was like verbal diarrhoea.

'A few days in heaven and she's ready to move in with me.'

Simon was enjoying this a little too much. I rolled my eyes.

'You know what I meant.'

He nodded, understanding. 'January will fly by. December did, after all.'

'And I packed a lot into December,' I agreed, reminiscing about the igloo and the ice skating, as well as my lovely family Christmas. 'I'm just going to Canada – to quit a job I haven't even started. That's normal, right?'

'For you, Evie Frost, I'm pretty sure you re-invent normality on a day-to-day basis. But…' Simon began, elongating the word and a seriousness cast over him. 'I know this may not be the right time but I want you to know that, if you enjoy it, you can stay if you want to. I won't be *too* upset.'

I smiled stiffly, moving a strand of his hair from his forehead as I considered his words. It was admirable of him to offer his support in such a way, but I knew that coming back to London was the right decision for me.

'Trust me, given how many times I've been emailed by Elijah about these bloody TV treatments over Christmas, I'm not going to enjoy it.'

The emails had been getting shorter, yet the demands had increased in each. The sign-off from Elijah had stopped being *best* and was just his initial 'E'. And as any office worker knows, that as close to saying 'fuck you, bitch' as is politely possible.

When I got a formal warning for slow performance, over Christmas and before my contract had even started, I knew I had made a very good decision to quit before I'd even started.

'I'm coming home. To London. And to you,' I promised.

Simon smirked and corrected my bag on my shoulder a little.

'I'm quite glad to hear that.'

I leaned up for one final lingering kiss. 'And I'm very glad to hear you say that.' I stroked his stubble a few more times and eventually pulled away. 'Right! I have to go or I'll miss my flight.'

'You foiled my evil plan,' Simon joked, still helping me with my bags as we headed towards the growing queue for check-in. 'Call me when you land, I don't care what the time difference is. I'll be awake.'

'Given how loudly you snore, I doubt you'll hear the phone ring.'

'Again, a few days and she's giving me lip about my snoring,' Simon said to no one in particular.

'It's what girlfriends or partners or…' I shook my head, not sure what to call myself. '… *lovers* do,' I finished lamely. 'I suck at this.'

Simon shrugged nonchalantly as if I had just asked what takeaway we were going to order. 'Girlfriend works for me, if boyfriend works for you.'

I grinned. 'You're so blasé about it.'

He smirked. 'I have to take after my dad in some way, I suppose.'

'I hope that was the *only* way.'

He smiled softly as we reached the cut-off points for goodbye. Queues to dismantle perfectly packed suitcases, removing all the liquids inside. I was so glad I had had the foresight to pack my washbag in my handbag for once. Mostly it was because Simon and I had left his flat so late I needed to do my make-up on the train.

Simon cleared his throat. 'I texted Dad last night, actually,' he said suddenly, a rather odd moment to admit it. 'You've inspired me. We've put in that lunch.'

'Without me?' I won't lie, I was suddenly envisioning a scene of plates flying and two men shouting in the middle of Côte Brasserie.

'It's just a coffee. For the three-course meal I might need you there as a buffer when things get awkward.'

'Me?' I said, shocked, pointing at my own chest. 'What can I do?'

'You can ask him twenty questions, like you said.' I vaguely remembered making that joke. Well, it would be interesting to get to know his father in a way other than through TikTok videos.

'Oh, quickly.' I pulled out my phone. 'Can you take a quick video of me at security?'

He sighed, not unkindly but with a slight *really?* tone. 'Am I your cameraman now?'

'Your *girlfriend*...' I stressed the word playfully, '... is a content creator, so yes. Add it to your CV.'

His hands were shaking with light laughter as he took a quick video of me poncing around in front of the growing queues.

'It's a good thing I like you more than a lot, Evie Frost.'

I took my phone back from him, grinning. 'I like you more than a lot too, Simon Holland. I'm glad I had my Christmas bucket list, so I could meet you.'

Simon nodded appreciatively, kissing my cheek with one final squeeze. I inhaled his cologne – which I may have stolen a bottle of and put in my washbag – and squeezed back. 'Wonderful things have happened since.' Lifting my chin up for one final *final* kiss. He lowered his face and hovered inches in front of mine.

'I support you too, no matter what,' I added. 'Whatever you need, I'm here for you. We can even make a list!'

Simon didn't release me but chuckled. 'Another list? What's this one going to include?'

'Things that make Simon happy? Number one: reconnecting with your dad. Number two…' I paused, waiting for his input.

'Meeting his girlfriend at the arrivals lounge four hours early.'

I beamed. 'Number three?' I prompted and his hands tightened around my waist.

'Spend a Christmas in London with his family?'

'Number four?' I leaned up just once more.

'Surprise me,' Simon said finally.

Oh, I would. I promised myself. He wouldn't have to worry about that.

EPILOGUE

TWO YEARS LATER

All was quiet about the house, not a creature was stirring, not even a mouse. Simon's face was buried in the pillow, peaceful and oblivious, while I stared at the ceiling, ticking off tasks in my mind.

'Stop thinking so loudly,' Simon moaned, his voice muffled by the pillow. I smiled.

'We need to get up.' I rolled onto my side and wrapped an arm around his chest, kissing his shoulders which were lovely and warm. I could have stayed there all day. But there was so much to do. 'I need a cup of tea.'

Simon didn't move.

'I said, I need a cup of tea.' Brutally I pushed myself up and pulled the blinds open in one swift movement, letting in a stream of harsh winter sunlight.

'Oh, bloody hell!' He burrowed back under his pillow like a mole, while I laughed evilly and kissed his bare shoulder again, since I couldn't get to his stubbly chin.

'I'm going to get the turkey on.'

'It's not even…' Simon squinted at the clock. '… eight o'clock.'

'The oven's not big enough for beef, turkey, roast potatoes, parsnips, Yorkshires, and pigs in blankets, you know.'

'And why do we have to have beef?' he called as I entered the landing and began slamming my feet down the flight of stairs as noisily as I could, just to be sure he wouldn't fall back asleep.

Our new place was in Sidcup, just outside of London – still close enough to allow us to say we're Londoners, far enough that we could actually afford a terraced house and not just a garage with 'charm'. I had had a list: I wanted a staircase, a spare bedroom, and Simon had wanted a garden so he could learn the manly task of barbecuing.

It had taken us nearly two years, two side hustles, and one mildly exhausting attempt at selling homemade Christmas jumpers on Etsy to save enough for the deposit, but we'd done it, miraculously, even after I'd torpedoed my big Canadian career move.

It seemed like a lifetime ago that I was due to work as a Broadcast Production Assistant at Salient, only to serve the most awkward one month's notice instead of starting my job at the station. Even for a limited time of working on bit-tasks, reality hit fast and I realised I had dodged a bullet. Elijah had bombarded me with so many last-minute *urgent* tasks that I began to suspect the real job description involved being psychic.

Quitting Salient, moving back to Kent, reuniting with Simon, and spending all my time in London – to the point I almost started decorating *his* flat like it was my own – felt like the universe finally giving me a nudge in the right direction, or rather a full-on shove. It was still the best decision I had ever made.

Now I was back where I belonged, in a job that didn't drain the soul out of me by 10.00 a.m., working as a Social Media Coordinator for the BBC. It was a move away from

Executive Assistant after my skill on TikTok grew to such a level that even my boss – who'd once called TikTok 'the slow death of civilisation' – couldn't ignore it, and marched me into an interview with the Social Media team instead. Now I balanced growing my own TikTok channel with getting paid to run actual TikTok campaigns; every day, going to work, was like putting on a new dress that fitted me perfectly in every single way *and* had pockets.

A whole new life had taken root.

Even Pim had re-invented herself. She and Alison had long since departed the shores of England for somewhere with micro-climates and mojitos on tap, and currently were happily working on the set of a film.

Pim had got the itch to act in front of the camera again after her talk-of-the-town event. Though the swashbuckling pirate flick she was shooting somewhere gloriously sunny in the Caribbean was an interesting choice, as Pim was only voicing the role of a parrot but had somehow managed to get an all-expenses trip to be on set to run lines with the actors, as they acted with a hovering tennis ball, ahead of special effects adding in some colourful plumage.

When we moved into our new home, Pim – or rather *Alison* – had sent a Fortnum & Mason's gift basket so large it came with its own driver. There was a postcard signed with a pawprint from Gerald the Chow Chow, whose own TikTok channel was flourishing, and occasionally I side-hustled as his social media manager, a gig which had boosted our deposit when Pim insisted on paying me a year's fee upfront. It was her subtle-not-subtle way of helping Simon and me over the line, and I would forever be grateful to her.

We had yet to unpack most of our belongings, but the bonus was the space we had without furnishings, which allowed us to host a full house during our first Christmas, with all our loved ones.

But only if I got the turkey in the oven on time.

Simon had insisted on unloading the Christmas decorations first. 'There's no such thing as a Christmas dinner if you haven't got a tree up,' he had argued. Though I pointed out the dining table was probably a better idea.

He had taken his role as content-creator cameraman to heart and had insisted that we throw a bauble into an empty room filled with packing boxes, before shutting the door and re-opening it to reveal our Christmas grotto – not styled by Josh, but definitely side-eyed by him.

The place now sparkled with tinsel, paper chains, hanging Christmas stars, and a tree that was as random and as beautiful as could be.

'Right, time to fire up the kettle,' he said, rolling up imaginary sleeves, while I stood against the door frame of our living room, admiring our green, red, and gold handiwork.

'My hero.'

'Have you basted the turkey?' I called to Simon from the entrance hall. The doorbell had just rung with our first guests but, thankfully, Simon and I had managed to get dressed in between our many preparations and were now sporting matching Christmas jumpers that I had knitted for us with smiling reindeer on – because we're that sickeningly domesticated now.

'Hello!' Denise and Bob shouted, arms laden with presents and a few random kitchen items.

'Hi! What's all this?' I said, kissing them each on the cheek, or as close as I could get to their cheeks given the amount of Christmas paraphernalia in their arms.

'I brought a few things, just in case you needed them,' Denise explained, pulling out a three-tiered vegetable steamer and a massive skillet.

'Oh, great!' I was amazed she could fit it all in her car, but also unsurprised at the same time.

Bob had already headed for the living room, depositing large sacks of presents near the tree, as they were hardly going to fit underneath our five-foot spruce.

'Did you want this table in here, Evie?' he called, getting straight to the business of moving the furniture that Simon and I hadn't yet got around to.

'That's the one.'

We flittered about, Denise filling me in on the latest gossip while shouting instructions to Simon on how best to make her homemade bread sauce.

'Use the packet!' I muttered loudly, and I saw his tell-tale smirk.

The house felt packed to the rafters already and we were only halfway filled. As Simon was serving the bowls of steamed vegetables, Denise pouring gravy and 'homemade' sauce into serving jugs, the door rang again.

'Is that Josh?' Denise asked, now stripping carrots with the peeler while I pushed over my phone to her.

'No, he's not coming.'

'What?' she gasped, aghast. 'Have you had a falling-out?'

'Read the text,' I said, hurriedly making my way to the door as the doorbell was pushed again and again.

Denise read the text aloud and laughed – Josh has bailed because he's shacked up with the Sexy Santa from Magic

Mike XXL – *'GUYS!! My God! The elasticity of this man. And the stamina! I'm in GAY CHRISTMAS HEAVEN! Send carbs, heat packs, and cans of whipped cream. I'm going to need them. XoXo'*

'Typical Josh,' she cackled. 'I hope he finds love. And a chiropractor.'

I opened the door.

'It's only us!' Megan said, letting herself in while holding the hand of Alfie, who was bouncing on his heels with excitement, clutching a Santa hat that was at least two sizes too big for his head and insisting on showing me immediately.

'Alfie, my angel!' I squeezed him tightly, kissing his tufty little curls as he squirmed to get away again, overwhelmed by the noise and scent of Christmas.

Alex followed his son with a small sack of presents and the leash of Megan's new chihuahua-Jack Russell cross, Jack-Jack, smiling awkwardly. He let Jack-Jack go – the little dog bounded off with a comically polite bark that was very endearing. Megan handed Alex her coat, without ever actually touching him. They had divorced the year before and were attempting to amicably co-parent Alfie, though it didn't mean the awkwardness of their situation had dissipated. It was obvious to everyone that they were still finding their new normal around each other as friends.

'I got a PlayStation!' Alfie shouted, and I looked to Megan, who was rolling her eyes at Alex.

'Alex bought *himself* a new PlayStation,' she explained after Alfie rushed into the living room to greet his grandparents. 'But told Alfie it was for him. I don't even think Alfie knows what a PlayStation is – he just thinks it's cool because his dad thinks it's cool.'

'I think I can get away with it for at least one more year,' Alex said cheekily, going in for a blink-and-you-miss-it hug with me before following his playful son.

'So long as it doesn't make its way into my house,' Megan whispered to me, her eyes tracking the two of them like a hawk.

'I'll defend your flat with my life,' I swore solemnly.

'It's just one day,' she repeated, a mantra to herself, as she wrapped an arm around my waist and we headed towards the kitchen. We could hear Alfie and Alex rough-housing in the living room, with Denise's calls to be careful.

Megan flinched.

'No flicking horseradish into his eye with a spoon,' I warned, pointedly reminding Megan of her previous Christmas with her ex, which had been much less amicable than this one.

'That was Alfie,' she insisted. It was not.

Simon was suitably red-faced and flustered, straining Brussels sprouts while also closing the oven door with his foot and balancing a jug of gravy with his spare hand.

'Let me take that,' Megan said, taking the jug before it spilled. Denise flew in instantly to claim it and place it on the table, all the while jabbering away to her beloved grandson from across the house.

Our home was a cacophonous bundle of noise and I was loving it.

In a moment of peace before the Yorkshires were due to be finished, I leaned into Simon's chest, and he wrapped his arm around me to savour the moment, but just at that moment the oven beeped. 'Oh, for Christ's sake!' he said, returning to his worker-bee status as the doorbell went for a final time.

'Do you want to get it?' I asked Simon, but he shook his head as the steam of the oven blasted in his face.

'Tell him I'll be out in a minute.'

Opening the door, Michael Holland stood awkwardly. Even after countless lunches, phone calls, and the occasional FaceTime, he still failed to loosen up, always appearing like he was about to grill you on the political nature of your decisions or shout about something unimportant.

It was a very bad case of resting bitch face, but I had grown to enjoy it.

Clearing his throat, he thrust a stunning bouquet of red tulips at my face. They were copious in number and clearly very expensive. 'My favourite. Thank you, Michael,' I said, moving aside to let him in.

He stepped in cautiously, dropping a few gift bags on the floor before he started to remove his coat.

'You can just leave it on the banister,' I said, gesturing to the other coats that had become mountainous with everyone's arrival. 'We haven't got the hooks on the wall yet,' I clarified.

Michael said nothing.

'Michael!' Bob said, entering the hallway and offering his hand. 'It's lovely to see you again.'

Michael shook Bob's hand, though he looked as if he had no idea who the hell he was.

'I'm Bob,' he reminded him. 'The Man City fan.'

'This is my dad,' I said over him – not wanting to get onto football before Michael had even had so much as a cup of tea. 'My *dad*,' I said warningly, re-using the term I had become more comfortable with using after returning to my childhood home in Kent for the first time since I was eighteen. For over a year, I lived with Bob and Denise, as Simon and I developed our relationship and I started my new job in White City. And in that year my love for them became so strong I asked the question if I could call them Mum and Dad for the first time. And their response was tears and tea. Which was a very British way of saying yes, while being unable to speak due to tears and strangled emotion.

I'd barely been home, too wrapped up in the bubble of first real love, but the time I did stay with them again was precious and changed our relationship only for the better.

'He'll show you where you're sitting,' I told Michael.

Who muttered, 'Of course,' his tone softening, mostly from embarrassment. 'Lead the way.' I let them go but distinctly heard Michael lean over and add in an undertone: 'What do you think of Pep's latest midfielder?'

'Now we're talking!' Bob slapped him on the back jovially, though he was distinctly shorter than Michael. It was like Danny Dyer inviting Stephen Fry in for a pint.

'Dad,' Simon said, suddenly appearing, tea towel in hand, as he wiped condensation off his wrists. Michael seemed to stand to attention, stepping forward and offering his hand for a shake. Simon looked at it, scoffed and reached forward, embracing his father before Michael could protest.

It was the briefest of embraces but it was done, and it broke the tension like a Christmas cracker being pulled.

'Do you need help with anything?' Michael offered.

'I could do with someone serving up the potatoes,' Simon said, immediately walking back into the kitchen grateful for the help. Michael rolled up his sleeves and got to work, while Bob wrapped an arm around my shoulders and smiled warmly at me.

'All's well that ends well,' he whispered.

'It took some time,' I said, thinking back to the many nights when Simon had raged at his father's lack of emotional ability and then to the days when he actually began to smile when he saw his dad was calling him on the phone.

But something had changed in recent months; the odd coffee became a regular habit, and Michael even figured out how to use emojis, though he still signed off every text with '*Michael*', as if he thought his son might forget who it was.

'If you two ever decide to get married,' he once began, while Simon was in the toilet during one of our post-work dinners. I very nearly choked on my tiramisu. He politely ignored the fleck of coffee cream now soaking into his shirt sleeve and added, without missing a beat, 'Don't sit me next to Pim Hardcastle.'

It was a wise request, and one I was slightly tempted to ignore *if* marriage was ever part of our future. It probably was, I thought deliciously that evening, my mind suddenly awash with fantasies and daydreams about what I'd like to do: a winter wonderland theme, with all of Simon's busker friends as our replacement string quartet, *lots* of glitter, and maybe even a wedding-cake race, with a themed-costume contest at the reception!

It would be an amazing day. *If* it ever happened. For now, a family Christmas was my daydream-come-true.

Sitting down at the Christmas table, surrounded by our family, arguing over the last of the roast potatoes and Yorkshires, it took me a moment to remember that not that long ago I thought that none of this would have ever been possible.

A family, a full life, roots.

Now, I looked at the tableau of faces from my parents-in-all-but-legal-status and my beloved nephew to Jack-Jack the yappy family pet, to a screen featuring Josh and Leo, the hunky Santa on FaceTime.

Not a face was out of place and, for the first time, it felt as if not a face was missing.

Over lunch, conversation flowed easily. Denise caught me up on her new piano lessons: 'I still sound like a toddler smashing their fists on the keys, but I have *fun*,' and Simon and Bob got into an intense debate about whether or not *Die Hard* was a Christmas film (it *was*).

'I feel like I should be paying my life coach for more than just gossip about reality TV shows,' Megan admitted between mouthfuls of trifle later in the evening. Nearly everyone else had left the table to half-sit-half-lie on our makeshift seats and sofa. 'How *is* the life coach?' I asked her, keeping her company on the sofa.

'He's fine.' She smirked, and I nudged her shoulder. We wouldn't discuss her latest beau with Alex still in the house, but I'd be sure to find the time later that evening. Sure, it was a bit weird to be dating your life coach, but the two of them seemed to be making it work at a pace that was remarkably slower than Megan's norm.

'And the job?' I asked. 'That new CEO driving you mad?'

She rolled her eyes, so yes. 'CEOs tend to get their positions through a lot of IOUs and this woman is the blatant example of that statement. I've never known someone to have so many fingers in so many pies.'

'Except you, you mean.' She had sold her business to a conglomerate and then gone to work with their competitor.

She wasn't exactly fingerless, and she knew it. She smiled proudly but authentically and it was uplifting to see her this way. The Megan I knew and loved from childhood to adulthood. She was returning to her true self after a few tough years. 'I love you,' I told her, because when else would I, if not Christmas Day?

'Ditto.'

Later, while washing up in the kitchen as Denise and Megan tortured the men in the house by singing 'Sixteen Going on Seventeen' during BBC's annual showing of *The Sound of Music*, Simon nudged me in the ribs lightly.

'So did you complete your Christmas bucket list this year?'

I thought about it for a moment. 'Mostly.'

'Mostly?' he repeated, confused.

'We had mulled wine in Covent Garden, went to that carol concert, took part in the Santa run—'

'My legs are still recovering from that, by the way.' But he was very proud of the medal he received for it; it held pride of place with the trophy from our Great Christmas Pudding Race.

'—and we went to a pantomime with Alfie.'

'I will never forgive you for seating us in the front row.' Yes, he would. He secretly loved being Dame Twinkie's boyfriend for the entire show.

'But there's one thing left.'

Simon raised an eyebrow. 'And that would be?'

I grinned, leaning up to whisper in his ear, soap suds dripping down my arm and onto the floor. 'Your old Grinch costume is upstairs.'

He groaned. 'Evie, no.'

'Simon, *yes*.'

He laughed, blushing already, but I could sense the intrigue and desire in him. We were still as playful as we had been two years prior, and I was hoping that wouldn't change for quite some time. He cleared his throat. 'And what exactly will you be wearing?'

I reached up and tapped one of my bauble earrings, making it jingle. 'Merry Christmas!'

Simon groaned again but he was smiling and, when he pulled me in for a kiss – slow, lingering, and warm – I knew without a doubt that this was exactly where I wanted to be.

Surrounded by love. Surrounded by family.

And, soon enough, surrounded by a very, very reluctant Grinch.

Acknowledgements

There is a village behind every book that comes into being and I wanted to give the team behind *Last Christmas in London* their flowers:

- Editor: Rebecca Weigler
- Production Editor: Polly Halsey
- Copyeditor: William Grandison
- Proof-reader: Millie Godwin
- Illustrator & Designer: Alexandra Allden
- Marketer: Callie Sutherland
- Publicist: Claudia Bullmore
- Sales: Laura Fletcher
- Literary Agent: Hannah Schofield

Thank you all for your support and involvement in making *Last Christmas in London* enter the hands of readers.

Further acknowledgement to Rebecca Roy for her initial feedback and structural guidance. To Freyja Hides-Westwood for always joining me on my Christmas adventures. To Grandad, who's always with us on Christmas Day. And to Piper, my auntie-depressant, thank you for giving me even more excuses to shop at Christmas, all my love Auntie La La.

And for Auntie Ann, the undefeated champion of Scrabble and the piñata, our Christmas plus one, who taught me the value of a good walk, *Anne of Green Gables* and the joy of having a home library.

About the Author

Eleanor Pilcher is an award-winning book marketer, content creator, podcaster and author.

Bedford Square Publishers is an independent publisher of fiction and non-fiction, founded in 2022 in the historic streets of Bedford Square London and the sea-mist shrouded green of Bedford Square Brighton.

Our goal is to discover irresistible stories and voices that illuminate our world.

We are passionate about connecting our authors to readers across the globe and our independence allows us to do this in original and nimble ways.

The team at Bedford Square Publishers has years of experience and we aim to use that knowledge and creative insight, alongside evolving technology, to reach the right readers for our books. From the ones who read a lot, to the ones who don't consider themselves readers, we aim to find those who will love our books and talk about them as much as we do.

We are hunting for vital new voices from all backgrounds –with books that take the reader to new places and transform perceptions of the world we live in.

Follow us on social media for the latest Bedford Square Publishers news.